The  ...

"Sorry about

"Somehow I don't think you are." Pete's voice was low, gruff, thick with arousal.

There wasn't a damn thing Olivia could do about the need throbbing inside her. She couldn't touch him, couldn't do anything but sit here, burning for him and wishing things were different.

The last light of the sun was fading now, leaving them in near darkness. The night pressed in around them, heavy with insect song and the crackling of desire in the air between them.

"I wish..." He brought her hand to his mouth and kissed it. Her skin tingled beneath his lips, and the fire deep in her belly raged.

"Don't. Don't wish. I'm the one who screwed up and got arrested." She pulled her hand back and stood.

"Don't sell yourself short." He stood and faced her. "You made a mistake. We all make them. Most of us just don't get arrested for them. If things were timed differently..."

He trailed his fingers over her cheek, and she felt it all the way to the depths of her heart.

"But they're not..."

Acclaim for the
Love to the Rescue Series

FOR KEEPS

"4 stars! With one super-hot cowboy, one spitfire of a woman, and several lovable dogs, Lacey draws readers into a tender story that will make your heart melt. An engaging plot and colorful, genuine characters make the author's latest a sweet, enjoyable read."

—*RT Book Reviews*

"Your heart will be captured many times by the genuine scenarios and the happily-ever-after for all, both human and canine."

—HeroesandHeartbreakers.com

"Lovable men and lovable dogs make this series a winner!"

—Jill Shalvis, *New York Times* bestselling author

UNLEASHED

"Dog lovers rejoice! The stars of Lacey's cute series opener, set in Dogwood, N.C., have four legs instead of two, and their happy ending is guaranteed."

—*Publishers Weekly*

"Delightful...a great story...You'll fall in love!"

—MyBookAddictionReviews.com

"Both the man and the dog will rescue your heart. Don't miss it!"

—Jill Shalvis, *New York Times* bestselling author

"Endearing! Rachel Lacey is a surefire star."

—Lori Wilde, *New York Times* bestselling author

EVER AFTER

EVER AFTER

RACHEL LACEY

FOREVER

NEW YORK   BOSTON

Forever
Hachette Book Group
1290 Avenue of the Americas
New York, NY 10104

www.HachetteBookGroup.com

Printed in the United States of America

First Edition: August 2015
10 9 8 7 6 5 4 3 2 1

OPM

Forever is an imprint of Grand Central Publishing.
The Forever name and logo are trademarks of Hachette Book Group, Inc.

The Hachette Speakers Bureau provides a wide range of authors for speaking events. To find out more, go to www.hachettespeakersbureau.com or call (866) 376-6591.

The publisher is not responsible for websites (or their content) that are not owned by the publisher.

To my sister, Juliana, for papering my child-hood with inspiration for this book. You are one of the most amazing people I know, and I am so lucky to call you my sister.

ACKNOWLEDGMENTS

As always, first thanks go to my family for all your love and support. I quite literally couldn't do it without you. Thank you to my husband for helping to juggle the many, many things we've had on our plate this year. And thank you to my son for being absolutely the best thing in my world.

So many thanks to my amazing agent, Sarah Younger. I ran completely off course about halfway through my first draft of this book, and you helped set me straight. I can't tell you how much your support and guidance have meant to me.

And to my fabulous editor, Alex Logan—I can't imagine having published my first series with anyone else. You helped make this experience a great one for me, and you always make sure my pages arc the best they can be. Thank you so much for everything you do!

Many thanks to everyone at Grand Central Publishing who had a part in the making of this book, especially

Madeleine Colavita, Julie Paulauski, and Elizabeth Turner (who designed this gorgeous cover).

I have so many friends in the writing community to thank. My critters—Annie Rains, Eleanor Tatum, and Nancy LaPonzina. Special thanks to Nancy for coming up with Olivia's hilariously botched graffiti message, and to Annie for critiquing this manuscript for me. My #girlswritenight crew—Sidney Halston, Annie Rains, Tif Johnson, and April Henry. You guys keep me sane and motivated and provide many much-needed laughs. Thank you all!

Thank you to Sidney Halston for helping me decipher the legal system for Olivia's court case. And to retired Detective Daniel Bates for answering my many law enforcement questions. As they say, all mistakes are my own.

To all the friends who have supported me on this journey, you guys are the absolute best. You have no idea how many times you have totally made my day with your awesome photos, tweets, and messages. Love you guys!

And last but certainly not least, a huge thank you to my readers. It is pretty much the greatest thing ever to know that people are reading my books. I am so incredibly thankful for each and every one of you!

EVER AFTER

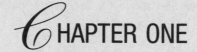HAPTER ONE

*R*ed paint dripped from Olivia Bennett's fingers. She tightened her grip on the metal canister in her right hand and gave it a solid shake. Beneath her feet, the ladder wobbled. With a startled squeak, she sent a burst of spray paint onto her boots.

"Sorry, Liv," Terence called from below.

"Watch it, will you?" She pressed her palm against the cool, corrugated metal of the factory wall and took a deep breath. Then she lifted her right hand and pressed the valve on the spray paint canister, forming a brilliantly red "S" on the side of the building.

"Almost done," Kristi said.

Easy for her to say, standing safely on the ground next to Terence. At the top of the ladder, Olivia fought to keep her balance as the remnants of several margaritas sloshed in her stomach. Hell of a way to end her twenty-ninth birthday.

The beam of Kristi's flashlight cast Olivia's shadow in stark silhouette over her red-painted message. She leaned right to spray another "S" but couldn't reach. She'd have to come down and move the ladder to continue, but a muffled sound captured her attention.

Mew.

The sound was soft yet keening. A kitten? Some other baby animal? She craned her head, peering into the darkness. "Did you guys hear that?"

"Hear what?" Terence asked, his tone wary.

"It sounded like a kitten."

Kristi panned the flashlight around them, plunging Olivia into darkness. She leaned a hip against the side of the building to steady herself.

"I don't see anything," Kristi said.

"Okay, put that light back on me so I can get down."

The flashlight's beam once more illuminated her, and Olivia scrambled quickly to solid ground. "I heard some kind of little animal crying while I was up there, so keep an eye out."

"Will do." Terence moved the ladder over so that she could reach the next section of wall to be painted and held it steady as she climbed back up.

Six letters to go, and they were out of here. Terence would drive them to his place for a post-graffiti celebration. Olivia was in no condition to drive herself anywhere tonight. Adrenaline mixed with trepidation as she stood at the top of the ladder yet again. The margarita buzz had faded enough to know she was doing a crazy, stupid thing that wasn't going to do a damn thing to help the chickens who arrived here daily, their only hope that death would be quick and merciful.

Based on what the undercover cameras had captured, that hope was slim.

She ground her teeth, her fingers clenched around the spray can. It was inhumane the way those birds were treated. Actually, it was inhumane the way most factory-farmed animals were treated, but this was happening right here in her little hometown of Dogwood, North Carolina.

Mew.

A flash of white fur caught her eye, disappearing into the bushes behind the factory. If it was a kitten, it was tiny. Was its mother nearby? There weren't any houses for miles around. Dammit. Now she was going to have to go on a kitten hunt before she went home. She couldn't leave it out here to fend for itself.

"Hurry up, Liv," Kristi called from below her.

Olivia raised the canister and let loose another blast of red paint. She'd just started "I" when the sound of an approaching vehicle reached her. Her finger slipped, and a fresh coat of paint soaked her hands.

Kristi and Terence must have heard it too, because the flashlight shut off, leaving her at the top of the ladder in pitch darkness, afraid to move. Headlights slashed through the night from Garrett Road, some two hundred feet to her left. They slowed, then tires crunched over gravel as the car turned into the factory parking lot.

Christ on a cracker.

"Get the hell down, Liv. We've got to get out of here!" Terence whispered.

A swirl of blue lights turned the night into a kaleidoscope of *oh, shit*. She pressed against the side of the building, stymied by paint-slickened fingers as she fumbled for the top of the ladder.

She was *so* not getting arrested on her birthday.

Except that she *so* was. A spotlight shone from the cruiser, illuminating her in a blaze of light so bright she could do nothing but press a hand over her eyes and count how many ways spray-painting Halverson Foods' chicken-processing plant had been a bad idea.

The ladder shifted beneath her, and she groped for the top rung. The combination of the spinning blue lights with the piercing glare of the spotlight was seriously disorienting.

"Hands where I can see them," a male voice boomed.

She shoved her hands into the air, managing to smack herself in the face with the can of spray paint in the process. It fell to the ground with a muffled thump. Oh, this sucked.

"Come down from the ladder, nice and slow, and keep those hands up," the cop instructed. He sounded nice-*ish*. Maybe he'd go easy on her. Maybe...

Awkwardly, she fumbled with her right foot for the next rung of the ladder. It swayed dangerously to the side. "Terence!" she hissed, her fingernails scoring metal as she tried to steady herself.

Silence. She looked down, but the spotlight's glare blinded her, preventing her from seeing past her own paint-spattered boots. "Terence? Kristi?"

She managed to get her foot settled onto the rung and took a step down. No answer came from her friends. *What the hell?*

She lifted her left foot to take the next step, and the ladder just dropped out from beneath her. One second it was there, the next she was plummeting through space.

"Oomph," came a masculine grunt, as she slammed

into someone's chest and big, strong arms closed around her.

"Terence?" Her voice was a squeak, because Terence was nowhere near this strong, and he didn't smell as good either. This man smelled faintly of cinnamon, his arms solid as steel behind her thighs, and based on the hard bulge stabbing into her kidney, he was also armed.

Oh, crap. Crap. *Crap!*

"Sorry," he answered her question, setting her roughly on the ground. "Not Terence."

"Oh." She staggered, still blinded by the spotlight aimed at her. Disoriented, she turned her back and blinked at her shadow on the factory's gray wall. Terence and Kristi had deserted her. *Bastards.*

"Keep those hands where I can see them," Invisible Cop said.

With a sigh, she placed them on the wall before her. Her hands glistened blood-red in the harsh light. She had been caught red handed. *Dammit.* She'd always hated being a cliché.

* * *

Deputy Pete Sampson reached for his cuffs. When he'd taken the call about a trespasser on Halverson Foods' property, he surely hadn't expected to find a teenage girl on a ladder, covered from head to foot in red spray paint. "You want to tell me what you're doing out here tonight?"

She kept her back to him. "It's fairly obvious, right?"

He looked up. The side of the building dripped with big, red letters. It was obvious all right, but he wouldn't be surprised if she tried to talk her way out of it anyway.

"Chicken ass?" he read. What the hell was that even supposed to mean? Kids these days. He shook his head in annoyance.

She made a choking sound, squinting up at her handiwork. "I wasn't finished."

"Do tell."

"It was supposed to say Chicken *Assassins*."

"Ah. Well I suppose you know this is private property."

She nodded, her shoulders slumping.

"What's your name?" he asked.

"Olivia Bennett."

"I have some bad news, Olivia. You are under arrest for trespassing and vandalism. You have the right to remain silent." Pete snapped cuffs around her slender wrists as he read her her rights. He could spare her a pat-down because there was no way in hell she had anything concealed beneath that purple tank top or the fitted jeans that hugged her willowy frame.

"It's my birthday," she mumbled.

"Sorry, kid. The law makes no exception for birthdays."

"Kid?" She turned to face him, and he saw he'd been wrong about one thing. She was no teenager pulling a back-to-school prank. This woman was mid-twenties, easily, and far too beautiful to be doing what he'd just caught her doing. Her long, blond hair was pulled back in a messy ponytail, and she stared at him from wounded brown eyes.

He shrugged. "Seemed a pretty juvenile thing to do."

Chicken Assassins. In retrospect, he realized he was dealing with an animal rights activist instead of a teenaged troublemaker.

"Do you have any idea what happens to the birds in there?" she asked, her eyes bright with emotion.

"They get slaughtered." He took her elbow and guided her toward his cruiser. Her breath smelled of alcohol. "You drive out here?"

She glanced over at the red Prius parked behind the building. "Um—"

"You're drunk."

"I wouldn't say drunk, exactly." She ducked her head as he tucked her into the back of the cruiser.

"Let's find out, shall we?" He took his portable breathalyzer out of the car and crouched beside her.

Her eyes widened. "Let's not. I know my rights, deputy."

Pete stood. Great. A drunk troublemaker who knew the law. He had zero tolerance for people who drove under the influence. He'd seen firsthand the damage they inflicted on society, the lives and families torn apart.

Zach Hill had been left without a father.

Pete's gut soured. "Fine. You'll take it back at the station. Where are your keys?"

Her brows creased, and she glanced at the empty seat beside her. "I must have dropped them."

She was lying. But why? He closed the cruiser door and walked back to the building, shining his flashlight over the gravel lot. No sign of car keys. He walked to the Prius and tried the door. Locked. No keys visible inside.

She'd been looking for someone when she fell off the ladder. Maybe she'd had an accomplice. He returned to the cruiser and opened the back door. "Who's Terence?"

"A friend." She studied her shoes.

"Was he out here with you tonight?"

She shook her head. "No, sir. Just me."

But he'd seen the flicker of truth in her eyes. She'd had an accomplice all right, probably a boyfriend, since she was protecting him. "That's unfortunate, you being out here alone and intoxicated. Judge might be inclined to think you drove drunk."

"I didn't—" She pressed her lips together and looked away.

Well fine, if that was the way she wanted to play it. He buckled her in and slid behind the wheel. Fifteen minutes later, he marched her into the Dogwood County Detention Center. Olivia kept her chin up while she was fingerprinted and photographed. She blew a .078 on the breathalyzer, which meant she had almost certainly been over the limit if she had driven herself out to that factory earlier tonight.

Pete wanted to know more about this Terence she was covering for. But for now, he was ready to let her sit and think over her foolish behavior for a little while.

"Judge Gonzalez will hear your case first thing in the morning," he told her, as he led her down the hall to the holding pen. Lucky for her, she was the department's only visitor tonight. "You got someone to come bail you out?"

"What?" She eyed the cell with its steel bench, toilet, and sink, her eyes wide and horrified.

"You've been arrested, Miss Bennett. Now you need to call someone to bail you out."

"Um, right now? It's like one o'clock in the morning."

He shrugged, fighting a smile at the incredulous look on her face. "You break the law in the middle of the night, you either rouse someone from bed to bail you out or you bunk with us."

She gripped his wrist as he propelled her inside the holding cell. "Wait! Okay, yes. I need to make a phone call."

"All right." He took her by the elbow and steered her down the hall to the phone.

"Could you?" She held out her cuffed hands. "Please?"

"Fine." He uncuffed her and sat on the bench against the wall while she made her call.

She stood there, looking forlorn and vulnerable for several long seconds, then shook her head and picked up the phone. He'd expected her to dial the boyfriend she'd been looking for earlier, but instead she called someone named Merry.

"It's Olivia. I'm sorry to bother you this late, but I didn't know who else to call."

Pete tossed an arm over the back of the bench and watched her. Olivia kept her back to him, her shoulders hunched. Her friend apparently hadn't picked up, as she left a message and ended the call.

"No luck?" he asked.

She kept her back turned. "Can I try someone else?"

"Go ahead." He watched as she dialed another number. She spoke in hushed tones, then hung up and rested her forehead against the wall.

He stood. "All right then."

She turned those wounded eyes on him again as he led her back down the hall to the holding cell.

He slammed the cell door behind her with a solid clang for effect. "Make yourself comfortable. We'll let you know if anyone shows up to bail you out."

And with a chuckle at her expression, he left her there.

* * *

What a jerk.

Olivia adjusted her head against the metal bench. He might be handsome as hell, but Deputy Sampson had looked downright gleeful when he'd locked her up, and that was just rude. Now she'd spent the night in jail, and oh, how it had sucked. Thank goodness she'd sweet-talked the young guy behind the desk into letting her use the ladies' room down the hall, because that toilet...

She eyed it with disgust. God help her if Deputy Hot Stuff were to come back and catch her with her pants down. No way. She'd sooner wet her pants. Almost.

"Ugh," she groaned out loud. Her head throbbed, and her back ached. Spray-painting the Halverson Foods chicken-processing plant was officially her worst idea ever. And assuming she got her ass bailed out of here before lunchtime, she was scheduled to work the afternoon shift at the Main Street Café.

Yep, she had learned her lesson. Big time. No more breaking the law. She just needed to get out of here and find a way to put this whole thing behind her.

"Mornin' sunshine," came a low, male voice.

She squinted up at Deputy Hot Stuff himself and...ah, Jesus, her head.

"Sleep well?" he asked, as the cell door clanged open.

"Just peachy." She sat up and rubbed her eyes.

He set two aspirin and a paper cup filled with water beside her.

"Oh, my God, thank you. I take back all the awful things I thought about you last night." She swallowed the aspirin and gulped the water greedily.

"Awful things, huh?" He didn't look like he'd been home—or slept—since last night either. His cheeks had darkened with stubble, and his eyes were weary.

"All forgotten." She leaned her head against the wall and looked at him. It hurt to focus her eyes, but no, her perception hadn't been altered by the margaritas. Deputy Sampson was one fine-looking officer of the law.

He stood tall and strong with olive skin, brown hair cut short and neat, and eyes as dark as coal. If he hadn't been the one to throw her in jail, she'd have definitely tried to get his number—or rather, get him to ask for hers.

He stepped back and motioned her to follow. She stifled another groan as she stood. Every bone and muscle in her body ached. And her head felt like someone was in there with an ice pick chiseling away at the backs of her eyes.

She gazed longingly at the ladies' room as he guided her down the hall, and he stopped with a sigh.

"Go on. Five minutes to freshen up. Don't make me wait."

"Thank you," she whispered, and darted inside. She made quick use of the facilities, then splashed cold water on her face and rinsed out her mouth. It wasn't much, but she felt slightly rejuvenated when she rejoined him in the hall.

He led her next door to the courthouse but stopped her outside the courtroom. He turned those ebony eyes on hers. "Let's get one thing clear before we go in there. I can't charge you with DUI since I didn't catch you behind the wheel, but unless you want to tell me who was out there with you last night, I'm left to assume you drove yourself. You ever have to walk up to someone's front door and tell them their loved one is dead? Killed by a drunk driver?"

Jesus Christ. "No."

"If I ever catch you driving under the influence, I will throw the book at you. Are we clear?"

"Crystal." The full implications of her predicament slammed into her sleep-deprived brain. She had not driven drunk last night, and if her jackass friends hadn't run off and left her to face the music alone, he might even believe her.

Well, she'd cover for Terence and Kristi for now, since the whole thing had been her idea and she'd done all the spray-painting herself, but if the sheriff's office tried to pin any kind of DUI charge on her, she'd fess up. No way was she going down for a crime she hadn't committed.

She'd never driven drunk. Not even close. If Terence hadn't agreed to be her designated driver, she wouldn't have even been there last night.

"Olivia?"

She turned at the sound of her father's voice. John Bennett stood outside the door to the courtroom, looking distinguished in a steel-gray suit, a black leather briefcase in his right hand, his expression stern. So he'd gotten her message.

Of course he had. She'd purposefully called his cell, knowing he turned it off when he went to bed, not wanting to face him in the middle of the night, half drunk and drowning in self-pity.

"I need a moment with my client, deputy," he said.

Deputy Sampson's eyebrows raised. Yeah, her dad was a big-shot local defense attorney, and no doubt her favorite deputy had just connected the dots between their shared last name. With a slight shake of his head, he walked away.

Inside the courtroom, Olivia's cheeks burned as she spotted her mother seated in the front row behind the defense table, her blond hair carefully styled in a sleek bob. She wore a black dress suit and offered Olivia a pinched smile.

God, this was humiliating.

Olivia sat behind the defense table, her back prickling under the weight of her mother's stare. She could imagine their conversation after this was over. *Well you really screwed up this time, didn't you, Olivia?*

Fighting the urge to hang her head, Olivia pleaded guilty to misdemeanor trespass and Willful and Wanton Injury to Property. John Bennett made his case to the judge for her good character and spotless record, while the prosecutor attempted to paint her as a troublemaker whose vendetta against Halverson Foods had escalated to breaking the law.

"Miss Bennett," Judge Gonzalez said. He looked down at her from behind black-rimmed glasses. "I must say that it is refreshing to have a defendant in my court who takes responsibility for her actions without making excuses. And your otherwise exemplary record in the community makes a strong statement for your character. I do, however, have some concerns about your history with Halverson Foods.

"Therefore, I am ordering you to make restitution by removing your graffiti from their property, and I'm placing you on a thirty-day probation, at which time we will reconvene here in this courtroom. If you've kept yourself out of trouble and demonstrated that you've learned your lesson, the charges will be dropped and your record will remain unblemished."

Olivia's knees wobbled in relief. No criminal record. She could absolutely stay out of trouble for the next thirty days. In fact, she never intended to find herself on the wrong side of the law again.

After the formalities had been worked out, her dad walked her out of the courtroom a free woman. "I've got to get to the office, Livvy. Do you need a ride home?"

Her friend Merry Atwater waved from across the crowded hallway, catching Olivia's eye. "No, I'm good. And thank you. Really."

"Any time, honey. But let's try to make this the last time we meet under these circumstances, okay?" He squeezed her shoulder and headed for the exit. Her mom, she noticed, had already left. She felt a pang in her chest—relief, or disappointment. She wasn't sure which.

Ten minutes later, she was in the passenger seat of Merry's SUV, headed home.

"Worst birthday ever." She burrowed into the upholstery and closed her eyes.

Merry snorted. "Definitely not your finest moment. What in the world made you decide to go out and spray-paint that place?"

"I had a few drinks, and it sounded like a good idea." Turning twenty-nine had put her into a bit of a tailspin. It meant there was less than a year left before she needed to get her act together and decide once and for all if she was going to finish law school.

Start acting like a grown-up.

Instead she'd decided to do something reckless and childish. If this went on her permanent record, she might have ruined her chances of returning to law school anyway, and well, she'd be pissed if she didn't get to make that decision for herself.

"Sweetie, nothing that started with 'I had a few drinks, and it sounded like a good idea' has ever ended well. The next time you break the law, make sure you do it sober, okay?"

Olivia scrunched her nose. "The next time?"

"Not that I advocate breaking the law, but I have been known to squeeze between the cracks when the welfare of an animal is at stake."

"Really? You?" Olivia couldn't imagine her straight-as-an-arrow friend breaking the law. Merry worked as a pediatric nurse and ran an animal rescue group in her spare time.

"Ask Cara to tell you what *really* happened to those dogs on Keeney Street sometime." Merry slanted her a look.

Olivia gasped. "You didn't."

Those two dogs, unwanted and neglected, had mysteriously disappeared from their owner's backyard after Animal Control refused to seize them.

Her friend shrugged. "Maybe I did, and maybe I didn't. Maybe they're living at a sanctuary in Virginia these days. Who knows?"

"Okay, I'm impressed. But at least you saved their lives. I didn't do a damn thing for the chickens at that factory. All I did is have a terrible birthday and possibly screw up my future with a criminal record."

"Well, take it from a pro: we all do dumb shit sometimes."

The problem was, Olivia tended to do dumb shit *most*

of the time. Her parents were probably right; she was never going to get her act together. Here she was a grown woman and still acting like a teenager.

Merry pulled into the driveway of her house. Well, Olivia's house now, sort of. Merry had recently moved in with her boyfriend and was renting her house to Olivia for dirt cheap on the condition that she foster for Merry's boxer rescue.

Consequently, Olivia now had a three-bedroom bungalow to call home and two foster dogs she was responsible to feed and take care of until they were adopted.

"I stopped by to walk them before I came to the courthouse," Merry said, as she led the way to the front door. "Bailey had peed in the kitchen again."

"Ugh, Bailey." Olivia pointed a finger at the dog as they walked into the kitchen. Bailey leaped at her in response, tail nub wagging. Then Scooby was pushing in for his turn, both of them barking and licking her for attention.

"I'll take care of them. You look like you need a shower," Merry said.

"Oh, my gosh, thank you." She glanced down at herself, still red-stained with paint. Her hair was greasy, and her mouth tasted like an old sock.

Wearily, she went upstairs. She brushed her teeth, then sat on the edge of the tub and scrubbed herself with nail polish remover until the majority of the paint had come off. She took a long, hot shower and, feeling like a whole new person, came downstairs to find the dogs gated in the kitchen and a note from Merry.

Had to get home to Jayden so T.J. could go to work. Call me later.

Merry, confirming her status as a responsible adult, was fostering baby Jayden while his birth mother finished up her time on probation and tried to earn back custody.

Olivia headed for the fridge and poured herself a glass of water, which she gulped between bites of bran muffin. Her poor brain was too tired and sore to figure out the solution, but her long-term problem hadn't changed. She needed to see the Halverson Foods chicken-processing plant shut down.

Never mind that the sheriff's office would be watching her back or that she was required to clean her graffiti off the damn chicken factory. She'd seen the video footage of the workers inside beating and otherwise abusing the chickens before they were slaughtered.

That wasn't okay, and she couldn't rest until she'd put an end to it.

Just let sexy Deputy Sampson try to stop her.

Olivia dropped her head to the table with a groan. She wasn't a coffee drinker—green smoothies were more her style—but she was going to need caffeine to make it through her shift at the Main Street Café. If only she could summon the energy to get up and fix herself a cup of tea.

Not happening.

She shuffled to the fridge for her emergency stash, hidden in the back of the empty meat drawer so that it wouldn't tempt her. Her fingers closed over its cold, smooth surface, and she let out a sigh of relief.

Diet Coke.

An addiction she'd kicked years ago, but she always kept one can on hand, just in case, for moments like this. She popped the top and took a long gulp.

Heaven.

She guzzled the whole can, then dropped it in her recycling bin and shooed the dogs out the back door. While they romped in the yard, she went upstairs to do her makeup and get ready for work. It took copious amounts of concealer to hide the shadows under her eyes.

Thirty minutes later, she clocked in at the Main Street Café.

"Tom wants to see you before you start your shift," Marla commented as Olivia tucked her purse into her cubby in the break room.

"Really?" A niggle of worry lodged in her stomach.

Tom Hancock owned the café, and *shit*. Was it possible word had already gotten out about her arrest?

She found him in the hallway outside the kitchen. He gave her a broad smile that didn't quite reach his eyes. Tom was a kind man and a fair boss, but he ran a tight ship. If you screwed up, you were out.

And Olivia had screwed up. Big time.

"Morning, Liv," he said. "I won't waste time because I know you need to get started out there. I heard you were arrested last night."

She nodded. Oh, how she hoped she wasn't about to get fired.

"I'm going to give you a warning because you're a good employee, but as a practice, I don't hire anyone with a record. Keep yourself out of trouble from now on, you hear? If I get any complaints from the customers or you find yourself in the custody of Dogwood's finest again, I'll have to let you go. Are we clear?"

"Crystal," she answered for the second time that morning. Her hands fisted inside the pocket of her apron. "It won't happen again."

$\mathcal{C}$HAPTER TWO

$\mathcal{S}$neakers squeaked against the polished floors of the Dogwood Community Recreation Center. A ball swooshed through the hoop, and the air filled with yells and cheers. Zach Hill, one of the youngest and shortest at thirteen, clenched his fists at the other team's success.

Pete watched from the sidelines. He'd stopped by the rec center to drop off some pamphlets on the Junior Deputy program for high school students interested in a career in law enforcement, but when he'd spotted Zach on the court, he'd lingered for a few minutes to watch the boy play.

Since losing his dad to a drunk driver three years ago, Zach had struggled to control his temper. It was hard for a kid growing up without a father figure to look up to. Pete should know.

"Yo, Pete!" Steve Barnes, the rec center's director, clapped him on the back. "Good to see you. How's your momma these days? Haven't seen her at church recently."

"She's doing well, thanks." The truth was, she got by. She hadn't been quite right since his father's arrest, but then, who could blame her?

"Well, you tell her to stop by this Sunday. I'll save her a seat." Steve's eyes crinkled as he smiled. He was a widower going on five years now, and Pete got the sudden feeling Steve's interest in his mom might go a little farther than friendship.

He shoved his hands into his pockets. "I'll do that."

"Hey, you played soccer in school, didn't you?"

"I did."

Steve nodded toward the boys on the court. "I've got this bunch three afternoons a week. You know, keep 'em busy, keep 'em out of trouble. But I'm short a coach on Tuesdays. Don't suppose you'd want to help us out?"

Pete watched as Zach shot the ball and missed. He shrugged. "My schedule's pretty unpredictable. Hard for me to commit."

"I hear you, man. You working next Tuesday?"

"I'm off at three."

"Help me out just this once? I'm really in a bind."

Pete knew the game. He might even be a decent coach. He looked over at Zach, saw the boy stalk off the court. "Just this once."

"Great. See you Tuesday around four."

Pete agreed and walked out to his car, ready to go home and kick back with some college football. His alma mater, NC State, was playing Virginia Tech tonight. He never missed a chance to cheer for his Wolfpack, even if it was from the comfort of his couch.

First though, he had one other bit of business to take care of. Well, not business exactly. He got in his cruiser and drove thirty minutes to nearby Raleigh. His GPS guided him to the brown-paneled apartment building where Derek Johnson lived. Derek was a K9 officer in the Raleigh PD and an acquaintance of Pete's.

He got out of his car and walked toward the second apartment on the right, number 109. Derek opened the front door and said something—probably hello—but his words were lost to the deafening din of a dog barking from within.

Pete flinched. What the hell had he gotten himself into? He followed Derek inside and found the source of the noise, a large German shepherd sitting in the middle of the living room. The dog bounded forward to greet Pete, thrusting his snout into Pete's palm for affection.

."Hey, buddy," Pete said.

"So this is Timber," Derek said. "Thanks so much for taking him, man."

Pete looked down at the dog. Timber sat at his feet and stared back through brown eyes brimming with intelligence and personality. He had flunked out of the Raleigh PD K9 program last week and had been staying with Derek since. Pete had agreed to adopt Timber to keep him from being dumped at the shelter. "Hell of a time for me to take him. I'm covering for Alvarez this week; I've barely been home."

"I know. I'm sorry I couldn't keep him for you until the weekend, but my landlord complained about the barking. He had to go tonight." Derek picked up a leash from the catch-all table near the door.

"All right then." Pete took the leash and clipped it to Timber's collar. Derek gathered the rest of Timber's things and walked out with them to Pete's car.

Pete loaded Timber into the back of the cruiser and filled the trunk with the dog's belongings, such as they were. He'd have to make a trip to the pet store when he had a chance, which wouldn't be any time in the next few days.

As they pulled out of the parking lot, the dog let out a high-pitchcd whine that made Pete wince.

"Easy there, Timberwolf." He hadn't hesitated to take in the dog when he'd heard about his predicament. Dogs who flunked out of K9 training were hard to place outside of law enforcement, and besides, Pete figured he could use the company. The house was feeling a bit lonely these days, since the divorce.

When they got home, he took Timber for a walk to calm him down. The dog had whined pretty much non-stop since they left Derek's apartment. Inside, Pete poured a bowl of kibble for Timber and fixed himself a sandwich, then kicked back on the couch with a beer and his new dog and turned on the TV. The Wolfpack were up by seven. He let out a whoop.

An answering woof came from the German shepherd at his side. Timber raised his wolfish head and looked at the TV, then at Pete.

"Go Pack," Pete told him.

Timber howled in agreement.

"You know it, buddy. You're a good luck charm for the Pack, Timberwolf."

Pete snapped a picture of Timber with his cell phone and texted it to his sister Maggie, who was no doubt dying for an update by now. His phone rang almost immediately.

"He's so handsome!" Maggie gushed. "How is he doing?"

"So far so good."

"I'm so jealous. I want a dog," his sister said.

"Then get one."

"Maybe I will," she answered. "In the meantime, can I come over tomorrow after work and meet Timber?"

Pete glanced over at the shepherd on his couch. The dog stared back with his ever-watchful eyes. "Sure."

"I'll bring wings from Jimmy's."

"Perfect."

He said good night to his sister and headed upstairs to call it an early night. Pete had worked thirty of the last forty-eight hours and was dead on his feet. He was covering a few shifts for Jimena Alvarez this week while her family vacationed at Disney World. As one of the few deputies without a family, he often volunteered to cover extra shifts. The extra experience, not to mention a few extra bucks, never hurt.

Last week, he'd taken the detective exam. It was something he'd wanted for a long time, the next step in his career. The sheriff would be promoting one of his deputies at the end of the year, and Pete wanted that spot. Except he hadn't officially applied for the position yet. The interview process would put a spotlight on his past and his family...

He squeezed away a day's worth of tension in the back of his neck and fell into bed, exhausted. The bed shook as eighty pounds of German shepherd hopped in next to him. Pete was too tired to object. As long as the dog didn't try to spoon him, they'd be just fine.

Timber, as it turned out, wasn't the problem. Restless, Pete eventually found himself back downstairs, updating paperwork until his eyes crossed. Sometime in the wee hours of the night, he dropped back into bed and drifted off to sleep.

He woke to the blaring of the alarm and four large paws on his back.

Timber woofed in his ear, then leaped to the floor.

"Who needs an alarm clock when I have you?" he grumbled. He staggered to his feet and stepped straight into a burning hot shower.

Thirty minutes later, he was dressed and on the road. He stopped in at the sheriff's office for an extra cup of coffee and to turn in some paperwork.

"Yo," Hartzler called from behind his desk. "Heard you caught our little vandal out at the Halverson plant night before last."

"Yeah." He'd caught her, in both senses of the word. He tried and failed to suppress the memory of Olivia Bennett in his arms after she'd tumbled from her ladder.

"Typical. You get the cute blonde, and I get the bar brawl. Ted lost two more teeth," Hartzler said.

"Ouch."

Ted Hackett, mid-forties and headed nowhere fast, had spent more than a few nights as their guest, sleeping it off after a bar fight. Pete couldn't help but be glad Ted hadn't been arrested this time and spent the night in the pen with Olivia.

Then again, one whiff of his whiskey breath might have been enough to scare her straight. A girl like Olivia had too much going for her to waste it with stunts like the one she'd pulled the other night.

Sheriff Linburgh poked his head out of his office. "Got a minute?"

"Absolutely." He followed his boss inside.

The sheriff closed the door behind him and motioned for Pete to sit. "That girl you arrested at the Halverson plant the other night—what's your read on her?"

"She's an animal rights activist who thinks slaughtering chickens is animal abuse."

"Animal rights activist. Hmm." Sheriff Linburgh tapped his pen against the blotter on his desk. "You know, someone cut loose a bunch of Frank Holloway's cows last month. Think it could be related?"

Pete's gut instinct said no, but he kept his mouth shut. He didn't know a damn thing about Olivia Bennett other than that she'd broken the law night before last and that he couldn't help but think about her long legs in those tight jeans. "Not sure. I'll take a look at the files."

"Do that. We have several open vandalism cases that I'd like to see closed. Find out if any of it is related. And in the meantime, keep a close eye on Olivia Bennett. She seems like a troublemaker, that one."

"You know her?" Pete's instincts rose to attention.

"I know her type." The sheriff stood, indicating their conversation was over.

Pete walked out of the office, an uneasy feeling in his gut. He'd keep a close eye on Olivia all right. In fact, one of his first orders of business today was to swing by and make sure she was out there removing her graffiti from that chicken factory.

* * *

As Pete pulled into the Halverson Foods parking lot, two things struck him at once. One, Olivia Bennett was not alone. And two, the sight of her gave him a thrill he had no business feeling about a woman he'd arrested night before last.

She was again at the top of the ladder, this time with a paper mask over her face, an aerosol can in one hand, dirty rag in the other, scrubbing her graffiti from the side of the building. A woman was on a ladder beside her, helping with the task as a man stood on the ground between them, holding their ladders steady.

Chump. Letting the women do all the work.

Several Halverson workers lingered near the back entrance of the building, smoking cigarettes and watching them work. At the sound of Pete's cruiser crunching across the gravel lot, they hightailed it back inside. Olivia and her friends turned in his direction and stared. He cut the engine and stepped out.

Olivia came down the ladder, tugged the mask around her neck, and stood with her hands on her hips as he approached. Her friends hustled over to their car and made a show of getting bottles of water from a cooler in the trunk.

Not too eager to talk to him. Maybe they were the ones who'd been here with her the night she was arrested. Maybe he ought to go have a chat with them after he was finished with Olivia.

"Come to check up on me?" she asked.

"As a matter of fact."

Her eyes were hidden behind oversized sunglasses, her hair pulled back in a loose ponytail. Sweat had beaded on her upper lip. Despite it being the first week of October, the temperature here in North Carolina had spiked into the mid-eighties, and she looked sun-baked in a red tank top and black shorts.

"Well you can report back that I'm doing what I'm supposed to."

"So I see." His gaze drifted to the swell of her breasts, the cleavage peeking from the lacy trim of her top. He yanked his eyes back to her face. "Hope it's the last time I catch you out here."

She let out a sound of frustration. "I'll try to keep myself in line from now on."

"See that you do."

"Seriously?" Her voice rose. "I don't need a lecture, deputy. Spray-painting this place may have been a stupid idea, but they've been abusing chickens in there for years, and no one has done anything to stop it."

"I hate to break it to you, but some animals eat other animals. Nature isn't always pretty. Halverson Foods is no different, but that doesn't make it abuse. People eat chickens. Always have, always will."

She sucked in a breath, and her cheeks bloomed red. "Yes, but that doesn't give the men in there the right to torture them before they're slaughtered. All living beings deserve our respect, even if they're destined for your dinner plate. The birds who come here are beaten and tormented needlessly, and that, Deputy Sampson, is abuse."

She spun on her heel and stalked off toward the ladder, leaving him at an uncharacteristic loss for words.

"Look it up if you don't believe me," she called over her shoulder. "Google 'Citizens Against Halverson Foods.' If the undercover videos don't make you sick to your stomach, then feel free to judge me. But I hope you're not that heartless."

Heartless? No, he had a heart. It might be withered and

hardened beyond recognition, but it was in there. "And how did spray-painting this place help the chickens?"

She paused at the base of the ladder and gave him a discerning look. "Well see, that's the stupid part. It didn't. And I've learned my lesson, I promise."

"Glad to hear it."

In fact, Olivia Bennett had just shocked the hell out of him. He'd had all manner of insults hurled his way in the line of duty. But not often did someone, much less a woman he'd recently arrested, stand up to him with such eloquence or intelligence while at the same time taking responsibility for her misdeed.

Olivia Bennett was much more than a pretty face. She intrigued him in ways that weren't purely professional, and that was a problem. He couldn't allow his judgment to be clouded by personal feelings, not by Olivia or anyone else. Not ever again.

* * *

Olivia gulped a breath and held it, waiting for the lecture, or worse, the cuffs. Because surely telling off a sheriff's deputy like she'd just done was a no-no.

Deputy Sampson regarded her from behind his mirrored shades, hands on his belt, feet shoulder-width apart, the casual yet alert stance of the law enforcement officer. He stared for so long, and so intently, that she could hardly keep from squirming.

"Have a nice day, Miss Bennett," he said, finally, and strolled back to his car, apparently unruffled by her words. He'd probably stop for chicken nuggets on the way home.

She blew out a breath and turned back to the ladder. "You can come out now," she called to her friends, who'd been huddled on the other side of Terence's Durango.

"Check the balls on you," Terence said with a cocky grin as he sauntered over. "I can't believe you told off a cop like that."

"Seriously." Kristi's eyes were wide. "You schooled him for sure."

"Whatever. He wouldn't think I was a drunk driver if y'all hadn't run off and left me here the other night." Her irritation had started to fade when they'd first come begging for forgiveness. Terence had a prior for smoking weed, and Kristi worked for the state. Neither of them could risk an arrest going on their record.

But now they'd left her to face Deputy Sampson on her own twice, and she was pissed. Terence and Kristi shared her passion for animal rights and her crusade against Halverson Foods in particular, but when it came down to it, they were pretty lousy friends.

And maybe it was time to start pruning the lousy friends from her life.

"I'm really sorry about that." Kristi at least sounded apologetic.

Olivia readjusted her mask to block the worst of the stink, then sprayed Goo Off onto her blood-red message, however ridiculous it had turned out. *Chicken Ass* had no doubt made her a laughing stock among Dogwood's finest. At least *Chicken Assassins!* would have gotten her intended message across. The letters dripped and ran down the side of the building.

She swiped at her forehead and scrubbed harder. She meant what she'd told Deputy Sampson. From now on, she'd limit her activism to the right side of the law. She'd become notorious among her friends for her Facebook war against Halverson Foods, and she'd generated a lot of attention for her efforts. The local news had even mentioned her crusade a few weeks ago.

She'd plead temporary insanity for her acts the night of her birthday.

Mew.

She spun on the ladder so quickly she almost fell, and this time Deputy Sampson wasn't here to catch her. There it was again, a flash of white bobbing through the tall grasses behind the factory. Just a tiny little thing.

"I think there's a kitten out there," she said.

"I heard it too." Terence squinted against the sun.

"I'm going to look for it after I finish washing all this stuff off. It's probably a stray, and I haven't seen any sign of a mama cat."

"I'll help," Kristi said, from her perch on the other ladder.

By the time they'd finished scrubbing, a handful of Halverson workers had gathered outside, smoking cigarettes and making rude comments.

"You like chicken ass? I'll show you my ass," a man shouted.

Several other comments followed, mostly in Spanish, but she got the gist. Despite her earlier annoyance with them, she was super grateful for Terence and Kristi's presence. She made the mistake of glancing over her shoulder. The man who'd shouted was waving at her, making kissy faces. He wore red-splattered overalls, and Olivia was pretty sure he hadn't been spray-painting anything.

Gross.

"Can you believe those guys?" Kristi whispered.

Olivia kept her eyes on the side of the building. She'd left the paint thinner behind and was finishing the job with good old soap and water to remove the last of the residue. Water ran down her arms as she worked, soaking her shirt.

The rumble of an approaching truck drowned out the voices of the plant workers. She glanced toward the road, and her stomach lurched. The big rig slowed and pulled into the parking lot behind her. Its freight bed was stacked high with wire crates.

A shipment of chickens to be slaughtered.

It pulled to a stop near the back of the building, where the workers had gathered. The putrid scent of animal waste wafted from the truck, making Olivia's eyes water.

Chickens were packed into wire crates stacked ten high, without room to stand or protection from the elements. They had likely traveled hundreds of miles to get here, without access to food or water.

The birds were silent as the truck's engine shut off, and a hush fell over the air. Olivia realized she was holding her breath, unable to move from the top of the ladder. A loud beep shattered the eerie silence as someone drove a forklift toward them to begin unloading the crates of chickens. One by one they were lifted from the truck and carried inside.

"Holy shit," Kristi whispered.

One of the crates slipped to the ground. The door popped open, and a chicken tumbled out. It lay on the ground, unmoving. Tears sprang into Olivia's eyes. Without thinking, she reached into her back pocket for her phone and snapped a quick photo of the fallen bird.

A worker grabbed the chicken by its feet and waved it in her direction. "You like chicken ass? I'll show you chicken ass."

She turned away, horrified. Birds squawked as their crates were jostled and moved. From inside the building came the clang of machinery. She swallowed past the urge to vomit. The last crate was lifted from the truck, and she watched helplessly as the birds were carried inside. It was wrong for humans to treat another living being with such a lack of compassion.

At the far end of the parking lot, the little white kitten darted out of the bushes after a butterfly. It hopped on three legs, keeping its left front paw tucked as if injured, its fur dirty and bedraggled. A factory worker shouted an obscenity and threw a rock at it, and the kitten ran around behind the building.

Several men loitered in the doorway, watching Olivia and her friends as they finished up.

"Liv," Terence said. "I think it's time to get out of here."

"No argument here." She scampered down the ladder and helped him fold it, then gathered their supplies and hustled for the SUV.

She thought briefly of the kitten, but there was no way she could look for it right now, and she'd been ordered to stay off Halverson Foods property once her cleanup was complete. That meant she had to find a legal way to save it, because she wasn't about to get arrested again. She couldn't protect the chickens from those men, but she could damn well make sure they didn't get their hands on that poor little kitten.

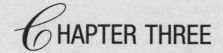

CHAPTER THREE

When Pete got off duty that evening, he went home and changed into gym shorts and a T-shirt and took Timber for a run. They headed for the paved jogging trail that ran around the outskirts of town and pounded out two miles down to the pond by the old mill.

Timber jogged obediently at his side, head up, eyes alert and watchful. If not for his *slightly* unpredictable personality, he'd have made a hell of a K9 officer.

Since they had the place to themselves, Pete unclipped Timber's leash and let him chase fish and frogs in the pond. The dog had been bouncing off the walls by the time Pete got off work. He knew enough about dogs— shepherds in particular—to know that proper exercise was essential to their sanity.

Pete knew the feeling. A good run always put him in a calmer state of mind as well.

Timber sloshed toward him. Pete bent and grabbed a stick, which he chucked into the middle of the pond. Timber raced down the short wooden pier and belly flopped into the water. He grabbed the stick and brought it back, a slightly rabid look in his eye when Pete tried to take it from him to throw again.

No doubt Timber's instinctual prey drive was off the charts, thanks to selective breeding and rigorous training to prepare him for work as a police dog. Pete waited for him to drop the stick on his own rather than grabbing it out of the dog's mouth.

He tossed the stick a few more times, then clipped the leash onto the dog and headed for home. Back at the house, he hosed Timber down then took a shower. He poured a bowl of chow for the dog and fixed himself a meatball sandwich, which he brought to the couch to enjoy with some football. A few minutes later, Timber joined him, still licking his chops.

After Pete had filled the gaping hole in his belly, he pulled out his laptop and typed in "Citizens Against Halverson Foods." A website popped up, filled with photos that, even to his nonactivist eye, were disturbing.

He clicked on a video. Three workers laughed as one of them tossed a chicken onto the concrete floor. It squawked as it lay there, unable to get up. What they did to it next made Pete's meatball sandwich rise into his throat. Olivia was right. That was animal abuse.

The website was filled with information on the efforts the group had made to have Halverson Foods' chicken-processing plant shut down. There was a link to sign a petition and access to the group's Facebook page, which had over four thousand "likes."

And the woman behind it all? Olivia Bennett.

She was smart, all right. Smart enough to have known

better than to break the law to further her cause. Smart enough to keep her pretty little self out of trouble from now on? He wasn't sure about that. The fact was, she remained Sheriff Linburgh's top suspect for a number of open vandalism cases around town.

Pete had his doubts. Olivia seemed pretty singularly focused on Halverson Foods. If anything else went down on their property, he'd be willing to bet she was behind it. But he didn't quite see her spray-painting a crude version of the Pillsbury Dough Boy with an erection on the front window of Beth's Bakery.

It was an election year, and Halverson Foods had backed Sheriff Linburgh in the last election. Certainly the sheriff's interest in this case could be related to a need to keep the company happy, but it didn't mean he was wrong about Olivia either. Had she turned loose Holloway's cows?

The sheriff had asked him to keep an eye on her, and hell, Pete's gut hadn't exactly been reliable lately, so he'd make sure she didn't fly anything beneath his radar. He couldn't afford another screwup.

* * *

Olivia kept her cheerful smile firmly in place as she approached Deputy Sampson's table. Sure, local law enforcement stopped in here sometimes for a cup of coffee or a meal after getting off duty. But Pete Sampson? He'd never eaten here before that she could remember.

Today he was here and seated in her section. He was checking up on her. Well fine, because that factory was cleaner than it had been when she'd found it. She'd done her penance, and she had nothing to hide.

"Deputy Sampson," she said politely, "what can I get you today?"

He looked up, his dark eyes searching her face. He was in uniform, his slacks and shirt pressed to perfection. But up close, he looked...tired. "What's good?" he asked, then gave her a devilish smile. "How's the chicken?"

She pointed her pen at him. "Ha ha, very funny. I would personally recommend the eggplant parm, but I hear the chicken is very good as well."

"So you're a vegetarian then." He leaned back against the red-patterned upholstery of the booth, his eyes never leaving hers.

"Yes, and maybe if you had checked out my website, you'd understand why."

"Oh, I checked it out." His gaze was steady and intent.

"Really?" That caught her by surprise. "And? What did you think?"

"Very informative." His eyes revealed nothing. They might have been discussing the weather for all he seemed to care.

"Informative? That's the best you can do?" If his intent had been to piss her off, he was succeeding. Big time. "You seem like a decent human being, Deputy Sampson. Did it not bother you to see those birds being abused?"

"I didn't say that." He looked down at his menu. "So the chicken parm, huh?"

"Seriously, you came here to order chicken from me?" She propped her fists on her hips and glared at him.

"You must serve chicken here every day. Do you get this worked up about it every time?"

He was baiting her. This had to be some kind of cop technique, and it was working because she was about to blow a lid, and he looked as calm as ever. "Do I get this worked up? No. Only when the deputy who arrested me comes in here making fun of my beliefs. Well, if you can watch those videos and not be bothered, then good for you. Enjoy your chicken parm."

"Did you say you got arrested?" Mr. Edgemont craned his head from the booth behind Deputy Sampson's. The old man came in here every day for lunch and was as much of a gossip as any woman she'd ever known.

"Yes, sir, I did." And dammit, she really hadn't meant to spread that information around town. Not that it wouldn't have gotten out anyway. Working at the Main Street Café, a lot of people knew her, and someone would have seen her mug shot on the local news website and spread the word soon enough.

Bad enough Tom already knew. This was exactly the type of scene he'd wanted to avoid. Olivia was teetering on a skinny wire right now, without a net.

"What did you do?" Mr. Edgemont's eyebrows were up, as if he expected her to confess something really scandalous.

"I spray-painted the Halverson Foods chicken factory," she told him.

He tsk-tsked her, and her fists clenched at her sides. "Aw well, honey, you've gotta come around sooner or later. People eat meat." He gestured at the remainder of his pulled pork sandwich. "You ain't never going to change that."

"I'll keep that in mind." She turned her back on him

to find Pete watching her, an annoying twinkle of amusement in his dark eyes.

"Anyway, if you're finished heckling me, I'll go put your order in." She tried to sound as nonchalant as he looked, but she failed. She sounded pissed.

"Aren't you going to ask what I want to drink?"

Oh my God. Her eye twitched. "Of course, Deputy Sampson. What would you like to drink?"

"You got Dr Pepper?"

She nodded.

"All right then. Dr Pepper, and why don't we make it the eggplant parm?" He winked.

Olivia's mouth fell open. She snapped it shut and stalked off to place his order. What the hell was his deal? All that and then he ordered eggplant?

He was entirely too obnoxious to be so good looking. She'd never actually been one of those women who lusted after a man in uniform—probably because of her dislike of authority figures—but Pete Sampson? Phew. Naughty images of him frisking her played through her mind, and her cheeks heated.

"Psst."

She whipped around to find Kristi standing outside the door to the kitchen, cell phone in hand.

"You've got to see this," Kristi said.

"See what?"

"There's a picture making rounds on the Internet today." She held her phone out.

Olivia took it, a tight fist of dread in her stomach, but it wasn't a picture of herself she saw on Kristi's screen. Instead, the photo showed a bunch of people wearing chicken costumes, standing beneath her botched *Chicken*

Ass message, mooning the camera. Someone had stamped clip-art chicken tails across the image to hide their bare butts from the Internet.

Kristi snickered, a look of pure delight on her face.

"What the hell is this?" Olivia asked.

Her friend shrugged. "Word is, some kind of fraternity prank. Funny, right?"

Funny? No. Her message had become a joke. She'd been arrested and possibly messed up her future so that a bunch of college kids could pull their pants down and become Internet sensations? "Where did you find this?"

"Anyone in town with a Facebook account has seen it. I'm surprised you hadn't."

This just kept getting better. "I've been here since this morning. Look, I need to get back to work. Call me later, okay?"

Kristi nodded and left with a wave.

Olivia walked to the soda fountain machine and stood for a moment with her eyes closed. She focused on her inner peace with an "on the go" meditation technique she'd mastered, using calm, deep breaths to banish her temper and frustration.

Then she filled Pete's Dr Pepper and carried it to his table. "Here you go."

She turned to walk away, but he placed a big, warm hand over hers, his eyes suddenly serious. "The videos bothered me, okay? I am not, nor do I intend to become, a vegetarian, but I don't like to think I'm supporting that kind of abuse when I buy my lunch."

So he did care. Well crap. Now she was *really* in trouble.

* * *

Pete saw surprise flicker in her eyes, covered quickly with more of that smartass temper he apparently enjoyed way too much for his own good. No other explanation for why he'd been needling her since he got here.

Sure, he could say it was for the case. He'd been trained to read body language, and sometimes it paid to push a little, helped him get a better gut impression on whether a person was guilty or not.

Olivia Bennett was guilty all right, but she'd made no attempt to hide it either.

"Your meal should be out in a few minutes," she told him, then walked off toward the kitchen.

He turned his attention to his cell phone, scrolling through messages. His eyes caught on the most recent email: the results from his detective exam. He'd scored an 86.34.

A thrill passed through him. Even if he was passed over for the promotion, that was a score to be proud of. This was what he'd been working toward since he was a little boy. More than a deputy, he'd wanted to become a detective. Solve crimes. Maybe even leave Dogwood behind once and for all and join a larger department somewhere else.

Charlotte, perhaps. But he'd never leave North Carolina, not with his mom and sister living here in Dogwood.

Sheriff Linburgh had hinted that Pete was his top choice to make detective at the end of the year, but it was far from a done deal. Three other deputies had tested with Pete, and there were several fine officers in the bunch. He slid his phone into his pocket, as Olivia approached with his lunch.

"Eggplant parm, as you wish," she said, as she placed a plate in front of him. The sandwich bulged with breaded eggplant, complimented by potato chips and a pickle wedge. The aroma made his mouth water. He'd always heard the food here was good, but he'd had his reasons for not visiting.

Reasons he'd overlooked today for the chance to see Olivia at work.

"Thanks," he said.

She didn't immediately walk away, so he decided to take advantage of the moment and keep her talking a little longer. "So you've been crusading against Halverson Foods for a while."

She nodded. "Over a year. I've even been able to get some national attention. There was a pretty big stink after those undercover videos came out, but still nothing was done to stop it."

"Seems hard to believe." With that kind of evidence, he would have expected charges to be filed. He made a mental note to look further into the case when he got back to the office.

Her brown eyes gleamed with emotion. "Well it's like you said, they're there to be slaughtered anyway. No one cares how they're treated beforehand."

All done up for work, with her makeup perfect, her blond hair long and straight over her shoulders, in black slacks and a snug pink top, she was absolutely stunning. He'd found himself attracted to her on that ladder in the sweltering sun, and today the pull was even stronger. Though he did kind of miss the shorts...

And he admired her passion. Stupid as she'd been to spray-paint that factory, her heart was in the right place. There were far too many people in the world who were inclined to let things slide instead of taking a stand for what they believed in or what was right. Olivia Bennett was not afraid to stand up for her beliefs, even if it made her a laughingstock, and he respected that.

"People care," he answered her. "But we can't enforce a law that hasn't been written. You seem fairly eloquent about the issue. Maybe you should be addressing your lawmakers."

"Hmph." She took a step back. "That's actually a really good idea."

"I have my moments." He picked up his sandwich and took a big bite.

"Well, thanks." She turned and walked off, giving him a backward glance that was sexy as hell. Everything about her was sexy as hell.

And he had absolutely no business lusting after a woman he'd arrested.

He devoured his sandwich, chips, and even the pickle, then polished off his Dr Pepper. The food was delicious. Too bad he couldn't eat here without wanting his waitress, and she was definitely not on the menu.

Olivia swung by and dropped off his check. He stuck a twenty on it and stood. He turned down the hall past the kitchen to visit the men's room before he went out to his car, but halfway there, he came face to face with Tamara Hill.

She wore the same uniform as Olivia, and she passed him without recognition. She had no way of knowing that Pete's testimony had put a habitual drug offender back on the streets, allowing him to take the fateful drive that had cost her husband his life. Nor did she know that Pete's own father had been the man driving that car.

Tamara didn't know who he was, and like a coward, Pete let her walk past, then pushed into the men's room. He stood there at the sink, sucking in breaths over the sickening clench in his stomach. Swallowing hard, he turned away, unable to face his own reflection in the mirror. Never in a million years could he repay his debt to the Hill family.

* * *

"Vandalizing a building, Olivia? What in the world were you thinking?"

Olivia winced at the rebuke in her mother's voice. "Obviously I wasn't."

Marlene Bennett sighed into the phone. "Well, thank goodness the judge was understanding. You've got to get the charges dismissed or you'll never get back into McKellon."

Olivia's mother was a prosecutor for the Wake County District Attorney's Office. Her father was one of the top defense attorneys in Raleigh. They'd argued for decades over which route Olivia should take: defending the innocent or prosecuting the guilty.

In the end, she'd decided to do neither. Two years into her studies at McKellon University School of Law, her longtime boyfriend died of an accidental overdose. Heartbroken, Olivia had taken it as a wakeup call to pursue her own happiness and quit living her life according to her parents' expectations. So she'd dropped out of law school.

Because truthfully, the more time she spent there, the more she wondered if she wanted to be a lawyer at all. She'd never truly fit in at McKellon. While her classmates were busy buying business suits and planning their path to partner, Olivia daydreamed about animal rights protests and meditation techniques.

Now she waited tables at the Main Street Café. Her parents were still waiting for her to come to her senses. They'd pay for her to finish her law degree as long as she re-enrolled before she turned thirty. That meant she had to decide this year if she wanted their help.

"I'll get the charges dropped." Olivia sank onto the couch and slung her feet onto the coffee table, suppressing a weary sigh.

"Don't you think this has gone on long enough?" her mother asked. "With your grades and your passion, you'll be on the fast track to make partner wherever you go. Or you could join the DA's office. You might even get to prosecute some animal abusers."

Olivia smiled, just a little. "But I'm not sure I want to be a lawyer."

"You have opportunities most people don't. You've got natural talent, and your dad and I have connections to get you started. Don't waste that. You're obviously bored with waitressing or you wouldn't be vandalizing buildings in your spare time."

Well, she was a little bored with waitressing, but that had nothing to do with the reason she'd spray-painted Halverson Foods' chicken-processing plant. "I'm not bored."

"Don't be foolish, Olivia. It's time to get your act together before it's too late."

"I will, Mom." Olivia hung up the phone and rested her

head in her hands. Everything her mother had said was true. She'd make an awesome lawyer. Except she didn't want to be one.

And that had to count for something, right?

Or was she being childish? Lots of people had jobs they didn't like. They did what they had to do to pay the bills and support their family. She could sure pay a hell of a lot more bills practicing law than waiting tables.

Bailey, one of her foster dogs, came over and licked her cheek. She was a four-year-old fawn boxer, available for adoption through Triangle Boxer Rescue. Olivia wasn't much of a dog person, but she'd promised to foster while she was renting Merry's house, so Bailey and Scooby—currently sprawled out flat on the couch and snoring loudly—were hers until they found their forever homes.

Her phone chimed a notification. It had better not be someone else tagging her in that fraternity prank picture, because if she had to see that thing one more time...

It was a text message from her friend Cara, who'd moved to Massachusetts earlier in the year. *Chicken ass? Handcuffs? Hot cops? Call me!*

Olivia snorted. If Cara still lived here, she'd have been at Olivia's birthday celebration and probably would have talked her out of spray-painting the chicken-processing plant in the first place. She was a good friend like that.

It's true. I'm a convict. I'll call you tomorrow, she texted back.

Because right now, she was going on a kitten hunt. It had been bothering her for days that she hadn't had a chance to look for the kitten yet, but tonight was the night. Technically, she wasn't supposed to set foot on

Halverson Foods' property now that she'd completed her restitution by washing off her graffiti, and she had no desire to run into the employees there again.

But she was hoping that, if she went over after they'd gone home and stayed by the road, she could lure the kitten to her. She'd bought a can of tuna for the cause, despite the fact she didn't eat it and the very smell was enough to make nausea rise in her throat.

The kitten was hurt, and it was hungry, and it needed a home.

She couldn't just turn her back and pretend she'd never seen it.

She put leashes on the dogs and took them for a walk, then loaded up her Prius with everything she thought she might need on her kitten-capturing expedition. She'd borrowed a cat carrier from Kristi, which she lined with a ratty old towel. That and the can of tuna were for her best-case scenario. Worst case, she had a cat-sized humane trap and a bag of kitten chow to leave behind.

If she couldn't catch it tonight, she'd leave the trap and check back tomorrow. With any luck, the hungry kitten would have taken the bait.

It was just past eight, and the sky above glistened with stars. She drove cautiously out to the factory but pulled over before she reached its entrance, instead parking on the side of the road.

She'd done her research earlier, finding where the edge of their property lay. No way was she getting caught trespassing a second time.

She stepped out of her car and popped open the can of tuna, letting its nasty fishy smell permeate the air. "Here, kitty kitty."

The air around her immediately filled with flashing blue lights and the blip of a siren. A cruiser pulled in behind her Prius.

"Christ on a cracker." She kicked her tire. Seriously, what were the chances?

Sure enough, Deputy Pete Sampson stepped out of the cruiser, looking every bit as crisp—and as hot—as he had at the diner earlier. He sauntered over, his expression stern. His gaze traveled over her, making her squirm.

He tipped his head to the side. "Mind telling me what the hell you're doing out here, fixing to break the law—with a can of tuna fish?"

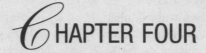HAPTER FOUR

$\mathscr{P}$ete watched her squirm. Disappointment battled curiosity as he waited for her explanation. He had to admit—he'd wanted to believe that the sheriff was wrong about her, that she would stay out of trouble and away from the Halverson plant. Yet here she was.

"I'm not breaking the law." Olivia raised her chin, still clutching the can of tuna fish.

"That's questionable. As you're well aware, trespassing is a crime."

She didn't blink, didn't look away. "I'm not trespassing. This is public property. Halverson Foods' property line lies about five feet past the entrance, right over there." She turned and pointed toward the driveway some twenty feet behind her.

"You sure about that?" He sure as hell didn't know where the property line lay, but as far as he was concerned, she had no business anywhere near here. And there she went again spouting facts that proved she was anything but a ditzy blonde.

"I'm positive. I told you I had no intention of breaking the law again."

"No offense, Miss Bennett, but a lot of people tell me that. They rarely mean it. So you never answered my question. Just what the hell are you doing out here after dark, carrying a can of tuna fish?"

She glanced down at the can in her hand and, if he wasn't mistaken, gagged slightly. "I'm looking for a kitten."

"A kitten?" Well that wasn't what he was expecting, but then again, Olivia Bennett had a habit of surprising him.

"I saw it both times I was out here. It's little, and something's wrong with one of its legs. It needs to see a vet, and, more than likely, it needs a home." Her chin was still up, daring him to challenge her.

He settled his arms over his chest. "A kitten."

She nodded. "I just want to see if I can catch it. I'm not going to trespass." She held up two fingers. "Scouts honor. So you can just be on your way."

He shook his head. "All the same, you have to admit, you're blurring a line. I'll just hang around and make sure you don't cross it."

She let out a sound of frustration. "Well if you're going to stand there, the least you can do is help me look for the kitten."

Was she serious about the kitten? He looked down at the open can of tuna in her hands. This woman was completely illogical yet totally logical at the same time. "I'm more likely to scare it off."

She rolled her eyes. "Which is why I suggested you be on your way. But if you seriously don't trust me..."

"Whether I trust you or not, I'm not leaving you out here by yourself." He gestured to their surroundings—dark woods to the right and the empty chicken factory on their left. It was no place for a woman to be alone after dark.

"I can take care of myself." She turned her back and walked a few steps toward the wooded buffer off the side of the road, waving the can of tuna and calling, "Here, kitty kitty."

Pete could almost see the cartoon lines of fishy scent wafting in the air around her. He pulled the flashlight from his belt and shone it in the bushes for her.

She poked around, crouching and calling for the cat. He would have thought he was being played for a fool, out here in the middle of nowhere in the dark, mere yards from the scene of her arrest, except for the fact he couldn't think of a single other reason for Olivia—a vegetarian no less—to be out here armed with nothing but a can of tuna fish.

After about ten minutes, he was about to tell her to pack up and be on her way. It was past time for him to resume his patrol, but she beat him to it, heading back toward her car.

"I knew it was a long shot," she said with a shrug.

He turned toward the cruiser. "All right then."

Olivia opened the hatchback of her Prius and pulled out a large wire cage.

"What are you doing?"

"Leaving a trap. I brought a bag of kitten chow to put inside. I'm betting his empty belly will get the better of him by tomorrow."

"And what if you catch a raccoon instead?"

She sucked her bottom lip between her teeth as if the idea of catching something other than the mythical kitten hadn't occurred to her. "Then I'll set it loose and try again."

"You're going to an awful lot of trouble over this. Why?"

She turned, her brown eyes bright in the beam of his headlights. "It's a tiny, helpless kitten. I can't pretend I didn't see it. I have to try my best to help."

"What if it has a home?"

She gestured to the darkness surrounding them. "Out here? More likely someone drove it here and dumped it."

"Hmm." Might be she was right. His first year on patrol he'd found a bag of puppies in a ditch, thrown out like trash.

Olivia carried the trap into the woods, then crouched and dumped a hearty helping of kitten chow inside. She carefully set the spring latch, then sat back to survey her handiwork. "I'll come out and check it in the morning before I clock in at the café."

"Not sure you want to be poking around out here on a Monday morning. Folks might get the wrong idea. I'm off tomorrow. I'll swing by and see if you've caught anything."

"Oh, um." She narrowed her eyes. "Really?"

"I'll give you a call." He turned and walked back to his cruiser before he'd had a chance to question his motivation.

* * *

Pete was still not thinking about it when he drove back out to the Halverson plant the following morning. He'd already gone for a long run with his dog, and now he'd do a cursory check on the trap Olivia had set. He could only hope he wasn't about to get his fingers gnawed off trying to free a rabid raccoon with a belly full of kitten chow.

He slowed his Subaru Forester and pulled over where he'd found Olivia the night before. The thought of her in his cuffs, looking forlorn yet devastatingly beautiful, had nothing to do with why he was here. Nothing. Not the scent of wildflowers in her hair. The fire in her eyes. Or the way she could sucker punch him straight to the gut with her passion for her cause.

The woman overflowed with emotion, with raw passion and unabashed determination. And Pete, well he did better when he kept his emotions firmly in check. Olivia was a firecracker all right, and he'd prefer to keep all of his fingers intact.

Therefore, he'd confirm that she hadn't caught anything in her trap, then he'd put her out of his mind in anything other than a purely professional capacity, which meant trying to connect her to any of the other acts of vandalism around town.

He stepped out of the Forester and crunched through leaf-strewn pine needles to the spot where she'd left the trap. "Well I'll be damned."

Inside the silver cage, a little white creature gazed at him from wide blue eyes. "Mew."

Pete shook his head. "You are one lucky furball."

He crouched to get a better look, and the kitten hissed at him. It was little, probably shouldn't even be away from its momma yet. Its white fur was dirty and matted with burs. He reached out to grab the handle on top of the cage, and the kitten went berserk. It ping-ponged from one end of the trap to the other, hissing and screeching like a wild animal.

"Whoa." He grabbed the cage and stood, careful to keep his fingers far enough from the bars as to be out of harm's way. Out of nowhere, he stifled a laugh imagining Olivia trying to tame this pint-sized terror.

They'd be perfect for each other.

Back at his SUV, he put the kitten in the back with an old towel underneath that he kept for Timber, then pulled out his cell phone and dialed her number. It rang through to voicemail, and he felt a flicker of panic. She'd mentioned having to work today. What the hell was he going to do with the kitten in the meantime? "It's Pete. I got your kitten. Call me when you get this."

He slid the phone into his pocket and stared at the creature in his car. It stared right back, eyes wide and terrified. He was tempted to drop it off on her doorstep and be done, but that wasn't right, and he knew it.

Therefore, with a heavy sigh, he got back into the Forester and headed home. The kitten meowed plaintively all the way there.

Pete put the cage against the wall in his garage and slung an old towel over the top. Covering the crate sometimes helped Timber settle down, maybe it would have the same effect on the kitten. It just hissed at him.

He went into the house and got a small bowl, filled it with water, and carried it back to the caged kitten. This would be tricky. He opened the trap just wide enough to slip the bowl inside.

The kitten hissed again, louder.

He slammed the door shut and made sure it had latched securely.

Now to wait for Olivia's call.

* * *

Olivia listened to the message on her phone, then punched five to listen to it again.

"It's Pete. I've got your kitten. Call me when you get this."

It's Pete. So they'd moved to a first-name basis now? She felt a little thrill at the prospect. She was attracted to him, which was silly because he certainly didn't date women he'd arrested. And that was a shame, because Pete was different from the guys she usually dated.

She'd always gone for the "lost cause" type, the boy her parents would be certain to hate, the one everyone said would end up being nothing but trouble.

And they'd been right.

Her dating life was nothing but a string of wrong-way collisions. She'd been in love once. She and Roger dated all through college, but while she was studying her butt off in law school, he was burning brain cells on cocaine. He was an addict, and she'd fought so hard to save him from himself, but in the end, he'd loved the cocaine more than he'd loved her.

He'd overdosed one sunny April morning, dead at twenty-four. Olivia had been heartbroken. And she'd vowed not to date another man with such demons. Unfortunately she hadn't always held true to that promise. It was in her nature to fight for a lost cause, and she'd wasted too many years on men who didn't have their act together.

Part of her pact with herself before she turned thirty was to get serious about this aspect of her life too. It was time to grow up, both personally and professionally. She needed a career, and she needed a man who respected himself. A man who might marry her and father her children, because her biological clock was starting to tick a bit more loudly these days.

Shaking her head, she lifted the phone to her ear. Pete had called at nine, almost five hours ago. She had no idea what he'd done with the kitten in the meantime, but she'd just gotten off shift. The thrill of excitement that ran through her this time had nothing to do with the sexy man she was about to dial.

They'd done it. They'd actually caught the kitten!

She pressed his number and hit send. It rang twice, then connected.

"Hello." He sounded irresistibly dark and sexy on the phone, his deep voice accentuated by the crackle of the airwaves.

"It's Olivia. I just got your message."

"'Bout time."

"Yeah, sorry. I just got off work. How's the kitten? Do you want me to meet you somewhere?"

"It's a feisty one, that's for sure. I'll drop it by your house in half an hour."

"Oh, okay. Thank you."

"Welcome." With a click, he was gone.

He hadn't asked where she lived. Hadn't asked for her phone number either. It irked her that he knew these things from her arrest. Blowing back a lock of hair, she headed for her car. Pete would be at her house in half an hour, which meant she had just enough time to buy a litter box and hurry home to put the dogs out back before he arrived.

Where should she put the kitten? Bailey and Scooby couldn't be trusted around it, not at first anyway. It might not even be tame and almost certainly wasn't house-broken. She flinched. Oh well, if there ever were a land-lord who'd forgive her bringing a kitten like this into her home, it was Merry.

She hurried to her car, then stopped short and stared. Someone had spray-painted chickens all over it.

What the hell?

She balled her fists. White paint dripped down the side of her Prius from the crudely drawn chickens stretching from her front bumper to the rear. It was the driver's side, which faced away from the diner. Someone had defaced her car in the middle of the day in the center of town. Who? Why?

Beneath the chickens were the words "Cluck you."

Classy.

Who had spray-painted her car, and what the hell was she going to do about it? Would it wash off? Should she go to the police? Swearing under her breath, Olivia slid into the driver's seat. No time to worry about it now. She had to get home and set up for the kitten. Fifteen minutes later, she turned into her driveway.

Inside, she let the dogs out of the kitchen and dodged slobbery snouts as she hurried upstairs to change. She tossed her uniform in the laundry basket and pulled on a pink tank top and shorts, thankful for the warm weather this far into October.

She put the dogs in the backyard and grabbed a bottle of water from the fridge when the doorbell rang. She smoothed her hair and adjusted the neckline of her top, which was ridiculous because it was *Deputy Sampson* at her front door.

If she knew what was good for her, she'd go scrub her makeup off and change into sweatpants before she opened it.

Instead, she pulled the door open and offered him her sweetest smile. And holy hell, she hadn't been prepared for the sight of him out of his uniform. He wore a red T-shirt and khaki shorts, his dark hair ruffled by the breeze, and oh, her heart tripped all over itself at the sight.

"Olivia." He looked down at the cage dangling from his right hand, then back at her.

So they were definitely on a first-name basis, and oh, the kitten! It looked up at her with wide, terrified blue eyes, crouched in the back corner of the trap.

"Thank you so much for doing this for me." She motioned him inside, trying to keep her eyes on the cat and not the man.

"You take up car graffiti in your spare time?" he asked, his dark eyes pinned on hers.

She sighed. "Someone did that while I was at work."

"You report it to the sheriff's office?"

She shook her head. "Should I?"

"Of course. Vandalism is a crime, as you know. Any idea who did it?"

"Nope. Maybe those college kids who achieved Internet fame last week with that picture of themselves mooning the camera."

A smile quirked his lips. "Could be. Do you know them?"

"No, I don't know them." She huffed in annoyance.

"Then how would they know who you are or what car you drive?"

"I don't know. It's a small town. Lots of people know me from the café. Anyway, thank you for bringing me the kitten." She reached for the cage.

He motioned that he would carry it inside. "I don't think it's tame."

In answer, the kitten hissed.

"Oh." She pursed her lips. What was she going to do with it? She couldn't very well turn a feral cat loose in the house. "I'll put it in the bathroom for now."

He nodded. "Probably best."

He followed as she walked to the half bath at the end of the hall. It was barely large enough to hold the trap and the small litter box she'd bought. But once the kitten came out of the trap, she'd have more room to set up supplies for it.

Pete's arm bumped hers as he set it on the floor. His skin was hot. It sent a jolt of awareness through her. And damn if he didn't still smell like he'd just stepped right out of a bakery. He made her hungry, in several different ways.

"So I'll be on my way then. Good luck with that." He gestured toward the kitten, still crouched and watching them.

"Thanks again. You really didn't have to do this."

He shrugged. "No problem. Make sure you stop by the sheriff's office later and report that vandalism on your car."

He strolled out her front door, leaving her with a healthy dose of unrequited longing and a decent amount of trepidation about the kitten in the bathroom. At least one of those could be easily fixed.

She went down the hall and set up litter, food, and water for her visitor, then unlocked the cage and closed the bathroom door. She'd leave it alone in there for a while to calm down, then check on it later.

In the meantime, she sat in front of her laptop to find out how to tame a feral kitten. Her search results suggested that, with a kitten as young as this one, the process shouldn't be too difficult. Nothing she couldn't handle. She also needed to get it to a vet. She suspected it had a leg injury, and it probably had a whole host of other issues, but she'd give it some time to settle in first.

In the meantime...

"Ugh." She closed her laptop and leaned back in the chair. The last thing she wanted to do was visit the Dogwood County Sheriff's Office, and that's exactly what she was about to do.

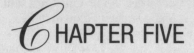

CHAPTER FIVE

Olivia walked out the front door of the Dogwood County Sheriff's Office, her pulse thumping an angry tap dance between her ears. The deputy who'd taken her statement had all but laughed at her.

"Do you own white spray paint?" he'd asked, as if she would spray-paint her own car and report it so that they could enjoy a laugh at her expense. They didn't take her seriously. And if the sheriff's office thought she was a joke, how was she ever supposed to get them to take action against Halverson Foods?

She hadn't thought anything could be more humiliating than her arrest last week, but this might be, because this time she hadn't done anything wrong. Now she had to go home and find out how to get spray paint off her car, then deal with the stray kitten in her bathroom.

That all sounded a bit lonely and depressing, which was not her idea of a good time in the least, so she picked up her phone to try to rustle up some company for later. No boyfriend at the moment, and she was trying to distance herself from Kristi and Terence. Her college roommate, Cara, had moved to Massachusetts. That left Merry. They'd been friends through Cara, but now that Cara had moved, she and Merry had been spending more time together.

Merry's phone rang through to voicemail, and Olivia remembered belatedly that her friend worked a twelve-hour shift at Dogwood Hospital on Mondays.

"Hey, it's Liv. If you feel like going out for a drink or something after work, let me know." She hung up and pushed the phone into her purse.

Ugh. This was so lame.

Olivia drove home in a huff. Phone in hand, she walked around the Prius taking photos of the graffiti. The sheriff's office might not take her seriously, but this was no laughing matter as far as she was concerned. It couldn't hurt to have her own documentation of the damage.

Once she was satisfied she'd taken enough photos, it was time to clean it off. A quick Google search suggested nail polish remover might be the answer. Unfortunately she'd used most of what she had scrubbing paint off herself after last week's debacle. She took what remained of the bottle outside with a dish towel and started rubbing at the chicken closest to her front bumper.

It smeared and began to come off. The rag quickly turned pink, but it looked like most of the car's red paint had stayed intact. She managed to remove the first chicken, leaving only a dull patch in the Prius's paint, before she ran out of nail polish remover.

Determined not to drive to work tomorrow in a chicken-covered car, she hopped in and drove down the street to CVS. She bought a half dozen bottles of nail polish remover, then drove back home and spent the next two hours scrubbing every last bit of graffiti from her car.

Her hands stung, and her head ached from the fumes. She turned on the hose and sprayed the rest of the residue from the Prius, then headed inside for a shower. When she got out, her phone was ringing.

She glanced at the screen, then answered. "Hey, Merry."

"Can I take a rain check?" Merry asked. "I work again tomorrow, and I usually go to bed super early on work nights. What if we go to The Watering Hole on Friday?"

"Oh, sure. That sounds great."

"Everything okay?"

Olivia swallowed a sigh. "Yeah. I just need a night out is all."

Merry made a sound of agreement. "That makes two of us. I've been a bit of a homebody since Jayden came to stay with us, but T.J. can handle bedtime when he needs to."

"Okay, I'll text you later this week."

"Perfect."

Olivia hung up the phone feeling as if the spring had returned to her step. Her car was clean, and she had fun plans to look forward to.

Now she just had to deal with the feral cat doing God-knew-what in her downstairs bathroom. She left the dogs gated in the kitchen, grabbed an armful of old towels, and cautiously cracked the door to the bathroom.

The trap was empty. She grabbed its handle and slid it into the hall, then stepped into the bathroom and closed the door behind her. A slight disturbance in the litter box indicated it had been used—*Hallelujah*—but where was the kitten?

Then she spotted a bit of white fur behind the toilet. The kitten was crouched against the linoleum, eyeing her. Olivia set about fashioning the towels into a makeshift kitten bed on the floor beside her. Then she sat and scooped the terrified creature into her lap.

The kitten hissed like a wild thing, struggling against her grip. Olivia pressed it against her chest and began stroking it behind its head. "Shhh. Sorry about this, but the Internet says I have to hold you and rub you several times a day to make you tame."

It didn't fight her but instead crouched, eyes wide and terrified.

Olivia kept rubbing it while she told the kitten all about her day, keeping her tone light and soothing. After she'd talked herself blue in the face, she set the kitten in the bed of towels she'd made. It ran behind the toilet again, hissing all the way. She made a show of freshening the food and water bowls, then said good-bye and slipped out of the room.

She'd keep at it until she won him or her over. It couldn't be that hard. Taming this kitten was the least of her worries.

* * *

Pete stepped inside the rec center and took a deep breath. It was quieter today. Maybe the boys had given up on him and gone home early. He could hardly blame them. It was four thirty, a half hour after Steve Barnes, the rec center's director, had asked him to be here to coach their soccer practice. Pete had gotten tied up with a traffic stop and subsequent paperwork. The story of his life.

He dropped his gym bag on the end of the bleachers and eyed the boys huddled at the other end of the gym. He cleared his throat loudly, and they scattered like drunks in a bar fight. One boy slunk off to put away the cell phone they'd all been ogling God-knew-what on.

They came to the rec center to stay out of trouble, and thanks to Pete's tardiness, that's exactly what they'd been up to.

"You boys ready to play soccer?" he asked.

"You're our coach for the day?" a tall boy with wavy blond hair asked.

Pete nodded.

"You're late. We already played. We're just about to clear out of this joint."

"According to Mr. Barnes, I still have almost an hour." Pete swallowed his guilt and grabbed a bag of soccer balls off the bleachers.

A couple of the boys groaned, while a few looked excited at the prospect. Zach Hill hung at the back of the group, head down and notably silent.

Pete started rolling balls toward them. "Take a minute to warm up while I get set up and see what you can do."

There was more groaning. One boy kicked his ball under the bleachers. Zach dribbled his ball to the goal and kicked. It sailed over the top of the goal. He scowled.

Pete set up some cones, then called the boys over. "You and you," he pointed at two boys. "You're a team. You'll stand here, and here. You two, there." He positioned the boys on four corners, partners diagonally from each other. "You two are in the middle." He brought two more boys in. "The object is to pass the ball to your team-mate without letting the guys in the middle steal it. If they get your ball, they get to move out to the corners. Got it?"

He set them up, then arranged the remaining boys to run the same drill at the other end of the gym. Soon the room filled with the sounds of sneakers squeaking against the floor and boys yelling as they worked together to pass the ball.

It didn't take long for the center teams to steal a ball and claim their turn on the corners. After everyone had a turn and the boys were focused and warmed up, he put them on teams and let them play a quick game.

"Sorry I was late today, guys. I got held up at work," he said as they were cleaning up.

"It's okay, Coach. We'll give you another chance," a lanky kid named Lonnie said.

"Well, actually—"

Steve Barnes came into the gym then, a big smile on his face. "Pete! Glad you made it. How'd it go?"

"I barely got here before it was time for them to go."

Steve shrugged. "Happens. Want to try again next week?"

"Oh, I don't think—" Pete turned away from the boys. "Probably you should find someone with a more reliable schedule."

"In a perfect world. But I have a feeling you could show these boys a thing or two about reliability, regard-less of what time you got here today."

"What's that supposed to mean?" Jason, the tall blond, asked.

"He's a cop," Lonnie told him, with a shrug. "I've seen him around town before."

"A sheriff's deputy, actually," Steve said. "Deputy Sampson was good enough to help us out today after he finished a full day's work serving our town."

"That's cool," one of the boys said, before they all headed to the locker room to change.

"Appreciate you helping us out today," Steve said. "I'm still in a bind on Tuesdays. I can't get over here early enough to do it myself, not to mention I don't know squat about soccer."

Pete wracked his brain and came up empty on a reason not to do this. "All right then. Pencil me in on Tuesdays for now."

And then he headed home to look up soccer drills. Because if he was going to do this, he was going to do it right.

* * *

Olivia sat on the bathroom floor and rested her chin on her knees. This had become her newest unofficial hobby: sitting in the bathroom talking to herself. "It's all your fault," she told the little white ball of fur in the corner.

The kitten lifted its head and stared at her.

She was making progress though. Yesterday they'd visited the vet, where Olivia had learned the kitten was a female and in overall good health. Naturally she had parasites and was underweight. The good news was that her lameness was caused by an infected cut in her footpad. A round of antibiotics ought to make her good as new.

In the two days since Pete dropped her off, Olivia had spent hours in here talking to the kitten and holding her despite much hissing and spitting. This morning, she had come close enough to sniff Olivia's hand. Surely she'd be tame soon, but Olivia wasn't the patient sort.

"Come here, furball." She held her hand out, and the kitten craned her neck to sniff her. "I blogged about you today."

She kept a blog on the Citizens Against Halverson Foods website, detailing the group's efforts to get the chicken-processing plant shut down. The kitten didn't technically have anything to do with Halverson, but she'd found it on their property and witnessed an employee throw a rock at it, so she'd put up a personal interest piece about how she'd captured it and managed to raise some money for future vet bills while she was at it.

She got a lot of visitors to her website and a lot of interaction through her blog and on Facebook. There were so many people supporting her cause. So why couldn't she seem to get any sanction passed against them?

Yesterday, she'd started a campaign to get her followers to write to all of their congressmen and other local representatives requesting a change in legislation to better protect factory-farmed animals and chickens in particular.

She'd included form letters and a handy little app that would generate an email to the appropriate representative if the person would just enter their name and address. If enough people wrote in . . .

Her top priority, though, remained finding an existing law they had broken and proving it. That would get them shut down a hell of a lot faster.

Her arrest had definitely shone a spotlight on the issue. She'd decided to milk it for all it was worth, owning up to her misdeed and detailing her struggles afterward. Traffic to the website had increased almost fifty percent, and she had over five hundred new "likes" on Facebook. So maybe her arrest hadn't been totally in vain.

If she could just keep the momentum going, she might finally be getting somewhere on her crusade against Halverson Foods. Feeling empowered, she reached out to rub the kitten beneath her chin. She jumped back, then came closer, sniffing Olivia's hand.

"That's right. I don't bite." She gave her a quick rub, rewarded by a thin purr. "I gotta get you tame so we can quit hanging out in the bathroom like this."

The kitten ventured closer, sniffing her bare toes and up her calf. Definite progress. They bonded for a few more minutes, then the kitten retreated behind the toilet, and Olivia left the bathroom. She took the dogs for a walk, then meditated for a few minutes in her bedroom to get her energy centered before work.

She hurried out to her car, then stopped dead in her tracks. The air whooshed from her lungs as she stared at the fresh graffiti on the side of her car. Again chickens had been crudely painted on the Prius, this time with the message *"Butt out."*

This time, someone had come onto her property. During the night.

And that was scary as shit.

Heart pounding, she stood there for several long minutes, unsure what to do. The sheriff's office had all but laughed at her last time, but this was more serious. Wasn't it? And what did "butt out" mean? Had someone from Halverson Foods done this?

Whatever and whoever, it would have to wait until after she got off shift tonight because she was going to be late if she didn't hurry. She was already one step away from losing her job. Tom wouldn't be happy if she brought more trouble his way.

Still rattled, she slid into the driver's seat and drove to the Main Street Café. She parked at the end of the lot with the driver's side facing the dumpster so that the graffiti wasn't visible from the street. No one needed to know about this but her and the Dogwood County Sheriff's Office.

She smiled her way through her shift. Eight hours later, she was smiling her way through another police report. The deputy behind the desk, Deputy Hartzler, was not the same guy who'd taken her initial report on Sunday, and if possible, he was even worse.

He flat out suggested she had brought this on herself when she spray-painted the Halverson Foods plant, and his promise that they would "look into it" left her fairly sure her report would never leave the corner of his desk.

Asshole.

"It's probably a joke," he said. "Chicken *ass*. *Butt* out. Get it?"

Oh she got it, all right.

She was going to need some serious meditation tonight to clear his negative energy out of her system. She hadn't driven half a mile down Main Street when she passed a Dogwood County Sheriff's cruiser headed in the opposite direction. It slowed, then made a U-turn to fall in behind her. Its lights turned on, and the siren blipped.

Christ on a cracker.

She pulled over, hoping against hope it was a coincidence and the deputy merely needed to get by on his or her way to an emergency. But no, the cruiser pulled in behind her and stopped.

She watched in her rearview mirror as Pete stepped out of the car and came toward hers. Her heart was racing, and not from fear. Actually, she had no idea what he wanted, but the thrill of seeing him made it clear her hormones had lost their common sense.

Keeping her eyes straight ahead, she rolled down her window and waited for him to make the first move.

"Who did this to your car?" he asked.

She shrugged, still refusing to look at him.

"Olivia?" His voice was lower, more intimate. And tinged with concern.

She looked up at him and saw her vulnerability reflected back at her in the mirrors of his shades. "Ask Deputy Hartzler."

"Why? You filed a report with him?"

She nodded, grateful to her own sunglasses for masking the hurt feelings she still harbored over her recent experience. "Your colleagues don't think very highly of me."

His lips thinned. "So tell me what you told him. This is different from what I saw painted on your car the other day."

"I washed that off after I reported it to Deputy Solomon, who also wasn't the nicest."

His expression betrayed nothing. It was so annoying how cops could do that. "Tell me."

"Someone did this last night while I was asleep."

His eyebrows pinched. "At your home?"

"Yes."

"The other was done while you were at work, correct?"

She nodded.

"I don't like this," he said, and her stomach immediately filled with butterflies. *He cared.* "Coming onto your property while you're at home is making things a lot more personal. The message is more personal this time too. Could be construed as a threat."

A shiver snaked down her spine. "Or a joke."

"I'm not laughing."

"Yeah, me neither." She looked down at her hands.

"I'll do what I can to look into it, but I have to be honest, Olivia. It's not likely we'll be able to make an arrest. There's no evidence to investigate, short of someone coming in to report seeing something."

He didn't sound optimistic, but she didn't care. She was elated by the thought of him looking into her case. At least he believed her and wanted to help. That had to count for something. "I really appreciate it."

"I'll ask around to see if anyone saw anything. And I'll see if I can get a car to drive down your street once or twice during the night to look for anyone who shouldn't be there."

"That would be great. Thank you."

"In the meantime, be careful. Make sure you're locking your doors at night."

She shivered again. "Definitely."

"I'll call you later," he said, stepping back from her car window.

She nodded, and then he was gone.

* * *

Pete walked into the station and zeroed in on Hartzler's desk. The older deputy could be a real ass when he wanted to be, and while vandalizing a vehicle was a minor offense, he was irritated that Hartzler hadn't taken Olivia seriously. "I need to see the report you just did for Olivia Bennett."

Hartzler looked up and adjusted his glasses. "What for? I haven't even finished writing it up yet."

"Well let me see it when you do."

"Hey, you're the one who arrested her last week out at the Halverson place, right? You think she's doin' this for attention?"

Pete clenched his jaw. "No, but I'm wondering if someone's retaliating against her for spray-painting that chicken factory. 'Butt out' could be a threat."

Hartzler shrugged. "Or a joke."

Olivia had said the same exact thing. Had she been repeating Hartzler's words? "How 'bout you treat it like a threat until you know otherwise? And let me see that report when you're finished with it." Pete strode toward his desk before the other deputy could question his objectivity on the case. Nonetheless, he was sure he'd be hearing from the sheriff about it.

He wasn't objective where Olivia was concerned. No doubt about it. But someone had vandalized her car, twice. They'd come onto her property during the night while she was asleep. But if the message was meant as a threat, who would have motive? Who wanted her to butt out?

A question he needed to ask Olivia.

Tomorrow. Because he was technically already off duty. He'd stopped by the office, as he always did, to catch up on paperwork before he went home.

An hour and one small tree's worth of paper later, he was finally on his way. It was almost five, and he'd been off the clock since three. In other words, an average day.

But somehow, instead of taking Walnut Street toward his townhouse, he found himself driving down Peachtree Lane to ride by Olivia's house. He'd always had a protective streak. It was part of what made him good at his job, and he needed to see that she was okay before he went home.

She was in the driveway, in red shorts and a pink tank top, her hair tied back, scrubbing at the graffiti on her car. He cruised past before he could give in to the temptation to stop and help. She glanced up, and their eyes locked for a moment—he nodded.

Then he turned the corner and headed for home.

* * *

Olivia sat on the floor in the bathroom, a tiny furball in her lap, feeling a bit like a superhero. She'd actually done it. She'd tamed the kitten. It hadn't even been that hard. She'd just sat in here several times a day for the last five days, talking and coaxing, and now she had a baby cat in her lap—of her own free will.

"You need a name," Olivia told her.

"Mew," she answered, those blue eyes wide and solemn. The sound of her itty-bitty purr filled the small bathroom.

"I was thinking Hallie, since I found you out at the Halverson plant. What do you think?"

"Mew," Hallie said.

"All right then, Hallie. Don't hate me for this." She stood with the kitten in her arms. There was something dark and sticky in her white fur that the kitten apparently couldn't clean up on her own. She needed a bath.

Olivia ran warm water into the sink, lifted the stopper, and lowered the kitten into the sink. Hallie's claws came out in full force as she fought to scramble to safety. But as she weighed all of a pound, it wasn't hard to hold onto her. Olivia kept one hand across her chest as she worked shampoo over the kitten's scrawny body. Hallie cried plaintively, scratching in vain at the sides of the sink, looking like the proverbial drowned rat with her hair wet and slicked against her body.

Luckily, the gummy mess in her fur came out fairly easily in the bath. When Hallie was clean and soap-free, Olivia wrapped her in a warm towel and plied her with treats as a reward for surviving the ordeal.

"What a good kitten," Olivia soothed as she settled her back into her lap.

Hallie gobbled the last of the cat treats, then set about licking her front paws.

From her back pocket, Olivia's cell phone chimed a happy tune. She shifted to the left to grab it without disturbing Hallie, then frowned at the unfamiliar number. "Hello?"

"Olivia, hi. It's Pete Sampson."

"Oh—" She sat up straighter against the bathroom wall. "Hi."

"Are you available this morning? I was hoping to swing by and ask you a few questions to follow up on your case."

Which case? she almost blurted. But she thought he

meant her car and not her arrest. Hopefully anyway. "I'm not working until three today."

"Great. Could I stop by in a half hour or so?"

"Uh, sure."

"Okay, see you then."

She stared at her phone, then at the kitten in her lap. "Looks like we have company coming, Miss Hallie. What do you say we get cleaned up for Deputy Hot Stuff?"

Hallie settled her head on the towel and closed her eyes.

"Okay, you take a nap, and I'll get cleaned up." Olivia set the kitten on the floor, still swaddled in the towel, and left the bathroom.

In the kitchen, she found two hyper and nosy boxers, still peeved that she hadn't allowed them down the hall to sniff at the bathroom door since the kitten arrived. They sniffed her up and down, licking and jumping. That's when she saw the puddle of pee in the kitchen.

"Bailey!"

The dog hung her head in shame.

"Bad dog. Seriously, you know better." Except possibly Olivia hadn't remembered to let them out since first thing this morning. She was *so* not cut out to be a dog owner. She led the way to the back door and put them in the yard, then turned her attention to cleaning and sanitizing the kitchen floor.

With that done, she jogged upstairs and changed into fresh clothes. She brushed her hair and put on some tinted lip gloss. Foolish, primping for the deputy coming over to ask follow-up questions on her case. Foolish because Pete Sampson wasn't interested in dating her.

There was probably a rule against dating people you'd arrested.

The doorbell rang, and she spritzed her neck with rose essence.

The thing was, she'd always been a foolish girl.

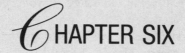

CHAPTER SIX

$\mathscr{P}$ete tucked his deputy's hat under his elbow as he followed Olivia into her living room.

"Would you like some water?" she asked.

"Sure, that would be great." Especially since his throat had gone dry at the sight of her. She wore a pink sundress, her hair long and loose over her shoulders. And she smelled like fresh flowers. He had the completely inappropriate urge to press his face against her neck and drink her in.

"I'll be right back," she said, and disappeared into the kitchen.

Dogs barked from somewhere nearby, out back maybe. Pete sat on the couch and leaned back to wait for her.

Olivia returned a minute later with two glasses of ice water. She handed one to him, then sat on the loveseat opposite the couch, one leg crossed over the other.

"Thanks." He took a grateful swallow. "You have dogs?"

"Two boxers, Bailey and Scooby. They're foster dogs. One of my friends runs a boxer rescue, so if you know anyone in the market, they're looking for homes."

"Ah. You really are dedicated to your cause, aren't you?"

Her nose wrinkled. "Actually, the dogs are just a favor for my friend Merry. They're a lot of work, and I'm not really a dog person."

"No?"

She lifted one shoulder in a half-hearted shrug. "No."

"So how's the kitten?" He'd been curious since he dropped it off here at the beginning of the week.

"Oh she's doing great. You want to see her?" The shift in her mood was like night and day.

"Sure."

Olivia stood and led him down the hall to the closed door of her half bath. Here she paused. "It's kind of a tight squeeze." Then she opened the door and slid inside, motioning him to follow.

He followed her into the bathroom, his back to the wall as Olivia pushed the door closed behind them then bent over a blue towel.

"I just gave her a bath." She lifted the towel, and he saw the kitten's scraggly white shape in its depths. It hissed at him.

"Looks like a rat," he said. The kitten's hair was still half-wet, stuck to its skin in places, sticking out wildly in others.

"I named her Hallie." Olivia stroked her head, and the kitten purred.

"Hallie for Halverson Foods?"

She nodded. "Seemed fitting, right?"

"She's tamed up nicely for you. Hard to believe that's the same kitten I brought you five days ago."

"Apparently it's easy when they're this little. And who knows, she might have had a home when she was born and been dumped outside town later on."

"Well, good work anyway."

"Thanks." She looked up and met his eyes.

She hadn't been wrong before—the bathroom did make for close quarters. Her floral scent filled his lungs and stole his breath. Her lips were pink and glossy, and he wanted to kiss her something fierce. His gaze slipped to her neck, where her pulse pounded, keeping time with his own.

Attraction thickened in the air between them, tightening around them like an invisible band. He pulled back and stepped into the hall before he lost his senses completely.

If he ever did kiss Olivia Bennett, it sure as hell wasn't going to be in the bathroom while she held a wet kitten in her arms.

She followed him out and closed the door behind her. Neither of them said a word as they walked back to the living room. He was no fool. They'd both felt it. He was reasonably sure they could go on behaving as rational adults despite it.

"So the reason I'm here is to ask you a few questions about that message on your car."

Olivia tugged her bottom lip between her teeth and nodded as she sat in the loveseat.

"Let's talk about 'butt out.' That mean anything to you?" He sat on the couch opposite her.

She shook her head. "Unless it was someone from Halverson Foods."

"Why would they write that? You haven't been back out there, have you?"

Her eyes widened. "Of course not! But anyone in town with Internet access knows I'm the one who spray-painted the factory. It's generated a lot of traffic to my website, which has put fuel on the fire for what I'm trying to do."

"Which is?"

"Have the chicken-processing plant shut down."

A light bulb blazed in his head. "So the Halverson workers actually have good reason to tell you to butt out. If you get that plant shut down, they're out of a job."

She chewed her lip and nodded again.

This put a new kink in his gut. He'd seen the men who worked at that chicken-processing plant, and he didn't like the idea of them hanging around her house after dark while she was asleep. Didn't like it one bit.

It also brought a new angle to the sheriff's interest in the case. If the Halverson Foods plant was shut down, it could hurt his chances in the upcoming election. He didn't like to think ill of his boss, but the man had been known to mix politics and police work in the past. The sheriff might be inclined to go harder on Olivia to keep her from making more trouble for Halverson.

"So are you taking over my case?" she asked.

"Not officially." Officially, he was supposed to be in-vestigating Olivia as a suspect in vandalism around town, but seeing as she was now the victim of vandalism her-self, maybe he could justify his interest by checking out whether the cases were related.

One way or another, there was a lot of vandalism go-ing on in Dogwood these days, and an awful lot of it involved the use of spray paint. Coincidence? Maybe. Maybe not.

"Well thanks for looking into it anyway," Olivia said.

"If it's someone from Halverson, then we can assume they meant this as a threat."

"It won't work. I'm not backing off. Someone has to stand up for those poor birds."

"Anyone else you can think of who might have written it?"

She shook her head. "Believe it or not, most people like me. I've given it a lot of thought, and since they drew chickens too, I feel like it has to be someone from Halverson. Probably some of the factory workers who saw me out there the day I washed my graffiti off their wall."

"I don't like the picture that puts in my head, Olivia." He stared at her, hard. "Not that you aren't perfectly capable of taking care of yourself, but those workers are all men, and there are a hell of a lot more of them than there is you. If anything else happens, you tell me, or someone else in the department immediately, alright?"

Her brows bunched. "Of course."

"And if you even think you hear a noise outside your house during the night, you call us."

She frowned. "Now you're scaring me a little."

"You probably have nothing to worry about. They haven't done anything violent, or even overtly threatening. Just be vigilant, that's all."

"I will be, and thank you."

"You're welcome." He stood and showed himself to the door.

Olivia followed, looking somewhat subdued.

"I'll do what I can to try to find out who did this, and in

the meantime, call me if you need me." He rested a hand briefly on her shoulder. "You'll be fine."

"Yes," she said. "I will."

* * *

Olivia sat behind the wheel of her Prius, headed for her favorite relaxation spot. She had an hour to meditate before she had to be at work. This morning's visit from Pete had been a twofold revelation. One, his concern had rattled her. She was a little freaked out to think of the men from Halverson's chicken plant hanging around her house during the night while she slept, or worse.

And two, her attraction was not one-sided. No, she'd seen the same awareness on Pete's face when they were in the bathroom together with Hallie, and again when he touched her shoulder before he left. He wanted her too, and that changed things completely.

Well, it made things more interesting anyway, if she did have to call him again about the vandalism. It almost made her wish for more trouble just for the chance to spend time with him. The way he'd gotten all protective on her behalf earlier had been pretty damn sexy.

She rolled the window down and let fresh air take the heat out of her cheeks. She turned into the entrance for MacArthur Park, once used as a cotton plantation, now a designated historic site open to the public and always crowd-free during the week.

She parked and walked up the hill behind the manor house to the towering pecan tree that was her favorite. From here, with her back against its trunk, she had a view of the old cotton fields and the trees beyond.

She raised her arms above her head and stretched, first her shoulders and arms, then her legs, loosening her body to let go of tension. Then she sat cross-legged beneath the tree, closed her eyes, and focused inward.

Long, deep breaths calmed her racing heart. As usual, she started with her toes and worked her way up, focusing on each body part as she relaxed it and let go of negative energy. By the time she'd reached her scalp, she felt the good energy flowing.

Fully relaxed, she turned her attention to the positive things in her life and the positive things she was working toward. By the time her phone began to chant that her hour was up, she felt rejuvenated and enthusiastic for the rest of her day. A good meditation session always reprioritized her for the best.

She arrived at the café ten minutes early. It was busy this afternoon, nearly every table occupied. Fall temperatures had finally arrived here in Dogwood, and Beatrice, their chef, had baked several of her famous fresh apple pies. There were a number of folks in town who stopped in just for a slice of pie and a cup of coffee.

Olivia sold five slices by the time she went on break and was starting to have a craving for some pie herself. She enjoyed a slice in the break room, then stepped outside for some fresh air before the second half of her shift. She'd be off by eight tonight, which wasn't bad. Still, she preferred working mornings so that she could have her evenings to herself. Oh well. Better tips from the dinner crowd.

"Hey you!" A couple of men pushed off from the pickup truck they'd been leaning against and walked toward her.

She recognized them from having been inside the café earlier that afternoon. They'd sat in Courtney's section and ordered some of the famous pie. "Can I help you?"

"You're Olivia Bennett, aren't you?"

"That's right."

They came closer, and that's when she saw the Halverson Foods logo embroidered on their overalls. "We heard you was the one who painted that message on the factory."

"Um—" She glanced around, but she and the two men were the only ones in the parking lot behind the café. "I need to get back to work actually—"

"We're hard-working people, Miss Bennett. It ain't always easy finding a job 'round here. I don't know if you understand that," the taller man said.

"Look, nothing against you personally, but I've seen the way the birds are treated inside that factory, and it's inhumane." She crossed her arms over her chest. "Now if you'll excuse me—"

They stepped between her and the door, and her bravado faltered. The taller man stared down at her, his dark eyes narrowed. "They're chickens. You eat 'em, I eat 'em. Someone's got to kill 'em. That happens to be us. Don't make it any of your business."

Her heart thumped against her ribs. "Step aside, please."

They did, one on either side of the door. "Back off, lady. Leave our jobs out of your little crusade."

Olivia slid between them to enter the café, then ran down the hall to the break room. She dug her phone out of her purse and dialed Pete.

* * *

Pete was never going to sleep tonight. He sat on a red barstool, sipping his second cup of coffee while he waited for Olivia to finish up and wishing he'd thought to order decaf. She'd sounded terrified in the voicemail she left him, but when he called back fifteen minutes later, she'd told him she needed to finish her shift before she could talk to him.

He'd been off duty for hours, had already been home to change and taken Timber for a run. He'd been in the shower when Olivia called, and now he'd spent two hours cooling his heels at the café, except no part of him felt cool when she walked past and gave him a tight smile. From what he'd gathered from her panicked message, a couple of Halverson employees had hassled her in the parking lot, which meant he wasn't letting her out of his sight until he knew exactly what had happened.

Finally, just past eight, she emerged from the hall behind the kitchen, apron free. "Sorry. I didn't mean for you to rush over here and spend all this time waiting for me."

"Not a problem. Why don't we go outside and you can tell me what went down earlier?"

She led the way out the back door into the parking lot. It was dark now, but the lot was well lit with halogen lamps around its perimeter. "So I came out on my break just before five to get some fresh air before the supper rush, and these two guys were out here. I'd seen them inside earlier having lunch."

"And they were wearing Halverson uniforms?"

She nodded. "I didn't notice that at first. I didn't notice them at all really until they started talking to me."

"So they initiated the conversation?"

She crossed her arms over her chest, chin up. "Of course they did. I wouldn't bother Halverson employees here where I work, or anywhere else for that matter. I was just going to go sit at the picnic table over there for a few minutes." She gestured toward a picnic table at the end of the lot.

He smiled at her burst of temper. "All right. So what did they say to you?"

"Something like, 'Hey, aren't you Olivia Bennett? You're the one who spray-painted the chicken plant.' And then they started telling me how they needed their jobs, and it was none of my business what went on there, and that I should back off."

"They said the words *back off*?"

She nodded. "And then they got between me and the back door. That was when I got a little worried."

"With good reason." He was a little worried himself.

"Anyway, I told them to step aside, and they did. So I went in and called you. But really, now that I've had a few hours to think it over, it's not that big of a deal. I don't think they meant me any physical harm." She hugged herself and shivered. The temperature outside had dipped into the fifties now that the sun had gone down, and she wore only a light jacket over her uniform.

"Like hell it's not a big deal. We're driving straight to the sheriff's office to file a report."

She groaned. "Do we have to? I told you everything that happened."

"And I appreciate that, but I'm off duty. You need to file an official report. What they did isn't grounds for any kind of a harassment charge, but it's important that it's documented in case there are any future incidents to show a pattern of harassing behavior."

"Future incidents?" Fear flickered in her eyes.

"They've defaced your car twice and hassled you in person all in a matter of days. I'd say it's likely you haven't seen the end of them, not unless you're planning to do as they asked and back off your campaign against Halverson Foods."

Her chin went up again. "Not a chance."

A smile tugged at the corner of his lips. "That's what I thought. The sheriff's office is just a few blocks away. You look like you're turning into a popsicle, so why don't I drive us over and then I'll bring you back here afterward and see you home."

She cleared her throat. "See me home?"

He reached out to tuck a strand of shiny blond hair behind her ear. "I'll follow you in my SUV and keep right on driving once I see that you're home safely with no unwelcome visitors hanging around."

"That's awfully chivalrous of you," she said.

They were alone in the parking lot and standing way too close for any good purpose.

"Just doin' my job." Although his job had nothing to do with the way he felt about her right then. He shoved his hands into the pockets of his jeans, trying to keep his mind off the way the street lamps reflected like little half-moons in her eyes or her flowery scent that toyed with his senses and hijacked his self-control.

"You're not even on duty right now, and I've taken up your whole evening. I don't think that's in your job description. Thank you." She went up on her toes and gave him a quick kiss on the cheek. Instinctively, he turned his head so that her lips met his. She sucked in a breath, her eyes wide. He'd startled her, taken a friendly gesture too far.

"Sorry," he whispered against her lips.

"Don't be," she said and kissed him back.

He drank in her scent and the feel of her lips on his. He wanted to taste every inch of her, more than he wanted his next breath, but not here, not now. Certainly not right before he marched her into the sheriff's office to give her official report.

He rested his forehead against hers. "I didn't mean to do that."

She laughed, and the sound loosened something deep inside his chest. "But I'm glad you did."

"I can't do this with you right now, not while I'm working your case—your other case." He held her hands in his.

"Well that's a bummer. Is it against the rules to date a criminal?"

He heard the laughter in her voice. "No, but as your arresting officer, it's against the rules to become involved with you before your court date."

"That's only three weeks away."

"Olivia." He lifted her hands to his chest. "It's not that simple. I'm about to take your official statement about what happened here in the parking lot earlier. It's unethical in so many ways to even contemplate what you're thinking about right now."

She slid her hands around his neck and pressed her cheek to his. "Fine. I get it. But you know, if I get off without a criminal record next month, maybe give me a call?"

He laughed, pulling her closer against him. "Maybe."

The back door of the café opened, and he spun her so that the Forester hid them from view. She burrowed closer, her head against his shoulder. Her fingers trailed down his back, driving him absolutely crazy with the need to kiss her again.

"Can I ask you a sort of personal question before we go back to a purely professional relationship?" she asked, her breath tickling his neck.

"Go ahead." He shifted his body so that she wouldn't feel what she was doing to him, how badly he wanted her.

"Why do you always smell so good, like cinnamon and spice?"

He flinched. "I bake when I can't sleep." It was the truth, the raw truth, and much more than he owed this near stranger with her arms around him in a half-lit parking lot behind the Main Street Café.

She tipped her face up to his. "You must have trouble sleeping a lot."

"Sometimes."

"You should try meditation."

He grunted. "No offense, but that sounds like a bunch of horseshit."

She giggled, and it vibrated through him. This woman, she affected him in a way he hadn't felt since... well, he wasn't sure anyone had ever had this kind of hold on him.

"It's not crap," she said. "It teaches you how to focus your mind, how to take control of your energy. It could help you relax."

He tensed. "I don't need help relaxing."

She slid her hands up to massage his shoulders. "Yes

you do. And since I can't help you the old-fashioned way," she brushed her lips against his, "I'd be happy to teach you how to meditate."

"I think I'll pass." If for no other reason, any time spent alone with Olivia promised to be anything but relaxing, given the effect she had on his body and his inability to do anything about it.

"Pig-headed man. Let me know if you change your mind."

"I'll be sure to do that."

Her back was against the side of the Forester, and he had caged her in with his arms. This had gone far enough. He needed to man up and let her go. He straightened.

Olivia sighed. "To remember tonight," she said, and then she covered his mouth with hers.

His barely leashed restraint came loose, and he kissed her with abandon. Her fingers tangled in his hair as she wriggled against him. He pulled her flush against him and kissed her until his heart felt like it was about to burst out of his chest.

"Olivia," he gasped.

She smiled, her lips glistening in the lamplight, breathless and absolutely the most gorgeous thing he'd ever seen. "Do you think it would be okay if I filed that report tomorrow morning?"

Reality crashed over him like a fifty-pound weight dropped on his shoulders. There was absolutely no way he could walk her into the sheriff's office right now without the body language between them revealing exactly what they'd been doing in this parking lot. "That's probably best."

"Okay. I'll stop by before my shift. Will you be there?"

"I could be, but it's probably better if I'm out on patrol and you talk to whoever's at the desk."

She scrunched her nose. "Even if it's Hartzler?"

"Even if. He's a good deputy. You have to understand how it looks from his perspective. He's a cynical guy, and he's been doing this a long time. But I'll make sure your case doesn't get swept under the rug."

"Thanks. I appreciate that."

"No problem." He forced himself to step back, putting a respectable distance between them.

She crossed her arms over her chest. "Okay, so I'll give my report to whoever's there. Should I mention that I called you?"

He cocked his head. "Never lie to the police."

"Right. Okay, thanks. Well, I guess this is where we say good night then." She leaned in to press one more kiss against his lips.

"Not so fast. I meant what I said about seeing you home."

She blinked. "Oh. Really?"

"I'll follow in my car. If all's quiet at your place, I'll keep on driving."

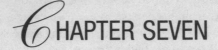

CHAPTER SEVEN

$\mathscr{O}$livia pulled into her driveway to find Merry's CR-V already parked there. The light in the living room was on. And maybe she needed to have a chat with her friend about using her key when Olivia wasn't home, even though it was Merry's house, after all.

She glanced at the clock on the dash. It was just past nine, and oops, it was Friday night. She and Merry had plans, and she was late.

Pete's SUV pulled in behind her, and he stepped out, looking all alpha male as he surveyed the extra vehicle in her driveway.

Olivia's cheeks flushed. She hustled out of the car to intercept him. "It's okay. It's my friend Merry. I forgot we had plans tonight."

"And she let herself into your house?" He eyed the light emanating from her living room window, then turned his dark eyes on hers, still looking all badass and protective, and *oh my God*, she was going to swoon right at his feet.

"She owns the house though, so she has keys."

"Well, all right then." He stood there another moment, looking like he wanted to kiss her every bit as much as she wanted him to, then he turned and climbed back into his SUV. With a wave, he was gone.

Olivia pressed a hand to her cheek. Her face was on fire, despite the chilly evening. Holy hell—that kiss. But what they'd shared afterward had been intimate on a totally emotional level. He'd revealed bits of himself she had a feeling he didn't share readily. She pictured him in his kitchen late at night, baking.

Wearing nothing but boxers. Flour smattered across his chest and through the stubble on his face. *Phew.*

Their chemistry was *hot*. She hadn't felt a connection like this in a long time, on an emotional or a physical level, and she and Pete had both. It was exciting, thrilling, but also scary. She hadn't felt anything like this since Roger.

Pete wasn't without demons. She saw them haunting the corners of his eyes and felt them bunched in the muscles of his well-sculpted body. But he was different. Pete was the kind of man who'd make some lucky woman a wonderful husband someday.

And Olivia was ready to look toward her future, not repeat the mistakes of her past. So while she might not have a shot at dating Pete, what with her recent foray into criminal behavior and all, maybe at least the fact that she was attracted to him meant she was ready to turn over a new leaf.

She stared after his car for a long moment. Then she marched in her front door to face Merry.

Merry sat in the middle of the couch, a dog on either side. "There you are. I was going to cry if you forgot about me entirely. Girls nights out are few and far between for me these days."

"Sorry. I got held up after work. And geez, why don't you make yourself comfortable?" Olivia laughed as she slung her purse on the end table and sank onto the loveseat.

"Well, you know." Merry glanced down at the half eaten bag of kale chips in her lap. Bailey and Scooby both had a suspicious smattering of green crumbs around their mouths, and they watched her with eager, adoring eyes. "You really need to keep better food in the house. These are good, but they're like, *vegetables*."

"My house, my food."

"*My* house, but..." Merry drifted off, staring at her intently. "You're all flushed and glowy. Just what were you doing after work anyway?"

"Um." She felt her cheeks flush hotter. "Let me go change, and I'll tell you all about it once I've had a drink."

"I'll drive. You look like you may need more than one."

"I love you," Olivia called over her shoulder, as she jogged up the stairs. She stripped in the closet and pulled on a clingy yellow eyelet dress. In the bathroom, she brushed out her hair and freshened her makeup.

Ten minutes later, she was in Merry's car, headed to The Watering Hole, a local bar where Merry's dad's bluegrass band played on Friday nights.

"Before you tell me about whatever naughty thing you were doing after work, why is there a kitten locked in the half bath?" Merry asked, eyebrows raised.

"She was a stray. I caught her at the Halverson plant and tamed her. You don't happen to list kittens for adoption on your website, do you?"

Merry shook her head. "Only boxers. I could do a courtesy post through Triangle Boxer Rescue though if you want to get her listed on Petfinder.com."

"Let me get back to you on that." She hadn't really thought about what to do with Hallie yet. The kitten was so little, so young, maybe she'd keep her. Dogs were a bit more responsibility than suited her lifestyle, but a cat . . . a cat she could handle. Maybe.

Merry turned into the parking lot of The Watering Hole. She parked, and Olivia followed her inside. She'd been here a couple of other times. The music was lively and cheerful, and the local beer on tap was just what she needed tonight. She ordered a blueberry ale and settled onto a barstool with a grateful sigh.

"So," Merry said. "Tell me what you were up to tonight. Are you seeing someone?"

"Not exactly. But I kissed Pete Sampson, the deputy who arrested me last week."

Merry took a swallow of beer and choked. "The deputy who arrested you? I thought he was a big jerk."

"Turns out actually he's not." She outlined what had been going on with the Halverson employees and how she'd ended up alone with Pete in the parking lot behind the café tonight.

"Wow." Merry sipped thoughtfully from her beer. "That sounds . . . complicated. But I'm glad you have him looking out for you, because that's kind of scary with the Halverson guys."

Olivia gulped from her own beer. "I know. I was pretty

scared there for a minute when they blocked the door to the café."

"They're not going to let this drop, you know."

"I know. And neither am I." Nobody was going to make her back off from what she believed in. She had taken it upon herself to find justice for those chickens, and she wouldn't rest until she'd gotten it.

"I'm behind you one hundred percent, you know that. I just wish your name hadn't gotten so negatively associated with the Citizens Against Halverson Foods effort." Merry rested a hand on her shoulder.

"I kind of wish that too, although my arrest has definitely brought a lot of attention to what's going on at Halverson. So maybe it will end up being a good thing in the long run."

"I hope so. And you and Pete?"

Olivia's pulse skittered into overdrive. "He says nothing can happen until after my court date. I want to jump his bones, but I wouldn't jeopardize his career for it. A cooling-off period is probably for the best. He's really not my type anyway."

Merry snorted. "Sweetie, T.J. wasn't my type either. Now I'm just waiting for him to put a ring on it. Speaking of weddings, we need to get our bridesmaid dresses fitted for Cara's."

"Yeah." She felt a twinge of guilt that she hadn't visited her friend in Massachusetts yet. It had been over six months now since she'd moved. Truthfully, a white dress didn't sound as hostile to Olivia now as it once had.

Maybe she was ready to grow up after all, ready to find her own Mr. Right. Just as soon as she got over her slightly-out-of-control crush on Pete Sampson.

* * *

Pete got her text as he sat in his cruiser, wrapping things up after serving an eviction notice at a well-to-do apartment complex to a man whose unit smelled like a horse's ass and looked even worse.

Report filed. Hartzler sends his love <3

He groaned. He should have warned her to be professional on his work phone, that the department monitored everything. He shouldn't have kissed her, shouldn't have lain awake last night wanting to do it again.

Stupid.

Good. Call the office if anything else happens.

She buzzed right back. *Will do. Let me know if you change your mind about meditation. Ohm.*

Okay, this was a problem. He radioed dispatch to let them know the notice had been served, then turned the cruiser around and drove down Main Street. Olivia's Prius was parked behind the café. He pulled in beside her and walked in the front door.

Heads swiveled. The uniform tended to have that effect on people, although at the moment he'd have preferred to go unnoticed. He approached the counter and ordered a large coffee to go.

Olivia breezed around the corner with a tray of sandwiches on her right arm. She stopped short at the sight of him, and the tray tipped dangerously.

He stuck his hand out and righted it. "I need to talk to you."

"Um." She gripped the tray, adorably flustered. "Sure. Give me a minute."

She delivered sandwiches to a table in the corner, then

refilled sodas for the table next to it. A tall brunette brought Pete's coffee, and he paid for it while he waited for Olivia.

She came his way and motioned for him to follow her. They walked out the back door, and she tipped her face toward the sun with a grateful smile. "What's up?"

"I should have told you that the number I gave you is town property."

Her brow bunched, and she gave him a blank look.

"So imagine that anything you text to me could be seen by anyone in the office."

"Oh." She giggled. "Sorry. I'm going to get you in trouble with the meditation, aren't I?"

"I'm your arresting officer on a case that's still open. It's a perception of impropriety."

She sobered. "Gotcha. Sorry about that. I have to get back inside, but I'll be good from now on. I promise."

It was on the tip of his tongue to give her his personal number, but that was a line he wasn't ready to cross. Instead, he watched her go, wishing it didn't have to be that way and knowing it was for the best.

* * *

Olivia worked until the café closed at nine. Way to spend a Saturday night. There was a time when she would have gone home to change and gone out to party with her friends. But she'd gone out with Merry last night, and tonight she wanted to catch up on social media.

Kristi had sent her a link to an article about a beef factory in Texas that had been raided and several employees arrested after undercover video showed workers kicking and prodding downed animals on their way to slaughter.

A loophole in the current laws on factory farming failed to provide similar protection to chickens. And tonight Olivia meant to blog her heart out about the injustice. She was going to renew her request for people to write to their lawmakers and also start a petition that she planned to send to the CEO of Halverson Foods.

She took the dogs on a long walk, sat in the bathroom and played with Hallie, and then settled on the couch with a veggie wrap and a glass of wine. She'd been on the go all day, and she was exhausted. That morning, she'd gone to the sheriff's office to file a report about the incident in the parking lot behind the diner. Deputy Hartzler had looked bored the entire time, but hadn't been as rude this time, so at least there was that.

Somewhere into her second glass of wine, as she added photos to her blog post, she dozed off on the couch. She was dreaming about Pete doing naughty things to her with his handcuffs when loud barking startled her awake.

She rubbed her eyes and rolled over to check the clock. It was three a.m., and she was on her couch, still dressed, her laptop on its side on the floor beside her. Ugh. Oh, and her fool dogs were barking.

Bailey and Scooby were at the front window, barking and growling to raise the dead.

Squinting, Olivia peered out the front window. In the yellowish glow of the street lamp, nothing stirred but a few moths.

"Come on, you guys, stop barking at raccoons." She herded them up the stairs to her bedroom, where she changed into pajamas, brushed her teeth, and climbed into bed.

The next thing she knew, sunlight was streaming in the windows. The clock showed it was just past nine, and Olivia sighed deeply into the pillow. Today was her first day off in eight days. Working at the café, she didn't have a regular schedule. Some days were early, some were late, some long, some short, but today, blissfully, she had nothing to do.

She'd go to MacArthur Park to meditate, maybe take the dogs on a jog, maybe think about letting Hallie out of the bathroom for the first time. Bailey and Scooby shoved their noses over the edge of the bed, looking for attention.

Merry'd been horrified when Olivia told her she didn't allow dogs in her bed, but *please*. She'd cleaned enough questionable stains off the couch. She didn't want to think about any of that nastiness in her bed.

"All right, all right." She slid out of bed and went into the bathroom. She freshened up, then tied a robe over the skimpy nightie she'd apparently put on in her three a.m. stupor and went downstairs to let the dogs out.

She'd just taken a big bite out of a bran muffin when someone started pounding on her front door. Her heart jolted in her chest. If it was one of the guys from Halverson...

Pressing a hand to her chest, she hurried to the door and peeked through the peephole. Pete stood on the other side of the door, in uniform and mirrored shades, his expression dark with anger or...something else, equally as intense.

Cautiously, she pulled the door open. "Um, hi?"

She glanced down at her bare feet. *Christ on a cracker.* She had on nothing but a thin terry robe over her nightie. Her hair was a mess, and she wasn't wearing any makeup. At least she'd brushed her teeth.

"Everything okay here?" he asked, his tone low and serious.

"Sure." She met his eyes with a shy smile, then watched as his gaze dropped to survey her lack of clothing.

"You been outside yet this morning?"

"No." She pinched the edges of the robe together in her fist to keep from giving him a peep show. Pete still looked awfully intense. She was starting to get the feeling she was missing something. "Should I have been? What's going on?"

He motioned her to follow him out the front door. "One of your neighbors called it in. They were concerned about your welfare."

"My welfare?" She padded after him down the walkway, confusion mixing with alarm.

Big, red letters dripped down the front of the house. *You didn't listen.*

"Oh, my God." She clutched her robe and stared. The entire side of the house had been spray-painted. Beneath the ominous words, a row of chickens had been painted.

"Your neighbor thought it might be blood," he said.

"Blood," she repeated. Holy shit. No wonder Pete had looked so spooked when he banged on her front door. She was feeling a bit woozy herself.

"Let's go inside." Pete put his hand on her elbow and guided her back through the front door.

She sank onto the couch and stared at him. "I just woke up. I had no idea."

"Did you hear anything last night?" He stood in the middle of the room, watching her.

"No. Oh!" She lurched upright. "I fell asleep on the couch. I woke up around three, and the dogs were at the front window, barking like crazy. I took them upstairs to bed. I thought it was a raccoon or something."

"Did you hear anything outside at that time?"

"No." She shook her head. "Only the dogs."

"Have you had any interaction with anyone from Halverson Foods since the last time we spoke?"

A shiver ran down her spine. "No. Do you think they were here last night?"

"Stands to reason." Pete shoved his hands in his pockets and looked out the front window, a different kind of tension on his face.

She glanced down and saw that the robe had gaped open to reveal the lacy, low-cut front of her gown. She yanked it closed. "Um, do you mind if I get dressed before we finish this conversation?"

"Not at all." He glanced at her, his professional demeanor betrayed by a flash of hunger in those dark eyes.

She shivered, and it had nothing to do with the message spray-painted on the front of her house. "Be right back."

* * *

Pete stood in Olivia's living room, hands in his pockets, willing himself to think of anything other than how sexy she'd looked all rumpled and fresh out of bed. He was here on business today, and he couldn't let himself be distracted, not by the fear in her eyes when she'd seen the message painted on her house or her breasts spilling out of her nightgown.

The barking at the back door had grown louder since she went upstairs. He heard paws scraping against its wooden surface. Curious since he'd never actually seen her dogs, he strolled over and peeked out the window. Two brown boxers sat at the top of the steps. As soon as they saw him, they reared up on their back legs, barking even louder, tail stumps wagging madly.

"They want their breakfast," Olivia said from behind him.

He turned. "I don't mind if you let them in."

She'd changed into a purple top and khaki shorts and added something pink and glossy to her lips. "Are you sure? They can get pretty rowdy."

"I can handle rowdy." He couldn't keep the slight double entendre out of his voice.

Olivia's cheeks heated to match her lips. "Okay then."

She opened the back door, and the two dogs bounded inside. They both went straight for him, barking and jumping on him, crazed with excitement. Olivia grabbed each dog by the collar and hauled them into the kitchen, where they quickly became distracted by the promise of food.

"What are their names?" he asked.

"Bailey." She pointed at the female dog. "And Scooby." She pointed at the male.

"Do you have somewhere else you could stay for a few days?"

She pressed her hands against the counter and faced him. "Jesus. Really?"

"This is twice now they've been at your home during

the night, and that's worrisome. You need to make your-self less accessible until the whole thing blows over."

She glanced toward the front of the house, her expression sober. "I fell asleep downstairs last night. They could have been looking in the windows, watching me. It's a little freaky."

"I'd feel much better if I knew you were staying somewhere else."

She sighed. "It's complicated. I've got these dogs, who aren't even mine or all that well behaved, and a kitten still living in my bathroom."

"What about the friends who ditched you the night you were arrested? I'd say they owe you a favor."

Olivia's mouth dropped open. "They—um. For the record, I have no idea what you're talking about."

He grunted. "One of them is named Terence. I'm guessing, if I searched the Citizens Against Halverson Foods website, I could probably find out his last name and maybe your other friend too. Is it Merry Atwater?"

Her eyes rounded. "Shit! No. Merry has nothing to do with any of this."

"Then who?"

She stared at the counter in front of her, her pretty lips pressed in a thin line. "You must think I'm an idiot for not turning them in. But they both could lose their jobs if they got arrested."

Yep, he did think she was an idiot on this particular subject. "And you? Your job isn't in jeopardy?"

She blew out a breath and glared at him. "It is. But I'm the one who was up on the ladder with a can of spray paint. It was my stupid idea, so I can handle the consequences."

"You're too smart to be so foolish."

Hurt flashed in her eyes. "Yeah, well, screwing things up is my specialty."

And now he felt like an ass. "Olivia—"

"But you're right, they do owe me a favor. Merry's already got a house full of dogs, but maybe I could have my other friends keep Bailey and Scooby for me so that I could crash at her place for a few nights."

"All right then. I just have a few more things to go over with you to finish up my report. The Halverson Foods factory is closed today because it's Sunday, but I'll stop by tomorrow morning to ask some questions, see if I can shake loose who might be behind this."

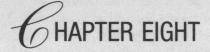

CHAPTER EIGHT

Olivia was halfway between homeless and a third wheel, and she was pissed about it. Merry had demanded she stay at the farm with her and T.J. until the graffiti incident had been sorted out, which she'd reluctantly agreed to. Kristi was keeping Scooby and Bailey for a few days, and Hallie the kitten had moved with Olivia into Merry and T.J.'s guest room.

But today was Tuesday, and Merry worked seven to seven at the hospital. Olivia was off at four, and there was no way she was going to the farm until her friend was home. T.J. was a great guy, but he was unlikely to appreciate having his girlfriend's troublemaking friend underfoot all afternoon.

So Olivia had spent an hour at the library doing some research for her next blog post. Now she was hungry and irritable, with two hours until she could go home. A plate of vegetarian sushi from Mikoto's might just take care of both of her problems.

It was only a few blocks from the library so she decided to walk. As she passed the rec center, the front door opened, and the man who came storming down the steps brought her heart right into her throat.

Pete was breathing hard, looking deliciously handsome in black athletic shorts and a red Wolfpack T-shirt stretched across his broad shoulders. Head down, he hustled onto the sidewalk. She put her hands out before he slammed right into her.

"Hi." She tried for a casual smile, but her hands were on his pecs, and holy hell, his muscles...

"Olivia?" His dark eyes flicked up to hers.

"Believe it or not, I was just walking by, and you... um, are you okay?" Because even for Pete, he looked intense right now. His brows were pinched, and his muscles were so tight her hands practically bounced right off him.

"I'm fine."

She lifted her hands free of his chest. "What were you doing in there, running a marathon?"

"Coaching soccer."

"Really? Because you look—" Actually, he looked angry. Or upset. Sometimes with a man it was hard to tell one from the other. Cautiously, she placed her hand back over his heart. It thumped hard and fast against her palm.

"Olivia—" His voice was rough, like he wanted to shake free of her and go stew alone.

But she couldn't let him do that, because she knew she could help. "Someone got under your skin today."

"There's this kid—" he said, then stopped and shook his head. "Never mind. I'll call you tomorrow to catch up about your case."

"Wait." She stepped in front of him again. "I need to show you something."

"Not now. I'll call you tomorrow."

"It's not about that. Come with me." She took his hand and tugged him in the direction of her car.

"Whatever it is can wait. " He pulled his hand free.

"No, it can't. Come." She took his hand again and half-dragged him down the block to her Prius, still parked at the library.

He gave her a long look, then folded himself into the front passenger seat.

"Trust me," she said. Then she put the car in drive and pointed them toward the outskirts of town. MacArthur Park would be closing within the hour so she'd settle for her second favorite meditation spot—a quiet overlook on Jordan Lake. It was too far above the water to be popular with fishermen, and this late in the day, unlikely to be occupied by any sightseers.

"Where are we going?" he asked.

"Someplace quiet." She glanced over at him.

His posture was tense, his hands braced against his thighs. "We can't. Even when I'm off duty, Olivia."

She snorted. "I'm not going to jump your bones. I just want to show you some meditation techniques. You look like you could use a little stress relief—or something."

"I shouldn't be seen with you outside of work."

"Then we won't be seen." She got it, she really did. So the tug of annoyance she felt must be directed at herself, because if she hadn't been stupid enough to break the law and get arrested, Pete wouldn't be afraid to be seen with her, wouldn't be compromising his professional integrity to be with her.

That just sucked. And it hurt a little bit too.

"Olivia—" His tone punched her right below her ribs.

Tears pricked behind her eyes. "I don't want to get you in trouble, Pete, with your boss or your conscience. Just let me do this for you tonight, and I promise I'll never contact you outside of work again."

* * *

Pete felt like a pressure cooker about to burst. He shouldn't have let Zach get under his skin like this. And Olivia...Olivia was driving him God-knew-where to do God-knew-what with him.

He was too angry to think properly or he never would have gotten in the car with her. Trapped inside the Prius, her flowery scent teased his nostrils. The sun was setting ahead of them, casting the interior of the car in its golden blaze. It created a halo effect around her when he looked over. "You're a little bit crazy, you know that right?"

She shrugged. "I like to live outside the box."

He rubbed his brow. This was ridiculous. He was a grown man, and he had totally lost it over a petty argument with a thirteen-year-old.

Zach Hill. The kid had started a fight, scuffling with one of the other boys over something he'd said. When Pete broke it up, Zach had told him to leave him alone.

"*You're not my father*," he'd shouted.

And that knocked the wind right out of him.

"Here we are," Olivia said, interrupting his thoughts. She pulled the car into a gravel pull-off along the banks of Jordan Lake. "Follow me."

She set off at a brisk pace down a dirt trail to the right.

He followed, trying to roll some of the stiffness out of his shoulders. He failed. But a new kind of tension was growing inside him now, one that had everything to do with the sexy woman leading him down this path.

"Here," she said.

They were standing at an overlook about ten feet above the lake, with a stunning view of the sunset beyond. She spread a blanket over the ground, then took off her shoes and stepped onto it.

"Olivia—" He stood in the dirt facing her. "I can't do this. I really just need to get out of here and go home."

She smiled, and goddamn she was gorgeous with the lake and the sunset behind her. She wore a blue top and a long black skirt that hugged all of her curves. All he really wanted to do right now was kiss her, lose himself in her until everything else faded away.

"Oh, come on now. You've come this far." She took his hand and tugged him toward her.

Reluctantly, he kicked off his shoes and joined her on the blanket.

"Good. I usually start with some stretches, but I think you might be too tense right now for that, so let's sit and focus on breathing first. Here…" She pushed on his shoulders until he sat, then she sat beside him. "Now close your eyes."

He did, but the blackness behind his lids brought him right back to the rec center.

You're not my father. My father's dead.

"Now I want you to concentrate on your breathing. Slow and steady. Deep breaths from your diaphragm. Feel the way your stomach moves in and out as you breathe. Focus on that."

He listened to the singsong tone of her voice, and he tried to do what she said. He drew in a breath and held it, then exhaled slowly.

"That's great," she said. "Keep doing that until you're comfortable with your breathing."

They sat in silence for a minute, and while he wanted to protest that this was silly, he did feel some of the pressure in his chest ease as his breathing slowed.

"You're doing great," Olivia said from beside him. "Now keep breathing slow and steady, but I want you to focus on your toes. Think about relaxing them. Wiggle them if you need to."

"There's nothing wrong with my toes."

"It's part of the process. You're going to work your way up, one body part at a time, until we've gotten all the tension out."

He wiggled his toes and silently cursed himself for coming here with her. But fifteen minutes later, when they finally worked their way up to his chest, he was feeling pretty damn relaxed. Listening to her soft voice, he let the bands of tension around his ribcage slip away.

She spent a long time on his neck and shoulders, talking him through the relaxation process without ever touching him. Then they moved on to his jaw, his cheeks, his eyes and forehead. Even his scalp.

"You're rocking this," she said. "I can feel the change in your energy. Can you feel it?"

"Yeah," he said. It was true too.

"Okay, so don't laugh, but since this is probably my only chance to give you a meditation lesson, I need to get it all in. We need to find you a 'happy place.'"

He did laugh, just a little. "If you say so."

"Think of someplace peaceful and calm. Someplace that makes you feel happy. The beach. The mountains. Where do you usually go when you need to blow off some steam?"

"The shooting range," he answered.

Olivia snorted. "Well that won't work. Start with this right here. Open your eyes and look out at the lake. Remember how it looked when we first sat down, with the sunset over the water? That was pretty breathtaking."

He opened his eyes. The sun was gone now, the sky a muted purple. Birds swooped over the lake's surface, fishing for their dinner. In the distance, he heard the rumble of a truck passing by on the road. And he felt Olivia's presence at his side, overshadowing everything else.

* * *

Olivia closed her eyes and soaked in the moment. Pete sat at her side. Calm. Peaceful. And she'd helped him get there.

"Do I have to call it my happy place?" he asked.

She bit her lip to keep from grinning. "You can call it whatever you want. And while you're at it, keep focusing on your breathing. Keep it slow and steady. Feel your belly move with each breath. Keep your muscles loose and relaxed."

"Yeah, okay."

"There's so much more I could teach you, but this is probably enough for today. Just remember the steps to relax yourself. If you don't have time to come out here and meditate like we are now, just take a minute in your car to concentrate on your breathing and relaxing your muscles.

Visualize your manly happy place. You can train yourself to work the effects of meditation into your day whenever you need them if you practice."

He was quiet, staring out at the lake.

She slid closer and rested a hand on his shoulder. He still felt tense, but nothing like the way he'd been earlier. "You might be sore tomorrow."

He grunted.

Slowly, she massaged the last of the tension from his shoulders. She pressed her fingers deep into his muscles, releasing the lactic acid that had built up in them.

Pete sucked in a breath.

"Better?" she asked.

"Yeah, but not entirely relaxing." There was a new tension in his voice, one that had nothing to do with stress or anger.

She looked down. In his gym shorts, there was no hiding the effect she'd had on him. "Oh."

"Yeah."

"Sorry about that." An answering tug of desire began to pulse inside her. She'd really love to slide into his lap and feel the bulge in his shorts up close and personal. Even more, she wanted to free him from his shorts and feel his bare skin on hers.

"Somehow I don't think you are." His voice was low, gruff, thick with arousal.

She squirmed. No, she wasn't. Well, she should be since there wasn't a damn thing she could do about the need throbbing inside her. She couldn't touch him, couldn't do anything but sit here, burning for him and wishing things were different.

"I'm not sorry either." He gripped her hand and pulled

it lower, so that she felt his heart pounding in his chest. "I didn't want to come out here with you tonight. I never would have done anything like this on my own. Thank you."

"You're welcome." The last light of the sun was fading now, leaving them in near darkness. The night pressed in around them, heavy with insect song and the crackling of desire in the air between them.

"I wish..." He brought her hand to his mouth and kissed it. Her skin tingled beneath his lips, and the fire deep in her belly raged.

"Don't. Don't wish. I'm the one who screwed up and got arrested." She pulled her hand back and stood.

"Don't sell yourself short." He stood and faced her. "You made a mistake. We all make them. Most of us just don't get arrested for them. But I have to say, from what I've seen, you're pretty damn honorable, Olivia. If things were timed differently..."

He trailed his fingers over her cheek, and she felt it all the way to the depths of her heart. "But they're not."

Feet heavy with regret, she took his hand and led the way back to the car.

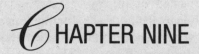

CHAPTER NINE

$\mathscr{N}$eed some help?" Olivia stood in the doorway to the kitchen, watching as Merry balanced a baby on her hip while she warmed his bottle.

"Sure." Merry passed the baby to her. "Thanks."

"No problem." Olivia cradled baby Jayden in her arms. He whimpered, tiny fists flailing. "Shhh. She's getting your supper ready right now."

"You think you'll do this someday?" Merry asked with a half smile.

"Fostering?"

"Well that, or one of your own."

Olivia looked down at him. She liked the feel of a baby in her arms, his warm, solid presence against her heart. "I'm certainly not opposed to the idea."

"Me neither." Merry led the way into the living room, bottle in hand. She lifted Jayden from Olivia's arms and sank onto the couch with him to give him his bottle.

"I'd settle for a man first." Olivia sat in the chair across from the couch.

"Any prospects?"

"No." Her mind was replaying every moment of her evening with Pete, the pride she'd felt in helping him re-lax and the way he made her body sizzle every time they got within a dozen feet of each other.

"What about the hot deputy?" Merry asked.

"He can't date me. It's a conflict of interest, seeing as he also arrested me."

Merry smiled. "Yeah, I guess I can see that."

"I think it's technically only until my court date, but I kind of get the impression I'm not good for his reputation either way."

"So you've had a conversation about it?"

Olivia sighed. "Yeah. The chemistry is hot. We'd be in his bed right now if not for the whole conflict of interest, but you know, it might be for the best."

Merry looked up. "And why is that?"

"Because I've been down the scorching chemistry road before, and I got burned. I think I'm ready to start looking for someone more serious. I want what you have."

Merry's eyes narrowed. "And you don't think T.J. and I have scorching chemistry?"

"What you guys have is much *more* than scorching chemistry."

And maybe things with Pete could go farther than chemistry too, but she couldn't shake the feeling that they were bad for each other in the long run. She lived to stir up trouble, and his job was to prevent it. There was a rea-son she'd never crushed on men in uniform. She needed a man with a wild streak, someone who could stand beside her on the picket line.

But damned if she wouldn't like to at least sample what Pete had to offer.

The front door opened, and T.J. stepped inside, six feet of strapping cowboy. He hung his hat on the rack inside the door, toed out of his boots, then crossed the room to kiss the woman he loved.

Olivia retreated to the kitchen for a glass of water. She was so grateful to her friends for taking her in, but she so couldn't wait to go back home to her own house.

"Hi, Olivia," T.J. called, from the other room.

Water glass in hand, she walked back into the living room. "Hi."

She saw the way Merry and T.J. were looking at each other. They hadn't seen each other all day, probably didn't get much alone time these days with Jayden staying with them. "Well as long as I'm crashing here, I may as well make myself useful. I can put him to bed while you guys catch up if you like."

"Are you sure?" Merry asked. "He goes down pretty easily. I usually just lay him in his crib and hum to him for a few minutes."

"I can handle that." Olivia extended her arms.

"Thank you." Merry stood and passed him over. "Remember to lay him on his back."

"No problem. I'm going to work on a blog post afterward so I'll be out of your way." She carried Jayden upstairs to the nursery. She changed his diaper and rocked him for a few minutes until his eyes started to droop. Then she laid him into his crib. She hummed a few lullabies, and his eyes drifted shut.

That was easy.

Motherhood wasn't easy. She knew that. Merry herself had lost a baby to SIDS. Bringing Jayden home, albeit temporarily, had been a huge step for her in overcoming her grief. But she'd done it, and with Jayden and T.J. beside her, she was healing from her painful past, moving toward a happy future.

Olivia didn't have a traumatic past. She'd led a fairly charmed life, aside from being a constant disappointment to her parents. But watching the baby sleeping before her, she felt a new urgency to get her act together and move forward as Merry had done.

She needed to figure out what she wanted to do with the rest of her life. It wasn't waitressing at the Main Street Café. She didn't think it was being a lawyer either. But what *was* it? What came next for her?

One thing she was sure of: she needed to wrap up this business with Halverson Foods and get on with her life.

* * *

Olivia woke the next morning to a strange tickling sensation in her nose. She opened her eyes to find a kitten tail across her face, and *oh gross*, kitten butt against her cheek. Cringing, she shifted Hallie to the side.

In response, the kitten purred loudly into her ear.

"You sure got the hang of domesticity pretty easily, didn't you?" Olivia rubbed behind her ears, and Hallie purred louder.

The kitten had been surprisingly well behaved here in T.J. and Merry's guest room. She'd taken right to the litter box and had only climbed the curtains once (that Olivia knew about anyway).

Hallie batted a paw against Olivia's nose.

"All right, go play then, little girl." She set the kitten on the floor. The guest room was where T.J.'s nephew slept when he stayed over, and as such, it was outfitted in blue with a huge bin of Legos in the corner. Hallie ran straight to it and began batting Legos around on the carpet. "I should go get you some kitten toys, shouldn't I?"

Olivia rolled out of bed and wrapped a robe over her pajamas so that she could venture down the hall to the bathroom without being indecent. Man, she really missed having her own place. On the other hand...

"I've got bagels," Merry called from downstairs.

"Be right down," she answered.

A few minutes later, she went down the stairs and found her friend on the floor in the living room, playing with Jayden. She had him propped against a pillow, rolling a ball across the carpet to him as he waved his fists and giggled.

"Bagels are in the kitchen," Merry said. "So are the dogs. Tank is too rough to be in here while I have Jayden on the floor."

"Gotcha." Olivia stooped to kiss the baby, then went into the kitchen. She let herself through the baby gate and was immediately assaulted by two hyper boxers, Ralph and Tank—appropriately named as he was the size of a small horse. She went to the counter and fixed herself a bagel and poured a glass of water. "Where's Amber?" she asked, as she rejoined Merry and Jayden in the living room.

"She's down at the barn with T.J." Merry's smile said

everything. That she'd helped T.J. overcome his fear of stray dogs to love Amber, a former stray herself, was a happily ever after moment for sure. "The house is being painted today."

"Oh really?" Olivia still felt bad about the graffiti that had defaced the house she was renting from her friend.

"The insurance company approved the claim. A fresh coat of paint will look good on it, don't you think?"

"Yeah." She took a bite of her bagel and chewed thoughtfully. "I want to go home."

"Not until the police catch whoever did that."

"We'll see." She'd been pretty thoroughly freaked out at the time, especially about the thought of them looking in the windows at her while she slept on the couch. But now, in the light of day and with a little time to think it over, she was ready to be in her own space. Well okay, she was still a little scared, but they hadn't hurt her or threatened to hurt her, and they shouldn't get this much power over her life.

"What's your plan with Halverson anyway?" Merry asked. She laid Jayden on his belly facing a little pop-up baby mirror. He smiled at his reflection.

"Good question. I've had a huge increase in traffic to my blog and Facebook page since my arrest. People are riled up. They want to see the place shut down. It's time for me to take this farther than Facebook, but I'm not sure how."

"Don't do anything stupid."

"I won't. No way am I getting arrested again or jeopardizing my probation. I've been having people write their lawmakers to try to get new legislation on the ballot, something to better protect factory-farmed birds. Maybe we need to organize a protest outside Town Hall."

Merry gave her a skeptical look. "Do you think that will help or just make you a bigger target for the guys at Halverson Foods?"

"It's better than doing nothing."

"*Nothing* is exactly what you need to be doing until your probation is over."

Olivia sobered. "You're right. No protesting until after my court date."

Merry lifted Jayden into her arms. "Not for nothing, Liv, but are you sure you aren't fighting a losing battle? I mean, I have to think the chances of getting that place shut down completely are pretty slim."

Olivia chewed and swallowed another bite of her bagel before she answered. "And has that ever stopped you when you were fighting for something for one of your dogs?"

"Point taken. But no one ever threatened me either. Be careful."

"I am, and I will be." Her phone rang, and she glanced at the display. Her heart beat a little faster. "Good morning," she answered.

"Morning." Pete sounded ridiculously sexy over the phone, his voice low and just scratchy enough to give her a thrill. "I wanted to check in with you about the vandalism on your house. You got a minute?"

"Sure." She stood and headed for the stairs.

"I went out to the Halverson factory on Monday and poked around. Spoke to the manager and several employees. Naturally, they all claim their innocence, but they're not the kind of guys who like having the police nosing around in their business. I promised to be back with reinforcements if anything else happened to you."

Olivia closed the door to the guest room behind her.

Hallie mewed from the bed, poking her head out to be petted. "Thank you."

"I may have also threatened to call a friend in Immigration."

She gasped. "I don't want to get anyone deported."

He chuckled. "It's a bluff. I just needed to get their attention."

"Well, good, because I'm ready to go home."

"I wish you didn't live alone, but I think it's probably okay."

She heard the protectiveness in his voice, and it spread something warm and syrupy through her chest. "I have guard dogs to protect me anyway."

"They didn't look all that vicious to me."

She sighed. "They're not. But they're big and loud, and that's better than nothing."

"Much better than that furball you call a kitten."

"Yeah. Well, thank you. Hopefully I can stay out of your hair from now on."

"Somehow I doubt that," he said.

And somehow, so did she.

* * *

Pete needed to get his head checked. And not just because he was voluntarily trying to meditate. Meditation was some kind of hippy-dippy crap he had no time for, and yet here he was, trying to recreate the magic he'd shared with Olivia.

Olivia. The real reason he needed to get his head checked. Because he was sitting in the dirt with his hands on his knees and a bored-out-of-his-mind German shepherd at his feet, mentally calculating how many days until her court date and wondering if he could possibly get away with dating her if she got off without a record.

The answers were: twelve days, and not unless he wanted to risk his good standing with the sheriff and subsequently his chances of making detective at the end of the year. So it must be some kind of self-punishing bullshit that he was thinking of asking her out anyway.

"Woof," Timber bellowed at a couple of geese below them on the lake. He'd finished the rawhide Pete had brought for him, and his patience with sitting here taking in the view was obviously wearing thin.

Pete huffed out a breath and started again at his toes. It was no use. He'd started over at least five times, and still he couldn't come close to recreating what he and Olivia had done here the other night.

"You've got to be kidding me."

As if he'd summoned her from his imagination, her voice came from behind him. He opened his eyes and looked over his shoulder. She stood a few feet away, dressed in blue yoga pants and a black jacket, staring up at the sky. "That's definitely a hawk, but have you seen any pigs flying up there? Because I could swear I just caught you sitting out here meditating."

"Maybe one or two pigs."

Timber leaped to his feet and rushed at her, yipping with excitement as his tail swooshed a happy dance in the dirt.

"Who's this?" she asked.

"Timber. He's a K9 flunkie so watch your fingers."

"Um." She lifted her hands out of reach. "Seriously?"

"He did flunk K9 training, but he won't bite you." He

couldn't take his eyes off her. He was in big trouble where she was concerned.

"You know, I really like animals. In fact, I'm an animal rights activist," she told the dog, her tone as serious as if she were talking to a person. "And I'm almost always a totally law-abiding citizen. So you'd have no reason to dislike me, even if you were prone to nibbling on fingers."

"Woof," Timber answered. He sat at her feet and gazed up at her adoringly.

Pete saw the way the muscles in his dog's haunches bunched. Any second now he was going to lose control and lunge up to kiss her face. "Down, Timberwolf."

The dog gave him a baleful look and slid down to his belly.

"Anyway, I think your human enjoys making fun of me. And that's not very nice. I bet you could talk some sense into him for me." She sat cross-legged beside Timber and stroked his neck. The dog let out an ecstatic howl and rolled belly up, halfway in her lap. Olivia rolled her eyes, even as she obediently began rubbing his belly. Timber groaned in appreciation, nipping at her arm while his tail beat the dirt behind him. "A bit of an attention whore, aren't we?"

"He loves the ladies." And what did it say about Pete that he was getting turned on just watching her play with his dog?

She looked at him. "So did you really come out here to meditate?"

"Does it make me less of a man if the answer is yes?"

"Not in my book." Her expression was equal parts admiration and the same flush of awareness he felt creeping over his own skin.

"Well, I'm failing miserably."

"Then let's meditate together. It's what I came here to do anyway."

"Okay." He closed his eyes and breathed in the flowery scent of her hair. Damn if he didn't feel more relaxed already.

"So I can kind of see why Timber got kicked out of K9 school," Olivia said from beside him.

He looked over to see his eighty-pound dog still canoodling in her lap. "I think he's in love."

Her eyes twinkled with laughter. "Well no offense, Timber, but I prefer men who still have their manhood intact."

Pete choked. Timber slurped her cheek, undeterred by her attack on his manhood.

"Timber, down."

The dog slunk out of her lap and gave him the stink-eye.

"I'm not sure he's all that conducive to meditation," she said with laughter in her voice.

"I brought him a bone, but he's finished it. He's bored."

"Sorry, Timber, but I don't know anything about meditation for dogs." She started rubbing him slowly, head to tail. Timber sprawled out in the dirt with a groan of contentment, tail thumping the dirt, eyes closed.

"And yet, I think he's just achieved total relaxation." Pete eyed his dog with more than a bit of jealousy.

"It's easier for them. They live in the moment."

"True."

"So since you have me here, let's see if we can't do the same thing for you."

She spent the next hour doing just that. She worked her

magic, banishing every last bit of tension and stress from his body. The truth was, Olivia Bennett was becoming his happy place.

"Thank you," he said, after he'd opened his eyes. The sun was starting to set again, sending orange and pink hues over the surface of the lake.

"You're welcome. I usually go to MacArthur Park, but for some reason, I came back here today." She looked over at him, and he saw the same yearning on her face. She'd come here because she'd been thinking of him.

The same reason he'd come.

This thing between them, it was more than attraction. He wanted her something fierce, wanted to lay her down right here and make love to her until they were sweaty and breathless and sated, but this...just sitting here with her felt intimate.

He'd only ever spent time like this with one other woman. His wife. And things with Rina had ended very, very badly. "After your court date..."

Her eyes heated. "Yes?"

He broke free of her gaze and looked out at the lake. "I'm up for detective at the end of the year."

"And I make you look bad."

"You're a bit...controversial." And he felt like an ass.

"I'm a troublemaker. I get it." An edge had crept into her voice, an edge that erased every bit of the relaxation he'd felt a few minutes ago.

"You make trouble where it needs to be made. You're smart, and passionate, and not afraid to stand up for what you believe in. I admire the hell out of you, Olivia, but the sheriff doesn't exactly feel the same."

* * *

Olivia fought past the tears pressing at the backs of her eyes. When had she become this person? The type of woman an honorable man like Pete Sampson would be hurting his reputation to be associated with? That's not who she was, not who she'd meant to be.

She'd only wanted to give a voice to the helpless animals who didn't have one, to bring light to the plight of factory-farmed animals.

Her mother was right. She was such a screwup.

"I always wanted to be a detective," Pete said. He was staring out at the lake, avoiding her gaze.

"You don't sound so sure about that." She rested a hand on his dog, letting Timber's thick fur occupy her fingers so that she wouldn't be tempted to touch the brooding man beside her.

"It's complicated."

"Most things in life are."

"Isn't that the truth."

"You'll be a great detective," she said. "I envy you knowing what you want out of life. I still don't know what I want to be when I grow up. That's a scary place to be when you're twenty-nine years old."

"You'd be a hell of a lawyer," he said.

She choked on a laugh. "You're joking, right?"

He shook his head. "Not at all. You're smart, passionate, headstrong. You make a damn good argument for your cause, even when your cause sounds completely crazy. You convinced me to meditate, for crying out loud."

She wiped a tear from the corner of her eye and

sobered. "My parents groomed me to be a lawyer from the time I learned how to talk. It's the only career they ever considered for me."

"Really?"

"My dad's a defense attorney, and my mom works for the prosecutor's office."

Pete's back straightened. "Okay, I knew about your dad, but Marlene Bennett is your mother?"

She nodded. "The one and only."

"Huh." He stared out at the lake for a long minute in silence. "So why aren't you a lawyer?"

"Because I don't want to be one."

"Good enough."

"It should be. Except everyone else—including you—seems to think I've missed my calling." She rested her head on her knees.

He shrugged. "Doesn't matter what I think, or anybody else. You have to be happy with your work. Life's too short not to be."

"And you? Are you happy?"

A muscle in his cheek twitched. "If I'm not, it's not because I chose to be a deputy."

"Why is it then?" She was pushing, but she couldn't help it. She wanted to know what caused the dark shadows that haunted the corners of his eyes.

"I made a mistake, and now I have to live with the consequences."

"Well I know that feeling." She fisted her hands in Timber's fur, and the dog rolled closer to her.

"What I did was much worse than spray-painting a chicken factory." His expression was grim. He carried a tremendous weight of guilt, for what she didn't know.

"We all make mistakes. It's what makes us human. I can't imagine you acted under anything but your own best intentions. Forgive yourself, Pete."

"Wish I could," he said. The tortured look on his face ripped at her heart.

She wanted to erase that look from his face. She wanted to make him happy, but the truth was, dating her would only hurt him, hurt his future with the sheriff's office.

And that was the saddest truth of all.

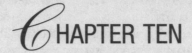

CHAPTER TEN

$\mathcal{P}$ete chewed meatloaf as Maggie chattered. His little sister had always felt the need to keep the conversation lively at the dinner table. He and his mom weren't big talkers, which usually meant Maggie kept a running commentary during their weekly family dinners here at Mom's house.

"So it's career day next week, and all the kids want to know if you'll come." She spooned a mouthful of mashed potatoes into her mouth and gave him her best puppy dog eyes.

"I don't know—"

"Well of course he will," his mother said. "Pete, you need to get out more. Do something fun for a change. Be social."

"Standing in an auditorium full of elementary school kids is not my idea of fun," he said. And she was one to talk. These last few years, his mother barely left the house other than to run errands. Her job as a medical transcriptionist allowed her to work from home, although it barely paid the bills. Pete and Maggie helped out whenever she'd let them with groceries and projects around the house.

"It's totally fun," Maggie said. "You're Superman to them. Enjoy it while it lasts." She grinned. Maggie was the art teacher at East Dogwood Elementary. She was also a talented artist who sold hand-painted crafts on Etsy.

"Not fun," he corrected her. "But for you, I'll come."

"Yay! Thank you." She took a big bite of her meatloaf. Maggie was three years younger than him at twenty-seven. They'd both gotten their father's dark eyes and hair. Maggie wore hers in a ponytail that made her look much younger.

"Speaking of getting out of the house," Pete said, turning toward his mom. "Steve Barnes says you haven't been to church in a while. You should go. I told you he offered to save you a seat."

His mother looked at him, her brown eyes empty, the way they'd been since his father's arrest. Maybe even before. "Maybe I'll go next week."

"Definitely go next week." Maggie nodded. "I'll even go with you."

Their mother smiled. "I would like that. Thank you."

Pete crossed his fingers under the table that she would actually go. It was past time for her to move on and start enjoying life again. Maggie was constantly scheming to get their mother out of the house, but this opportunity had just fallen into his lap and seemed like it might actually work.

Speaking of Maggie, she was bent over suspiciously, her back to him. A long black tail protruded from beneath the tablecloth.

"Don't feed the damn dog from the table," he said.

"Shush. He likes meatloaf." She turned sheepishly.

Timber pranced out from under the table, licking his chops, and gave Pete a victorious look.

"Sure he does, but you're teaching him bad manners. If you have to feed him meatloaf, at least put it in his dog bowl."

Maggie scowled at him. "You are such a spoilsport."

He grunted. "I've been called worse."

They finished their meal, and Pete headed home while his mom and Maggie moved into the living room to watch some reality show train wreck they were both addicted to. It was their Thursday tradition.

He couldn't go for a run after eating meatloaf, so he took Timber for a long walk instead. The dog was hyper, despite a belly full of beef. Sometimes Pete wondered if a dog like Timber needed more attention than he had time to give.

But they'd make it work. He enjoyed the companionship. Enjoyed having someone to come home to. And he didn't plan on trying marriage again, so he and Timber were just going to have to make do with each other.

A cat streaked across the street ahead of them, and Timber nearly yanked Pete's arm out of its socket.

"Okay, okay. I'll make time for a long run before work tomorrow. Deal?" And this time he would stay far the hell away from Jordan Lake.

* * *

"Nothing on the car or the house?" Merry asked.

Olivia shifted the phone to her other ear to disentangle

a kitten paw from her hair. "I went out and checked again first thing this morning. No spray paint. I think it worked when Pete went out and talked to them."

"Well I hope so, although I still don't like you being at home by yourself."

"Don't worry. I have Dumb and Dumber here to protect me." Olivia had been gating Scooby and Bailey downstairs at night, partly so that they could alert her to anyone lurking in the bushes and mainly to keep them from terrorizing Hallie, who had moved into the bedroom with her since she'd come back home.

"That's a terrible way to talk about Bailey and Scooby," Merry said. "It's not Bailey's fault she's not all the way potty trained. Her last owners obviously didn't train her right."

Or the damn dog just enjoyed peeing in the kitchen. "Well anyway, they'd raise quite a ruckus if anyone came around here again. Scooby's got a protective streak. I don't think he'd let anyone hurt me."

"Gracious, Olivia. Don't even say that or I'll make you move back in with us."

"It was just spray paint. I'm fine. Don't worry."

"I do worry," Merry said. "But I understand too. If I were in your shoes, I'd probably be doing the same thing."

Not for the first time, Olivia was grateful that Merry had come into her life. They'd become friends over the summer when they'd worked together at a camp on T.J.'s farm, and now Olivia counted her as one of her best friends.

"I'll call you later," she told Merry.

She slid the phone into her back pocket and extracted

Hallie from her hair, only to have a kitten attached to her wrist, biting and kicking for all she was worth. "Ouch. You're a little rabid this morning, aren't you?"

Hallie purred as she continued her attack, a lovable little rogue.

Olivia pried herself free and went downstairs to deal with the dogs. They were hyper and annoyed at having to spend the night downstairs by themselves, so since she had a few hours before work, she took them for a run.

It was chilly today, finally starting to feel like October. Many of her neighbors had put Halloween decorations out, pumpkins on their front porches, big fake spider webs across their doorways. One even had a giant inflatable witch hooked up. Bailey barked at it as they passed.

As they rounded the final corner and her little gray house came into view, Olivia stumbled. A Dogwood County Sheriff's cruiser was parked out front. She slowed to a walk, resisting as the dogs tugged her forward. What now?

Pete got out of the cruiser and stood facing her, wearing his unreadable cop face. A different man than the one she'd found at Jordan Lake the other night. "Where were you last night?"

"Here at home. Why?" She stopped in her tracks, her stomach clenching uncomfortably. Had there been more vandalism? She glanced over at her house and car but saw nothing out of place.

"You been out to Frank Holloway's farm recently?"

"Um, no." And she was starting to get a bad feeling about the direction this conversation had taken.

"Mind if I take a look in your car?"

"Knock yourself out." Now she was really getting

pissed because he sounded like he was about to accuse her of a crime...and this time she was *not* guilty.

He walked around the Prius, looking at her tires, then popped the trunk and poked through its contents, which was slightly embarrassing because—as she was reminded when she saw him lifting it up—she'd left a big pack of toilet paper in there after her last trip to the grocery store.

"What the hell's going on?" she demanded.

He turned toward her, his expression somewhat softer. "Someone spray-painted a bunch of Holloway's cows last night."

"Spray-painted cows?" she sputtered. "Why would anyone—wait, you think *I* did it?" Her stomach flip-flopped as rage pushed its way through her belly.

"The words 'Don't eat me' were painted onto about a dozen cows."

She fisted her hands on her hips, only to have them yanked away by her errant dogs. "That's actually quite clever. Wish I could take credit for it, but I have no intention of breaking the law ever again, and I'm certainly not stupid enough to risk my probation by spray-painting a bunch of cows the week before my court date."

The corner of his mouth quirked. "You're anything but stupid, but I had to eliminate you as a suspect, given your previous arrest."

"Hmph." That took some of the wind out of her sails.

"Have a nice day, Olivia." With a wink, he got back into his cruiser and drove away.

She stood there for a moment, still halfway pissed off, then went inside. Who had spray-painted those cows? Hopefully it wasn't anyone from her group. Because if

her act of vandalism had inadvertently encouraged someone else to do the same, that made her feel even worse.
Maybe she needed to do a blog post reminding people to
keep things legal.

Besides being the right thing to do, it was the only way
they'd ever get the sheriff's office to take them seriously.

She took a hot shower and dressed in an emerald-
colored sweater and skinny jeans, with her leather-free,
fake Uggs. Since she still had a few minutes before she
needed to leave for work, she sat on her bed and twirled
a feather-duster toy she'd bought the other day for Hallie.
The kitten lunged through the air chasing the feathers,
eyes dark with mischief. She really was fun to have
around. Olivia had never had a cat before, and as she
hadn't actually tried to find another home for Hallie, it
was time to admit that she had one now.

"You're mine. You know that, right?" she told Hallie,
who purred then launched herself through the air in another attack on the feather toy.

The doorbell rang, followed by booming barks and the
scuffle of dog toes over hardwood floors. See? They were
a decent alarm system. Olivia set down the feather-duster
and glanced out her bedroom window.

The Channel Two news van was parked in front of her
house.

What in the world?

She walked downstairs and checked the peephole,
spotting a familiar-looking blonde on her doorstep. She
slid back the deadbolt and opened the door.

"Hi. I'm Diana Robbins from the WJBV Channel Two
news. Are you Olivia Bennett?"

Olivia nodded slowly. "Yes. What can I do for you?"

"The town's been buzzing since your arrest out at the Halverson Foods plant, and now some of Frank Holloway's cows have been spray-painted as well. Care to give us a comment?" Diana asked, her green eyes gleaming with interest.

"Um." Olivia noticed for the first time the cameraman standing beside Diana, the red light lit, camera rolling. "I don't know anything about the cows, so I really can't comment on that."

"What about your ongoing battle against Halverson Foods? Can you give our viewers the inside scoop?"

A segment on the news highlighting her campaign against Halverson Foods? This was too good to be true! Olivia pulled the front door shut behind her and smiled into the camera. "It all started about a year and a half ago when I came across some undercover footage showing conditions inside the Halverson Foods chicken-processing plant."

* * *

Pete spent the weekend working, and Monday too. He was satisfied that Olivia hadn't gone anywhere near Holloway's farm, although her name hadn't been officially removed from the list of suspects. He didn't believe she was guilty of anything but spray painting the Halverson factory, and the quickest way to prove that was to catch the actual culprit or culprits.

And so he'd spent every spare minute investigating the other open vandalism cases. He'd tracked down and talked to every convicted vandal in town. He even scoured Olivia's website for names of her fellow animal rights activists and checked to see if any of them had a criminal history that suggested they might have spray-painted "Don't eat me" on those cows.

So far he'd come up with squat, but he'd keep digging until he caught whoever was responsible. When he finally got home that night, he took Timber for a quick run, then settled on the couch with a plate of leftover pizza to catch the end of the ten o'clock news.

He choked on a piece of pepperoni when he saw Olivia's face on the screen. She wore a green sweater and jeans. The front of her house was visible behind her.

"It's barbaric," she was saying. "Those birds deserve to be treated humanely, even though they're destined to be slaughtered."

A newscaster stood beside her, microphone in hand. "I think that most of us imagine the chickens we eat roaming around happily outside on a farm before they head to the slaughterhouse, but that's not the reality of it."

Olivia shook her head. "No, and it hasn't been for some time. But the fact is, the chickens that arrive at the Halverson Foods factory each day are beaten and subjected to other horrific forms of abuse before they're killed. And that shouldn't be allowed to happen, not anywhere, but especially not here in Dogwood."

The newscaster faced the camera. "You can find more information on our website at WJBV.com."

Pete picked up his cell phone and dialed. "What the hell was that?" he asked when she answered.

"You saw me on the news?" Olivia asked.

"I just caught the end of it. Liv...this was a bad move."

She sighed dramatically into the phone. "It wasn't the

best timing, but she just showed up on my doorstep with the camera rolling. What was I supposed to do, send her away?"

"Yes."

She growled at his blunt answer. "Well that would have been a bad move too, because I might not have gotten her attention again later on. This news segment is going to drum up a lot of new support for my cause."

"That may be, but you shouldn't have gone on TV a week before your court date. You need the judge to see you as someone who's learned her lesson."

"And I have." There was a new edge in her tone. "The last time I checked, it isn't illegal to talk to a reporter."

He rubbed his brow. "It's a matter of perception. Not to mention, you've probably just pissed off all those workers again."

"You know what? I don't need a lecture. If I'd had a chance to think it over ahead of time, maybe I wouldn't have done the interview, but she caught me off guard, and I went with it."

"Olivia—"

"I have no regrets, so don't you dare have them for me." She paused, and the sound of dogs barking echoed through the phone. "What the—"

Alarm zipped up his spine. "What happened?"

"I don't know. I heard a noise outside, and the dogs are going nuts."

He stood from the couch, sliding his mostly uneaten pizza onto the coffee table. "Hang up, and dial 911."

"So your esteemed colleagues can laugh at me again? No offense, *deputy*, but I'll pass."

He gripped the back of his neck. "Stop fucking around,

Olivia. There could be someone outside. Call the police, *now*."

"You know what?" Anger snapped over the line. "I think I'll take my chances."

The line clicked, and she was gone.

* * *

Olivia kicked the toppled trashcan and laughed. For a moment there, she'd been really scared. So scared that if she hadn't glanced out the window and seen the snooping raccoon, she might have actually called the police.

And she was *so* glad she hadn't. She could only imagine the many ways they'd have laughed at her for calling 911 over a raccoon in her trash.

Bailey and Scooby were still putting up a ruckus loud enough to wake the whole neighborhood, alternating between poking their heads in the trashcan and lunging in the direction the raccoon had run when they'd come outside.

She hustled them toward the front door, eager to get back inside and get them quiet. With the door closed and locked behind her, she collapsed in a fit of hysterical laughter at the very idea of her taking on a bunch of disgruntled Halverson employees with only Bailey and Scooby for protection.

She was a terrible person for letting Pete think the worst. She should call him back and let him know she was okay.

The thought had no sooner crossed her mind than she heard a vehicle pull into her driveway, followed by the slam of a car door. Her heart fired back up, but it was Pete's SUV parked beside her Prius.

Pete stormed toward her front door.

She pulled it open ahead of him. "I already handled it."

He stopped in front of her, dark eyes flashing, oozing protective alpha male from every pore. And oh, her poor hormones were so confused. She was still mad as hell at him, and yet it was all she could do not to fist her hands in his black T-shirt and kiss him.

"Handled what?" he demanded.

She shrugged. "Oh, half a dozen Halverson employees."

He raked a hand through his hair. "Shit. You foolish, headstrong—"

She put a hand out. "Stop before you really piss me off. I'm kidding. It was a raccoon."

He stared. "What?"

"A raccoon knocked over my trashcan. The dogs scared it away."

Pete looked like he'd just had the wind knocked out of him. "A raccoon."

"Yep." Her nerves twitched, humming with residual fear, anger, and lust.

"And you just—" He grabbed her shoulders. "Fuck."

And then he kissed her. All the restless energy she'd been holding onto spontaneously combusted at the feel of his lips on hers. She flung herself into his arms and kissed him back. His tongue danced with hers, igniting a fiery need that pulsed inside her, growing stronger and more urgent with each stroke of his tongue.

She slid her hands over his chest, feeling the hard contour of his pecs. His muscles tightened as her fingers roamed across them. A low groan rumbled through his chest, tickling her nerve endings. He smelled fresh like soap and aftershave, like he'd just taken a shower.

His hands cupped her ass, yanking her up against him. She felt his hard length against her belly, and she whimpered with frustration. He was so tall, and she was too short. She needed to feel him right where her body burned for him. She went up on her tiptoes, but it was no use. She couldn't align their bodies.

"Olivia." His voice was a growl, thick with lust.

They couldn't do this. She knew that as well as he did. But she wanted him. God, she needed him more than she'd ever needed anything. Just one more minute...

He pulled away, breathing like he'd just scaled a mountain. The expression on his face was one of desperation. He swore under his breath, and with one final, scorching look, he strode out her front door, slamming it behind him.

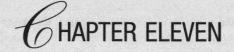HAPTER ELEVEN

*P*ete gritted his teeth and gripped the steering wheel. He couldn't go home, not like this. The Forester had a full tank of gas so he pointed it toward the miles of country roads outside of town limits. He rolled the window down and let the cool air hit him like a slap in the face.

Maybe Mother Nature could slap some sense into him and help him regather his reins. Pete had always prided himself on being a man in control. And tonight he'd lost it. He'd gone off half-cocked, racing over to Olivia's house as if a woman like her needed a Knight in Shining Armor. Olivia Bennett was more than capable of taking care of herself.

And then he'd kissed her.

And he was really fucking sorry that he wasn't still kissing her, that he wasn't in her bed right now, taking them both right out of their minds with pleasure. Instead he was driving around aimlessly, trying hard to forget how sweet she'd tasted and those soft, little whimpers she'd made as she tried to climb his body.

He'd barely found the strength to pull away. This was a problem.

He'd had a few one-night stands after the divorce, but they'd only left him feeling empty. Hollow. He hadn't felt anything with those women, and it had scared him, so much that he hadn't been with a woman in over a year.

That was the root of the problem with Olivia. He felt things with her, too many things. Things that went much deeper than their fiery chemistry or the fact that it had been way too long since he'd gotten laid. Olivia made him feel *everything*. And that might be even scarier than feeling nothing.

He made it home just past one a.m., exhausted and miserable. He fell into bed, knowing already that he wouldn't sleep. An hour later, he rose and went into the kitchen to bake muffins. The women's shelter would be getting a fresh delivery in the morning.

Sometime before dawn, he fell back into bed and slept a few restless hours. He rose with the sun and took Timber for a long run, grateful today was his day off because, mentally, he was spent.

He dropped off his batch of cinnamon muffins to the shelter, then spent a few hours at the shooting range, burning through his frustrations the only safe way he knew how. It was Tuesday, and he had to coach the boys' soccer again this afternoon. He'd debated coming up with an excuse to skip it, but he'd never been one to shirk an obligation. Steve Barnes was counting on him to keep those kids occupied for a couple of hours, maybe even teach them a thing or two.

He was still troubled by his argument with Zach last week. The kid was struggling, and Pete wanted to help him.

By the time he got to the rec center that afternoon, he was feeling less sure about that. He arrived early to set up balls and cones for drills and found Zach sitting out back. Based on the smell clinging to his clothing and the frantic stubbing of his sneaker in the dirt, the kid had just smoked a cigarette.

"That shit will ruin your lungs, you know," Pete said, as he sat beside Zach on the bottom step.

Zach looked over, defiance in his dark eyes. "Oh yeah? You gonna arrest me?"

"Nah. I'm just your soccer coach. But let me tell you what got me to quit smoking."

"You smoked?"

Pete nodded. "In high school, for a bit. Who didn't, right? But then I realized none of the girls wanted to kiss me because my breath stank. So I quit."

"Sienna smokes. She gave me one to try. Wait—" Fear rose in Zach's eyes.

Pete chuckled. "Seriously, quit thinking of me as a cop right now. I'm not here to get anyone in trouble. Just the opposite."

"Well I never saw her smoke, so maybe she does, and maybe she doesn't," Zach hedged.

Pete stared out at the trees on the other side of the parking lot. "You're a smart kid. I'm sure you'll make the right decision."

"I don't like cops," Zach said.

"What about soccer coaches?"

"Not sure I like them either."

"You want to help me set up?"

Zach shrugged. "Yeah, okay."

They walked back inside together. Pete showed him how to set up the cones and ran through a couple of drills with him before the other kids arrived.

"You're good, you know," he told the boy. "If you ever want to play, give me a call. The field behind the playground on Main Street is usually free in the evenings."

"Maybe." Zach sauntered off to chat with the other boys, who had arrived and been goofing off over by the locker room for the last five minutes or so.

Pete followed, bag of soccer balls in hand.

* * *

Olivia sat on the front steps of the rec center, hugging her knees. She was not at all sure Pete would want to see her, but she wasn't one to run away from an awkward situation, and last night had definitely ended awkwardly.

"Olivia?"

She heard his voice behind her, and she stood to face him. He wore a blue T-shirt and gray athletic shorts, and he didn't look at all like he had last Tuesday when she'd bumped into him leaving soccer practice.

The night she'd taken him to Jordan Lake.

"I just wanted to apologize," she said.

"For what?" A smile creased the corners of his eyes. "The way I remember it, I kissed you and ran out on you, not the other way around."

A rush of heat flooded through her. "That's true. But I was being a foolish, headstrong—what else were you going to call me?"

He grimaced. "Pain in the ass?"

"I should have told you it was just a raccoon."

His eyes narrowed. "Next time you hear a noise outside, you'll call the police."

Of course she would, but for some reason, she couldn't resist messing with him. "As a compromise, I'll punch in 911 and bring my phone out with me."

He looked pained. "How am I supposed to sleep at night thinking about you running around outside chasing vandals in the dark?"

"There were no vandals." And Pete didn't look like he'd slept well regardless.

"Here's an idea. Why don't you get a motion-activated surveillance camera for the front of your house?"

Her brow wrinkled. "That sounds expensive."

"The equipment isn't that much. I'd be happy to come out and install it for you."

"I'll think about it."

"Liv—" he said, and her heart softened at the sound of her nickname on his lips.

"I really should be apologizing for screwing things up before I even met you. If I hadn't broken the law, you wouldn't have had to walk away last night."

He didn't blink. "If you hadn't broken the law, I never would have met you, and I wouldn't have even been there last night."

She huffed an angry breath. "Well, I'm pissed at myself for it anyway."

He touched her cheek. "You apologize too much. I wouldn't change a thing about you."

For a moment, she thought he was going to kiss her right there on the sidewalk outside the rec center. But the tenderness and affection in his eyes left her feeling just as breathless.

She gulped air, afraid to look away and break the connection between them.

"Your court date is on Monday. If the judge dismisses the charges against you..." The look in his eyes made her shiver with anticipation.

Her heart pounded. "If the charges are dropped?"

"I want you. You know that. But I can't promise anything long-term. I'm divorced, and I don't want to go there again."

Her spine stiffened. She *did* want to go there someday, and now that he'd put the thought in her head, she couldn't shake the image of him waiting for her at the end of the aisle, looking drop-dead gorgeous in his dress blues. "Okay."

"I just wanted to be clear about my intentions."

"I appreciate that."

"And I totally understand if it changes your feelings for me."

"It doesn't." And that was true. She didn't need a promise of forever, not yet anyway. And right now a fling with Pete sounded pretty damn irresistible. "You working on Monday?"

"Until three."

"Meet me up at the lake around six. It's time for your next meditation lesson."

* * *

Pete watched her go, hoping like hell she had plans for something more exciting than meditation at the lake. He wasn't sure it was even possible to meditate with a hard-on, and he sure as hell couldn't be alone with her without getting aroused.

Reluctantly, he headed for his Forester and drove home. For once, exhaustion seemed to have overtaken everything else. He walked Timber outside to pee, then collapsed into bed, asleep before his head even hit the pillow.

He dreamed of Olivia, naked beneath him. He buried his face in her hair, thrusting inside her until the weight of the world lifted away. He woke with a start, his body damp with sweat, his dick hard enough to cut steel.

With a groan, he rolled to his back. The clock on the bedside table read one twenty-two, which meant he'd slept a solid six hours, the longest stretch of sleep he'd had in weeks.

If only it hadn't ended with him alone in bed in the middle of the night, sporting one hell of a hard-on.

Timber leaped onto his chest, those enormous paws knocking the breath right out of him. When he'd recovered enough air to speak, Pete cursed his dog and rolled out of bed. He shrugged into a pair of lounge pants over his boxers and headed for the stairs.

Pete baked until the sun rose. The women's shelter would be getting another batch of muffins later that morning. He showered, then checked his bank account balance from his phone. His paycheck had cleared, right on time.

He got ready for work a few minutes early and took an envelope from the catch-all in the kitchen. As he did every payday, he drove to the ATM and withdrew a hundred dollars. He pushed five crisp twenty dollar bills into the envelope, sealed it, and dropped it into the mailbox down the street from his bank.

His way of giving back to the Hill family. It wasn't enough, but it couldn't be easy for Tamara, raising Zach on her own. The least he could do was help.

He was on his way to the station when his cell phone rang. Olivia's number showed on the display.

"Are you on duty?" she asked when he answered, and a bad feeling took hold in his gut.

"Yes. Why?"

"I need to file another report."

"What happened?" He shifted into the left hand lane, preparing to turn back toward her house.

"More of the same."

"I'll be there in five minutes. Stay inside and lock your doors."

He turned onto Peachtree Lane three minutes later, and as he approached the little gray house at the end of the street, under any other circumstances, he would have laughed.

Someone had hurled dozens of eggs, splattering the entire front of the house in slimy, dripping yellow goo. A harmless prank, except in this case, because eggs came from chickens, this was most likely tied into her feud with Halverson Foods.

Olivia met him on the front porch, her eyes flashing with anger. "This is disgusting."

"Good morning to you too."

"Sorry. Come in." She stepped back, and he followed her into the living room. The sound of dogs barking and toenails clattering against linoleum came from the kitchen.

"Did they bark during the night?" he asked.

"They've barked every night since I started leaving

them downstairs. I heard them around three, but when I peeked out the window in my bedroom, I didn't see anything."

"This is where that motion-activated camera would have come in handy," he said.

She pressed a hand to her forehead. "We had that discussion *yesterday*. I didn't get a chance to look into it yet."

"Well let's get it done now. I can get a camera and install it for you tonight."

Olivia folded her arms over her chest. "I'm working tonight."

"Tomorrow then."

She stared at him for a moment then released a weary sigh. "Okay. I'll buy the camera; you just tell me which one to get."

"I'll text you a link. In the meantime, let's get this written up." He gestured toward the front of her house.

"I feel like I'm wasting my time even filing a report. A lot of good it's done me so far."

"Reporting a crime is never a waste of time. At the very least, you need a paper trail, a record of every incident showing a pattern of behavior in case anything more serious happens later on."

"They're mad because I went on TV."

"Probably." And this was exactly why he'd wanted her to lay low.

He took her statement and photos to document the scene, all the while fighting the urge to beg her to back off Halverson Foods for a little while. He knew it would be a waste of breath. Nothing was going to change her mind. "Be careful," he said instead.

"I am. I have been." Her chin was up, defensive.

"And let's get that security camera installed."

She nodded.

"All right. I'll be in touch about the camera. Call if anything else happens before then."

* * *

Pete installed the camera for her on Thursday afternoon. She'd be able to view the feed on her television or her phone, so at least he wouldn't have to worry about her running around in the dark chasing criminals anymore. And if anyone vandalized her house again, they'd have the fuckers on tape.

When he arrived at the station the next morning, Solomon gestured down the hall toward the sheriff's office. "Linburgh wants to see you."

"Thanks." Pete set the paperwork he'd been carrying on his desk. Somehow he doubted the sheriff wanted to praise him on his most recent arrest. He found Linburgh in his office, door open and talking on the phone

Linburgh motioned him in. "Absolutely, Tom. I appreciate your cooperation. It was great talking to you. Give Marcia and the girls my best."

Pete stood inside the doorway. He stared idly out the window, watching the sky darken with impending rain.

"Sampson, thanks for coming in," Linburgh said, after he'd ended his call. He motioned for Pete to close the door.

He closed it and turned to face his boss. "No problem. What can I do for you?"

"I hear you've been spending a lot of time with our little vandal, Olivia Bennett." Linburgh leaned back in his chair and clasped his hands behind his head.

Pete's skin prickled with misgivings. "I've been looking into the vandalism on her property, trying to see if it's tied into the other vandalism around town."

"And installing a home security system for her." Linburgh's eyebrows lifted.

How in God's name did he know about that? Didn't matter. "Just helping out a citizen."

"Olivia Bennett is a troublemaker, and if I have any say in the matter, she's going to pay for that in court on Monday."

Pete rocked back on his heels. "I'm not sure what you're getting at, sir."

Actually, he knew exactly what the sheriff was getting at, and it pissed him off royally. Linburgh had no reason to take an interest in Olivia's case or care whether Pete installed a security camera for her. Her crime was a petty misdemeanor, which she'd already made restitution for.

The only explanation was Linburgh's connection to Halverson Foods. He was going hard on her to kiss ass with his biggest campaign supporter.

It might not be illegal, but it sure as hell made Pete's skin crawl. Politics had no place in police work as far as he was concerned.

Linburgh leaned forward and poked a finger in Pete's direction. "Just remember, your objective here is to tie her to the other vandalism in town, not to get in her pants."

CHAPTER TWELVE

Olivia stood in the courtroom Monday morning, dressed in a black pencil skirt, white shirt, and gray blazer, her hair pulled back in a simple bun. She'd gone for the mature, law-abiding citizen look this morning, and she was about to find out if it had worked.

"Miss Bennett," Judge Gonzalez said. "You've completed your thirty days of probation, and it's time for the court to rule on whether or not to press charges against you for your acts of trespass and vandalism at the Halverson Foods chicken-processing plant last month."

Olivia drew a breath and crossed her fingers beneath the desk before her. At her side, her dad rested a hand on her shoulder.

"I gave you a chance to demonstrate that yours was a one-time mistake. However, I've learned that you're still causing trouble for Halverson Foods. Just last week, you appeared on the Channel Two news speaking against them. And the sheriff's office tells me you are

currently under suspicion for an act of vandalism at
Frank Holloway's farm. This leaves the court with some
concern about future actions you might take. Therefore,
I hereby find you guilty of misdemeanor trespass and
Willful and Wanton Injury to Property."

Guilty.

Panic rose up to clog her throat. She would have a
criminal record for the rest of her life. She might even
have to serve jail time.

Oh God.

She glanced over at Pete, sitting near the back of the
courtroom, but he was staring straight ahead, his expression set in stone.

The judge cleared his throat before continuing.
"You've already made restitution to Halverson Foods by
removing the graffiti. The remainder of your sentence
may be served in the form of one hundred and twenty
hours of community service, to be performed here in
Dogwood County over the course of the next year. The
court will provide you with a list of approved charities
you may choose from."

Olivia closed her eyes. A slow breath leaked from
her lungs. Community service. She could handle that.
She embraced that. Her throat constricted painfully. How
could she have been so stupid? The judge should have
dropped the charges against her.

But he hadn't. And it was because she'd pissed off
the powers that be at Halverson Foods. They wanted her
to back off. Well, fuck that. Her hands tightened into
fists.

The judge banged his gavel, and everyone started
talking at once. Her dad muttered reassurances as he

gathered his papers and stuffed them into his briefcase. The clerk started calling the next case. Somewhere, a baby cried.

Olivia looked over her shoulder to the row where Pete had been seated. He was gone.

Her dad placed a hand on her shoulder and guided her through the throng of people in the aisle toward the door. She had a criminal record. Her legal career was probably over. Not that she'd wanted one. But she hated having the decision taken away from her.

Hated knowing that she'd brought all of this on herself.

As for Pete, she had no idea where this left them. Would he still meet her at the lake after work? She'd had such high hopes for tonight too. She was really overdue for some great sex, and she had a feeling he could deliver on that, and then some.

"It's all right." Her dad patted her on the back as they reached the front steps of the courthouse. "Community service isn't so bad. I bet you can volunteer at the animal shelter."

She forced a smile. "Not bad at all."

"What's this about Frank Holloway's farm?" His brows knitted.

"Someone spray-painted cows, but I had *nothing* to do with it, Dad. I guess I'll be Suspect One for all the vandalism around town for a while."

He shrugged. "This'll all die down soon enough. Can I take you to lunch?"

No rose immediately on her tongue, but she'd taken the day off from work, she hardly ever saw her parents, and some company might be nice. "I'd like that, Dad."

She followed him down the street to where he'd parked

his Mercedes. Her legs felt heavy, and she still couldn't swallow past the lump in her throat. *A criminal record.*

Her dad started the car, then rested his hand on her knee. "It's not that bad, you know."

"This will make it even harder for me to get back into law school. You must be so disappointed in me." She stared down at her lap.

"Oh, honey. I'm sorry your mom and I put so much pressure on you. I know you never wanted to be a lawyer. Maybe this is a blessing in disguise. You can stop beating yourself up over not wanting to be what we wanted you to be. You're a wonderful, smart person, and I'm proud of you, no matter what you decide to do with your life."

She blinked back tears. "Really?"

He gave her a serious look. "I've always been proud of you. I'm sorry if I didn't show it."

"But I'm just a waitress. I haven't found a career, or gotten married, or any of the things I'm supposed to do."

"You're a smart young woman who's not afraid to speak up for what she believes in. You give voice to the animals no one else cares about. That's something to be proud of, Olivia."

And then he reached across the center console and gave her a hug.

* * *

Pete's Monday had gone from bad to worse. First he'd watched Olivia be charged with vandalism and sentenced to community service. He'd then spent the rest of the morning sorting out a domestic dispute in which the wife refused to press charges against her abusive scumbag of a husband.

A handful of traffic stops later, he'd been about to clock out for the day when he caught a traffic accident near the high school. He'd had to watch as a seventeen-year-old girl was zipped up in a body bag, her life cut short because she'd felt the need to send her boyfriend a text message as she drove home from school.

Having to deliver the news to her parents, having to watch their hopes and dreams dissolve in utter devastation, had left him somewhere between empty and ready to punch a hole through the nearest wall.

When he finally made it home, he took a long, hot shower. Belatedly, he looked at the clock. It was almost seven. He'd been supposed to meet Olivia by the lake at six.

The charges against her should have been dropped. But she'd had to push the damn envelope and piss off the management at Halverson Foods with that TV interview.

He shouldn't go anywhere near her. She wasn't good for his reputation even if she'd gotten off today. And with charges on her record? It didn't violate a written rule, but it might make the sheriff think twice about promoting him, especially after their conversation on Friday.

She probably hadn't gone to the lake anyway. And even if she had, she'd probably gone home by now. But tonight he needed a distraction from the grim realities of life. He needed to feel alive. He needed Olivia.

If she was there at the lake, he'd take whatever she would give him.

* * *

He hadn't come. Of course, Olivia had known he probably wouldn't. He shouldn't be with her, not now. But she'd come anyway, hoping against hope. When he hadn't arrived by six thirty, she indulged herself in a few tears, but they'd only made her feel worse. So she dried her cheeks, sat in front of what remained of the sunset, and meditated.

She worked the tension out of her body inch by inch until she no longer felt the weight of today's many disappointments on her shoulders. She looked ahead to a fresh start for herself. She would achieve what she needed to with Halverson Foods and begin a new chapter in her life.

Start a new career. What would it be?

Tension coiled in her shoulders, and she shook it free. She didn't have to decide today. But it was time to start looking around for ideas. Something involving animals. Animal advocacy would be a dream, but there weren't many paying jobs, and she needed to pay her bills.

"You're still here." Pete's voice came from behind her, and Olivia jumped about three feet in the air, landing in a heap.

She scrambled to her feet, brushing dirt and leaves from herself, her heart throbbing in her chest. "I didn't think you were coming."

"I just got off work." He was a voice in the darkness, like the night they'd met. Tonight though, there was a hard edge in his tone. "I'm sorry I'm late."

"Long day?" She took a step toward him, outlined in the last light of the setting sun.

"Yeah." That one word said it all. This had nothing to do with her court appearance this morning. He saw things, did things in the line of duty that she'd never want to imagine. He yanked her against him and buried his face in her hair. "Promise me you'll never text and drive."

Oh God. "Never."

"She was only seventeen." The pain in his voice was palpable.

She wrapped her arms around him. "Oh, Pete."

He fisted his hands in her hair and kissed her, rough and raw. She went up in flames for him, just like that. His tongue thrust against hers while his hands roamed down her back to her ass, which he gripped, pressing her into him.

She whimpered with need, pulsing with it, desperate to strip him naked and give him release from his pain, to find pleasure together, to lose her fucking mind with what was sure to be some of the hottest sex of her life. But—"Wait."

He froze, hands still on her ass, his chest heaving for breath.

"Should we—I mean, I was convicted this morning." Shame flooded through her, burning in her blood, mixed with the fire Pete had ignited.

"No, we shouldn't, but I don't care." His voice was low and rough.

She groaned, letting her head fall against his shoulder. "I want this—you—more than anything, but you can't sacrifice your career for sex. That's stupider than me spray-painting a building on my birthday."

Laughter rumbled through his chest. "I'm not sacrificing anything for you. Are you good for my career? No. But neither are a lot of things. I need you, Olivia."

She felt how much he needed her, pressed hard against

her belly, and dammit, he was still too tall. She went up on her tiptoes and kissed him. "Then have me. Please."

He let out something similar to a growl, once again crushing his mouth against hers. She gripped his shoulders and jumped, wrapping her legs around his hips. She wiggled against him, his erection pressed right where she needed it. *Finally.*

Then they were kissing and groping frantically until she thought she might spontaneously combust in his arms. Her skirt had come up around her waist, and the friction of his jeans against her panties was almost too much. The throbbing need inside her overtook all her other senses.

Pete sank to his knees on the blanket she'd laid out to meditate on. He laid her on it, then followed her down, one powerful leg thrust between her thighs. The night air had cooled, spreading goose bumps over her flushed skin. She shivered with delight as he kissed his way down her neck.

A blanket of stars covered them. Somewhere over the lake, a hawk called. It was absolutely the most romantic setting she could have ever envisioned.

She pulled him closer, drinking him in, totally intoxicated with the man in her arms and the nightscape around them.

He rested his forehead against hers. "We can't do this, not here."

"What?"

"Public indecency and all that." He smiled against her lips.

"Please." Her voice was a needy whisper, and she thrust her hips against his.

He groaned. "Come to my place. Stay the night."

"Yes." She held in a groan of her own, as he untangled himself from her, pulling her up to stand beside him. "Just give me one minute."

She pulled out her phone and texted Merry. *Huge favor?*

Shoot, Merry answered.

Will you feed the dogs and take them out for me tonight?

Why...? She could almost see the playful twinkle in Merry's eyes.

You'd approve, I promise.

It's a work night for me, so this better be good.

Shit. I'm sorry. I'll babysit for you later this week. You pick the night.

"What are you doing?" Pete slid his arms around her.

"I'm trying to bribe Merry into taking care of my dogs tonight."

"Hurry."

She heard the urgency in his voice, and it fueled the aching need inside her.

You'll babysit, and you'll give me a full rundown on whatever you're up to tonight, Merry texted back.

Deal. You rock. Gotta go.

Olivia slid her phone into the pocket of her jacket, grabbed the blanket, and hustled after Pete toward the road.

"Follow me," he said. He kissed her, then slid behind the wheel of his SUV.

She didn't have to be told twice. She jumped into her Prius and cranked the engine.

The ride into town had never taken so long. Pete annoyingly hugged the speed limit, somehow steady and calm when she was ready to jump out of her skin with the need to feel him inside her.

He turned down Townsend Drive and pulled into the driveway of a gray townhouse near the end of the street. She pulled in behind him, painfully aware of how obvious her red Prius was in his driveway. As much as she wanted him, she did not want to keep him from being promoted to detective.

And despite what he'd said, her reputation had the power to do just that. She backed out of the driveway. He stepped out of his car, watching, hands on his hips.

She drove down the street and around the corner, parked, and walked back to him.

"What the hell was that?" he asked.

She shrugged, then led the way to his front door.

"Seriously, Olivia." He grabbed her elbow, turning her to face him.

"Half the people in town know that's my car. I don't want to get you in trouble."

"And I told you that you won't." His expression hardened.

She shrugged. "Then call it me not wanting to advertise this night to the world, okay? Maybe I'd like some privacy for once."

He shook his head. "You're thinking way too hard about this."

He opened the front door, greeted immediately by loud booming barks from the back of the house. She followed him in and stood for a moment in his foyer.

Then Pete had her pressed against the wall, kissing her senseless. "Give me five minutes," he whispered against her neck.

"If you insist." But she knew he had to tend to Timber. It would have been the same at her house.

He pulled free and disappeared down the hall toward what she presumed was the kitchen. She poked around in his living room, finding photos on the mantel of what looked to be his mom and sister. No evidence of a father. She filed that away as another piece of Pete's puzzle.

While she waited for him, she ducked into the hall bathroom to freshen up. When she came out, he was just coming in the back door with Timber at his side. The dog literally leaped for joy when he saw her. She went into the kitchen to greet him, and Timber twirled and howled his pleasure.

"No offense, buddy, but you're cramping my style right now." Pete gave his dog a long look, which Timber completely ignored. Pete fetched a hollow bone from a box in the corner, stuffed it with peanut butter, and tossed it onto Timber's bed. "Have fun," he said.

He pulled a baby gate across the doorway to the kitchen and tugged her toward the stairs.

"Finally." She went up on her toes to kiss him.

Pete scooped her into his arms and carried her up the stairs. She clasped her hands behind his neck, nibbling beneath his jaw as he walked. He tossed her into his bed, on a gray quilt that smelled intoxicatingly like him. Then he kicked off his shoes and lowered himself on top of her, bracing on his forearms so that he didn't squish her.

She slid her hands beneath his T-shirt, skimming them over his hot, firm skin. Muscles bunched beneath her touch. Sometime later, she wanted to enjoy the fine sight of him without clothes, but right now, she couldn't wait another moment, and based on the hard evidence in the front of his jeans, neither could he.

"Please." She shimmied out of her panties and reached

for the zipper of his jeans. "Hurry." She was burning for him, aching to finish what they'd started by the lake.

"We should slow down," he whispered against her neck, even as his hands explored her bare skin, stroking and teasing.

She whimpered. "We have the rest of the night to take it slow."

Something in her tone must have broken his control because he gripped her ass, thrusting his pelvis against hers, making stars dance behind her eyes. She unzipped his jeans and freed him. He was hard, so hard, and he thrust into her hands with a groan of pleasure.

Her body clenched with anticipation. "Now."

"Christ, Olivia." He sounded half-strangled. He pushed his jeans and boxers down, crushing his mouth against hers, his cock straining against her belly. "You have no idea how much I want you."

"That makes two of us." She wiggled beneath him, desperate for release. "Hurry up and get a condom."

He froze, then collapsed onto the bed beside her, cursing a blue streak.

"No condoms?" She rolled to her side, letting him suffer from his own lack of planning for several long seconds.

"Fuck." He pulled his boxers back up, grimacing as if the action caused him severe pain.

"I have one in my purse. It's downstairs."

He gave her a look that could only be described as panty-melting (if she'd been wearing any in the first place), then kicked off his jeans and, wearing only his boxers and T-shirt, practically ran out of the room.

This was taking *way* too long.

When he returned, he held her purse in his right hand. He handed it to her, then shucked his boxers and dropped onto the bed beside her. She fumbled through her purse until she found the condom, then ripped open the packet and rolled it over his hard length, letting her fingers tease him as she went.

"You are something else." He stared deep into her eyes, and then with one long stroke, he slid inside. There was no more talking then. They were frantic, clinging to each other as he thrust inside her, hard and fast. Sensation swamped her, pleasure filled her to bursting, and she was coming...

Pete gripped her hips and pushed even deeper, taking her even higher. She writhed beneath him, completely undone. He thrust into her again and again until, with a groan, he went still as he found his own release.

They lay tangled together, gasping for breath. Aftershocks of pleasure hummed through her. Pete rested his forehead on hers, eyes closed. The tension had gone out of him, the dark cloud lifted, at least for now.

Her heart pinched as she remembered what he'd witnessed tonight. Death was hard enough to stomach, but the death of a kid...She cupped his face and kissed him.

His eyes opened, burning into hers. "You are so fucking amazing."

"I could say the same." She smiled playfully, even as she felt the pull of something deeper between them, an undercurrent of emotion neither of them wanted to acknowledge.

He kissed her again, then rolled out of bed to get rid of the condom. When he returned, she put a hand out to stop him before he slid back into bed.

"Wait." She went up on her knees and tugged his T-shirt over his head. *That's better.* She ran her hands over his chest, shamelessly enjoying the sight of him naked. He was all tanned skin and taut muscle, and she wanted to touch every inch.

"My turn," he said.

Olivia was still basically dressed, her skirt bunched around her waist. Pete peeled it down her legs, stroking fire with his fingers as he went. He lifted her shirt over her head, leaving her in nothing but a pink lace bra. He traced the edge of the lace, then popped the clasp and kissed his way down her neck and over her breasts.

"You are so beautiful." His voice was low and rough, thick with lust but also heavy with emotion, as if he found her equally attractive inside and out.

And that touched a vulnerable spot in her heart, the place where she harbored insecurities about her career and her future. In his arms, she felt worthy of whatever dream she chose to chase, no matter how whimsical or foolish.

They lay together in his bed, kissing and touching, taking time where before they had been rushed. Desire built inside her, a slow burn that grew hotter with each kiss, each movement of their bodies together.

"We have a problem," she said between kisses.

"I know. That was our only condom." His cock pressed against her inner thigh, hard and ready.

"For a guy, you aren't very well prepared." She gave him a teasing smile.

"I got off work later than I'd expected." He paused, and his expression changed. "I don't do this that often."

She absorbed the vulnerability he'd just shared, tucked it away in her heart. He didn't have casual sex, yet he didn't want a committed relationship. Baggage from his divorce? She touched his cheek. "Since your wife?"

He nodded. "I've dated since the divorce, just not lately."

"How long?" She had no right to ask, but he'd brought it up after all.

"A year. Maybe a little longer."

Wow. "That's a long time."

He chuckled. "Tell me about it."

Oh, Pete. His scars ran deeper than she'd realized. She'd lost a little piece of her heart to him tonight, and she could only hope he'd give her the chance to help his heal.

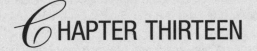

CHAPTER THIRTEEN

*P*ete felt like he'd been knocked flat on his back. It had been so long since he'd felt anything but pure physical release during sex, followed by an all-encompassing sense of emptiness. With Olivia, he felt protective. He felt vulnerable. He felt *alive*.

She'd taken him in her arms and rocked him to his very core. He wanted her. *Needed* her. And he had no fucking idea where they went from here.

As if she'd read his thoughts, she smiled softly. "You know, there's a twenty-four-hour Walgreens over on Hanover Street."

He laughed in spite of himself. "In a minute."

Because he wasn't quite finished with her yet. He wanted to taste her, wanted to watch her come, not hard and fast like the first time, but slow and fierce. He slid his hand between her legs, feeling how hot and wet she was.

She moaned, arching against him. He stroked her slow and steady, watching the blissful look on her face and loving every moment. Then he dipped his head and settled between her legs. He gave her pleasure with his tongue until she writhed against the sheets, each breath a needy gasp.

He brought her closer and closer to the edge, drawing out her pleasure for as long as he could. She begged. She panted. And finally, she came apart with a scream.

"Holy shit." Her voice was hoarse, her body limp and trembling.

He smiled with satisfaction as he kissed his way back up her belly to her mouth.

Their little problem was now his *big* problem. He pulled back with a grim smile. "I think it's time for me to take that trip to the drug store."

And it was going to be one hell of an uncomfortable trip.

Olivia looked up at him, her eyes still glazed with satisfaction. "Not so fast. I can't send you out in this condition."

"No?" If it was possible, he got even harder just imagining what she might have in mind.

"No." She pushed him down flat on his back.

He was breathing heavy, and she hadn't even touched him.

"You are—" She kissed his neck. "The sexiest—" Her lips brushed over his collarbone. "Man I have ever known."

He fisted his hands in the sheets, desperate for her touch. She took her sweet time trailing feather-light kisses down his chest and over his stomach. Her fingers brushed against his shaft, and he squeezed his eyes closed, unable to breathe.

"You're so hard." Her breath teased him, and his cock throbbed painfully. "So big."

Her fingers gripped him, stroking up and down his shaft in one long, slow movement, and he thrust against her, unable to hold back, completely lost to her touch.

"So hard," she whispered again, and then she took him in her mouth.

He swore roughly, his hips arching off the bed. Her tongue circled his head in a swirling motion while her fingers continued to stroke up and down in a painfully slow pace that had him ready to beg. But then it would be over, and he wasn't sure he'd ever felt anything as exquisite as the swirl of her tongue, the pressure of her lips as she urged him on.

He fought to hold himself back, to let her take the lead, but his need was too great. His whole body tightened, swamped with sensation, pulsing with it. *More.* He needed more. He swore again, fighting to keep his hips still, not to thrust too hard against her.

She must have sensed she'd pushed him to his breaking point because she picked up the pace then. Her hand tightened around him, stroking hard and fast as she applied a gentle suction with her mouth.

And like that, he broke. He came so hard he lost his senses. A guttural groan tore from his chest as she sucked him dry. Wave after wave of red-hot release pulsed through him, leaving him limp, spent. Sated.

"Holy fuck." He pulled her up against his chest.

She smiled sweetly. "Better than driving to Walgreens with a hard-on?"

"Fuck." Apparently he'd lost the ability to do anything but swear. "That was—" Well, it was one of the most intense moments he'd ever experienced.

She kissed his nose. "I'm glad."

He held her close as he caught his breath, wondering how he was ever going to let her go.

* * *

Olivia woke before dawn, exhausted but exhilarated. After a trip to Walgreens, they'd made use of their new box of condoms (and the chips and candy bars he'd bought to go with them). They'd finally fallen asleep sometime after midnight, but Pete had woken her in the dark hours of the night to make love to her again.

He was like no man she'd ever been with, and already she wanted more. She wanted this to be more than a casual fling, but he'd laid the ground rules, and she'd agreed to them, so she would be happy with this... for now.

The sky outside was beginning to lighten, and an idea took hold. She rolled on top of him to kiss him awake.

"Mornin'." He snaked an arm around her waist and pulled her closer.

"Good morning. I have plans for us," she said.

"So do I." He shifted her hips so that his cock pressed between her legs. Hard. Ready. And so was she. A burning need took hold inside her at the feel of him.

"Okay, your plans first." She reached for the bedside table and grabbed a condom.

"Slow down, babe. There's no rush."

"Yes," she said. "There is. We need to be at MacArthur Park by sunrise."

"What?" His brows drew together.

"My plans." She sheathed him in the condom, and there was no more talking as they succumbed to the desperate desire that only seemed to grow more intense each time they made love. When they'd finished, they stepped into the shower together.

By the time they got dressed, she was rushing him along. Timber, hyper and miffed at having been left downstairs, made his displeasure known with his howls and a frantic dance across the linoleum.

"Bring him," she said.

Pete leashed his dog, and they walked outside. The air was cold and invigorating, crisp with the arrival of fall. They rode in his SUV, arriving at MacArthur Park just as the sun peeked over the horizon.

She led him to her favorite spot by the old pecan tree. The sunrise gleamed golden over the field before them. She spread her blanket, and they sat together on it as Timber frolicked in the field.

"You know, I don't need to meditate anymore. I think I've discovered a better method of stress relief." Pete gave her a teasing smile.

She punched his shoulder. "Sex isn't everything. Meditation is good for your soul. I could teach you ways to incorporate it into your day, just a few minutes here and there when you need to find your center."

"My center, huh?" He looked out over the field, and they sat quietly for several minutes. "It's nice here."

"I come here almost every day."

"I can see why." His hand closed over hers. They sat together, watching the sun rise. "I'm on duty at eight," he said finally.

"And I need to get home to my dogs. I just wanted to start our day here together."

"Thank you."

"You're welcome. This is what I picture when I close my eyes." She gestured to the field before them, glistening with color as the sun rose above the treetops. "If I'm having a tough day at work or whatever, I just close my eyes, wherever I am, and picture this. Try it sometime. The more you practice, the better it works."

He gave her a long, dark look, as if here, in the light of day, he wished she didn't know as much as she did about him. "I'll keep that in mind."

"Okay." She stood and led the way back to the car.

Pete loaded Timber into the backseat. Olivia climbed into the passenger seat as Pete cranked the engine. Timber stuck his head around her headrest, first on one side, then the other, making a series of comical faces at her.

"I'm not really a dog person, but I like you," she told him. Timber woofed his approval, then craned his head to lick her cheek. "Don't push your luck."

He let out a high-pitched whine before settling down on the backseat.

"I'm off at three, then coaching soccer until five thirty. Dinner?" Pete asked.

She shook her head. "I'm working until nine."

"When will I see you?" He sounded awfully possessive for a man who'd claimed to want nothing but a physical relationship.

"I took yesterday off for court, so I'm working the rest of the week. Tom put me on noon to nine today and tomorrow. Why don't we play it by ear?"

He pulled into his driveway. "Let me see your phone."

She handed it to him with a questioning look. He typed in some numbers and handed it back. "My personal number."

She looked down to see that he'd added himself to her address book, and a warm feeling spread through her chest. She gave him a quick kiss, grabbed her purse, and pulled open her door. "I'll call you."

She walked quickly down the street and around the corner to where she'd parked her Prius, unable to wipe the silly grin off her face.

Last night had been amazing, crazy, overwhelming—so many things. She could fall for him if she wasn't careful, and that would be dangerous. He'd already warned her not to, and she knew better than to try to get more than a man was willing, or able, to give.

She drove home to find two dogs, a puddle of pee, and a pile of poop waiting in the kitchen. Scooby gave her a wounded look, as if it offended him that she'd left him here to sleep among Bailey's accidents.

Bailey herself could care less, ecstatic to have Olivia home. She put both dogs out back, grumbling as she got out a bottle of cleaner and paper towels to clean up the mess. Seriously, who was ever going to adopt the damn dog if she wasn't potty trained?

Guilt settled heavy in Olivia's stomach. If she was home more, if she spent more time working with her, she'd have Bailey potty trained by now.

The dogs were banging at the door so she let them in and fed them, then went upstairs to check on Hallie. The kitten was sprawled in Olivia's bed like a queen, but evidence of her was everywhere. The curtains were ripped, and the vase on her dresser had tipped onto the floor and broken, leaving glass and flowers everywhere.

"Mew!" Hallie leaped up and pranced down the bed in a sideways kitten dance, as if not yet certain whether she'd present herself for petting or attack.

"Well, you certainly kept yourself busy, didn't you?" Olivia flopped onto the bed. She'd hoped for a nap before work, but nope. These crazy animals were making her pay for spending the night at Pete's.

Okay, so she'd learned her lesson. Maybe.

Then again, maybe not.

* * *

Pete was learning to plan ahead. He stopped by the rec center around lunchtime and left instructions for the boys to set up and start running drills when they arrived, in case he got held up at work again.

Luckily, his shift was fairly uneventful because he was semi-distracted thinking about Olivia. Fairly sleep deprived too, although that was nothing new. No muffins for the women's shelter this morning though. No tension either.

He almost made it out on time, but the sheriff called him into his office as he was getting ready to change for soccer.

"I hear you've been poking around out at Halverson Foods," he said.

Pete nodded. "I was investigating a string of vandalism at Olivia Bennett's property. It looks like some of the factory workers may be behind it. They may be trying to intimidate her into backing off her campaign to get the place shut down."

"That's your assumption." Linburgh's face said he didn't agree. "From what I hear, you've lost your objectivity where this case is concerned. Pass it off to Kirk."

"Sir—"

"That's an order, Sampson. I don't want you anywhere near Halverson Foods or Olivia Bennett. Are we clear?"

Pete had undoubtedly lost his objectivity where Olivia was concerned, but he had no intention of staying away from her. This was a low profile case that wouldn't ordinarily warrant such an order. He'd seen a photo of the sheriff with Jim Beggs, the General Manager of Halverson Foods' Dogwood factory, in the paper just yesterday, taken at a fund-raising event for Linburgh's campaign. "I understand," he said.

Pete understood that the sheriff didn't want trouble for Halverson Foods, not this close to an election. He'd lost some popularity last year after the office was accused of mishandling an underage drinking scandal at one of the local colleges. Recent polls showed the Democratic candidate, Dale Walker, gaining in popular opinion.

How deep did Linburgh's loyalty run? Was he willing to look the other way where Halverson was concerned to keep their support? That didn't sit well with Pete, not at all.

When he walked into the rec center at four fifteen, the boys had set up cones and were busy dribbling soccer balls in and out of the zig-zag configuration Pete had drawn for them. He watched them for a minute, unobserved. He made note of how Lonnie had a tendency to swing wide when he dribbled. Zach fell behind during dribbling but had a hell of a kick when it came time to put the ball in the goal.

"Coach Sampson!" Leroy waved, tripped, and sent his ball careening into the bleachers.

So the group wasn't destined for soccer stardom, but they were good kids who needed a place to hang out in the afternoons to keep them on the straight and narrow. Most of them were kids from lower income families, with no parent at home when they got off the school bus. Pete was thankful the Dogwood Community Recreation Center was here to keep them busy.

"Watch this, Coach Sampson." Zach kicked and scored a goal from a good twenty feet down the court.

"Not bad," Pete said. "You boys have been busy. Let's practice some interceptions before we break it out into a scrimmage."

He put them through their paces and ran them through a practice game, ending at five thirty. He ought to go home. His neighbor's teenager had walked Timber at lunchtime, but by now the dog would be hyper, lonely, and ready for some real exercise.

And for some reason, Pete had a hankering to stop by the café for supper on the way home. There was leftover lasagna and a cold six-pack of Yuengling in his fridge. So he had no excuse other than a burning need to see Olivia.

And that was good enough.

He showered, changed, and drove down Main Street. Olivia's red Prius was in the lot behind the café. Other than a slightly dulled paint job on the driver's door, no trace remained of the graffiti. It still bugged him that she'd parked around the corner last night, although she wasn't wrong. The sheriff had ordered him to stay away from her, after all, but Pete had never consulted his boss on who he dated in the past, and he didn't intend to start now. And if it cost him his shot at detective this year, he would accept that consequence with his dignity and conscience intact.

When he walked inside, he didn't immediately see her so he asked the hostess to seat him in her section. The girl, a brunette, gave him an appraising look as she did so. Almost as if she didn't approve of his being here, although he had no idea why.

He'd barely settled into his booth when Olivia came around the corner, menu in hand, eyes wide with surprise. "Pete?"

"I was hungry," he said with a shrug.

Her left eyebrow lifted. "And a bit lonely perhaps?"

He decided to ignore that. "Last time I was here, I let my waitress con me into a vegetarian meal. Don't suppose that's common practice around here?"

She grinned. "I can't say, but your last waitress sounds pretty awesome. We have a new special—a loaded omelet made with local cage-free eggs. It's delicious."

"You've had it?"

She nodded. "I had the kitchen make me a vegetarian version. I do eat eggs and dairy if I know they were humanely raised."

"So would my waitress be offended if I ordered the nonvegetarian version?" Because a loaded omelet sounded pretty damn good.

"No she wouldn't."

"Great then. I'll have that and a sweet tea."

"I'll be right back with your drink." She sashayed off toward the back. He found himself watching the sway of her hips and the swing of her ponytail across her shoulders. Yep, he was pretty hung up on his waitress.

Still hoping there was a chance he'd have her in his bed tonight too.

She returned a minute later with his drink and a warm smile.

"I don't suppose you had anything to do with the new local cage-free eggs?" he asked.

"I've been trying for years to get Tom—he's the owner—to buy humane meat and dairy, but I finally figured out the right angle. I convinced him that supporting a local farm would be good for business. A lot of people are into that right now. He's giving it a try. If it's popular, he may agree to switch more of our products over. I'd love to see him create a niche with local, organic, and humane products. He's kind of stuck in his ways, but we'll see."

Pete shook his head, amused and impressed. "You are something."

"Something more than a pain in the butt, I hope." She winked, and then she was gone.

His omelet was perfection, bursting with cheese, spinach, mushrooms, ham, and pretty much everything delicious that could be put inside an omelet. He cleaned his plate and sat back, full and content. Maybe he'd stop by here more often.

"Pete Sampson?"

He looked up to find Tamara Hill standing at his booth, dressed in the café's uniform of pink top and black pants, her black hair carefully styled. His food instantly congealed into a cement block in his belly.

"Yes," he answered. She'd recognized him. She'd connected the dots and figured out his dad had killed her husband.

"Zach told me you've been coaching the boys on Tuesdays," she said.

He nodded tightly. "That's right."

"He thinks highly of you, and that's a lot from him. You know, his dad died a few years ago, and he's—well he's had some trouble handling everything."

"Yeah, he mentioned that." His stomach curdled.

Tamara flashed him a warm smile. "I just wanted to say thank you."

"You're welcome."

She didn't know, and he'd never felt like a bigger fraud.

* * *

"You two know each other?" Olivia handed Pete his check, still secretly thrilled that he'd stopped by for supper—and to see her.

"I'm coaching her son at the rec center."

"Oh. Cool." A simple enough explanation, and yet, Pete looked anything but simple right now. He was pulsing with tension, his eyes dark and haunted. What was it about Tamara that had triggered this? Or had something else happened that she'd missed? A call from work perhaps?

"Well, I should go." He slid some cash inside the bill holder and passed it back to her.

"Do you need change?"

"No."

"Hey." She put her hand on his shoulder before he could stand. "I was just thinking about the sunrise this morning. It was really beautiful. Maybe we can do that again sometime."

His expression softened. "I'd like that."

So would she, but that wasn't why she'd brought it up. She hoped to subtly put the image in his head, in case he needed to visualize it later.

He slid out of the booth and went on his way, and Olivia returned to her shift. Things stayed busy during the dinner rush, gradually tapering off until the café closed at nine. She was fortunate not to have any stragglers in her section tonight, so she cleaned up and clocked out, walking to her car alongside Tamara.

"How's Zach these days?" she asked. She'd known Tamara about three years; she'd started working here shortly after her husband was killed in a car accident. A former stay-at-home mom, Tamara had found herself suddenly thrust back into the workplace, struggling to make ends meet for herself and her son, while going to school nights to finish her bachelor's degree.

"He's been keeping himself out of trouble, mostly." Tamara smiled. She exuded a kind of effortless style and presence that seemed suited to much bigger and better things than the Main Street Café. "He goes to the rec center most days after school."

"That's good. You should bring him in sometime soon. It's been ages since I've seen him."

"I'll do that. Good night, Olivia."

"Night." Olivia waved. She slid into her Prius and drove home, exhausted. She took care of her animals and fell into bed, asleep before her head hit the pillow.

The next morning, after a flurry of text messages with Merry, she headed out to the farm to have breakfast with her friend. Dinner would have been more fun, but Olivia was working noon to nine again today.

"Perfect timing," Merry said as she opened the front door. "I just put Jayden down for a nap. We should have a solid two hours." She crossed her fingers.

"That's all I have anyway before I have to get to work." Olivia followed Merry into the kitchen, setting down a bag of fresh muffins from the café.

"Mmm, those look awesome. Help yourself to coffee or whatever you want to drink." Merry set a couple of plates on the counter and sipped from her own coffee mug. "So I have two things to tell you, and then I want to hear all about the other night."

"Okay." Olivia poured herself a glass of water and put a strawberry muffin on her plate.

"First, I'll take you up on babysitting on Friday night. T.J. and I haven't had a date night in ages."

Olivia nodded. "You got it." She enjoyed babysitting, and she owed Merry big time for taking care of her dogs after working a twelve-hour shift.

"Thanks. So my other news is that I have an approved adopter interested in Scooby. They should be calling you later today."

"Sweet! But are you sure they wouldn't be interested in Bailey instead?"

Merry gave her a steely look over her chocolate chip muffin. "You've got to crack down on her with the potty training. And she needs to know some basic obedience."

Olivia picked at her muffin. "You're right. I'll work with her, I promise."

"Good. So," Merry wiped a chocolate smudge from her mouth and settled back in her chair, "tell me all about Monday night, and please let it involve Deputy Hot Stuff."

Olivia grinned. She'd missed having a girlfriend to

gossip with since Cara moved. "Oh it most definitely involved him."

"In sexy ways that had nothing to do with handcuffs?" She paused and seemed to consider this. "Unless you were using them for, um, recreational reasons."

"No handcuffs. I spent the night at his place."

"And?" Merry prompted.

"And it was amazing. He's, well..." Olivia fanned herself. "You know."

"I can imagine." Merry winked. "And it's not a problem for him that you were convicted?"

Her smile faded. "He says no, but I get the feeling it's still not good for him to be associated with me, and he's trying to make detective this year."

"Then why would he get involved with you? He strikes me as a smart man."

She set her half-eaten muffin down with a sigh. "Good question. He says he's only looking for a casual relationship, so maybe this is too short-term to matter."

"Oh, honey." Merry rested her hand on Olivia's.

"All this business with getting arrested has made me realize maybe I am ready to grow up after all. I'm ready for a more settled job, whenever I figure out what that is, and I'm ready for this—" She gestured around the kitchen. "A house, a husband, a family."

Merry laughed. "I'm not married yet."

"Oh please." Olivia rolled her eyes.

Her friend sobered. "A few months ago, I wasn't ready for any of this stuff either. It took T.J. practically hitting me over the head with it to realize we were meant to be together. So you're already ahead of me in knowing what you want. Are you sure Pete isn't that person?"

"He's divorced, and he doesn't want to get married again."

"Well I give him props for being up front about it at least. So will you see him again?"

Olivia felt a tug deep in her chest. "Probably. The fire definitely hasn't burned out yet. And it's not as if I'm a stranger to casual relationships, so I'll enjoy this while it lasts. Maybe it'll be my last hurrah before I settle down."

"Atta girl. Maybe I can find you a cute doctor at the hospital."

"Oh yeah?"

Merry tapped her finger against her lips. "There is a really hot surgeon. I'm pretty sure he's single."

Olivia shrugged. "Doctors seem kind of stuffy to me, like lawyers. I need someone who'll go camping with me and meditate."

"Does Deputy Hot Stuff meditate?" Merry asked.

"It just so happens I've taught him a few things."

Merry's eyes rounded. "Really?"

"His job can be stressful so I took him out to Jordan Lake and introduced him to meditation."

"Wow. That sounds...intimate."

"It was." Olivia remembered just what it had led to, and her cheeks heated. But she knew what Merry meant: it was intimate on another level. And Pete had already warned her not to go there, not with him.

* * *

Two hours later, Olivia walked into the café, ready for her shift. She found Tom waiting in the back hall.

"I need to talk to you." He motioned her into his office at the end of the hall.

Uh-oh.

A heavy feeling settled in the pit of her stomach as he closed the door behind her.

He looked at her with sympathetic eyes. "I'm very sorry, Olivia, but I'm going to have to let you go."

"Oh no." Her face felt hot, then cold. *Fired.* "What— why?"

"There have been complaints."

Complaints? About her? Her heart thudded against her ribs until she felt sick. "I'm sorry."

He put a hand on her shoulder. "So am I. You've been a hell of a waitress."

"Thanks."

"I'll walk you out." He opened the door and escorted her down the hall and into the parking lot.

Olivia walked ahead of him, numb. Her job, her friends at the café...

Gone. Done. Blinking back tears, she got into her car and pointed it toward MacArthur Park.

CHAPTER FOURTEEN

$\mathcal{P}$ete walked up Olivia's front steps promptly at six thirty Thursday evening. A break-in at the card store had held him up at work, but he'd had just enough time to go home and get ready to take her to dinner. On time. He'd been late to plenty of dates—a fact that was sometimes overlooked due to his profession—but tonight would not be one of them.

He was ridiculously glad about that. And ridiculously thrilled to be taking her out to dinner. In fact, he'd changed into khaki pants and a green button-down shirt, which was about as dressed up as he ever got. He'd even picked up a bouquet of wildflowers for her from the flower shop. Yesterday he'd worked overtime, so he hadn't seen her since Tuesday, and right now that felt like an eternity.

Flowers in hand, he knocked on her front door. A dog barked from inside.

Olivia pulled the door open a few seconds later, wearing jeans and a T-shirt that read *Tofu Never Screams*, her hair pulled back in a loose ponytail. Her eyes widened, and she clapped a hand over her mouth. "Oh, my God. Look at you."

Well that wasn't the reaction he'd expected, and now he felt a bit overdressed. Usually Olivia was decked out in one of her cute dresses while he wore jeans. He held the flowers toward her. "These are for you."

She took them and buried her nose in their depths, a blissful smile on her face even as her eyes welled with tears. "They're beautiful. They're perfect. Thank you."

She went up on her tiptoes and kissed his cheek.

"Is everything okay?" he asked.

"I lost my job."

"You *what*?" He followed her inside, where only one dog greeted them in the living room.

"I got fired." Her eyes flashed, a mixture of hurt and anger.

"Shit. Why?"

"Apparently there were complaints about me." She crossed her arms over her chest and looked away.

"Complaints?" That was ridiculous. Olivia was nothing but professional at work. "What kind of complaints?"

"He didn't say."

"That's bullshit. I'm sorry."

"Yeah, well, know any place that's hiring convicts? Because I need a job."

"What are you looking for?"

Her chin went up. "That would be helpful to know, wouldn't it?"

"Christ, Olivia." He touched her cheek. "Don't do that."

"Don't you dare feel sorry for me." Her tone was hard,

but with the faintest quiver that filled him up with all kinds of warm and mushy things.

"Never." He wanted to wipe the hurt off her face, to do something for her the way she'd helped him when he was feeling low. But he had nothing.

So he kissed her.

Olivia kissed him back hungrily, her body pressed to his, all soft curves and the scent of wildflowers. He backed her against the kitchen counter.

"You're dressed like you had bigger plans for tonight than to seduce me," she whispered against his cheek.

"I made us a reservation at Torino's. I'll cancel it." He lifted her onto the edge of the counter.

She slid forward, pressing against his erection. "I could still get dressed."

"Or I could get you *un*dressed." He skimmed his hands beneath her T-shirt.

"What time is our reservation?" she asked breathlessly as his fingers slid inside her jeans.

"Seven."

She hooked her legs around him. "Let's do both."

He nibbled her neck. "Both?"

"You undress me." She lifted her T-shirt over her head. "And then I'll get dressed."

Well shit. He didn't need that invitation twice. He lifted her from the counter and carried her upstairs to her bedroom, where they scrambled out of their clothes and fell onto the bed. Twenty minutes later, and a whole lot sweatier, Pete lay panting beside her, his body humming with satisfaction.

"God, that was perfect," she whispered, her arms around his neck, legs still entwined with his.

Perfect. He rested his forehead against hers, completely blindsided. It had been perfect. Everything about her felt perfect. Except nothing about this was. It was about as far from perfect as a relationship could be.

She gave him a quick kiss and rolled out of bed. "We'd better hurry if we want to make our reservation."

"Right." He shook his head to clear it.

He joined her in a quick shower then went downstairs while she fussed with her hair and makeup. He rummaged through her cabinets until he found a vase, put the flowers in it, and set them on her kitchen table. Her dog followed him around, wagging her nub of a tail.

Ten minutes later, Olivia came down the stairs, breathtaking in a pale green dress and strappy sandals, her hair long and loose over her shoulders.

His throat went dry. "You look amazing."

"Thanks. You look pretty dashing yourself." She crossed the kitchen to him, dodging slobbery kisses from her overzealous boxer.

Pete pointed at the dog. "Where's the other one?"

"Scooby got adopted," she said. "So only Bailey the un-potty-trained remains."

He grimaced. "Sounds like there may be a reason for that."

"I know, I know. Merry said the same thing. I just haven't had time to work with her on it, but I do now, so she's about to get her little butt trained."

She gated the dog in the kitchen and followed him out to the Forester. He drove the short distance to Torino's, where they were seated in a romantic booth in the corner. Olivia sat across from him, still glowing from their romp under the covers, a ray of sunshine in the dimly lit restaurant. He couldn't figure why everyone else in the place didn't turn around and stare.

She sipped from her glass of wine. "Catch any bad guys today?"

He shook his head. "Hunted for a couple of them though."

Someone had broken into Cathy's Card Boutique and dumped a bucket of purple paint over the Halloween card selection. A stupid prank that was causing the property owners a huge headache, not to mention the fact that they were going to take a financial hit.

This was one more act of vandalism in the already long list of incidents plaguing Dogwood this fall. He didn't like it, and neither did the sheriff. There was a lot about the recent goings on that Pete didn't like, but he would put his misgivings aside until tomorrow. He took a sip of his own wine. It was bold and spicy, like the woman across the table.

"Did you always know you wanted to be a law enforcement officer?" Olivia asked.

"Since I was a teenager." That was the short answer. The long answer was that he'd decided to become a cop the first time he'd seen his dad come stumbling in the front door, high as a kite, car keys dangling from his fingers. He'd wanted to be the one to put his father in jail, where he couldn't disappoint Pete or Maggie by forgetting their birthdays and missing family events, where he couldn't hurt their mother with his lack of a steady job and frequent drug-induced rages.

Instead, Pete had been the one to put his father back on the street, to get high and drive one last, fatal time.

"I envy you that," Olivia said. "Knowing what you want from life."

"What did you dream of being when you were a little girl?" he asked.

"For a little while, I had a secret dream of being a vet. I wanted to help sick dogs and cats, but then I realized I'd have to go through veterinary school and dissect all kinds of dead animals. Plus, I'm not really into bloody, medical stuff."

"And your parents wanted you to be a lawyer."

Her brows bunched. "Well that dream is over. McKellon would probably never take me back after all this time with a criminal record."

"Maybe it's just a way of clarifying things for you."

"Everything happens for a reason. I know." She took another sip of her wine. "I just wish I knew what came next."

"What do you want?" he asked.

The waitress interrupted them then to take their dinner orders. Olivia ordered linguine with roasted vegetables in a lemon and caper sauce. He went with traditional lasagna. She made no comment on the meat content of his dinner choice.

"You asked the million-dollar question," she said after the waitress had left. "What do I want? Not what my parents want or my so-called friends in the animal rights group. What do *I* want?"

And that question spoke volumes. He saw the turmoil in her eyes, and also the anger. It was obviously eating her up that she hadn't figured it out yet.

He shrugged. "It'll come to you when it's meant to. Whatever it is, you'll be great at it."

She took his hand across the table. "Thanks. In the meantime, I'll probably look for another job waiting tables or something similar. Maybe the Dogwood Diner is less picky about the criminal history of their employees."

"Is that why you were fired?"

"I think it must have played a part. Tom told me he didn't hire people with a record. But he also said there had been complaints."

And that was the part that was sticking with Pete. A really dark, cynical side of him remembered that the sheriff had once gotten Tom Hancock's daughter out of a sticky situation. Linburgh needed to keep Halverson happy, which might include hurting Olivia.

He didn't like to think ill of his boss, but he'd seen Linburgh play dirty in the past. Tomorrow Pete would do a little poking around and see what turned up.

In the meantime, he and Olivia stuffed themselves on pasta, polished off their bottle of wine, and strolled hand-in-hand down Main Street to check out Halloween decorations. He couldn't even remember the last time he'd dressed up, but he loved the ambience of fall—the pumpkins, colored leaves, and tacky decorations with winking lights and fake spider webs.

"This is my first Halloween in a house," she said, her body pressed close to his against the chill of the evening. "I probably should have stayed home and bought candy for the trick-or-treaters."

He pulled her closer. "I'm glad you didn't."

Here and there, a few kids were still out. He spotted Darth Vader and some newfangled action hero running across the town square.

"Be glad you didn't know me when I was a teenager." Olivia giggled. "When I was fifteen, I dressed up as a slaughtered chicken and snuck out of the house. I passed out PETA pamphlets at every doorstep. I didn't get much candy that year."

"Fifteen is too old for trick-or-treating anyway, but I guess the candy wasn't what you really wanted."

"No. I was just going for shock factor."

"Animal rights has always been your passion then."

She looked up. "Yeah."

"Then you need to find a career that lets you follow your passion. It's the only way you'll be happy."

* * *

Olivia absorbed the truth of his words. Of course, she'd love a job that let her follow her passion for animal rights. "But there aren't many paying jobs."

He looked down at her, his dark eyes serious. "One is all you need."

Well, shoot. When did he turn into a philosopher?

They reached his car, and he opened the passenger door for her. She swooned a little inside. Who said a strong, independent woman couldn't still enjoy a little chivalry from time to time? Thank goodness she'd decided to go out with him instead of moping around at home.

No moping. It just wasn't her style.

Pete climbed into the driver's seat and turned to her. "Is Bailey social with other dogs?"

"Totally. Just prone to accidents and a bit short on manners."

"I was just thinking, if she and Timber got along, it would make things easier. You know, no rushing home to the dog."

"Oh." She finally caught up with his train of thought, and she liked what he was thinking. "You mean like if we stopped by your place right now to get Timber?"

"How do you think that would go over with Bailey?"

"She'll be fine, although she might pee on the kitchen floor in her excitement." And she was only half joking about that.

Pete made a face. "How is it that you haven't potty trained that dog yet?"

"I'm never home." She sighed. "I suck at dog ownership. To my credit, the kitten is totally trained."

"Oh yeah?" He laughed as he pulled onto the road. "And let me guess, she trained herself while you were keeping her locked up in the bathroom."

She rolled her eyes. "Pretty much."

They pulled into the driveway of his townhouse, and she followed him inside. Timber greeted them in the kitchen, howling and letting out ear-piercing squeaks to show his joy at their presence.

"Just wait," she told him. "You're going to have a sleepover with a girl. It should be very exciting."

* * *

Pete woke in Olivia's bed with her hair in his face, her scent wrapped around him like a warm cocoon. He felt refreshed. In fact, he hadn't woken a single time during the night, not to make love to Olivia or for any other reason.

Her hair tickled his nose, and he reached up to brush it away. Something sharp poked his finger. Ouch. And what he'd thought was Olivia's hair didn't feel right at all. What the hell?

He felt another prick, then pain everywhere in his hand. "Fuck!"

He lurched upright to find the little white kitten hanging from his index finger, biting and kicking for all she was worth. Olivia lay blinking up at him from the other side of the bed, not nearly close enough for her hair to have been in his face.

It had been goddamn kitten fur.

"Hallie, stop it," Olivia mumbled, swiping lazily at the kitten with one hand while she buried her face back into the pillow. "What time is it?"

Good question. He rolled over, looking for a clock. "Seven thirty." And a good damn thing the kitten had woken him, because he was on duty in thirty minutes. "Don't take this the wrong way, babe, but I've gotta run." He pulled her in for a kiss, and damn she was sexy first thing in the morning, all rumpled with sleep.

"Work?" She snuggled in close, reminding him they were both naked. And he wanted her.

A dog barked downstairs.

"Shit." He pulled back. "I forgot Timber was downstairs."

"Leave him here," she said.

"Really?" He slid out of bed regretfully and headed for the bathroom.

"I'll keep him. Plus it means I get to see you later." Her smile held all kinds of promise.

He stepped into a two-minute shower, then shaved and dressed in his uniform, complete with Kevlar and belt. He'd brought it with him last night, planning to get ready for work at her place, then drop Timber off at home on his way to the sheriff's office.

Olivia still lay in bed, watching. "You look sexy in uniform."

"Thanks for watching Timber. Wish I didn't, but I've got to run."

"Go," she said. "I'll see you later."

"Bye." He kissed her and jogged down the stairs.

He'd been taken off the Halverson case, but that didn't mean he couldn't keep digging into other aspects of the goings on in town. It was pissing Pete off royally that he hadn't figured out who was behind all the vandalism yet. There must be an angle he hadn't explored.

It was time to ask some more questions, see if he couldn't shake loose what was really going on in Dogwood.

* * *

Olivia watched him go, hoping he'd still be in uniform when he came back later. Because she had all kinds of naughty ideas about how to take it off him. The dogs were barking downstairs. She'd left Bailey in her crate overnight since the dogs didn't know each other, so hopefully they weren't getting into trouble, but with those two, who knew?

She went into the bathroom to freshen up, then pulled on her robe and walked downstairs. Timber sat at the gate, alert and maybe even a little bit unsure about being left here in a stranger's house. He whined in that high pitched shepherd squeak that hurt her ears.

"Your dad's coming back," she told him. "It will be more fun to spend the day with me than being home alone, right?"

She went through the gate and patted him. He spun and whined, following her as she went into the dining room to get Bailey out of her crate. Bailey barked and wiggled, but her crate was dry. Well how about that?

Not wanting to push her luck, she put them both out back, then sat on the deck with her arms hugging her knees. Merry had taught her enough to know that she couldn't leave two dogs unsupervised together until they knew each other.

Another thing Merry had told her was that keeping Bailey in her crate would help with potty training. But Olivia had been gone so much of the time she'd felt bad keeping Bailey crated. Now she was second-guessing that decision. And also she'd be home more now, at least until she found a new job.

She'd put in a few applications yesterday, and today would be more of the same. She needed a new job. Like, yesterday. She had bills to pay, and while she was sure Merry would give her leeway on rent until she got back on her feet, that wasn't Olivia's style.

While she waited for the dogs, she typed "animal rescue" into the job search engine and opened the search area to the whole United States. Fifty-three jobs came up. Fifty-three paying jobs helping animals in the whole country. Wasn't that sad? Maybe later, just for fun, she'd submit her résumé for a few of them.

Timber finished his business in the yard and came to press his face in her lap with a squeak. He looked up at her with those rich chocolate eyes. They were alive with personality, twinkling with mischief.

"You're a whiny one, aren't you?" She stroked his fur, and he licked her arm. "I like you though. There's a lot of spirit in your eyes. You've got a story, I can tell. And hey, you got kicked out of K9 school. So we're both rejects. Kindred spirits."

He wagged his tail and shoved his head further into her lap. Bailey trotted up the steps and shoved in for her own share of the love.

"So I kind of get why people keep dogs," she said. The wholehearted affection was pretty cool. The level of care, not so much. Then again, she was thinking about kids sometime in the future, so...

"How about breakfast?" She herded them inside.

She fed them and exercised them, then got ready for her day. She kept Bailey in the bathroom with her while she showered, Timber downstairs in the kitchen. Then she crated Bailey before she left on her job hunt.

She wasn't terribly worried about remaining unemployed. There were plenty of job openings in Dogwood or nearby Raleigh at businesses who could care less that she'd been convicted of vandalism. But she wanted something at least semi-enjoyable. She was good with customers. She was smart. She had a bachelor's degree for crying out loud. So what if it was in Political Science?

Dressed in a very practical blue dress covered in a white wrap-around sweater, she headed out. First on her list was the local thrift shop. They were hiring for a full-time salesperson, and while the pay was less than ideal, the work would be interesting. She knew a bit about fashion and loved finding beauty in repurposed ways.

The girl behind the counter took her application with a bored "thank you," much more interested in whatever she was reading on her cell phone. No wonder they were hiring for a new daytime employee. Olivia lingered for a few minutes in the shop, admiring a vintage incense burner. No impulse shopping until she'd received a paycheck, but if she got the job here, she was *so* buying that.

In the meantime...

She applied for a waitress position at the diner, a hostess position at Finnegan's Pub—which served way too much meat for her taste, but at least she wouldn't be the one serving it—and a cashier job at the Walgreens where Pete had made his infamous late-night condom run. Not for nothing, but she didn't want to stand behind a cash register all day.

Somewhat demoralized, she headed home to fix herself a salad. A veggie wrap from the café sounded better, but there'd be no more eating out until she got a job, and she doubted she would ever set foot in the café again anyway.

So home she went. The dogs were ecstatic to see her. She let them out while she ate, visited Hallie upstairs, then crated Bailey and hit the road again. Having exhausted her list of jobs to apply for, she headed first to MacArthur Park to meditate.

She imagined finding Pete here, taking a few minutes of relaxation on his lunch break, but of course he wasn't. He was out busting bad guys, doing whatever it was he did all day. And hmmm, she actually knew very little about what he did all day. Or what he did in his off time, other than coaching the boys at the rec center on Tuesdays.

But his dog was at her house, so that was kind of a big deal. And maybe it was best if she didn't know too much about him, since they were trying to keep this casual and all that.

Banishing him from her mind, she meditated for over an hour until her mind was cleansed and her energy buffered. When she got back into her car, it was just past two. Pete was off duty at three, that much she did know. But he often worked late. She knew that too.

She'd be home by three, just in case. Timber would be eager to see him, after all.

She drove back into town and cruised down Main Street, eyeing the various storefronts for any *Now Hiring* signs she hadn't already applied for. Jimmy's Wing Hut was hiring for a line cook, but ewww...no thanks. Not that she was qualified anyway.

She turned down Dogwood Road, headed for Peachtree Lane. There were other storefronts here, not as high profile as the businesses on Main Street, but there were some off-color places she adored like the thrift shop she'd applied at earlier, a paint-your-own pottery shop, and a vacant storefront with a *Now Hiring* sign.

Intrigued, she pulled over. The poster in the window read: *The Lavender Moon: holistic and alternative remedies. Now hiring for experienced sales staff. Inquire within.*

And Olivia had the feeling she'd just had her first big break in the job hunt.

* * *

Pete finished his shift on time for once and drove to the office to drop off some paperwork before he headed to Olivia's to get Timber. He was slightly uncomfortable with the fact he'd left his dog with her all day. Not that he didn't trust her. More like...it felt way too cozy for a woman who was supposed to be nothing but a casual fling.

He needed to get his dog and head home for the evening, maybe take a step back and slow things down before they both got in over their heads.

His phone rang and, speak of the devil—Olivia's name showed on the screen.

"Pete, oh my God—" Her words tumbled through the phone, shrill and panicked.

"What happened? Are you okay?" His heart pounded. If those assholes at Halverson Foods had so much as touched a hair on her body...

He was already striding toward the back door when she answered.

"It's Timber."

"Timber? What happened?" A new kind of fear twisted inside him.

"Someone threw chicken carcasses in my backyard, and the dogs ate them before I realized, and Timber choked on a bone." Her voice broke.

"Choked? Is he—is he okay?"

"I gave him the best doggy version of the Heimlich maneuver I could, and it moved enough that he could breathe, but it's still stuck in there. I'm at the vet now."

Pete blew out a breath. "Where?"

"Dogwood Animal Hospital. Hurry."

"I'll be right there." He disconnected the phone and strode toward his car. Timber was still breathing, and he was at the vet. Surely that meant he would be okay.

Five minutes later, he walked in the front door of the animal hospital.

Olivia sprang from the nearest chair, looking poised to

fling her arms around him, but at the last moment, she stopped short and hugged herself instead.

Fuck. He reached out and pulled her against his chest. "What's going on?"

She looked up, her eyes suspiciously bright. "They were playing in the backyard. I was on the deck applying for jobs on my laptop. They were hanging out by the back fence, but I wasn't paying attention because they were being quiet. Then Bailey threw up. That's when I found the chicken carcasses. They were—" She put a hand over her mouth. "There were at least three birds, whole. Raw. The dogs had really done a number on them. Timber started gagging... that's when I realized he couldn't breathe."

"Jesus." His throat tightened.

"I just grabbed him around the chest, under his diaphragm, and heaved. He made a choking sound, and he started breathing, but it was raspy, and he was drooling and acting all weird still, so I rushed them both here—I'm so sorry, Pete."

"What are you sorry for? You probably saved his life."

"But if I'd been paying attention instead of working on my laptop—"

"Stop that. You had no way of knowing those chicken carcasses were there. And I want to talk more about that, but how is Timber now? Have you seen Dr. Johnson?"

"He's been back there with him since we got here. I brought Bailey too, to be checked out."

"I'll go check for you," the vet tech behind the counter said. "You guys can wait in exam room three, and I'll send Dr. Johnson in." He led them into the empty exam room and closed the door.

Pete sat next to Olivia in the two plastic chairs against

the wall and clasped her hand between his. He'd only had Timber a few weeks, but already the thought of losing him hurt. He couldn't imagine coming home without that damn whiny shepherd there to greet him.

Dr. Johnson came into the room a few minutes later. "Good to see you, Pete."

Pete stood. "Dr. Johnson. How is he?"

"I was able to remove the bone from his esophagus using the endoscope, which was minimally invasive. I expect him to make a full recovery."

Pete swallowed hard. "That's great news."

The vet nodded. "He's a lucky dog. Olivia saved his life."

She gripped his hand, looking as relieved as he felt.

"He's still sedated," Dr. Johnson said. "We'll want to keep him for observation. His esophagus is quite abraded, so I've inserted a feeding tube for the time being, but I do expect him to recover relatively quickly."

"Fantastic."

Dr. Johnson turned to Olivia. "I've examined Bailey as well. She doesn't appear to have any blockages, so she's free to go home with you. Just keep a close eye on her for the next forty-eight hours. If she has any difficulty eating, drinking, or going to the bathroom, bring her straight in."

She nodded. "I'll do that. Thank you."

"Okay. I'll have the tech bring Bailey in, and you can see Timber for a few minutes before you go if you'd like."

"I would. Thank you."

"Right this way." Dr. Johnson led him to the back room, lined with metal crates of various sizes. Timber lay in one of the largest crates, unconscious, an IV taped to his front leg. A thin plastic tube protruded from an incision on his right side.

"Oh," Olivia said softly from behind him.

Pete felt a punch to the gut as he looked at his dog. He sat in front of the crate, opened the door, and stroked Timber's fur. "It's going to be okay, buddy. The doc says you're going to be fine."

"Oh, Timber." Olivia crouched next to him. "I'm so sorry, honey."

"Don't listen to her," Pete told his sedated dog. "She saved your life."

She reached in to pet him. "You get well soon so that I can spoil you rotten to make up for this, okay?"

"Hang tight, Timberwolf. I'll be back to see you tomorrow." He stood and took Olivia's hand, pulling her up beside him. She was shaking, her hand like ice in his. "I'll drive you home. Let's go have a look at those chickens they got into."

"My car's here," she said, but she didn't look in any shape to drive. Her normally vibrant eyes were glassy, her cheeks pale. Aftereffects of the crisis.

"We'll get it tomorrow." He led her to his squad car and motioned for her to get in the passenger seat. "You get to ride in front this time. Behave yourself."

She glared at him. "Any other time, that *might* be funny."

He shrugged. "It was funny."

She loaded Bailey into the back of the car, then climbed in beside him, sitting with her eyes closed as he started the engine. Her phone rang, and she pulled it from her purse. "Hi, Merry." She paused. "Bailey's fine, and it looks like Timber will be too, although he has a bit of recuperating to do."

Pete turned the car toward Peachtree Lane. Now it was

time to figure out how those chickens had gotten into her backyard. This might have been intended as just another harmless prank, but Pete's dog had almost died. And someone was going to pay for that.

"No, I don't know where the chickens came from," Olivia was saying. "But ten bucks says they're from Halverson Foods. We're on our way to my house now." Another pause. "Yes, he's with me. I'll call you when I know anything okay?"

She hung up the phone and stared out the window, silent as he turned into her driveway.

"All right then, let's go have a look."

She followed him inside with Bailey. "You're staying inside," she told the dog, then followed Pete into the backyard.

He walked toward the back fence. It wasn't hard to tell where it had all gone down. The back corner of her yard was strewn with chicken carcasses, in various states of destruction. The birds could have come from the supermarket—they were already plucked, heads and feet removed. But he'd bet Olivia was right. They had probably come from the Halverson Foods chicken-processing plant.

She made a sound of disgust from behind him. "I can't believe someone put these in my yard. Why would they do that?"

"To make a point, I guess. I'm off duty, so I'm going to have to call it in."

And then he and Olivia were going to have a little talk. This had gone too far, and she wasn't staying here alone again until the vandals had been caught.

CHAPTER FIFTEEN

Olivia felt like she'd been swept up in a tornado, and it was not a feeling she enjoyed. She closed her eyes and pictured the landscape at MacArthur Park until her pulse had slowed. When she opened them, the sheriff's deputies were still there. Pete stood in the corner with them as they finished up their paperwork.

"We'll be in touch," the tall one—whose name she'd forgotten—said.

She stood. "Thank you."

Pete walked them to the door. He still wore his uniform, his expression dark and brooding. Guilt pinched her stomach. Because of her, he'd almost lost his dog.

He closed the door behind them, then slid his arms around her. "You okay?"

She leaned into him. His body was hard and unyielding behind her, separated from hers by all of his law enforcement gear. She turned in his arms, placing a hand against his chest. Hard. She frowned.

"Kevlar," he said.

"Really? You wear that every day?"

He nodded.

The knowledge sent an uncomfortably cold tingle down her spine. "Have you ever been shot?"

"No."

"Ever shot anyone?" Now she was just being nosy, but to be perfectly honest, she'd never thought that much about the dangers of his job. Not until now, and it was freaking her out.

"No," he answered.

"That's good." She pulled back and wrapped her arms around herself.

"Been shot at. Once. He missed." Pete cracked a smile.

"If that's meant to make me feel better, it doesn't." On the contrary, tears stung her eyes, and she didn't even know why.

"Hey." He took her hand. "I need to go home and change. Why don't you come? Stay the night."

She glanced at the clock, and her heart sank. "Crap. It's Friday night. I'm supposed to be babysitting for Merry and T.J. right now."

"I'm sure Merry, of all people, understands."

"Of course she does but—" She shook her head. This was just one more screwup to add to the long list of her life screwups. "I better call her." Olivia dialed Merry's number.

"Any news?" her friend asked when she answered.

"Bailey's home. Timber's stable. And I'm standing you up right now, but why do you sound like you're at the bar anyway?" A buzz of music and conversation carried over the line.

"Amy and Noah came over to watch Jayden for us. You didn't stand me up. You were busy with the police and with Bailey."

"Oh, I'm glad you guys still got to go out." Olivia was grateful that T.J.'s sister and nephew had been able to fill in for her. "I'll babysit for you next week. Just pick a day."

"Don't worry about it. Are you spending the night at Pete's?"

She looked over at him, thumbing through emails on his phone. She didn't want to be alone tonight. "Yes."

* * *

Olivia followed Pete into his townhouse. They stopped for a moment in the foyer, absorbing the emptiness inside. Quiet. No howling, whining German shepherd waited for them in the kitchen.

Even Bailey was subdued, standing silently beside them, her tail tucked.

Olivia set her backpack on the floor and put her hand on his shoulder. "I'm so sorry."

"Please stop apologizing. It wasn't your fault. On the contrary, you saved Timber's life. I should be thanking you." He pulled her into his arms and kissed her, long and deep, then he picked her up and carried her up the stairs to his bedroom. He set her on the edge of the bed and unfastened the belt that held his gun, cuffs, and all his other law enforcement gadgets.

She forced herself to take a long look at it. As a practice, she hated guns. Anything that led to violence of any kind went against the fiber of her soul.

"You're looking at me like I'm holding a snake," he said, a touch of amusement in his voice.

She looked down at her hands. "I don't really mind snakes."

"But you don't like guns."

She shook her head. "No. Sorry."

"Most women find it a turn-on." He still sounded amused.

She raised her head and met his eyes. "I'm not most women."

His dark eyes heated. "Isn't that the damn truth."

He hauled her off the bed and kissed her until every cell in her body was on fire for him. She worked her way down the buttons of his uniform shirt and tugged it open.

"And I hate that you have to wear *this*." She ran her fingers over the unforgiving surface of his Kevlar vest.

"You'd rather I didn't wear it?"

"I'd rather you didn't put yourself in the way of bullets at all."

He reached behind himself to unfasten the vest, then lifted it over his head. Now he stood before her in a sweat-dampened white undershirt and slacks, his hair rumpled from her fingers. He was the opposite of what she wanted in every way, and yet...he was the most perfect thing she'd ever seen.

"I have no idea what to do with you." He bent his head to nibble at her neck, and she shivered from her heart to her toes.

"I can think of a few things." She tugged at the waistband of his pants, pulling him closer against her.

He laid her on the bed, covering her body with his.

"You'll stay here until this mess with Halverson gets sorted out."

She braced her hands against his chest. "Wait—what?"

"I'll sleep a hell of a lot better if you're here. Stay." His eyes filled in the gaps between his words. He was worried about her, worried for her safety.

And she should probably be offended. She should argue that she could take care of herself—because she could—but right now she was too busy feeling all warm and fuzzy. "I'm staying tonight. After that we'll see."

Because she couldn't let herself get too comfortable here in his house. This was only temporary, and she couldn't let herself forget that.

"You'll stay," he said. Then he tugged down her pants, and she forgot what the hell they were talking about.

Thirty minutes later, and a whole lot more relaxed, she followed him downstairs. He went into the kitchen to order takeout, and she took Bailey outside to potty. Then she settled on the couch to work on a blog post

Pete strolled in, looking dangerously sexy in relaxed jeans and a worn NCSU T-shirt. He sat next to her and turned on the TV. "You're not stirring up more trouble for Halverson, are you?"

"Just blogging about what happened today, but I'm not backing off. They can't bully me like this and get away with it."

He changed the channel to football. "I just think you may need to adjust your expectations slightly."

"What's that supposed to mean?"

"That plant isn't going to be shut down, Olivia. Even if it was, the chickens would still be slaughtered somewhere else. Halverson Foods is a lot bigger than you, and the town needs those jobs. Why don't you push for changes to their worksite practices instead?"

She sighed as she closed her laptop. "Because Dogwood is my hometown. We're better than to be known as a place where chickens are slaughtered."

He smiled. Not patronizing, much as she wanted to be annoyed by him, but more like he understood, even appreciated her. "We're not known as a town where chickens are slaughtered. We're known as the charming little town that half of North Carolina wishes it could be. Dogwood is a wonderful place to live, and like it or not, Halverson Foods employs a lot of our citizens."

"Agree to disagree?"

He nodded and turned his attention to the football game.

She sat, staring at the TV but not watching the game. *He was right.* The realization spilled over her like a bucket of ice water. She was fighting the wrong battle. Even if she got the plant shut down, those chickens would be slaughtered somewhere else. People would always eat chicken—hadn't most of the people in town told her that at one time or another?

But if she focused all of Citizens Against Halverson Foods' energy into a push for revamped workplace practices and elimination of the abuse shown in those undercover videos? That could actually work.

"You're right," she said.

Pete gave her a sideways glance. "I am?"

"About Halverson. I'm fighting the wrong battle."

He smiled smugly. "I like the sound of those words."

She punched him. "That I was fighting the wrong battle?"

"No, that I was right."

"You're a jerk." She rested her head on his shoulder, exhausted by the day. Also...starving. "What did you order for supper?"

"Vegetarian pizza from Gino's," he answered.

"Thanks." Her heart melted a tiny bit more. He'd ordered vegetarian. He hadn't even complained about it, and she knew he would have ordered meat if not for her. She'd dated a lot of men who'd given her grief for her beliefs.

Pete never had. And when he disagreed with her, he did it with respect. The truth was, she felt right at home here on his couch.

"I'll stay," she whispered.

* * *

Pete tightened his arm around her shoulders. "Good."

"Just until we get things sorted out," she said.

"Right." He hadn't defined exactly what needed to be sorted out before she went home, and neither had she. He'd never lived with a woman other than Rina. No need to change that, certainly not with Olivia.

"I'll have to bring Hallie."

Shit. He'd forgotten about the kitten. "Can't you just stop by the house and feed her?"

She tilted her head to give him a dirty look. "Not unless I want her to rip my house to shreds in the meantime."

"I'd rather she not rip *my* house to shreds."

"She's pretty well behaved as long as she has people to play with."

Clearly he'd lost his ever-loving mind because he heard himself saying, "Fine. You can go get her tomorrow."

After they ate, he brought her out back and lit a fire in the fire-pit on his patio. Olivia brought out a blanket, and they sat in front of the flames.

"This is nice," she said with a sigh, snuggling closer against him. "Like camping from the comfort of home."

He'd hardly used the fire-pit since he bought it, but he could imagine sitting out here with Olivia every night. They sat and talked. They roasted marshmallows. And when they went upstairs, they slept together, in both meanings of the word. Because with Olivia, he actually slept. Deep and dreamless.

"Wake up."

He heard her voice, filtering through the fog of sleep. He grunted. Her hair tickled his chest, and he reached out and yanked her closer against him.

Her fingers wrapped around his cock. "I woke you in time for this," she whispered.

Sweet Jesus. If he'd still been half-asleep before, he was wide awake now and rock hard in her hand. He cracked open an eyelid to peer up at her. "Mornin'."

"Good morning." She slid over, straddling him. Behind her, the sky was still a deep purple.

"What the hell time is it? Did I happen to mention to-day is my day off?"

"It's six o'clock. We're going to MacArthur Park to watch the sunrise."

"We are?" He slid his hands down to cup her ass. Olivia Bennett was officially like no other woman he'd ever known. She absolutely boggled his mind.

She nodded. "We are. We both need to find our center again after everything that happened yesterday."

"I think I've found my center." He rocked his pelvis against hers.

She narrowed her eyes at him. "I'm being serious. Your dog almost died yesterday."

Yeah, he knew that. The knowledge weighed heavy in his chest. He was more fond of Timber than he cared to admit. "You're right."

Her lips twitched. "I like the sound of those words."

He bent his head and kissed her. She reached into the bedside table for a condom, and they made love in the predawn light.

After a quick shower, she hustled him to the car, and he drove them out to MacArthur Park. It was peaceful. He could see why she came here to watch the sunrise. To meditate. To find her center, whatever that meant.

But he didn't need all that. The unsettling truth was that he felt centered whenever he was with her.

He was getting the hang of this meditation thing though. He sat beside her, relaxed and quiet as they watched the sun rise over the treetops. The last time they'd been here, Timber had been with them, frolicking in the field. Pete hoped he'd done well overnight, that he could come home today. He missed his dog.

When he and Olivia left the park, it was just past eight o'clock.

"I'm going to call the vet for an update," he said.

"I'll call. You drive," she answered. He put the Forester in gear and drove, subconsciously pointing the car toward Dogwood Animal Hospital. He wanted to see Timber, wanted to bring him home.

She spoke to someone at the hospital, answering with too many "mm hmms" and "oh reallys" for his taste.

"Well?" he asked when she hung up.

"He's doing well overall, but he's not able to eat without the feeding tube yet so they want to keep him a few more days. They said we can stop by to see him though." She smiled when he turned into the parking lot.

"So let's go see him." He swung out of the car and followed her inside.

A vet tech greeted them in the lobby and promised to be right back with Dr. Johnson. Pete slid an arm around her shoulders, because it was chilly and she wasn't wearing a jacket, not because he needed to feel her close against him.

The vet came out a few minutes later. "The bone left behind quite a bit of irritation in his esophagus. He's having difficulty swallowing. I expect he'll be feeling much better in a day or two, but in the meantime, we'd like to keep him here so that we can keep the IV and feeding tube in."

"Okay," Pete said. "Thank you."

The vet motioned them to follow him into the back. Timber lay on his side in his crate, his head up and alert. He whined when he saw Pete, his tail thumping loudly against the wall behind him.

Pete opened the crate and rubbed his head. "Hey, buddy. It's awfully quiet at the house without you."

Timber whined, thrusting his head into Pete's lap. He sat with his dog for a while, petting him while he and Olivia talked. Timber was overjoyed that Olivia had come to visit him too. And while it tore Pete up to leave him there, he knew his dog was in good hands and would be home soon.

Didn't stop him from wanting the punks who'd done this to him to pay.

"I'll call this afternoon with an update," Dr. Johnson promised when they stood to leave. "I expect he'll be ready to go home on Monday."

"Thanks," Olivia said.

"We appreciate it." Pete put his hand on her shoulder as they walked through the reception area and out to his car. "I'm starved. You dragged me out of the house this morning before I even got a cup of coffee."

"But I gave you something better than caffeine."

His blood heated at the memory. "That's true. But I'm running on empty now. Let's get something to eat. We'll stop back by here to get your car on the way back to my place."

"Okay." She slid into the front seat of the Forester, and he climbed in beside her.

"The diner?" he asked.

"Sounds good."

He cranked the engine and pulled onto Main Street. "I'll call the sheriff's office later, find out what's going on with the investigation."

She scoffed. "I bet they won't laugh when you call."

"We're going to get to the bottom of this, Olivia, I promise you."

He turned into the parking lot of the Dogwood Diner, a tired looking building with blue clapboard siding, and pulled into an empty spot near the back.

"I applied for a job here yesterday," Olivia said.

"Really?"

"I've applied most anywhere in town that's hiring."

"Any leads?" He followed her through the front door.

Inside, the hostess led them to a booth by the front window and handed them each a menu.

"Thank you," Olivia told her, then turned to Pete. "Not really. Truthfully I don't want to wait tables anymore, but I'll take whatever I can get to pay the bills until I find something better."

"You'll find something." He looked down at the menu in his hand. He was hungry enough to eat everything on there.

"I will. So today's your day off, hmm?"

He met her eyes across the table, completely captured by their chocolate depths. "Spend the day with me."

A soft smile curved her lips. "Well as it happens, I'm free today too."

A million ideas tumbled through his head, most of them involving Olivia naked and writhing beneath him.

"We should go hiking," she said.

His mind went blank. "Hiking?"

She nodded. "I know some great places."

Yep, Olivia Bennett was one of a kind. And he'd follow her to the moon if she asked. Their waitress arrived, and he ordered a bacon, egg, and cheese biscuit and grits with a large coffee. Olivia ordered a bran muffin and water with lemon.

"A bran muffin?" He didn't try to hide the disdain in his voice.

"A green smoothie would be better. They make great ones at the café." Hurt shone in her eyes.

He resisted the urge to cover her hand in his. "No offense, but that sounds disgusting."

"I'll make you one sometime. They're delicious and so good for you. It's much better fuel for your body than the greasy breakfast and coffee you ordered."

"We'll see about that."

"I need to stop by my place for some more clothes and to get Hallie after breakfast."

Right. Because he'd agreed to keep the cat. "Okay."

He was seriously rethinking that decision an hour later as they entered Olivia's bedroom. One of the curtains had been shredded and the picture frames on her dresser were knocked helter-skelter, while the kitten herself lounged in the middle of the bed, giving them a wide-eyed innocent look.

Olivia pinched her lips together, a poor effort at hiding her grin. "She, um, gets a little crazy when I leave her alone for too long."

"Jesus Christ." He ran a hand through his hair and glared at the kitten.

In response, she raised her rear leg in the air and started licking her ass.

"You are a little heathen, aren't you?"

"She'll be good," Olivia promised. She went into her closet with a duffel bag.

Pete sat hesitantly on the edge of the bed, remembering the way the little fiend had attacked his fingers yesterday morning to wake him. How things had changed in a day. Hallie crept toward him. Her butt wiggled, and then she pounced, landing in his lap in a mixture of teeth, claws, and wild purring. After he'd disentangled her from his fingers, she rubbed her head against his chest, purring louder. "I do not understand you. Not one bit," Pete told her.

Olivia flitted in and out of the room, packing. Finally, she set the duffel bag on the bed, fully stuffed. "Looks like you two have bonded."

He looked down at the kitten asleep in a tiny ball

in his lap. "I decided this was safer than risking her claws."

Olivia gave him a knowing smile. "I'll just go get her things." She returned with a large reusable shopping bag and a cat carrier. She lifted the sleeping kitten from his lap and placed her inside the crate. "Okay, we're ready."

"All right then." He led the way downstairs.

Hallie mewed all the way to his townhouse.

"Poor thing," Olivia said as she carried the kitten inside. "This is already the second time I've had to cart her off to someone else's house to stay. It's a wonder she's as well behaved as she is."

He let that one go rather than debate the kitten's manners, or lack thereof. And then he let Olivia convince him that Hallie should stay in the master bedroom with them, on the somewhat questionable assumption that the kitten would get into less trouble that way.

Once she'd gotten Hallie settled, he pressed her up against the wall. "Now let me tell you what I think we should do with the rest of our day."

"Oh yeah?" She went up on her tiptoes and kissed him.

"That's an excellent start." He lifted her off the floor so that his pelvis matched hers, his cock pressed between her legs.

"I like what you're thinking, but hold that thought." She unwrapped her legs from around his hips and slid to her feet.

"Hold that thought?" He sat on the edge of the bed and watched her.

"I'll make it worth your while, I promise. You change

into something comfortable for hiking while I get a back-pack ready."

So she was serious about this hiking thing. "Babe, I don't think anything's going to be comfortable right now." He gestured to his lap.

She grinned. "Sorry about that."

"You could take care of it for me." Because the last thing he wanted to do was go hiking with a hard-on.

She shook her head. "Incentive. We can do it in your bed anytime. This will be special."

So she had more than just hiking on her mind, and he liked that. He *really* liked that. But— "I can't do what you're thinking of doing."

Her brow wrinkled. "What?"

"Public indecency. I'm a cop, Liv. I can't break the law."

She sighed dramatically. "Your job can be such a downer sometimes."

"You know, surprising as it may be, most women find my job to be a turn-on."

She gave him a long look that made his dick even harder. "Well, I *am* pretty turned on right now."

He grabbed her and pulled her into his lap. "You drive me absolutely crazy."

"Wait—" She pulled back. "What about in a tent? Is that legal?"

"You want to have sex with me in a tent?"

"I really want to show you this place. Come with me?"

He rolled her beneath him on the bed "Baby, I can come with you right here."

He thrust his hips against hers, rewarded by a whimper of need from Olivia.

"You're not playing fair," she protested.

At that, he fell still. True, she'd been trying to plan something special for their afternoon, and he was too busy trying to get in her pants to listen. "I'm sorry."

"So, yes in a tent?" She looked so hopeful that his heart clenched.

How could he ever say no to this woman? "Yes, in a tent, as long as it's legal to camp there."

"It is. I've camped there before. I packed a picnic for us while we were at my house. We'll just need to stop back to get my tent."

"I have a tent."

Her eyes lit with interest. "Really? You go camping?"

"Yeah. I like being out there under the stars." He liked the solitude. Usually. Now all he could think about was getting Olivia in his tent. Naked.

"Me too," she whispered. "So let's go."

She slid off the bed and went downstairs. He went into his closet to change into hiking boots, then followed her down.

She was in his kitchen, shoving things into her backpack.

"You bringing Bailey?" he asked.

"Ordinarily I would, but she's supposed to take it easy today while she gets all that chicken out of her system, and besides, she might get in the way of what I have planned." She winked.

Pete pulled her in for a lingering kiss. "Wish we could stay the night."

"Me too. But I need to get back to Bailey, and you need to check on Timber."

"And I'm on duty tomorrow morning at eight."

"Right." She pulled free, put Bailey in her crate, and

led the way to the front door. "Let's get going so that we can be home by late afternoon."

"And where are we going, exactly?" he asked.

"Loblolly State Park."

He nodded. He knew it, had even camped there before. It was just outside Dogwood, with miles of scenic trails and plenty of loblolly pines. Swift Creek ran through its center.

The drive took about twenty minutes, and they were hiking by eleven.

"It should take us about an hour," she told him as she led the way down the Dogwood Trail. She carried the backpack. He carried the tent.

"Incentive, huh?" He repeated her earlier words. He'd never gone to this much effort to get laid, but neither had he felt the intensity of anticipation she'd created. She was right. This was going to be special, an afternoon they would always remember. So much more than a quick romp in his bed.

She smiled over her shoulder. "You brought condoms, right?"

He paused, drawing a total blank as dread crept its way up his spine.

She tossed her head back and laughed. "You're terrible at this! Good thing I have you covered."

He exhaled roughly. "Yeah. Good thing."

"So who do you usually go camping with?" she asked, sliding her hand into his.

"No one. I camp alone." He'd gone often as a teenager, needing the space from his family, from the drama at home.

"I like to camp alone too." She squeezed his hand. "It's

so peaceful. There's nothing like meditating under the stars with nothing and no one nearby but nature."

It was a stunning image she'd created. But he didn't quite like the idea of her out here all alone overnight either. Call it the overprotective deputy in him. He'd seen too many women fall victim to violent crime.

"I come a lot with my friends too," she said. "My friend Cara and I used to camp together all the time."

"Used to?"

"She moved to Massachusetts earlier this year. She's getting married in the spring." Olivia sounded wistful.

A cold feeling crept through his chest. "You want that? Marriage? Two point five kids and the white picket fence?"

"Maybe. Someday. Probably not the white picket fence though. Not quite my style."

"Nah. I see you more with a little ranch out in the country. Wide open spaces. No fence."

"I'd like that." She squeezed his hand.

He wondered if she was picturing him there with her on that ranch in the country, because he sure as hell was, and he had no idea why. He'd been there, done that. And failed miserably.

"We're almost there," she said.

Their trail had followed Swift Creek for a while then meandered up into the pine forest. Beneath the bushy treetops, a bed of pine needles coated the ground.

"This way." She led him off the path and into the woods.

"You're sure you know where you're going?"

"Positive." She led him through the trees alongside a smaller creek. They crested a hill, and here she stopped in a small clearing. Before them, the world opened in a perfect panoramic view of the valley beyond, with Swift Creek at its base. It was breathtaking.

"Wow" was all he could say.

"I've camped here before. It's pretty much perfection, don't you think?"

"Yes." He pulled her into his arms and kissed her. "Thanks for bringing me here."

"Worth the wait?" she asked.

"Hell yeah." He forced himself to let her go, then shrugged out of his backpack and pitched the tent against the bed of pine needles. After inspecting his work, he unfurled the sleeping bag and laid it across the floor.

Olivia took a blanket out of her backpack and spread it out in front of the tent. She sat on the blanket and took off her hiking boots, then motioned for him to join her.

He took off his boots and sat beside her.

"Hard to feel anything but breathless taking in this view," she said.

He was breathless, and not entirely from the view. The woman beside him was just as breathtaking. He brushed his fingers through her hair, turning her face to his. She leaned in, and he kissed her, slow and thorough. He kissed her until his chest heaved and his heart hammered against his ribcage. Olivia slid into his lap. Her fingers scraped down his back, igniting the fire inside him from a slow burn to a white-hot blaze.

"I want you so much," she whispered. Her hips thrust against his.

He held her tight. "This is your dance. You lead."

Her eyes gleamed wickedly, and he knew he was in for the most delicious kind of torture. She laid him on the blanket so that he was flat on his back, staring up at the sweeping loblolly pines above. The scent of pine needles filled his lungs, mixed with Olivia's flowery perfume. An intoxicating combination.

"I always thought this would be the most romantic place in the world," she said, kissing her way down his neck as her fingers roamed over his chest. "It's kind of been a fantasy of mine to bring a guy here and have my way with him."

"I like your fantasies." His voice was gruff because he was so turned on he could barely breathe.

"I fantasized about making love here under the pines." She straddled his erection.

He gripped her hips, rocking her against him. She wasn't wrong. The sweeping landscape around them, the whisper of the pines, the distant gurgle of the creek, was almost enough to make him forsake the law and strip her naked right here on this blanket.

"I don't believe this breaks any laws." She lifted his shirt over his head. Her hair tickled his chest as she bent over him, kissing her way from his throat to the waistband of his shorts.

He hissed out a breath.

She pressed a light kiss against his zipper, then lay beside him, her body pressed firmly against his, her brown eyes as alive as the forest behind her. And dear God, he'd never seen anything more beautiful.

He ran a hand through her hair, cupping her cheek. "You are so amazing, so beautiful." So much more than he could ever put into words.

They lay together on her blanket, kissing, touching, teasing, for as long as either of them could bear.

"Sex in a tent is another fantasy of mine," she whispered against his neck. "I think it could rival sex here beneath the pines."

"I promise it will be even better."

She sat up and tugged him with her as she crawled inside the tent. He followed, too weak at the knees to stand if he'd tried.

He zipped the entrance closed behind them, and they fell on each other in a wild scramble to get naked. He tugged on her shirt while she fumbled with his pants until they were panting and giggling like a couple of teenagers in the backseat of a car.

"Olivia," he pressed her against him, body to body, skin to skin.

"Pete." She gripped his cock, and he thrust into her hand.

He pulled her down on top of him in a frantic tangle, groping hands and the friction of hot skin. He slid a hand between her legs, feeling her heat, loving that he had this effect on her.

He couldn't give her two point five kids and a ranch in the country, but he could show his feelings the only way he knew how. He thrust two fingers inside her, and she cried out.

His own need was overpowering, but first, he wanted to see her come. He bent his head and kissed her, devouring her with his mouth while his fingers stroked, slow and steady.

"Please—" she whispered. A shiver rippled through her body, and his balls tightened. *Goddamn.* "Now, Pete."

"Right now's all about you, babe. Take your time."

Her hips bucked against his hand, and a needy whimper escaped her lips. He slid his free hand beneath her, drawing her closer so that he felt each movement of her body on his, letting it fuel the need already pulsing hot and heavy in his dick.

Olivia squeezed her eyes shut, gripping him with trembling legs as she panted his name. "I can't—"

"Go ahead, baby. Let go." He circled his thumb over her clit, and she screamed as she came, writhing against him, eyes closed and so beautiful.

So fucking beautiful.

"Wow." She went limp in his arms, glowing with pleasure.

He gave her a moment to catch her breath, then he drew her closer, his cock straining against her belly. "I need to be inside you. Now."

She reached behind them and handed him a foil packet. Hands shaking slightly, he sheathed himself in the condom. Olivia kissed him, then rolled him to his back and sank onto him with a soft moan. A desperate breath hissed from his lungs.

She surrounded him, hot and wet, gripping him and taking him right out of his mind as she began to move. He gripped her ass and gritted his teeth as she rocked, each movement of her hips taking him deeper. She gyrated in his lap with a needy gasp, and his control snapped. He flipped her beneath him, thrusting hard and fast inside her until she screamed again.

"Oh, my God, Pete!" Her body clenched around his, and he was lost. The orgasm took him hard until his whole body shuddered, and he collapsed against the sleeping bag in a boneless heap.

"Fuck." He flung an arm around her and pulled her against his chest.

"I seem to have that effect on you."

Yeah, she did. She'd taken him right outside himself, and he was awfully afraid his world would never be right again without her.

Fuck. He was so screwed.

CHAPTER SIXTEEN

Olivia lay on her back on the blue and yellow checked blanket she'd had since college, her fingers entwined with Pete's, staring up at the majestic pines overhead. Everything about the moment was perfect. Her nostrils filled with the scent of fresh pine. The wind rushed through the trees with a steady whisper, while in the distance a hawk called.

Peace. If she could take a picture to illustrate the word, this was it.

She looked over at Pete. He lay with his eyes closed, his chest rising and falling in a slow, steady rhythm. He was a part of her peace. He calmed the part of her that had been restless and reckless.

She'd fallen in love with him. And for however long they lay together on this blanket, she was going to revel in it. For these moments were separated from the real world, and she could enjoy the rush, the thrill, the *joy* of loving him.

She rolled onto her side and pressed her face against his neck. No cinnamon smell today. Nor had she seen him bake, but then again he hadn't seemed to have any trouble sleeping either. His arm came around her, drawing her even closer.

"Did you have a nice nap?" she asked.

"Mm hmm. I sleep a lot around you." His voice rumbled up through her.

She thought of how tired he'd looked when they met. "Maybe that's a good thing."

"Maybe. What time is it?"

She looked down at her watch. "Just past two."

After their romp in the tent, they'd dressed and come outside to eat the picnic she'd packed: peanut butter and jelly sandwiches, apples, and chips. Neither of them kept their pantries particularly well stocked so it was the best she'd been able to come up with on the spur of the moment. After eating, they'd stretched out to enjoy the view.

"That means we have time for this—" He tugged her on top of him. "Before we head back."

She bent her head and kissed him. "You are insatiable."

"I always wake up hungry."

They crawled back inside the tent and made love to the rhythms of the forest around them. It was magic. No matter where things went from here, this was a memory she would keep and cherish.

She hoped he would too.

It was pushing four o'clock by the time they made it back to his car. They were both in pretty serious need of a shower but decided to stop at the vet to check on Timber first.

It was a harsh reality check after their magical afternoon.

One of the vet techs took them back. Olivia knelt in front of Timber's crate, and the dog looked up at her, letting out a high-pitched whine. Pete crouched beside her, and Timber's tail wagged harder, whacking against the metal bars of his crate. The IV was gone now although the feeding tube remained, barely visible behind a fold of vet wrap stretched around Timber's abdomen.

"He's probably ready for a walk if you guys want to take him out for a few minutes," the tech said.

"You bet," Pete answered.

He clipped a leash on his dog, and they walked outside together. Timber raised his leg on a sign, then walked about aimlessly for a minute and whined.

"Your throat hurts, huh?" She crouched next to him. Timber thrust his head into her lap and whined some more.

They spent about ten minutes outside with Timber then brought him back inside and said good night. Hopefully they'd be bringing him home in the next day or two. And then what? How long was she going to play house with Pete?

* * *

Pete walked upstairs. Hallie sat in the middle of his bed, staring at him like a queen from her throne. "Don't get too comfortable," he told her. "You're not staying."

She pounced, grabbed his sneakers, and held on, biting and kicking. Kind of like the woman downstairs. She'd leaped right into his life and gotten all tangled up. She couldn't stay either. But damned if he wanted her to go.

Olivia came into the bedroom behind him. They showered, then sat at the kitchen table together and ate some kind of Asian noodle dish she'd ordered from Mikoto's. It was nothing he would have ever chosen for himself, but not half bad.

After they'd eaten, they watched TV together for a little while. Then Olivia turned to him. "I want you to show me how to bake."

"Excuse me?" He'd come to expect the unexpected where she was concerned, but even so, this caught him off guard.

She leaned closer. "You don't smell like cinnamon anymore. I miss it."

He pulled back. He'd never baked with a woman he was dating, not with anyone since he was a kid helping his grandma in the kitchen. Baking muffins and cookies with her was one of his few truly happy childhood memories. She'd died when he was twelve, but he'd never forgotten the time they spent together, the way she'd helped him escape the pain at home. And so when he couldn't sleep, when his mind buzzed with things he'd rather not think about, he baked.

Olivia was looking at him now, brow wrinkled, those warm eyes focused on his. Something told him she knew exactly what she was asking for. She understood things about him he didn't even fully understand himself. And she wanted to do this. She wanted to bake with him.

"Okay," he said.

She smiled, a simple smile that did funny things to his chest so that it was hard to draw breath. She leaned forward and pressed a kiss to his lips, then took his hand and led him into the kitchen.

"So what do you want to make?" she asked. "What's your specialty?"

"I bake a lot of muffins."

She slapped his arm. "And you made fun of me for eating a muffin just this morning."

"I don't eat them." He wanted to take the words back as soon as they'd left his mouth.

Her eyes widened. "Why not?"

He shrugged. "I don't really care for them. It's just something I do when I can't sleep."

"So what do you do, throw them all away?"

"I give them to the women's shelter."

"Oh." Her brain was spinning so fast on that tidbit he could practically hear it. "So what kind of baked good do you like to eat?"

"Well I do like chocolate chip cookies."

"Then let's make those."

"I don't have chocolate chips."

She propped her hands on her hips. "And why not? When's the last time you baked chocolate chip cookies?"

He squeezed the back of his neck. "I don't know. A couple of years?"

She looked like she had plenty to say about *that*, things he probably—definitely—didn't want to hear, but instead she said, "Then let's go down the street to Walgreens and get some."

So they did. They bought chocolate chips, and they baked cookies together in his kitchen. And it was one of the most intimate experiences he'd ever had with a woman.

And he probably—definitely—didn't want to think too hard about *that*.

* * *

Olivia watched him dress for work from the safe haven of his bed. For once, she hadn't dragged him out to MacArthur Park to watch the sunrise. They'd both slept until his alarm had gone off, and truth be told, she was in no great hurry this morning.

So she lay there, watching as he layered up in all his protective gear, the vest, the crisp uniform, the belt. His gun. And she still didn't like that part. But she respected what he did, respected pretty much everything about him.

"Here." He held out a silver house key. "I should be home around four."

"Thank you." She took it, wishing it meant more than it did.

"See you later." He bent to give her a kiss, and then he was gone.

She lay in his bed, and since she had no job of her own to get to, she closed her eyes and went back to sleep. When she woke, Hallie was tangled in her hair, scurrying around like a frantic little mouse.

"You're a freak, you know that?" She disentangled the kitten and set her on her chest. Hallie pressed her forehead against Olivia's chin and purred. "A lovable freak, though."

She put Hallie on the bed and went into the bathroom. She showered and dressed in a purple sweater and jeans, feeling somewhat out of sorts here in Pete's house without him. It was Sunday, which limited her options as far as job hunting.

Tomorrow she'd go to the courthouse to pick up the

paperwork for her community service. Now was as good a time as any to get started fulfilling her community service hours while she was between jobs.

She was tempted to text Pete and tell him she'd eaten chocolate chip cookies for breakfast, but stopped herself when she remembered what he'd said about his work phone being public. His personal phone lay forgotten on the nightstand. And anyway, it felt a little too familiar, when she and Pete were... well, she wasn't sure what she and Pete were.

But they sure as hell weren't a couple living together, no matter how it felt right now. He was just being overprotective after what had happened at her house, but once the culprit was caught, he'd expect her to go.

Which left her with a limited window of time to break through his barriers. She wanted more than just a fling with Pete Sampson. Yeah, she'd agreed to a casual relationship, but surely even he knew that ship had sailed. They'd shared things that went far past casual, whether he wanted to admit it or not.

She wasn't giving up without a fight, and she was damned good at fighting for what she wanted.

* * *

Pete walked out of the station at four fifteen. He couldn't wait to get home to Olivia. He'd been thinking about her all day, imagining her lying in his bed or baking in his kitchen. For tonight at least, she was his, and he intended to take full advantage of that fact. He was pulling into the driveway when his cell phone rang.

"Hi, Maggie," he answered.

"Hi," his sister said. "I was just calling to remind you about dinner at mom's tonight."

"Tonight? But it's Sunday."

"I know, that's why I called to remind you. We didn't do dinner this Thursday because I had a work thing, remember?"

Well now he did, but shit, they were going to have a field day with him if he brought Olivia to family dinner. "Rain check?"

"Are you still at work?"

"Just got home."

"Well, Mom went to church with Mr. Barnes this morning. I don't know about you, but I can't wait to hear how that went."

"Really?" He stepped out of his cruiser and clicked the locks.

"Yep. So I'll see you at six?"

"I, ah, may bring someone with me." He held the phone away from his ear and cringed.

"Someone, as in, a girl?" Maggie's voice rose.

"Yes a girl, but don't get too excited. She's just staying with me while she gets some things sorted out."

Maggie squealed. "But you are sleeping with her?"

He cringed again. "Jesus, Maggie."

"I'll take that as a yes. Tonight's dinner is going to be epic. What's her name?"

"Olivia." And she was probably going to hate him when he told her what he'd just gotten her into.

"Well, I can't wait to meet Miss Olivia. See you at six."

Pete shoved the phone into his pocket and opened his front door. He followed the sound of cabinets closing and found Olivia in the kitchen, putting away groceries. Bailey lay on a dog bed in the corner, asleep.

"You didn't have to grocery shop," he said.

She turned with a smile so warm, so bright, that he lost his breath. "Well, I had a lot of free time on my hands today so I stocked up on some essentials. I was thinking about making a stir fry tonight."

"My sister just called to remind me I'm supposed to have dinner with her at my mom's tonight."

Olivia's brow wrinkled. "Oh."

"Want to come with me?" he asked.

Her face brightened. "I'd love to."

He was never going to live this down, not with any of the women involved. He was so screwed. Bailey scampered over to say hello, tail wiggling, and he bent to pet her.

"I sat with Timber for a while today. Dr. Johnson thinks he'll be ready to come home tomorrow," Olivia said.

A knot in his chest loosened. "That's good. Real good."

She clipped a leash on Bailey and walked to the back door. "Hang on. I'm trying to walk her more regularly to keep her from peeing in your kitchen."

"I appreciate that." He went upstairs to change, only to be reminded of the rabid kitten that now inhabited his bedroom. His house had been taken over by Olivia and her critters. When he came back downstairs, she was sitting at the kitchen table, typing something on her laptop.

"I'm organizing a protest," she said.

"What?" He wasn't sure he liked the sound of that.

"We're going to protest outside Town Hall on Friday. And before you ask, I've been planning it since before what happened to Timber. That undercover video was swept under the rug. Halverson Foods is getting away with abuse, and now they're trying to scare me into backing off. Well, it won't work."

"Liv—" But he couldn't say it. He couldn't tell her the sheriff would have a fit when he heard about this, even more so if he knew Olivia was staying with him.

"This has gone on long enough. I'm ready to end it. The abuse has to stop." She stood and closed the laptop. "But I know you don't approve, so I'll work on it later. What should I wear to dinner? And what do we need to bring?"

He looked down at her purple sweater and jeans. "You're fine, and we don't need to bring anything. My mom loves to cook."

"And *my* mom taught me you never go to someone's house for dinner empty handed. We still have about a dozen of those cookies left. Will that do?"

Another thing he'd never live down, once his mom and sister realized he'd baked with Olivia. "Yeah, that'll do."

"Okay." She started rummaging through his cabinets then, coming up with a large white plate, which she started arranging cookies on.

"I have to say, I didn't expect this domestic side of you."

She gave him a smile over her shoulder. "I'm full of surprises."

And wasn't that the damn truth. An hour later, he stepped through his mother's front door with Olivia at his side.

"You must be Olivia." His mom came and took Olivia's hands in hers. "I'm Elizabeth, Pete's mom."

"Elizabeth, it's so nice to meet you." Olivia gave her a genuine smile, reminding Pete that she was a chameleon of many colors. She was just as at ease here in his childhood home as she was with her animal rights group, raising hell against Halverson Foods.

"And I'm Maggie, Pete's sister."

The women went into the kitchen. Pete trailed after them. Maybe this would go smoother than he'd thought.

"So how did you and my brother meet?" Maggie asked.

And then again, maybe not.

CHAPTER SEVENTEEN

*O*livia's cheeks burned. How in the world could she answer Maggie's question?

So how did you and my brother meet?

For one of the first times in her life, she felt ashamed. Ashamed to tell Pete's mother and sister that they'd met when he arrested her. More than anything, she wanted to make a good first impression on his family. But she'd never been one to make excuses for herself, so she lifted her chin to face the music.

"We met through a case at work," Pete answered.

"Oh," Elizabeth said. "That sounds interesting."

"Anything you can tell us about?" Maggie asked.

And now Olivia was annoyed. She might not be proud of her actions, but she was frustrated that Pete had covered up the truth.

"No," he answered his sister, just as nonchalant as he could be. He took the plate of cookies from Olivia's hands and set it on the kitchen counter. "It smells delicious in here. Lasagna?"

"Baked ziti," his mom answered. "With salad and garlic bread."

Pete glanced at Olivia, then back at his mom. "Does that have meat sauce?"

"Not tonight. I sautéed some fresh spinach and peppers instead. Hope you don't mind."

"Nah, that's perfect," he answered. "Olivia's a vegetarian."

Maggie snickered. "Maybe you can actually get my carnivorous brother to eat some veggies now and then."

Olivia winked. "I've had some luck."

Maggie's eyes widened, and she pointed a finger in Olivia's direction. "Oh! I knew your name was familiar. You're the one who—" She slapped a hand over her mouth.

"The one who what?" Elizabeth asked.

"I was arrested for spray-painting animal rights propaganda on the Halverson Foods chicken-processing plant." And *phew*, she was glad the truth was out.

"Arrested?" Elizabeth gasped.

Maggie grinned.

Pete grimaced.

"Not my finest moment," Olivia said. "But I'd been trying to bring attention to the abuse happening to the birds there for months, and in a roundabout way, getting myself arrested has actually done just that."

"And Pete arrested you?" Maggie looked like she might start tap dancing with glee.

Olivia nodded. "Yes."

He cleared his throat. "That case is now closed."

"And yet you've brought her with you to meet the family." Maggie clapped her hands in delight. Their mother looked less thrilled.

"It's not like that," Pete said. "Olivia just needed a place to stay for a little while."

And that stung. Her cheeks heated again. "Right. My house has been vandalized several times. The other day someone left chicken carcasses in my backyard, and the dogs got into them. Timber choked on a bone and almost died. Pete didn't think it was safe for me to stay there until the sheriff's office caught who did it."

Elizabeth pressed a hand to her mouth. "Pete, you told us Timber had gotten into something, but you didn't say he almost died."

"He's going to be fine," he said.

"And your dog, Olivia?" Elizabeth asked.

"She was lucky. No ill effects."

"Well my goodness. You've had quite a month." Elizabeth ushered them toward the living room.

The house gave Olivia warm, homey feelings. Its wood-paneled walls and floral print couch and loveseat were right out of the eighties. It reminded her of the little house she'd spent her first years in, before her parents started bringing in enough money to move them into a brick-front colonial in a fancy neighborhood with snooty kids who'd teased Olivia for her tomboy ways.

She sat on the loveseat next to Pete, while his mom and sister took the couch.

"Sorry for putting you on the spot," Maggie said. She had brown hair and dark eyes like her brother, but unlike Pete, she had a fun, playful air about her that made Olivia think they might be good friends if the situation were different.

"Not at all." Olivia shook her head. "I'm glad that you know. I'm pretty much an open book. I don't like keeping secrets."

Maggie darted a look at Pete, reminding Olivia that there were entire chapters of his life that she didn't know. He'd given her a few glimpses inside, but he wasn't, and probably never would be, an open book.

"Well." Elizabeth clasped her hands. "I'd better go check on supper. It's almost ready."

"Is there anything I can help with?" Olivia asked.

"No thank you, dear. I just need to pull everything out of the oven." Elizabeth stood and walked into the kitchen.

"I'm not sure your mom likes the idea of you bringing a criminal to dinner," she whispered.

"She may be hesitant about the idea," Maggie said, suddenly sober, "but she doesn't dislike you. It's just—our dad got into a lot of trouble when we were growing up."

"And she doesn't want her son to end up with someone like him?" Olivia felt her chest cave in on itself.

"You're nothing like my father," Pete said, breaking his silence. His eyes burned into hers with shocking intensity. "Nothing."

Olivia didn't know what to say, but the way he was looking at her right now, all proud and protective, made goose bumps rise up and down her arms.

"Pete's right," Maggie said. "Our dad is an addict. He was high, or out looking for a way to get high, for most of our childhood."

Well, Olivia was starting to get a clearer picture of things now. "And they're ... divorced?"

Maggie shook her head. "Our father is in jail."

In jail. No wonder his mom didn't like the idea of Pete dating a criminal. "Oh."

Elizabeth appeared in the doorway, a forced smile on her face. "Dinner's ready."

* * *

Pete should have known better than to bring Olivia to dinner at his mom's. Maggie hadn't stopped talking since they sat down at the dinner table. She and Olivia had definitely hit it off. They were alike that way—eternal optimists who'd never met a stranger.

And he admired them for it, he really did. But he took after his mom. They were both more inclined to sit back and watch, to keep their emotions bottled deep inside. Every once in a while, he wished he could be a little bit more like Olivia and Maggie.

"So, Mom, how was church this morning?" Maggie asked between bites of ziti.

Their mom smiled. "It was nice, thank you."

"And your date?"

Elizabeth blushed. "Well my goodness, Maggie. It wasn't a *date*. Steve Barnes is an old friend. It was very kind of him to invite me to sit with him."

Pete watched with interest. His mom had actually blushed. He'd seen the interest on Steve's side too. "You know, maybe it's time to go ahead and file for divorce."

His mother blanched. "Well, I—you know—your father—"

"Is not getting out of jail for at least ten years. It's time to move on, Mom. Even if he weren't in jail, you deserve better."

"Well, that just feels disloyal. I promised to stand by him, for better or for worse." She fidgeted with her napkin.

"And he promised to love and cherish you," Maggie said quietly. "Pete's right. You deserve better. We want to see you happy."

"Well for goodness sake, I am happy." She looked between them. "I am. The two of you are all I need."

"In all fairness, Mom, you deserve more," he said.

Olivia squeezed his hand under the table. She'd been quiet throughout the conversation, but he knew she was absorbing every word and would use it to sharpen her already uncanny ability to read him.

And that didn't make him squirm nearly as much as it should have.

* * *

"Thanks for bringing me." Olivia watched Pete's face as they pulled into the driveway of his townhouse. He'd been quiet much of the drive home, broody or just tired, she wasn't quite sure. She'd learned a hell of a lot about Pete Sampson tonight, and it only strengthened her resolve to fight for him.

Pete gave her a look, as if he knew every thought she'd just had. "Thanks for tagging along. I completely forgot I was supposed to have dinner with them tonight."

That was a jab, and it hurt. "Tagging along? Don't be a jerk."

Maybe he didn't want her to read anything into tonight, but too bad. If she were just a random hookup, he never would have brought her to his mom's house. By the looks on Elizabeth's and Maggie's faces, it wasn't something he did often.

And whether he liked it or not, it *did* mean something. "Liv—"

She got out of the car and slammed the door behind her. Maybe she was overreacting, but her feelings were hurt, dammit.

Pete caught up to her at the front door. "I didn't mean—"

"Then what *did* you mean?" She turned on him. " 'It's not like that. Olivia just needed a place to stay.' I'm not your fucking pity case. If that's all I am to you, then I'll pack my bags and be out of your hair tonight."

"Stop it. You know that's not true." He took her hands and tugged her toward him, but she yanked them free.

"No, I don't know that." Her voice wobbled. "I have no idea where I stand with you."

He raked a hand through his hair. "You're only the second girl I've ever brought to family dinner, okay?"

She heard the desperation in his tone, and her heart softened. "Your wife being the first?"

He nodded.

She leaned in close so that her lips brushed his cheek. "Then stop treating me like I don't matter to you."

He clutched her fingers in his. "You matter."

She swallowed over the ache in her throat. "Good. Because you matter to me too. A lot."

Then he was kissing her as if his life depended on it, and she was putty in his arms. When he held her and kissed her and made love to her, she felt like the most important thing in his world. But his words told a different story, and she was tired of being brushed aside. This was no casual fling, and it was about time for him to man up and admit it.

She tugged free and went inside. Bailey waited in her crate in the kitchen, her butt wiggling like crazy. The crate was dry. "What a good girl! Let's get you outside."

She leashed Bailey and rushed her right out the back door. After she'd walked and fed her dog, Olivia went looking for Pete. She found him upstairs, just stepping out of a shower.

And heavens.

She stood in the doorway of the bathroom, just drinking in the sight of him, all tall and strong and *naked*. He reached for a towel and ran it through his hair, then slung it over his shoulder and pulled her up against him for a kiss.

"I'm way overdressed for this situation." She ran her hands over his naked butt and squeezed.

"Easy problem to fix." He lifted her in his arms and carried her to his bed.

By this time he was fully aroused, and so was she. After a frantic tumble to get her out of her clothes, they made love with moonlight streaming in through his bedroom window. She wanted every night to end this way.

The next morning, Pete went to work, and Olivia drove to the courthouse to get her community service paperwork. There was a long list of approved nonprofits she could volunteer with. The Dogwood County Animal Shelter was one, and she'd be stopping by later this morning to see what they had available.

The Dogwood Women's Shelter was on there too. She paused, thinking of Pete bringing them the muffins he'd baked. The muffins he never ate himself. Was there a reason he was partial to that particular charity? Had his family once sought refuge there?

Maybe she'd stop by the women's shelter too. She did have one hundred and twenty hours of community service to fulfill, after all. It almost felt like cheating to serve them all at the animal shelter. Maybe she should broaden her horizons and help people in need as well.

Maybe it would even earn her some brownie points with Pete.

* * *

Pete stared down at the middle-aged woman he'd just pulled over for driving forty-eight in a thirty-five. Tears stained her cheeks, and she'd been blubbering nonstop about the Facebook class at the local library she was running late for.

"Consider this a lesson, ma'am," he said, as he handed her a written warning. As she'd had a squeaky clean record and seemed remorseful, he'd decided to let her go without a ticket. He must be in a good mood this morning. Maybe thanks to the way he'd started it, with Olivia in his bed.

"Thank you—I'm so sorry—it won't happen again," she spluttered.

"See that it doesn't. Have a nice day, Mrs. Franklin."

"Thank you. You too, deputy."

With a nod, he walked back to his cruiser. He watched her drive off—nice and slow—then sat back to finish entering her citation into the system. His phone rang. It was Hartzler.

"Thought you'd want to know. Word on the street is

that goings-on at Olivia Bennett's place were a fraternity prank," Hartzler said.

"A fraternity prank?" Pete pinched his brow.

"Apparently one of the fraternities over at Carolina U uses chickens as some kind of mascot, and they've been having a field day with this shit with Halverson."

Pete frowned. He vaguely remembered a photo a few weeks ago with some fraternity guys pulling their pants down in front of Olivia's *Chicken Ass* graffiti. This fit, and it wasn't sinister. But it didn't sit quite right with him either. "I don't see why they'd target Olivia specifically."

"Why do college kids do any of the things they do?" Hartzler sounded bored. "I'll go down there tomorrow and read them the riot act. That ought to be the end of it."

"Well all right. Let me know if anything else turns up."

"Like what?" Hartzler asked.

"I don't know. Just ask around and see if anything sounds off."

"Don't read more into this than there is just because you're banging her, Sampson."

Pete bristled. "And don't write her off just because she's caused trouble in the past."

He hung up the phone, frustrated and pissed off. Hartzler wasn't going to ask any questions when he visited the frat boys. In his mind, the case was already closed. Yet Pete couldn't shake the feeling that there was more to the story.

He was going to have to pay his own visit to the Omega Chi fraternity at Carolina University to get the answers he needed. Never mind that the sheriff had warned him to stay away from this case, and Olivia.

CHAPTER EIGHTEEN

Timber's high-pitched whine drowned out the radio on the ride home from the Dogwood Animal Hospital. His cold snout pressed into the back of Olivia's neck, sending shivers down her spine.

"You did not enjoy your stay at the vet, did you?" she asked the woebegone shepherd.

"Woof," he answered, his head cocked to the side, brown eyes crinkled.

"I didn't either," Pete said. "Thank goodness for pet insurance."

"Will it cover his bill?"

"Most of it." He pulled into his driveway and shut the car off.

Timber whined again. Olivia felt like joining him. Deputy Hartzler had called earlier. He told her that the vandalism to her house, including the dead chickens in the backyard, had been a fraternity prank. Which meant she could go home.

Surely Pete knew this, but he hadn't mentioned it. She nibbled on her bottom lip as she followed him and Timber into the house.

Bailey waited in her crate in the kitchen, squealing with glee. Olivia opened the crate and ushered her straight out the back door. It had been days since the dog had had an accident. Crating her when she was left alone and more frequent potty trips seemed to have totally turned her around.

Olivia tried not to feel guilty for how long it had taken to get her to this point. She'd have had the damn dog adopted out weeks ago if she'd just spent a little time training her.

Lesson learned.

She walked back inside with Bailey only to have Timber fling himself against her legs, squeaking at eardrum-piercing levels, giving her the kind of super-sad puppy dog eyes no one could resist. "You are so pathetic." She sat on the kitchen floor to coddle him.

"Man up, dude. No wonder you got kicked off the force. The vet says you're good as new." Pete stared down at them, but his tone belied his words. He sounded like he wanted to give his dog a big hug.

"It's okay," she said. "I think he's earned himself at least one night of pampering after his ordeal. I picked up some wet food for him earlier, figured it might be easier for him to swallow while his throat's still healing."

"Yeah, the vet mentioned that would be a good idea. Thank you."

"You're welcome." She placed a kiss between Timber's eyes then stood. "I was planning to make stuffed peppers tonight. Sound good?"

"Yeah." He yanked her up against him and kissed her hard. "You don't have to cook for me, you know."

"I know." She kissed him back. "But I like to."

In truth, staying at Pete's townhouse made her feel all kinds of domestic. She didn't want it to end. She'd fallen for him, hard and fast, and there was no way out, not for her at least.

But did he feel the same?

* * *

Pete closed his eyes and kissed her while his heart hammered against his ribs. Olivia was terrible at hiding her feelings. It was all there on her face, in her eyes. She was falling for him. And well, he didn't want to look too hard at his own feelings, because there was no way he and Olivia could ever be more than they were right now.

He'd already tried marriage, and it had been a disaster.

"I spoke to Hartzler today," he said.

Olivia pushed backward out of his arms, which had been his intent, but still he fought the need to reach out and pull her back against his chest.

"He called me too," she said.

"He's pretty sure the Omega Chi kids are behind it all, although we don't have enough evidence to charge them."

She looked away. "So I can go home."

"Tomorrow." He gave in to the urge to pull her against him, her chest pressed to his. "No rush."

"Tomorrow," she spoke against his shirt.

He ought to make a clean break with her here, let her go home and back to her own life before things got any messier between them. It was selfish of him not to. She deserved her happily ever after, and he couldn't promise her happiness.

So he had no idea why he heard himself saying, "I'm off on Wednesday. Maybe we can do something."

She tilted her head up to meet his eyes, giving him a searching look. "I'm volunteering that morning at the women's shelter, but I'm free in the afternoon."

The women's shelter? Pete thought of the night he, Maggie, and their mom had spent there after his dad came home stoned out of his mind, smashed his fist through the china cabinet, and then—convinced they had turned against him—threw them out of the house. "I thought you'd spend your time at the animal shelter."

"I was there today, and I'll be there again tomorrow, but I thought maybe I should spread myself around a little."

"You'll be finished with your community service hours in no time."

She shrugged. "Might as well try to finish it up before I go back to work."

"Any leads there?" he asked.

"A few. If nothing pans out by the end of the week, I'll lower my standards." She backed out of his arms and bent to rub Timber behind his ears. Bailey sat behind her and whined.

He squeezed the back of his neck. "Don't do that."

"I need a paycheck, Pete. If I have to bag groceries until I find something better, so be it."

She shouldn't have to lower her standards with him either, and yet he found himself hoping she would, just a little while longer, because he wasn't strong enough to give her up. Not yet. "Something will come along, hopefully something much better than working at the café."

"I hope so." She turned her full attention to the dogs, fussing over them as she fixed their suppers. Once both dogs were happily stuffing their faces, she went to the refrigerator and took out ingredients for the stuffed peppers.

Pete stood there, watching her work. Olivia had made herself right at home here, had made his house feel like a home with her presence.

The truth was, he might not ever be ready to let her go.

* * *

Tuesday morning, Pete finally made it out to the Carolina University campus to have a chat with the fraternity brothers, face to face. He pounded on the front door of the frat house for a solid five minutes before he finally heard a shout from within.

"Dogwood County Sheriff's Office," he called and was rewarded by heavy footsteps approaching the door.

The kid who opened the door wore low-slung athletic shorts and nothing else, his disheveled hair hanging in his eyes. "Can I help you, Officer?"

"Deputy Sampson with the Dogwood County Sheriff's Office. I need to have a few words with whoever's in charge."

"Uh." The kid looked at him for a moment through eyes reddened from sleep, or pot. "Just a minute." He turned and walked upstairs.

Pete stood in the foyer, hat tucked under his right arm. Minutes ticked by. Finally another kid came down the stairs, this one dressed in jeans and a CU sweatshirt, his hair combed back and damp, as if he'd just splashed water over his face.

"I'm Justin Wendell, president of the CU chapter of Omega Chi," he said, extending a hand.

"Deputy Sampson with the Dogwood County Sheriff's Office."

"How can I help you, deputy?" Justin gestured for Pete to join him in the living room.

Justin sat on the battered-looking couch, and Pete chose a black leather recliner across from him. "I'm investigating a string of vandalism around town, in particular on the property of a woman named Olivia Bennett."

"Oh, sure. Another deputy came out earlier this week to ask us about that. And like I told him, we don't know anything about it."

Pete questioned the kid for a solid thirty minutes, and he didn't like the vibe he got at all. Justin Wendell was cocky and evasive, like a privileged rich kid who didn't think the laws of the real world applied to him or just didn't care.

"So if I had a look at your cell phone, I wouldn't find any pictures of your boys egging Olivia Bennett's house or spray-painting her garage?" Pete asked.

"No, but you'd need a warrant for that, deputy."

Pete shrugged. "Unless you voluntarily handed it over, you know, to clear your name."

"No, thanks."

"Have it your way. But we'll be paying close attention to your fraternity. If anyone steps out of line, we're going to nail your asses." Pete stood to leave.

"Good luck with that," Justin said. He walked Pete to the door. "Funny thing, you asking about this. I would have figured you guys at the sheriff's office would be thanking us."

* * *

Olivia spent Tuesday morning at the Dogwood County
Animal Shelter. She'd been given doggy duty today,
which meant she was responsible for visiting with and
walking as many dogs as possible before it was time for
her to leave, cleaning their kennels when necessary.

"They haven't been walked since last night," Darlene,
the woman at the front desk, told her. "The ones that are
potty trained are marked at the front of their kennels, so
try to walk them first. If you don't want to take them outside, there's an exercise pen out back you can let them run
around in."

"But it's okay to walk them around the neighborhood
if I want?"

Darlene leaned back in her chair and gave Olivia an
amused look. "More than okay. Most of them would love
the chance for a real walk."

"Okay. Great." Olivia unlatched the wire-mesh door
leading to the dog kennels, greeted by an onslaught of
barking and clanging as the dogs vied for her attention.

Truth be told, yesterday was the first time she'd ever
set foot in the Dogwood Shelter. She'd spent the morning
cleaning out the cat enclosures and playing with kittens. It
hardly felt like work. This was different. Dogs looked up
at her, eyes bright and hopeful, tails wagging, paws thrust
through metal bars to get closer to her.

Remembering what Darlene had said, she glanced
around until she found a kennel marked with a bright pink
card that said "I'm potty trained! Please walk me first."
Inside was a brown and white dog of dubious heritage,
bouncing up and down like a wind-up toy.

"You're first, it looks like," she said, then glanced at his ID card. "Barney, huh? Who named you? You're not a purple dinosaur."

She attached a leash to the little dog's collar and led him through the lobby onto the shelter's front lawn. Barney tugged her toward the nearest tree to relieve himself, then trotted happily at her side as she walked him around the neighborhood. Here and there he stopped to sniff at mailboxes and trees. He barked at falling leaves and tried to chase a squirrel. In short, he had a blast.

His stride slowed as they circled back around toward the shelter.

"You're not ready to go back inside yet. I get it. I wish I could keep you out longer but there are a whole bunch of other dogs who're still waiting for their turn."

He hung his head and followed her inside.

Olivia reached into the treat bowl on the front desk and passed him a cookie. "You're a good little dog, Barney. I bet someone will take you home soon."

She put him back in his kennel and took out the next dog, a bouncy pit mix named Annabelle. After Annabelle was a Lab mix named Luke. And so on. By lunchtime, she'd walked twenty dogs.

Thirty more remained, most of them waiting in soiled pens for a chance to see the sunshine and pee outside.

Olivia had planned to leave at noon so that she could spend the afternoon job-hunting, but she couldn't leave those dogs unwalked. "Am I seriously the only one here walking dogs today?" she asked Darlene.

The other woman nodded. "We have two other volunteers who usually come in on Tuesdays, but one's on vacation and the other one called in sick."

So Olivia got a bag of chips and a Diet Coke out of the vending machine and kept going. She scrubbed out kennels for the ones who hadn't made it outside in time. She was bringing a Golden Retriever named Earnest back to his kennel when she saw a couple walking through, looking at the dogs.

She'd seen several families here today. Some had found their new best friend, some hadn't. But it was fascinating to watch the process.

"Excuse me. Do you work here?" the woman asked.

Olivia closed and latched Earnest's pen. "I'm a volunteer. Would you like me to get the Adoption Specialist for you?"

"Oh, she's with another family right now. I just thought you might be able to give us some pointers in the meantime."

"I'd be happy to try," Olivia said. "What kind of dog are you looking for?"

"Something on the small side. Maybe an older dog. We're no spring chickens ourselves so we don't need to be training a puppy." A smile creased the woman's cheeks. "And gentle, good with kids. Our granddaughter visits often. I'm Deborah Willis, by the way. This is my husband, Gerald."

"Olivia Bennett. Nice to meet you." Olivia shook hands while she ran through a mental list of all the dogs she'd walked that morning, trying to think who might be a good match. "Are there any breeds in particular that you like or dislike?"

Deborah shook her head. "I don't really pay attention to breed. All of our dogs have been mutts. We just want a good family dog."

Olivia clapped her hands together. "I think I know just the dog."

She led them down the aisle to Barney's pen. "His tag says he's a terrier mix, but I'd call him a mutt. I walked him this morning, and he was good on the leash, very well mannered. It says here that he's good with children and other dogs."

Barney pressed his snout through the bars of his cage, and Deborah rubbed him gently.

Gerald bent down beside her. "Reminds me of Scout, our first dog."

"He does look like Scout," Deborah said. Barney licked her fingers.

"Well I'm not really supposed to be helping you since I'm just a volunteer and this is my first day working with the dogs, but I can't see the harm in letting you guys take him out back in the exercise pen if you wanted to spend some time getting to know him."

"Oh, we'd love that," Deborah said.

"Great." Olivia grabbed a leash and opened Barney's door. The little dog trotted right out, wagging and greeting the Willises like he'd known them forever.

Olivia led them down the hall to the exercise pen and left them there tossing a ball with Barney. She walked out to the reception desk to tell Darlene where they were, then went back to walking dogs. By the time she'd walked them all, she felt like the potty-trained ones needed another quick trip before she left.

The shelter was closing for the day as she walked out.

"Olivia, wait up," Tracy, the Adoption Specialist, called from behind her.

"Hi, Tracy. What's up?"

"The Willises adopted Barney. They said he was the first dog you showed them. You're a natural." She smiled.

Olivia shrugged. "Lucky guess. I'm really happy for them though. Barney seems like a great little dog."

"He is, and he had been here a long time."

"Then I'm extra thrilled for him." She and Tracy walked together toward the parking lot. "I don't suppose you guys are hiring?"

Tracy snorted. "I wish. We're on a skeleton crew right now, and funding is scarce. You looking for a job?"

She nodded. "And as much as I enjoyed walking the dogs today, I need to be able to pay my bills."

"I hear you. Well, if anything comes up, I'll let you know."

"Thanks. I appreciate that. Have a good night!" Olivia waved as she stepped inside her Prius. She ought to be exhausted after walking dogs all day, but truly she felt invigorated. It wasn't any more tiring than waiting tables, and it had felt good to be working.

She drove home, determined not to be sad that she would be spending the night at her place tonight and not with Pete. That was silly. She was an independent woman, and this was where she lived. It was good that she wasn't in danger, that the whole thing had been nothing but a fraternity prank.

And then she turned the corner and saw Pete's Forester in her driveway. He and Timber sat on her front steps.

* * *

Pete watched as she got out of the Prius. He tried not to feel the way his heart lifted just at the sight of her. That messy blond ponytail of hers had always turned him on.

"What in the world?" She crossed her arms over her chest and stared at him.

I missed you. He cleared his throat. "I went and talked to the Omega Chi boys today. Thought maybe you'd want to hear about it."

"Sure." She motioned him in after her.

He followed her into the house. Timber tugged him down the hallway to the kitchen where Bailey waited in her crate.

"Oh what a good girl." Olivia praised her as she opened the crate and ushered her out the back door.

Pete unclipped Timber's leash and let him join her in the yard. Then he stepped Olivia back against the wall and lowered his mouth to hers. She yanked him closer, her fingers raking through his hair.

He drank her in, losing himself in the feel of her lips on his and the way it felt to hold her in his arms. Truth be told, when he'd come home to an empty house tonight, he hadn't liked it a damn bit. And when he got to her house and realized he had no idea where she was or when she'd be home, he hadn't liked that either.

"How was your day?" she asked, her lips tickling his cheek.

"Pretty average. How about you? Any luck on the job front?" He ran his hands down her back, pressing her flush against his body.

She shook her head. "I spent the whole day at the shelter."

"The whole day?"

"Mm hmm. Consequently, I'm starving, and I need a shower. Care to join me?" She cocked her head to the side, and he went from halfway aroused to hard as steel, just like that.

"For which?"

"Both." She was on her tiptoes, wiggling against him, and he lifted her so that her legs wrapped around his hips, his cock pressed between her legs.

"I could use a shower."

She giggled. "You look like you just got out of one."

True. He'd showered when he got home from soccer practice. "But I think you're about to get me all sweaty again."

"Maybe." She grinned, then slid out of his arms. "Let me just get the dogs back inside before we go upstairs."

He watched as she brought Bailey and Timber inside, rubbing them and chatting with them in that effortless way that had them both fawning all over her. She was mesmerizing to watch.

Then he took her upstairs, and they got naked and breathless together in the shower, rinsed, and repeated. When they got out of the shower, Olivia flopped dramatically on the bed. "Dude, I've had nothing but a bag of chips since breakfast. I need food."

He dragged his eyes from the gorgeous sight of her sprawled naked across the bed. "Why haven't you eaten?"

"I told you. I was at the shelter all day. I didn't plan on it, so I didn't bring lunch." She bit her lip and looked away.

"What?"

"Nothing. I have tofu downstairs, and some veggies. I can make a quick stir fry."

He grunted. "That hardly sounds filling. Let's go out."

"I can't—"

"You can't what?" He frowned. Was she worrying about money? *Dammit.* "Christ, Olivia. Let's go to Torino's and get you a big plate of pasta or something."

She slid out of bed and pulled on a shiny pink bra and panties, which she covered with jeans and a matching pink sweater. "Tomorrow's a week since I lost my job, and no eating out until I fix that."

"Well I'm paying for your supper, whether or not you have a job. So let's go."

She huffed an indignant sigh and followed him downstairs. She put Bailey back in her crate and gated Timber in the kitchen, then grabbed her purse and walked out to the Forester with him.

He got it. Really he did. It had to be frustrating that she couldn't pay her own way, even though he would have paid for supper regardless. Olivia was strong and independent, used to taking care of herself. She was quiet on the way to the restaurant, blond hair tumbling across her face, her pink lips set in a pretty pout.

He decided to leave her be until he'd put some food in her. She'd had a long day on nothing but a bag of chips.

Thirty minutes later, she was halfway through a plate of cheese ravioli and a glass of Riesling, and the Olivia he loved was back.

He choked on a bite of lasagna.

"You okay?" she asked.

"Fine." He coughed. Not entirely in control of his own thoughts, but fine. And not in love with Olivia Bennett. It was just a meaningless phrase that had flitted through his mind.

"You look funny." She cocked her head, her brown eyes twinkling. "Is your lasagna bad?"

"No, it's great."

"Okay. The ravioli is good too."

He cleared his throat. "So I talked to the boys in the Omega Chi fraternity today."

"Right. Anyone confess to a penchant for spray-painting chickens?"

"Not exactly. They're guilty for sure, although we don't have enough evidence to charge them."

"Figures." She rolled her eyes. "A bunch of frat boys can get away with vandalizing my house repeatedly and almost killing your dog. Me? I spray-paint *one* building, and I spend the night in jail and wind up with a criminal record."

He shrugged. "Life's not fair sometimes. Chances are they're not smart enough to keep getting away with it, so I wouldn't be too jealous."

"True."

"Anyway, there was a lot of deceptive body language. I didn't quite like the vibe I got from them." Almost like they were hiding something, something more than what he suspected them of.

What if it wasn't just a college prank? What if someone at Halverson Foods had paid them to harass Olivia?

"Then nail their asses," Olivia said.

"I'll do my best." Officially, the case wasn't his to investigate. But his dog had almost died. Olivia's peace of mind had been shattered. And he couldn't let that rest.

CHAPTER NINETEEN

Olivia polished off her wine—and her ravioli—and stared at the man sitting across from her. The man she loved. "Thanks for dinner." She reached across the table to take his hand.

"Any time." He smiled, and the candlelight from the votive on their table danced in his eyes. Goodness, he was handsome. He stood, and they walked hand-in-hand out of the restaurant.

"You brought Timber with you. Do you want to stay the night?" she asked.

His fingers tightened around hers. "I probably shouldn't."

"You missed me," she whispered against his ear, pushing her luck. Truthfully, he probably hadn't even had time to. After all, she'd only moved out of his townhouse that morning.

"Maybe a little," he admitted.

His words hung in the air between them, and she

tried—really tried—not to read more into them than he'd probably intended.

She bumped her shoulder against his. "Admit it, you just couldn't face a night without Hallie to tackle you awake in the morning."

He gave her a long look, his lips twitching with amusement. "There is not one damn thing about that cat that I miss."

"Oh come on. She's sweet."

"And possibly rabid."

"Not rabid." She let go of his hand to step into the passenger seat of his SUV. "She doesn't even have fleas. So you'll stay?"

"Well, I am off from work tomorrow." He went around to the driver's side and climbed inside.

She pressed her hands beneath her thighs, chilled by the cool November evening. "I'm volunteering tomorrow morning at the women's shelter. Want to come with me?"

He cranked the engine and backed out of the parking spot, his expression unreadable. "Maybe."

They drove home in comfortable silence, both tired and stuffed full of Italian food. When they got to her house, they took the dogs for a short walk, then snuggled on her couch together and watched an episode of *Mythbusters*, which was apparently one of his favorite shows.

She was hard-pressed to say she'd ever seen an episode, but she enjoyed it. The guys spent the entire episode building things out of duct tape, and she and Pete laughed until their sides hurt. Then they went upstairs and got naked.

Pete was inside her and thrusting hard when something cold and wet brushed against her hip.

"Ah!" She lurched beneath him.

Pete froze, his eyes crinkled in concern. "What's wrong? Did I hurt you?"

"No—" She glanced to the side and found two canine faces watching them with rapt attention. *Christ on a cracker.*

Pete followed her gaze. "Fuck. Get lost, you two."

In response, Timber leaned forward to lick Pete's thigh. He recoiled, shooting his dog a deadly look.

Olivia covered her mouth to stifle a giggle. Timber was staring comically at the spot where hers and Pete's bodies joined. "You are a pervert!" she told him.

The dog whined. Bailey huffed a dramatic sigh and left the room.

Pete withdrew and chased his dog out of the room. He closed the door behind them, then flopped back onto the bed. "Fuck."

"Next time we'll remember to gate them in the kitchen." She rolled against him so that his erection settled between her legs.

"That dog is not quite right." He leaned in to kiss her.

She giggled again. "He's a dog. He doesn't know the meaning of modesty."

"I'm hardly modest, but I draw the line at having an audience." He thrust inside her, and they stopped talking, both eager to finish what they'd started.

Pete groaned, settling into an easy rhythm that sent her right over the edge. She clenched around him as she found release. Pete swore roughly. He rolled to the side, and a white kitten tumbled from his back.

Hallie landed right on her chest, then leaped off the bed and ran into the closet. Olivia's body quivered, missing the heat and weight of Pete's body on hers. He was sitting on the edge of the bed, looking pissed.

Hallie's well-timed leap had interrupted him at the worst possible moment.

He shrugged into his jeans and left the room. Olivia pulled a nightie over her head and followed him downstairs. She found him in the kitchen, pouring himself a glass of water.

"Sorry about that," she said.

He grunted. "Damn animals."

"They make our sex life more interesting, that's for sure." She kissed his cheek, then moved to the counter to pour her own glass of water.

"Interesting is not the word I would use." He gulped from his glass.

They munched on some vegan cookies in her pantry and called it a night. And when they woke in the early hours of dawn, she made it up to him. Then she dragged him out with her in the chilly morning air to watch the sunrise over the trees in MacArthur Park.

"So you'll come with me to the shelter?" she asked, her head on his shoulder.

"I should really get some stuff done at home."

"Okay." She threaded her fingers through his.

"But maybe I'll come with you for just a little while."

"That would be nice." She couldn't explain why she was pressing him on this. Maybe it was a greedy need to pry further into his history, his childhood. She wanted to understand what made him tick. But also, she just wanted to spend more time with him, time that had nothing to do with vandalism and police reports and everything to do with her and Pete.

So they stopped by his place for a change of clothes, and then they drove together to the Dogwood Women's Shelter.

"Good morning, Pete," Nancy, the shelter's director, said with a warm smile as she greeted them at the door. "And you must be Olivia."

"Nice to meet you." Olivia returned her smile.

"Nancy." He nodded. "Good to see you."

"Have you brought us some more muffins? We've been missing your baking these last few weeks."

Pete looked chagrined. "I've been busier than usual."

Olivia hid her smile. He hadn't had trouble sleeping since he started dating her. Her gain was the shelter's loss. But surely they could bake some muffins for the shelter together during daylight hours.

"Well don't you worry about it," Nancy said. "We've got plenty to eat. So you're both here to volunteer then?"

She and Pete nodded.

"Well, as you probably noticed when you got here, we're buried in leaves right now. I was hoping to put you to work out here in the yard this morning if you don't mind."

"No problem." Pete rested his hand on Olivia's shoulder as they followed Nancy to the shed in back. She handed them each a rake and a fistful of plastic bags.

They settled into an easy rhythm together, raking and bagging leaves. And Nancy wasn't kidding—the shelter's lawn was covered with them. Olivia's heart pinched as a couple of little girls raced through the yard. One of them paused to give her a shy smile, then leaped into the pile of leaves she'd just finished.

"Sophie! Ella!" a woman called, and the girls were off and running.

Olivia paused to watch them go. "Hard to imagine living here. Not having a home or belongings of your own."

"It's not a bad place to be." Pete raked leaves into the pile the little girl had demolished. "And they can bring some of their own stuff with them, clothes and things. What most of these families come from…this is a big improvement. They're safe here."

She turned to look at him.

His dark eyes were expressionless. "I place a lot of women and children here after we remove them from abusive situations. Last week I brought a teenage girl who'd been living with her much older, drug-addicted boyfriend."

"Why didn't you take her home to her family?"

"She'd just turned eighteen, and she didn't want to go back. Probably the situation at home was no better than what I took her out of."

"Damn." Olivia ran her rake over the ground. The scent of fresh earth and damp leaves filled her nose, reminding her of so many childhood afternoons spent raking leaves and leaping into them, of riding around the neighborhood on her father's garden cart collecting bags of leaves to add to the compost pile in their backyard.

"You had a pretty cushy childhood, didn't you?" Pete said.

"I guess I did." And she felt very, very humbled now.

Pete didn't comment on that. He just kept raking.

The van from the senior center pulled up to the curb behind them. Its doors opened, and a parade of women piled out, each carrying a casserole dish. Apparently the elderly citizens of Dogwood had quite a penchant for cooking for the less fortunate. And Olivia was starting to feel totally selfish for never having done anything charitable for her own species before.

"Your childhood wasn't cushy," she said. Pushing again. She just couldn't help it.

He glanced over at her. "No."

"I'm sorry."

He shrugged. "It was what it was."

"It must have been hard for your mom, raising you two."

"She did the best she could."

She thought she heard the faintest hint of resentment in his words, as if he thought his mom could have done better. "Did you ever stay someplace like this?" she asked.

"Once."

She absorbed that quietly. Pete had seen things, lived things, that she never had and never would. "Was your dad abusive?"

"Not with his fists."

She wasn't sure exactly what that meant, but figured it had to do with drug abuse and the chaos that came with it. "Why is he in jail?"

"Because he killed a man." His voice remained expressionless, but his eyes flashed with anger. He carried the last bag of leaves to the curb and walked quietly around the side of the house, toward the shed.

Olivia stood there, rooted to the spot with shock. Pete's dad had killed someone?

She ran after him, eventually finding him on the back porch playing with the girls they'd seen earlier. One of them had put a tiara on his head, and the other was bandaging a "booboo" on his finger. He looked relaxed and at ease with the pampering so she left him there and went to find Nancy and get her timesheet signed.

Nancy met her at the front door. "Thank you so much for your help this morning." She took the timesheet from Olivia's hand. "I don't usually let people come to the house who are fulfilling community service hours, but I know your dad and I heard what you were arrested for, so I figured you're good people."

"Oh." Olivia blanched. "Yeah, you can consider it a one-time screwup."

Nancy smiled kindly. "Well don't we all have those? Say, I wanted to ask you about something. We get a lot of families here who have to leave pets behind. I do what I can to help them find someone to watch the animals, but most often they're either left behind or end up at the shelter. I wondered if you knew of an animal rescue that might be able to help us out."

Olivia's heart hurt to think of these families, already leaving so much behind, not being able to bring a beloved pet with them. "I know a lot of people in animal rescue; I'm sure we could figure something out. Let me ask around and get back to you, but in the meantime, call me if you have someone coming with a pet that needs watching."

Nancy's eyes shone. "That would be wonderful. Thank you so much, Olivia."

Olivia left that afternoon knowing for sure she'd be back, and not just to accumulate more hours on her community service timecard.

* * *

"So what next?" Pete asked as they climbed inside his Forester.

Olivia had been quiet since they left the women's shelter. "I need to do some more job hunting."

"Any leads?" He pulled onto the road and turned the car toward Olivia's house.

She shook her head, thumbing through messages on her phone. "Wait a minute. The manager of the thrift shop wants me to come in for an interview."

"That sounds promising."

"Yeah. I'd like it there, I think. Let me call him." She tapped the screen, then held the phone to her ear. "Mr. Henneby? Hi, it's Olivia Bennett. You emailed me earlier about the daytime position at the thrift shop."

Pete kept driving toward her house as she talked. When she hung up the phone a few minutes later, she was smiling.

"He wants me to come in this afternoon. I kind of got the impression the job was mine as long as I don't screw up my interview."

"That's great. They'd be lucky to have you."

"Thanks."

He pulled into her driveway. "I need to take Timber for some exercise and get a few things done at home, but maybe we can get together later."

"Okay." She gathered her purse and led the way to her front door. Inside, Timber waited exuberantly in the kitchen while Bailey danced in her crate.

He bent to clip Timber's leash to his collar, then pressed a kiss to Olivia's lips. "Good luck."

"Thank you."

"Call me later," he said.

"I will."

He took his dog and went home, determined to ignore

the feeling that his home didn't feel quite the same without Olivia sharing it. When he got there, he changed and took Timber for a walk. The dog was itching for a long, hard run, but it would have to wait until his body had finished healing.

After their walk, Pete showered, dressed, and was about to tackle the mountain of laundry in his mudroom when his cell phone rang. Hopefully it was Olivia—with good job news. He rushed to answer it.

"Hi." It was Maggie.

"Hey, Maggie. What's up?"

"Mom got divorce papers in the mail this morning. I thought you'd want to know."

"What?" Pete reeled backward, anger raging inside him. His dad had filed for divorce? Of all the selfish, jackass things . . . His mom had stuck with him through thick and thin, and there had been a lot of thin, and this was how he repaid her loyalty?

"Yep. She's pretty upset." And by the sound of it, Maggie was too.

"I'm off today. I'll go over and see her."

"That would be great. I've got art camp this afternoon with the fourth graders so I'm busy until dinnertime."

"I'm on my way."

Pete left Timber in the kitchen and drove straight to his mom's house. She opened the door wearing an apron and with flour clinging to her fingers. She'd been baking.

He nodded toward the kitchen. "Want some help?"

"Sure. I was just making a batch of banana bread. It always was your father's favorite."

"That's a little masochistic, isn't it, Mom?"

Her gray eyes grew misty. "I'll go visit him tomorrow and get this all sorted out."

"Sorted out? Mom, he filed for divorce. I think that's pretty clear-cut."

"Well it's not. We haven't even discussed it yet. He's hardly in a position to be making life decisions right now."

Pete raked a hand through his hair. "I can't believe you're defending him! This is so typical."

"And you've always been too hard on him." She brushed away a tear. "He has a disease, Peter. Sometimes it gets the better of him."

"He killed Troy Hill."

"And he will have that on his conscience for the rest of his life. He's paying for his sins. When's the last time you visited him?"

"It's been a while," he admitted. Truthfully, he hadn't been able to bring himself to visit his father behind bars. He couldn't bear the sight of him there, knowing what he'd done and the role Pete had played in it.

"You should go. He's a different man. You'll see."

* * *

Olivia drove home from the thrift shop with her head in the clouds. The job was hers. She started on Monday. Regular, dependable hours. The salary was nothing to celebrate, but at least she was no longer dependent on tips to pay her bills. And she would enjoy helping people find new love for older things. It wasn't a career, but it was a step up from what she'd left behind, and that would do for now.

She fist-pumped the roof of the Prius. Then she dialed Pete. "I got the job."

"That's fantastic." The sound of his voice sent the best kind of chills down her spine. "Can I take you to dinner to celebrate?"

"You took me to dinner last night," she reminded him.

"You're good company. And this definitely deserves celebrating."

And those chills turned to heat. "Twist my arm, why don't you? I'm on my way home now, so stop by whenever."

"I'll be there in half an hour."

She went inside and hugged Bailey, then took her for a quick walk. She went upstairs and changed into a pink dress and boots. She even added a little bit of shimmer to her makeup.

She *did* feel like celebrating tonight. Maybe she'd even have champagne.

Pete knocked on the door just as she spritzed some rose essence on her neck. She hurried down the stairs to let him in.

"Wow." His gaze drifted from her eyes to her toes, lingering everywhere in between. He swallowed hard. "You look stunning."

"Thanks." She stepped back to invite him in. He wore dark jeans and a gray Henley shirt, and he was pretty much the handsomest thing she'd ever seen. God, she loved him. She was so filled with emotion tonight that it was all she could do not to blurt those words out right here in her entrance hall.

"So where do you want to go?"

"Anywhere." Anywhere with him.

In the end, they went to Mikoto's, where she had vegetarian sushi and he had the real thing. Then they took a bottle of champagne and a bag of chocolate truffles and drove out to Jordan Lake to have a romantic picnic under the stars.

She spread a blanket across the ground while he brought out a second one to wrap around their legs. Now that the sun had set, the chill in the air was headed toward flat out cold. Olivia lay on her back on the blanket, staring up at the stars. Behind her, Pete popped the cork on the bottle of champagne.

"I'm probably the first person ever to celebrate a job at a thrift store with champagne."

"And that is one of my favorite things about you." He sat next to her, two plastic cups fizzing with champagne in his hands. "You never do what's expected."

"Thanks, I think." She sat up and took one of the cups from him.

He tapped his cup to hers. "To your new job."

"To my new job." She took a long sip, letting the champagne tickle her tongue. "It'll be fun helping people find treasures in what someone else gave away. It's right up my alley. Plus regular hours."

"There's a lot to be said for regular hours." There was humor in Pete's voice. "And I agree. This job suits you."

"For now," she clarified.

"For now. And you'll figure out the forever part soon. I know you will."

"Thanks for the vote of confidence." She rested her head on his shoulder and drained her cup of champagne. "This is maybe the most romantic thing anyone's ever done for me."

His arm tightened around her. "Maybe you should raise your standards."

"Maybe."

He lifted the bottle, and she held her cup out for him to refill it. Then they opened the bag of truffles. She bit into one and let out a little moan of pleasure. Possibly she was already tipsy from the champagne. Possibly she didn't need to raise her standards at all, because she'd already achieved nirvana.

What could top this?

She lay back on the blanket, staring into the depths of the universe above. The stars winked down at her, crystal clear here away from the lights of the city. A shooting star zipped across the sky, and she squeezed her eyes shut.

I wish I could be this happy forever.

She opened her eyes and looked over at Pete. He lay beside her, also gazing up into space. In the dark, she could make out only his profile and the glitter of his eyes.

"You make me happy," she said with a sigh. The champagne warmed her belly and sent a happy haze through her system.

He turned his head to stare at her in the darkness. "I don't think anyone's told me that before."

"Then maybe you need to raise *your* standards."

He didn't say anything to that, but he took her hand in the darkness. And when the next shooting star blazed across the heavens, she wished Pete could be her happy-ever-after.

"I didn't think my night would end like this," he said finally.

"Rough day?"

"My dad filed for divorce."

"Really?" She absorbed that for a minute through her champagne fog. "Is that good or bad?"

"I don't know." He was silent for a long minute, and she thought the topic had closed. Actually, she was surprised he'd brought it up at all. It said something, a lot really, that he was willing to talk about his personal life with her. "Mom's upset. I hate him for putting her through this. He's the fuck-up. It should be her decision to leave. Not his."

"Would she have? Ever?"

He let out a rough sound. "Probably not."

"Do you visit him?"

There was a twinge of guilt in his voice when he answered. "I haven't seen him since he was arrested."

"Do you think you should?"

"I don't know."

"It might help you come to terms with everything that's happened." She took his hand in the darkness.

"Might."

"Wanna tell me about it? I'm a pretty good listener." She gave his fingers a squeeze.

"I told you. He killed a man."

"And I'm guessing it wasn't quite as simple as that."

"He got high and drove. He might as well have played with a loaded gun."

"But he didn't. And maybe he feels terrible about what happened."

"He damn well should."

She heard the hurt in his voice. "Yes, he should. But drug addiction is a disease. He did a stupid, horrible thing, but it doesn't mean you can't still love him."

"It's not that simple."

"Not many things in life are."

* * *

Pete couldn't explain why he was still talking. Lying there in the dark, side by side, was something like sitting in a confessional. He couldn't see her, couldn't look into her eyes. And so he spilled his secrets into the night. "Four years ago, my dad turned over a new leaf. Cleaned up his act. He was a good husband, a good father. We were already grown at that point, but he seemed to really have his act together."

He paused. Olivia squeezed his hand in the darkness. She was right. She was a damn good listener. Maybe it was true what they said: clearing your conscience was good for the soul.

"For a year, he was the husband and father we'd always wanted him to be. Then he got arrested on an old charge. They'd finally run some prints on an old drug bust and linked him to the case.

"I testified on his behalf at the trial. I told them the man who'd once bought and sold crack on Cassidy Street didn't exist anymore. My father deserved a second chance. They let him go with probation. Two months later, he got high and killed Troy Hill."

Olivia sucked in a breath. "Oh—"

"Yes, Tamara's husband. Zach's dad. My father destroyed that family."

She moved closer to him on the blanket, her body nestled against his. "Zach's on the soccer team you coach."

"Yeah."

"And you blame yourself for what happened. Because you testified." She laid it out for him the way she was so good at.

"If I hadn't testified, he'd have gone to jail. Troy Hill would still be alive."

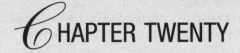

CHAPTER TWENTY

Olivia lay next to him in the darkness. They polished off the bottle of champagne, ate way too much chocolate, and shared more personal stuff than she'd ever dared hope for. It was a terrible weight of guilt he carried, blaming himself for Troy Hill's death.

He had to find a way out from under it before it crushed him.

The champagne had made her all warm and fuzzy so she ignored the little warning bells clanging in her head. Maybe Pete had bigger demons than she'd realized, but he was far from a lost cause.

And when he dropped her at her house and went home with Timber, she refused to read anything into that either. Because they didn't live together. It was perfectly fine for him to sleep at his place while she stayed at hers.

She woke the next morning with Hallie sprawled across her face. The kitten had grown exponentially since

Olivia took her in. At her last checkup, she had tripled in size from one pound to three.

As Olivia shifted beneath her, Hallie stretched, purring loudly into her ear.

"Hard to believe you used to be feral," she said as she rubbed the kitten. Hallie bit her finger, then hopped down and headed for the bathroom, where her food bowl was.

Olivia rolled over and went back to sleep. She woke again around nine. It was one of her last mornings to sleep in. Tomorrow she'd be up early for the rally she'd planned outside Town Hall. And on Monday she'd be starting her new job at the thrift shop.

After a lazy start to the day, she got up, took Bailey for a walk, and headed out to MacArthur Park to meditate for a little while. To center herself before life got busy.

She'd just settled on her blanket beneath the pecan tree when her cell phone rang. Pete. His personal line, not his work phone. And that funny little flutter in her chest must have been her heart cheering in anticipation of hearing his voice.

"What's this I hear about a protest outside Town Hall tomorrow?" he asked.

"I told you about it earlier this week." She heard the rebuke in his voice. It really was a pain in the butt sometimes dating a cop. "I'm tired of being brushed aside. It's time for the town to realize what's going on at Halverson and do something about it."

He made a sound of frustration. "The sheriff asked for extra deputies to be on duty to keep things under control."

"Well that's silly. We aren't going to cause any trouble."

"These things rarely go as planned." He still sounded annoyed.

And that was starting to piss her off. "On the contrary, I've protested several times, and we've never caused any trouble. I know what I'm doing."

"Don't make me arrest you again," he warned.

"I won't."

She hung up completely furious. Her pulse pounded, and she had the strong urge to hurl her phone as far as it would go down the hill before her. But that would only break it, and she couldn't afford a replacement. And she'd come here to meditate, after all.

Tricky thing, meditating while pissed off.

Even trickier holding onto her anger because, if she let it go, she just might cry. And she was *not* going to cry. Nor was she going to drive across town and strangle Pete for being such a pain in the ass, because then he'd get his wish to arrest her again.

Argh.

She gave in to the need to stomp her feet against the cold ground beneath her. Then she closed her eyes, took a deep breath, and started at her toes.

Thirty minutes later, she was calm and in control. Ready to take on whatever came her way.

Starting with tomorrow's protest outside Town Hall.

* * *

Olivia checked her appearance one last time in the mirror. Her hair was blown straight, her makeup polished yet understated. She'd chosen a blue corduroy pea coat to go over her sweater and jeans. Like it or not, she was the face of Citizens Against Halverson Foods, and she'd likely be on camera today.

The doorbell rang, and she hurried downstairs to answer it.

"Ready to kick some politician butt?" Merry held up a hot pink sign that read *Dogwood Doesn't Stand for Animal Abuse*.

"Thank you so much for coming with me." Olivia motioned her inside. "I think we're going to have a great turnout today. Over three hundred people RSVPed on Facebook."

"I've got to hand it to you, Olivia. You are good at what you do."

She shrugged. "I try."

"Really," Merry said. "Donations to Triangle Boxer Rescue are through the roof since you took over our social media accounts. I hope today gives you a big push in your battle against Halverson."

"I just want to quit being shoved under the rug. I want people to know what's happening and hold them accountable for the conditions at their plant here in Dogwood."

"What happened to having the place shut down?" Merry asked as she stooped to pet Bailey, who was dancing around her, begging for attention.

Olivia thought of Pete and how he'd helped her adjust her expectations. "I realized that wasn't realistic. Halverson Foods is a nationwide company, and their plant in Dogwood provides a lot of jobs. It's not getting shut down, and even if it did, those chickens would still get slaughtered somewhere else. What I need to do is get them to revamp their workplace practices. They can slaughter chickens without abusing them."

"That's very mature of you."

"I have my moments." Actually Olivia felt like she'd

done a lot of growing up in the last month or so. She was not the same girl who'd drunkenly spray-painted that chicken factory on her birthday.

"You've always had your moments," Merry said. "The difference is that now you're starting to believe in yourself."

"What?" Olivia turned, *Stop Halverson Chicken Abuse* sign clutched in her hands.

"You're a star, Olivia. The only person who thinks you're a screwup is you."

"Well, I—" She cut herself off, because it had been on the tip of her tongue to argue that she *was* a screwup. "Maybe there's hope for me yet."

Merry put a hand on her shoulder. "Oodles of it."

"All right then. Let's go kick some butt." She put Bailey in her crate, grabbed the box of pamphlets she'd had printed, and led the way to her car. It was just past nine o'clock. The protest didn't start until ten, but she wanted to be there early since this was her brainchild.

She drove downtown and parked in the public lot near the sheriff's office, then she and Merry walked to Town Hall. The deputies had put out metal barricades in anticipation of the crowd, keeping them back from the street and away from the entrance.

She and Merry took their places right up front, and soon their supporters started trickling in. Terence, Kristi, and various other members of Citizens Against Halverson Foods filled the area. They each took a stack of pamphlets, passing them out to everyone who walked past.

Several of Dogwood's finest stood nearby, keeping watch, but this was as peaceful as a protest could be. Olivia and the other protesters held up their signs, passed out pamphlets, and chanted various catchy phrases like "Treat them with respect" and "Down with abuse in Dogwood."

"Will Pete be here?" Merry asked.

"Not on this side of the fence. He's working today."

"Is he working the protest?"

Olivia wished she knew. "I don't think so. He'll probably keep his distance if he can. He was not terribly pleased I'm doing this."

Merry pursed her lips. "Puts him in kind of an awkward situation, I guess."

As pissed as Olivia was about it, Merry was probably right. No matter his personal opinion on her actions, it would be awkward for him to work crowd control at a protest with his girlfriend standing behind the picket lines.

Around ten thirty, Olivia felt someone tap her on the shoulder. She turned to find Pete's sister Maggie standing there, sign in hand.

"Maggie, hi! I didn't expect to see you here today."

Maggie smiled sheepishly. "It sounded kind of fun. I've never protested anything before."

"This is my friend Merry Atwater." Olivia turned to Merry. "Merry, this is Pete's sister, Maggie."

Merry's eyebrows raised. "Nice to meet you, Maggie."

"You too," Maggie said. She turned to Olivia. "After we met the other day, I looked up your website. I was pretty grossed out by what Halverson is doing."

Olivia thought pushing her brother's buttons might be part of the reason Maggie was here too, but either way, she was glad for the company. "Shouldn't you be at work?"

Maggie shook her head. "It just so happens today is a

teacher work day. I'll stop by this afternoon, but I'm the art teacher so I don't have as much lesson planning to do as the primary teachers."

"Well, we're so glad you're here."

Maggie turned out to be quite an asset too. She knew a lot of people in town and handed out a lot of pamphlets. Around eleven, Diana Robbins from Channel Two news arrived with her film crew. They shot some footage of the protest, and then Diana interviewed Olivia.

"So this is just the latest battle in your war against Halverson Foods," Diana said.

Olivia nodded. "Changes need to be made. The chickens inside that factory are being beaten and subjected to other horrible forms of abuse before they're slaughtered. All living beings deserve respect and dignity, even if their purpose in life is to feed us."

"But nothing's been done."

Olivia shook her head. "No. We have undercover video showing the abuse going on in there, and still no charges were filed."

"You were in fact arrested for vandalizing their factory last month," Diana said.

"Yes I was. I made a bad decision, let my emotions get ahead of my better judgment. I broke the law, and I've suffered the consequences. I was arrested, and I'm serving my community service hours. Halverson Foods is breaking the law, and no one is holding them accountable."

When the protest ended just past noon, Olivia felt euphoric. They'd made a big splash, passed out over three hundred pamphlets, and secured another eye-catching segment on the news. She'd been checking the Facebook page from her phone, and already she was up over fifty new "likes."

To celebrate, she, Merry, and Maggie walked down Main Street to Red Heels, her favorite martini bar and site of many a girls' night out. They ordered a table full of vegetarian appetizers and a round of martinis.

"To Olivia." Merry lifted her glass in a toast. "You rocked that protest today. I hope it gives you the leverage you need."

"Thanks." She took a sip of her strawberry martini and sighed. It had gone well.

Maggie grinned. "Maybe I should hang out with you guys more often."

"You totally should." Merry nodded wisely. "We have a lot of fun. You like dogs?"

"I love dogs."

Olivia brightened. "Want one? I bet you'd love Bailey."

"Who's Bailey?" Maggie asked.

"She's my foster dog. Merry runs Triangle Boxer Rescue, and I foster for her."

"Well I have thought about getting a dog," Maggie said. "Maybe I'll come over and meet Bailey sometime."

"Or if you're not ready to adopt, we can always use more foster homes." Merry waved her glass in Maggie's direction.

"I'll think about it."

"Speaking of foster homes, I volunteered at the women's shelter the other day, and the director, Nancy Sheerin, mentioned that she'd been looking for an animal rescue who could help with families who have pets. Animals aren't allowed in the shelter, and a lot of families have to leave their pets behind."

Merry blanched. "That's horrible. Why doesn't she allow pets?"

Olivia rolled her eyes. "She saves *people*, Merry. Women and children. And she wants to find a way to help their pets too."

Maggie swirled her martini. "Nancy is amazing. Did Pete tell you we stayed there once?"

Olivia felt an uncomfortable pinch in her chest. "Sort of."

"Sign me up," Maggie said. "I'd keep someone's pet for them while they stay there."

"Really?" Olivia sat up straighter in her chair. "Me too. Let's do it."

They toasted their decision with a second round of martinis as they munched their way through vegetable spring rolls, stuffed mushrooms, edamame, and mozzarella sticks.

"Pete didn't bring you to supper last night," Maggie commented, as she popped another mushroom into her mouth.

"I moved back home a few days ago." Olivia tried to dull the sting by downing the last of her martini. It didn't work.

"Well Mom and I would love to see you next Thursday, if my brother's not too pigheaded to invite you."

"I don't think he meant to bring me last week," Olivia confessed.

Maggie scrunched her nose. "Maybe he didn't, but you're the first girl he's brought home since Rina. That means something, whether he knows it or not. So don't give up on him. Sometimes he can be a little slow on the uptake when it comes to matters of the heart."

Olivia blew out a shaky breath. "I won't give up on him."

                              * * *

Pete felt his jaw drop as he watched the news coverage of the protest. His sister was standing right next to Olivia on the picket line.

What in the world?

He dialed Maggie.

"You saw the news," she said with a giggle when she answered.

"Yeah, I saw it. Why were you on it?"

"Because it was fun."

"Fun?" Pete squeezed his neck. His sister was starting to sound an awful lot like Olivia, and he wasn't sure at all how he felt about that.

"I like your girlfriend. We made plans to hang out again this weekend. You'd better bring her to dinner next week. Gotta run!" Maggie hung up with a solid click.

Pete just sat there staring at his phone in disbelief. Then he walked outside to his Forester and drove across town to Olivia's house.

She greeted him at the front door, wearing jeans and a loose sweatshirt. "I'm still a little bit pissed at you, you know."

Yeah, he'd been a total ass on the phone yesterday. The sheriff had read him the riot act when he'd gotten wind of their relationship, and Pete had taken it out on her. "I'm sorry I gave you a hard time about the protest."

She took a step back. "Really?"

"Really." He narrowed his eyes. "You're corrupting my sister now?"

She gave him a wry smile. "I had nothing to do with that. I think Maggie has a bit of a wild streak in her."

She did, at that. He followed Olivia inside. "I'm glad it went well."

"Thanks. I know I put you in an awkward situation, and I hate that, but I can't change who I am."

"And you shouldn't have to." Pete didn't like it either, didn't like the pressure Linburgh had put on him about it or the way the sheriff talked about Olivia and her fellow protesters. The truth was, they had all behaved perfectly. Not a single person had broken the law or even stepped out of line.

And he'd probably lost his shot at detective for defending her. He'd do it again in a heartbeat. He pulled her against him and stood there for a long minute just absorbing the feel of her in his arms, inhaling her scent, fantasizing about tents and wildflowers and champagne under the stars.

She wound her arms behind his neck and pressed her cheek to his. "I'm sorry that me-being-me makes things awkward for you at work."

"You should never apologize for being yourself." Because she was amazing, the most amazing woman he'd ever met. And he should have broken things off with her long before they got to this point. "But in the long run, it won't matter anyway."

"Why?" She pulled back and stared into his eyes. Neither of them said a word for a long minute, but she was good at reading him. She always had been. And whatever she saw, she didn't like. "Because you and I are only short-term?"

He looked away. Bailey watched them from the doorway. She wiggled her tail stub hopefully. There was no way out of this for him without hurting Olivia. "I told you I can't commit to anything more than that."

"And you honestly think that's all we have going on here?"

Not even close. "Liv—"

To his horror, tears pooled in her eyes. "You're a jackass, Pete Sampson."

Yeah, he was a jackass. Because he'd known better than to lead her on the way he had. He'd treated her like this was something special, because she *was* special. So damn special. "You're right. I am. I wish I could give you all the things you want, but I can't."

"That's where you're wrong." She swiped a tear from her cheek. "All I want is you. And you could. You did."

"It's not that simple."

Her nostrils flared. "Sure it is. We need each other. We're good together. So why won't you give us a chance?"

"I—" He clenched her hands in his. How did she always manage to muddle him up until he'd forgotten all the reasons he shouldn't be with her?

Her eyes softened. "Is it your ex-wife?"

No. He couldn't pin this on Rina. "Leave her out of this. My fuck ups are my own."

She lifted her chin. "Then don't fuck this up."

"I already have." He shoved his hands into his pockets to keep from reaching for her again. "I'm sorry, Liv."

"So you're just going to walk away?"

"It's the right thing to do."

She shook her head, then planted her fists against his chest and pushed him backward out her front door. "Wrong again. If you ever come to your senses, you know where to find me."

The door closed behind him with a solid thunk, and he was left with the sinking feeling that he'd just made a stupid, horrible mistake. Maybe the worst mistake in his entire life.

CHAPTER TWENTY-ONE

After he left, Olivia indulged herself in a good cry. As hurt as she was, she was mostly mad at herself. She ought to have learned her lesson by now where men were concerned. Why did she always fight the losing battles?

But even if she was destined for a lifetime of heartbreak with the men in her life, she was *not* losing her war against Halverson. If she kept fighting and making noise for long enough, sooner or later, someone would listen.

And she was really good at making noise.

Even when her heart was broken.

She went upstairs and splashed cold water on her face, then freshened up her makeup. She'd drive out to MacArthur Park and meditate until she'd made peace with things. Her phone had been dinging like crazy in her purse since before Pete left, one notification after the next.

So many people showing their support after the protest this morning. It really had gone well, and the news segment was the icing on the cake. She was going to ride this momentum all the way to the finish line.

She pulled her phone out to have a quick look. She could use some warm and fuzzies right about now.

What in the world? This is very disappointing to hear, the most recent comment said.

Traitor! We believed in you.

The corporate buck wins again. Sad. Sad indeed.

Olivia frowned. What in the world? The recent flurry of comments all stemmed from a posting two hours ago, which was weird because she hadn't posted since lunchtime...

She thumbed furiously to the original post.

After much time and consideration, I've decided to end my efforts against Halverson Foods. It was brought to my attention that some of my findings were inaccurate, and I've realized I was wrong to pursue these actions against them...

It went on for three paragraphs, detailing how she'd come to this decision, how she'd been mistaken in accusing Halverson Foods of animal cruelty, and how the Citizens Against Halverson Foods website and Facebook group would be closing shortly.

And *what the actual fuck*...she hadn't written a word of it.

She'd been hacked. And not just any old hacking. No, this person hadn't posted porn all over her Facebook page or sent spam emails to her contact list. This was personal This was the work of whoever had been trying to shut her up since the vandalism started last month.

Already sick to her stomach, she clicked on her website. It was gone. Every last picture and blog post. In its place was a message reiterating what had been posted on her Facebook page.

Hands shaking, she got in her car and drove to the sheriff's office. Pete wasn't there, of course, but she didn't want to see him anyway. Instead she headed straight for Deputy Hartzler's desk.

"Miss Bennett," he said with a curt nod.

"I've been vandalized again, but this time it's my website and Facebook page."

"Ma'am, we don't handle cyber crimes. If someone hacked your website, you'll want to report it to the cyber crimes division at the SBI, but unless they're peddling kiddie porn or something, it's unlikely they'll be able to do anything about it."

"But—" She stopped herself and sucked in a deep, calming breath. "What's the SBI?"

"The state bureau of investigation. People's Facebook pages get hacked all the time, unfortunately. You'll want to change your password and set up stronger security checks. A buddy of mine is a real whiz at setting up firewalls. I could give you his number if you're interested."

"Um, I guess. But this wasn't just any old hack. They posted a message saying I was ending my efforts against Halverson Foods."

"Reckon you've made some enemies around town. I'll make a note in your file about it. Wish I could do more to help you, Miss Bennett, but it's outside my jurisdiction."

Fuming mad—and with the name of Hartzler's computer geek friend tucked away in her purse—Olivia stomped out of the sheriff's office. Today had gone from awesome to crap in the space of an hour.

She went home and changed her Facebook password,

then deleted the offending message and posted one instead saying that she'd been hacked, Citizens Against Halverson Foods wasn't going anywhere, and that, on the contrary, her efforts were stronger than ever.

Unfortunately things weren't quite as simple for her website. After a lengthy phone conversation with her web host, she found out that her blog posts weren't backed up anywhere—that cost extra, and she hadn't sprung for the extra cost when she opened her account. So while she was able to default back to the basic layout of her website, everything she'd blogged about for the last two years had been lost.

Someone was going to pay for this. And one way or another, Halverson Foods was going down.

* * *

"Have you talked to Olivia yet today?" Maggie asked.

Pete frowned into the phone. "No, why?"

"I'll let her tell you. Call her." The line clicked, and she was gone.

Pete swore at the all-too-familiar prickle of awareness that snaked its way up his spine at the mention of Olivia's name. He'd spent Saturday morning burying himself in work that had nothing to do with her or Halverson Foods, desperate to get his head back on straight. To quit thinking about her. To ease the pain that had been in his chest ever since she'd pushed him out the front door of her house last night.

But what did Maggie mean? Had something happened?

He dialed Olivia. "Something going on?" he asked when she answered.

She made a sound that vaguely resembled a dog growling. "Nothing that concerns you. I've already talked to Deputy Hartzler."

He sat up straighter in his seat. "Tell me."

"My website was hacked. But apparently that's not your jurisdiction."

"Hacked?"

She sighed into the phone. "Someone hacked my website and Facebook page with a message that said I'd been wrong about Halverson, they weren't evil after all, and I'd be shutting down Citizens Against Halverson Foods."

"That's not a random hack." His mind was churning over this latest bit of information. Who would have done that? Frat boys? Why? As far as he could tell, they had no motive to mess with her website.

"Nope. Lucky me. Well it won't work. I generated a lot of positive press for our efforts yesterday."

"This doesn't make sense."

"Of course it does," she said. "I obviously pissed off someone at Halverson, and they hired someone to hack my website."

"Olivia—" He didn't like anything about this, not one damn bit. This felt personal, and that sent all his protective instincts into overdrive.

"Just don't. You're not even assigned to this case, and it has nothing to do with the fact that you and I are no longer a thing, so really, we have no reason to even be talking about it. You shouldn't have called."

He scrubbed a hand over his face and swore. "I still care about you, okay? And I care about this case. I don't want to see you hurt."

She sucked in a breath but said nothing.

"I want to see those assholes locked up as much as you do," he said. "And I need to know that you're safe. So I'm still involved whether you like it or not."

"Fine," she said. "And when you're ready to take a look at why you're really still involved in this case, let me know."

He couldn't answer that one. He had feelings for her, feelings that went much deeper than sex. He felt empty and restless without her, but it didn't—couldn't—change anything.

Being married to Rina had been a wakeup call. They'd been madly in love when they eloped the summer after high school graduation. So friggin' happy those first few years. Poor as dirt, but they'd put themselves through college and survived on ramen noodles and sheer determination.

Things were still good when he started as a rookie in the sheriff's office. But it hadn't been long before Rina started complaining about the hours, the danger, how emotionally unavailable he was. And after his father's arrest, things had really gone to hell. There'd been so much yelling, so much anger and resentment.

Sometimes it was hard to remember how young and in love they'd once been.

His job, his lifestyle, was not suited to marriage. And Rina was right—he was emotionally unavailable. Half the time he didn't even know what the hell he was feeling, let alone try to explain himself to someone else. Olivia lived, breathed, *pulsed* with emotion. She was passionate and caring and never afraid to take a risk.

He needed to see her through this mess with Halverson, but that had to be the end of it. He couldn't offer her the life she wanted, the life she deserved.

Still brooding over past mistakes, Pete finished out his shift and then, instead of pointing his cruiser toward home, he got on the highway, headed toward the state penitentiary.

Toward his father.

At the desk, he surrendered his weapon. He was taken to a small visitation room outfitted with a gray table and two chairs, whitewashed by the fluorescent lights above. He sat there for a while, long enough to question what the hell he was doing here. Why now, of all times, was he finally visiting his father in jail?

The door clanged open, and his dad shuffled in, escorted by a guard. He looked thinner, older, than he had three years ago. But his dark eyes were still bright, and they were fixed on Pete's with surprise and maybe even relief.

"Pete," he said. "When they said I had a visitor, I thought it would be your mother."

"It's me." Pete stood, and the two men stared at each other in awkward silence.

"I'll be right outside. Knock on the door when you're ready to leave," the guard said.

"Thank you," Pete answered.

"You look good, son. How have you been?" His dad sat at the table.

Pete sat in the chair across from him. "You know why I'm here."

His dad nodded. "Because I filed for divorce from your mother."

Pete's hands fisted beneath the table. "After all you've put her through, and she stood by you through all of it, this is how you repay her?"

His dad shook his head, his expression pinched. "I did it for her, you know."

Anger blurred his vision. "How so, Dad? How does this help her? You haven't had to see how miserable she is this week, how she still defends you, even now. It's pathetic."

"Because I'm in here, and she's out there. Because she deserves better." His dad's weary eyes glistened with tears. "Because she was never going to leave me on her own."

Pete sat there, stunned. His dad's words were all true. His mom did deserve better. She deserved to start living her life again and maybe even find a man who could love her the right way, where she wouldn't play second-string mistress to drugs and booze.

"I'm sorry for the way I was when you were growing up. I wish I could say I tried to be there for you, but it's not true." He hung his head. "I cared more about where to get my next fix than I did about my own family. I was addicted, but that's no excuse. A stronger man would have done better."

Pete watched him in silence. His dad had apologized for everything four years ago, when he'd turned himself around for that briefest of times. "I don't know how to respond to that, Dad."

His dad nodded. "That's fair. And whatever you're feeling toward me, I deserve it. I was an asshole, plain and simple. I screwed up all of your lives. Sitting in here day after day has given me a lot of time to think." He grimaced. "A lot of *sober* time to sit and think."

"Jail tends to do that," Pete said.

"I killed a man. I have to live with that for the rest of

my life. But I can set your mother free from the weight of my mistakes. Maybe she'll even start over again, find someone new." He looked pained at the thought.

"Jesus." Pete looked away.

"I still love her, you know. I've always loved her. So next time you see her, tell her not to fight the divorce, okay? She needs to get on with her life."

"I'll tell her," Pete said.

"You're a good man, Pete. You're a stronger man than I am. You won't repeat my mistakes. You'll make a lucky woman very happy someday. I know it."

* * *

Olivia blinked and rubbed her eyes because they had to be playing tricks on her. Her Facebook page and website were gone. Deleted. Deactivated. Whatever she wanted to call it, they no longer existed.

How could that happen?

Obviously she sucked at password protection. And now everything she'd worked so hard to create was gone. Not just her blog posts, but her followers— everyone who'd subscribed to or "liked" her page. All the people she'd reached yesterday at the protest...if they'd gone home and looked up the links on the pamphlet she'd handed out, they'd seen either the message saying she'd given up the fight and Halverson wasn't so bad after all or nothing but broken links.

This was so much worse than eggs or spray paint on the front of her house. This was a disaster. And she was heartbroken.

She wasn't giving up. She'd *never* give up. But for the

first time since this whole mess started, she honestly had no idea where to go from here. What came next?

Her cell phone rang, and she fumbled for it in her purse.

"Hi." It was Cara. "Something's wrong with your website."

"I know." Olivia flopped back onto her bed. "I got hacked. Someone posted a message on there yesterday saying that I'd decided to quit fighting Halverson, which I deleted, and so today my pages are just gone."

"Holy crap," Cara said. "They can do that?"

"Halverson's henchmen are apparently a lot more tech savvy than I am."

"Aw, honey. This sucks. Can you get them back?"

Olivia shook her head. "They don't keep backups. I guess that was my job."

"I could have Jason look into it for you, if you want," Cara offered. Her future brother-in-law was quite the cyber sleuth.

"I would appreciate that. The police don't seem to care about website hackings unless it involves something seriously illegal."

"No problem. I'm sure he could track it down. Maybe he could even retrieve your web files for you, who knows."

"That would be awesome. Thank you."

"You got it. Wish I could come visit. I miss you." Cara sounded wistful.

"I miss you too. You're coming down for Christmas, right?"

"Yep. We're spending Thanksgiving here with Matt's family and Christmas in North Carolina."

Olivia smiled. "Good. We're overdue for a girls' night at Red Heels."

Cara laughed. "We certainly are."

Olivia hung up the phone feeling a tiny bit better. Friends had a way of doing that for each other. For a little while, she'd forgotten that it was Saturday night and she was sitting home moping about the fact she'd been dumped by the man she loved yesterday and her entire life's work had just been erased.

And... *oh God*, she was pathetic.

This wouldn't do. She changed into jeans and a sweater, fastened her hair in a messy bun, and freshened her makeup. Maybe she'd go to The Watering Hole and listen to some live music. Maybe she'd go to Jordan Lake and meditate. But she was definitely *not* going to mope around on a Saturday night feeling sorry for herself.

She was halfway down the stairs when she heard someone knocking at the front door. Bailey danced in the entranceway, barking and wiggling her nub, but Olivia didn't share her excitement. She wasn't in the mood to deal with reporters, disgruntled Halverson employees, or anyone else tonight.

She tiptoed to the front door and pressed her eye to the peephole.

Pete stood on the other side.

CHAPTER TWENTY-TWO

$\mathscr{P}$ete stood on Olivia's doorstep, feeling like his heart was going to jump out through his throat. He had no business here, not after the way they'd left things last night. But he missed her, especially tonight when she was sure to be smarting over what had been done to her website.

The door opened, and Olivia stood there, looking at him with eyes not nearly as warm or vibrant as usual. "What are you doing here, Pete?"

Good damn question. Since he had no answer, he pulled her into his arms instead. Then he was kissing her, and his chest loosened for the first time since he'd left here yesterday. She let out a little moan, her hands tangling in his hair as she stumbled backward into her house and kicked the door shut behind them.

She dragged her mouth from his. "This is stupid."

"I know." His arms tightened around her. "I just needed to see you."

"You dumped me, remember?"

He flinched. "Yeah, I remember."

She pulled back and stared at him for a long time in silence, waiting for him to make the next move. He could take it back, tell her he'd made a mistake. But as much as he needed her—and he needed her *so fucking much*—he still couldn't offer her the future she wanted.

She chewed her lip and looked away. "My website is gone."

"What?"

She nodded. "Gone. The Facebook page too."

"The hacker deleted them?"

"Yep."

"Dammit." He pulled her back into his arms.

She sighed against his chest, and the sadness in that one sound stabbed deep into his heart.

"I'm sorry. The sheriff's office has really let you down." He ran his fingers through her hair, burning with the need to find justice for her.

She peeked up at him with a wry smile. "It looks like Halverson Foods might get their wish after all. I've lost all my blog posts and all my followers. There's no recreating that."

"Come on, now. The Olivia I love wouldn't give up, no matter how tough things get." He heard the words leaving his mouth, but his brain was too sluggish to stop them. A hot, prickly sensation came over his face and spread through his chest.

She sucked in a breath, her eyes locked on his. Seconds ticked by, punctuated by the pounding of his heart and the electricity shimmering in the air between them.

It was just a phrase, it doesn't mean . . . but he couldn't say the words out loud.

He cleared his throat. "You'll fight back. Start a new blog, do one of those kick-ass posts you're so good at. Call the news to run a follow-up story about what happened to your last site."

She blinked. "I could do that."

"You will."

"I will," she whispered.

They were still standing in the entrance hall, her arms around his neck, his hands tightly anchored at her waist. She buried her face against his neck. "Stay with me tonight."

"I shouldn't." Because in the long run, he'd only end up hurting her more.

"I don't want to be alone tonight. Please."

"Then you shouldn't be." And he walked with her toward the stairs.

* * *

Olivia woke in her own bed, one arm draped across Pete's chest and a kitten purring in her hair. She shouldn't have asked him to stay, but she didn't regret it either.

The Olivia I love.

Maybe it had been merely a slip of the tongue. Or maybe he did love her. He might not even know it yet. For now, she was going to hold on tight and hope he came to his senses before it was too late.

His cell phone buzzed from the bedside table, reminding him to get up and get ready for work. She gave him a nudge, and he grunted, rolling toward her.

"Hold that thought," she whispered against his lips. "But it's seven."

He groaned and buried his face in her hair. Hallie bopped him on the nose. "Goddamn cat."

"She likes you," Olivia told him.

"Mm hmm." He rolled out of bed and dressed in his clothes from yesterday. Then he bent over the bed and gave her a quick kiss. "I'll call you later."

She nodded.

For a moment, he just stood there, staring at her, guilt heavy in his eyes, so heavy she had to look away. Then he went downstairs and left.

"What are you looking at?" she asked the boxer in the corner.

Bailey gave a dramatic sigh.

"Don't judge," Olivia told her. "Someday you may find yourself in this position with a man. Probably not though, seeing as how you're missing some of your girl parts. What you need is a family."

Merry had already been talking about sending Olivia a new foster dog, since Scooby had been adopted. Olivia had put her off since things had been so crazy, what with losing her job and moving in with Pete. But today was Sunday, which meant she started her new job at the thrift store tomorrow, and things seemed to be back to normal here at home too. So it was probably time to face the inevitable.

Not that she hated fostering. It just didn't bring her the same joy it brought her friends Merry and Cara. Olivia would take a picket line over a foster dog any day.

"You're growing on me though," she told Bailey.

Then she got out of bed, dressed, and put Bailey out back. She hadn't had an accident in over a week now, but Olivia didn't want to push her luck.

She fixed herself a green smoothie and sat in front of her laptop. Today was all about damage control. She needed to get her website back online with a message about what had happened, a scathing blog post that made it clear she refused to be silenced.

Facebook wouldn't be as easy. Sure, she could start a new page. But there was no way to bring back the thousands of people who'd followed the old one.

But as Pete said yesterday, Olivia had never been one to back down from a challenge. And with that thought, she called Channel Two news and left a message for Diana Robbins, the reporter who'd covered the protest on Friday.

Take that, Halverson Foods.

She typed Citizens Against Halverson Foods into Facebook and was told it was already taken. Yeah, it was. *By her.* She growled and punched the couch. But what if, since she had to start over from scratch, she made this bigger than Halverson Foods?

On a whim, she typed in "The Face of Factory Farming," and *ding ding*, she had a new Facebook page. For a cover photo, she uploaded the picture she'd taken of the chicken that had fallen off the Halverson delivery truck the day she'd washed off her graffiti. A worker held the bird by its feet, with a truck full of birds visible behind.

She wrote a post describing her efforts to gain better protections for factory-farmed animals, chickens—and Halverson Foods in particular and then set about creating a brand new website for her project.

Around noon, as she was elbow deep in her return-to-the-web blog post, her phone rang. Olivia didn't recognize the number.

"It's Maggie," Maggie said when she answered. "I got your number from Pete."

"Oh, hi, Maggie. It's great to hear from you."

"I was wondering if you wanted to get lunch?"

"That sounds great." Olivia smiled. She liked Maggie a lot.

"Cool. I'll stop by and pick you up so I can meet your foster dog, if that's okay."

"Sure." Olivia glanced at Bailey, lounging in the sun by the front window. "I'll see you in a little bit."

She hung up the phone and snapped her fingers at Bailey. "Someone's coming over to meet you. Let's get you primped." She brushed the dog's teeth and trimmed her toenails, then gave her an appraising look. "You're cute. I'm not sure if she's actually interested in adopting you, but it never hurts to make a good first impression."

Ten minutes later, the doorbell rang. Bailey barked, dancing in circles in the foyer while she waited for Olivia to open the door.

"Hi." Maggie stood there in a red pea coat and jeans, her dark hair pulled back from her face in a matching clip. She looked down at Bailey. "Oh, you're adorable!"

"Come in." Olivia stepped back, motioning her inside. "This is Bailey."

"How in the world could you not keep her?" Maggie asked. She squatted and rubbed Bailey's chin while the dog wiggled with glee.

"I just treat them like I'm dog sitting. I like them, but they're not mine."

"Hmmm. Interesting." Maggie stood. "I've been wanting to get a dog. Figured I might go by the shelter sometime and check them out. I don't really know breeds."

"You should do that," Olivia said. "I've been volunteering there as part of my community service. They have a lot of great dogs."

"When will you be there next?" Maggie asked.

"This afternoon actually. I'm scheduled to walk dogs from two to four."

Maggie's eyes brightened. "Maybe I'll come with you."

* * *

Pete was winding down an uneventful shift when his phone showed an incoming call from Olivia. His stomach tightened, excitement or dread, he couldn't say. Had something else happened? Or was she just calling to make plans after work?

"Do you know someone named Justin Wendell?" she asked.

"Yes. Why?" Warning bells clanged in his head. There was no good reason for her to know the name of the president of the Omega Chi fraternity.

"He's the one who hacked my website."

"How the hell do you know that?" he demanded.

"A friend of a friend is a private investigator who specializes in cyber stuff. He checked into it for me."

"Fuck." He slammed his fist into the steering wheel.

"So who is he?" she asked.

"I really can't discuss it with you, but since, as you probably know, the information you've gotten isn't admissible in court, he's connected to the fraternity. And I don't want you going anywhere near him. No phone calls, no protests outside the frat house. Are we clear?"

"Don't go all alpha cop on me." Her tone snapped with

irritation. "I don't want to go to his house. I just thought *you* might want to know in case, you know, it helped solve the case."

"Let me call you back." He hung up, an uneasy feeling churning in his gut.

There was no reason for Justin Wendell, or anyone at Omega Chi, to hijack Olivia's website. This had nothing to do with their chicken mascot or any kind of stupid prank. People didn't do shit like that without a motive, and Pete needed to know what it was. Justin's last words had been haunting him ever since he left the frat house.

"Funny thing, you asking about this. I would have figured you guys at the sheriff's office would be thanking us."

At the time, it had made no sense. But now an uncomfortable suspicion had taken hold in his gut. On a hunch, he turned to the laptop in his cruiser and pulled up Linburgh's bio on the sheriff's office's website. Sure enough, he was a Carolina University alumnus and a member of Omega Chi. A search of the fraternity's website listed Donny Linburgh as a longtime supporter.

Funny how Linburgh's name kept popping up where Olivia was concerned, except he didn't think there was anything funny about it. He'd been out to the Halverson plant a number of times and never gotten the prickly feeling he'd felt when he visited the Omega Chi frat house.

His gut said the frat boys had indeed been behind all the vandalism at Olivia's place, but it had little to do with their chicken mascot and everything to do with Sheriff Linburgh. If Pete's gut was right, Linburgh had asked, or even paid, his buddies at Omega Chi to hassle Olivia in an effort to shut her up, all to keep his good favor with Halverson Foods before the election.

And that meant Linburgh had broken the law. He'd dirtied his nose to win the election, that no-good piece of scum. Pete would spend the rest of the day gathering what evidence he could. Tomorrow morning he'd pay a visit to the district attorney's office.

Linburgh wasn't getting away with this. Not on Pete's watch.

* * *

Olivia and Maggie volunteered together until the shelter closed, walking dogs and cleaning out their kennels. Olivia helped another couple pick out a dog to join their family. She'd done it several times now, and while it wasn't part of her duties as a volunteer, no one at the shelter seemed to mind. Plus, it was fun.

"Wow," Maggie said, as they headed for the front door. "That was kind of horrible and awesome at the same time."

Olivia nodded. "It can be hard seeing all the homeless animals, but I like to think of the situations a lot of those dogs came out of, being abused, or starved, or homeless. Now they have kindness, a warm bed, and access to food and water."

"That's true." Maggie opened the passenger door of the Prius.

"It's not for everyone."

"But it doesn't bother you."

Olivia shrugged. "I wouldn't say that. But it's a hell of a lot better than what goes on at the Halverson plant, so that puts it in perspective for me, I guess."

Olivia drove them back to her house, and Maggie played

with Bailey for a bit before going home. Olivia felt twisted in knots inside over her relationship with Pete and his sister. She wanted them both to stay in her life. And yet she feared she was fighting a losing battle.

The next morning, she got up, got dressed, and headed to the Dogwood Thrift Store for her first day of work. The owner, Bruce Henneby, was an older man and not much of a talker. He showed her how to work the register and gave her a rundown on the workings of the store, then retreated to his office in the back.

There was a steady stream of customers throughout the day, and Olivia enjoyed helping them. She rearranged a few displays and dusted off a tray of antique earrings that looked like they hadn't been touched in years. All in all, it was a good day. She'd be happy here until something better came along.

And oh how sick she was of waiting and wondering what that something better would be, in her personal and her professional life. She was ready for all of it, now.

$\mathcal{C}$HAPTER TWENTY-THREE

$\mathcal{P}$ete stepped out of the courthouse and placed his hat on his head. He'd just finished a second day of meetings with the district attorney and his staff. He'd presented a variety of evidence of the sheriff's dirty doings, and the district attorney's office was assembling a team to further investigate.

If it was true, if the sheriff had broken the law to stay in good favor with Halverson Foods ahead of the election, well, at the very least, he needed to be removed from office. He might even face jail time.

Pete had also passed along Olivia's tip about Justin Wendell to a colleague at the SBI. Wendell was an Information Technology major at Carolina U, and if he was already using his skills to break the law, he needed to face charges as well.

When Pete got off work, he headed straight to the rec center to coach the boys' soccer. They'd found their footing together now and worked easily through drills and a practice game. Even Zach seemed to have lost some of his bad attitude.

Pete showered and changed at the rec center, then drove to Olivia's house. He needed to bring her up to date, and he needed to do it in person. But when he got to her house, she wasn't there.

He called her cell. "Where are you?"

"In your living room," she answered, sounding annoyed.

"In my . . . *what*?" He rubbed his brow.

"You gave me a key, once upon a time, and you never asked for it back." The sound of Timber barking carried over the line.

"Okay." He remembered that. Vaguely. "And why are you at my house, exactly?"

"Because I hadn't heard from you, and I want to know what's going on with the case. Two days ago, you said 'let me call you back,' but you never did."

"Well, as it happens, I'm at your house right now," he told her.

"Then come home."

"On my way." He hung up, trying not to feel irrationally turned on by the thought of Olivia lounging on his couch, doing God knew what. And also a little bit pissed that she'd used that key and let herself into his townhouse like this. They weren't even seeing each other anymore, technically. Hell, he had no idea what he and Olivia were doing.

When he got home, he found her with her feet up on the coffee table, brows furrowed, blogging her heart out.

"I gave you that key to use while you were staying here," he said.

She rose from the couch, brown eyes snapping. "Oh,

so I've overstepped the bounds of our dysfunctional relationship. Is that it?"

"I—" He shook his head. It was pointless to argue, not now. Not when he'd been the one to complicate things by showing up on her doorstep the other night after he'd already walked away. "Forget it. Look, I'm sorry I haven't been in touch. I can't discuss the case with you until things are resolved, but I'm pretty sure I know what's going on and who's behind it."

She rolled her eyes. "Duh. Justin Wendell. Which you wouldn't know if I hadn't found it for you."

"Justin was most likely hired by someone else."

Her eyes widened. "Someone at Halverson?"

"I really can't discuss an ongoing case. You're going to have to trust me."

"I do," she said. "Always with police stuff."

But not with her heart, which was smart because he'd probably break it.

* * *

The rest of the week passed uneventfully. Olivia worked days at the thrift store and came home to work on rebuilding her online presence. She'd posted messages on several local Facebook groups inviting people to "like" her new page and had over two thousand followers by Friday, which was a lot, but far fewer than she'd had originally.

Oh well.

If Halverson Foods had hoped to shut her up, they must be sorely disappointed. She taped a follow-up segment for the Channel Two news, talking about how she'd been vandalized and her website hacked. When it aired Friday night, she had a rush of new traffic to her website and Facebook page.

Take that, Halverson Foods.

She wouldn't stop until they faced the music, no matter how long it took or how hard she had to work. She was midway through a new blog post when her phone rang, an unknown number with a 212 area code. Wasn't that New York City? She didn't know anyone in New York.

Frowning, she answered. "Hello?"

"Hi, is this Olivia Bennett?"

"This is Olivia."

"Olivia, this is Jane Samms from the Tri-State Animal Welfare Coalition. You applied earlier this month for a position as our Director of Marketing and Publicity."

Olivia's mouth fell open. She'd completely forgotten about the afternoon she'd applied for a bunch of random animal rights jobs all over the country. "Oh, wow. It's nice to hear from you."

"Your résumé caught our eye so we've been reading up on your efforts there in North Carolina for the last few weeks, and, Olivia, we are more than impressed," Jane said.

"Really?"

"Yes. I'd love to do a phone interview with you, if you're still interested, that is."

"Oh, well yes. Sure." Olivia drew a deep breath. Was this actually happening?

"Great," Jane said. "I'm sure we're both busy people, but since I have you, is now a good time?"

Olivia spent the next hour talking to Jane. They talked about Olivia's efforts against Halverson Foods, her legal background (she'd made it halfway through law school after all), and in depth about her fund-raising and social media experience. Jane wasn't fazed by her recent arrest, and in fact, they shared a laugh about it. It was probably the best, and by far the most interesting, interview she'd ever had.

"Thank you so much for your time today, Olivia."

"You're welcome. It was my pleasure."

"You have a way with people, and with animals too, it would seem," Jane said. "We'd love to have you visit our office here in New York, and if you think it's a good fit, the job is yours."

"Oh, my God." She sank to her knees in the middle of the living room floor.

Jane was still talking, discussing salary and benefits, and Olivia pressed a hand over her mouth. This was the job she'd always dreamed of. A real paying job doing what she loved, advocating for animal rights. She'd be putting all of her talents to work.

And New York? New York! She'd never been, but she'd always wanted to. The big city sounded exciting and terrifying and wonderful.

"I don't know what to say, Jane. Thank you so much. This is absolutely amazing."

"The office is very casual, everyone brings their dogs to work with them. You'd be spending a lot of time networking with local rescues. We run several large benefit events each year that you would be in charge of organizing. And of course social media."

Of course social media. Olivia grinned. "It sounds perfect. I do need to think about the logistics of it, moving to New York."

"Absolutely. Take the weekend to think it over, and let me know on Monday if you'd like to come up and visit us or if you have any other questions I could answer for you. We'd be honored to have you join our team."

Olivia hung up the phone in a daze. She jumped up and hugged Bailey, then danced in a circle around the living room.

Her dream job. This was it!

Reality started to filter through her euphoria, and she sank back down on the carpet. Her friends, her family. Pete. She had so much here in North Carolina. Could she leave it all behind to chase her dreams in the Big Apple?

Could she convince Pete to take a leap of faith and follow her to New York?

* * *

Olivia bellied up to the bar with a cold beer. Beside her, Merry took a long drink from her own Blue Moon.

"So what is your gut telling you?" Merry asked.

Confused and conflicted and with Pete working late again on whatever secret thing he was doing to close her vandalism case, Olivia had turned to Merry for help. "My gut says this is the dream job I've been waiting for. It's perfect. It's that mythical paying job in animal rescue." She sipped from her beer. Behind them, Merry's dad's band played bluegrass over the noise of the bar.

"How's the money?"

"About what you'd expect when working for a non-profit: not great. But neither you or I have ever been in it for the money."

Merry nodded. "True. So let's talk about the real issue here: you moving to New York."

"Yeah." Olivia gulped beer and closed her eyes. "Me moving to New York."

"I object vehemently on the grounds that Cara moved to Massachusetts earlier this year, and if you leave too, I'll be seriously out of friends. So there, you can't go." Merry set her mug down with a solid clunk.

It reverberated through Olivia's chest, compounding the ache that had been there since she got off the phone with Jane. She'd make new friends in New York, but... "I know. I don't want to leave you either."

"Or Pete," Merry said.

She stared into the amber depths of her beer. "Or Pete."

"Where do things stand with you two right now?"

"I'm in love with him." A lump rose in her throat, and she swallowed painfully.

"Oh, honey." Merry touched her shoulder. "Did you tell him?"

She shook her head. "But I will, before I go. If I leave. I want him to come with me. Or I'd stay if he'd fight for me."

"You'd give up your dream job for him?"

Olivia scoffed. "Not to stay home barefoot and pregnant. But to stay here in his hometown, in *my* hometown? I would. If he asked me to."

Merry stared pensively into her beer. "Hmm. I hope he's man enough to ask."

"Me too." And she was terrified that he wasn't. "And if he's not, then maybe New York will be the fresh break I need to get over him."

"No offense, but I don't quite see you as a city girl."

"I've lived in Dogwood my whole life. The city always sounded exciting though. There'd be so many other vegetarian crunchies like me. I could see myself doing it."

"But what about hiking? Meditating? You love to be outside in nature."

"I hear Central Park is nice." She polished off her beer and signaled the bartender for another.

"It is nice. I visited one summer during college," Merry said.

"So what should I do?" Olivia heard the note of desperation in her voice.

"Well, first you have to have a serious talk with Pete. But ultimately you have to follow your heart, wherever that leads you."

And yet, Olivia had a sinking feeling she'd be leaving her heart behind with Pete here in Dogwood. He called just before she and Merry left The Watering Hole, and her heart jumped into her throat.

"Where are you?" he asked.

"At The Watering Hole with Merry."

"I need to see you."

"Well, Merry and I rode over together, so I could have her drop me off at your place, if you want, when we leave."

"I'll come pick you up." He sounded intense, even more intense than usual, and it sent a little zing up her spine.

She hung up and looked at Merry. "Now or never, right?"

Merry squeezed her shoulder. "Go for it, girlfriend. He'd be stupid to let you go."

Ten minutes later, Pete strode into the bar. He'd obviously been home to change since work and now wore a navy blue Henley shirt and jeans. "Hey." He bent to give her a quick kiss.

"Hey yourself." She closed her eyes and inhaled his scent, no longer cinnamon but fresh and minty like after-shave.

He nodded toward her friend. "Merry."

"Hi, Pete."

"You ready?" he asked Olivia.

"Yes. Bye, Merry. Thanks for the ride, and the chat."

Merry raised her beer in Olivia's direction. "Anytime. Good luck."

"Thanks." She hooked her arm in Pete's and followed him out to his SUV, parked around the corner on Pine Street. "You've been working late this week," she said, as she climbed into the passenger seat.

He nodded. "Big things are going to happen on Monday."

"Really?" Monday was a big day for her too, the day she would call Jane back to give her decision.

"I can't say much more than that, but I think you'll be pleased with how everything pans out."

Oh how she hoped she would, with his news and hers. He turned the SUV toward his townhouse. His jaw was set, as if he'd already picked up on the fact that she had something important to say.

Neither of them spoke as he parked in the driveway. The night was cool, the sky above glittering with stars. She followed him through the house—past one very hyper shepherd—to the back deck. Pete busied himself lighting a fire in the fire-pit. They were in sync that way, needing fresh air and open space, especially when important things needed to be said.

Her heart was pounding as she watched him, tears already gathering behind her eyes. It was going to suck if she professed her love, and he turned her down, and then she still had to let him drive her home.

Poor planning, Olivia.

The story of her life.

He spread a blanket across the ground in front of the fire, and they sat on it, side by side, shoulders touching, absorbing the warmth of the flames. She stared into their flickering depths. "I got a job offer today."

"Oh yeah?" He turned toward her. "Something better?"

"Way better. Director of Marketing and Publicity for an animal rights organization. I'd be planning fundraisers and events, running their social media. Drumming up money and awareness for animal rights."

He pulled her in and kissed her. "That's amazing. I'm so proud of you. You've found that one-in-a-million job."

Her breath hitched. "There's a catch."

He slid his fingers through her hair, anchoring her face to his. "I figured."

"It's in New York." She closed her eyes and pressed her forehead against his.

His exhale was audible. "You should take it. This is your dream job, Liv. It's the chance of a lifetime."

"It is, but this is my home. I can find a job that makes me happy here in Dogwood. I know I can." Because a job was only a job, and there was more to happiness than work.

He kissed her hard. "You should go. If it doesn't work out, you can always come home. If you don't, you'll stand in the thrift store every day wishing you were in New York, saving animals for a living."

Two tears rolled down her cheeks. "I'm in love with you."

He jerked backward, his black eyes glittering in the darkness. "Liv—"

"Don't you dare tell me this is just sex for you." She fisted her hands in his shirt.

His chest heaved beneath her fingers. "You know it's not."

"Then tell me what it is." A tiny bubble of hope bloomed in her heart.

"I don't know." His voice was rough, raw. Desperate.

"So take a chance on us, whatever we are, and come with me. I'm quite certain New York is always in need of law enforcement officers." She tightened her grip on his shirt, anchoring him to her, even as she felt him slipping from her grasp.

"I can't," he spoke into the darkness, and she heard the finality in his words, although she refused to pop that bubble of hope still lodged in her heart.

More tears slid over her cheeks. "Then tell me not to go, Pete. Ask me to stay."

"I would never do that."

"You're more important to me than a job. Please. Ask me to stay."

"Go, Olivia." He tugged her to her feet and pressed her face against his chest. "You should go."

The bubble popped then, and her heart collapsed. It shuddered and quivered, but it kept beating. And as she shoved him away, she almost laughed at herself for predicting the awkward drive home.

CHAPTER TWENTY-FOUR

Pete thought this must be what it felt like to take a bullet, and it fucking hurt. He rubbed at his chest. Olivia stood a few feet away, her back to him, typing furiously into her phone.

"What are you doing?" he asked.

"Calling a ride."

A ride? "I'll drive you home."

"No thank you. Good-bye, Pete." She went inside his house, closing the door behind her.

He yanked it open and hustled after her through the house and onto his front porch. He reached out but stopped short of touching her. "Let me drive you home." He paused. "Please."

She shook her head, her back still to him. "My friend will be here in a few minutes."

"Olivia—"

"Don't you dare say you're sorry." Her voice quivered.

That's exactly what he'd been about to say. And this whole thing sucked, because he was *so fucking sorry*. For everything. For taking things too far, for letting it get to this point when he'd meant to keep it simple and uncomplicated.

Most of all, for hurting Olivia.

"Go inside, Pete." She crossed her arms over her chest and leaned against the front bumper of the Forester.

So, like a coward, he did. He went inside and left her out there, although the cop in him made him stand in the darkened living room, watching as she waited for her ride to arrive.

It killed him to think of her hundreds of miles away in New York City, living her dream without him, to think of not seeing her. Maybe not ever again.

A few minutes later, a black Kia sedan pulled up in front of his house. Olivia climbed inside without so much as a backward glance, and just like that, she was gone.

* * *

Olivia woke early on Saturday morning, her eyes sore and scratchy with a dull headache throbbing behind them. The pitfalls of crying oneself to sleep.

"Ugh." She rolled over and wrapped her arms around Hallie, who purred loudly into her ear. "If I bring another man around here anytime soon, remind me it's a bad idea, okay?"

Hallie pressed her nose against Olivia's cheek in a show of support.

"You'll come with me to New York, won't you?" she asked the kitten.

Hallie rolled belly up as if to say she had no choice in the matter.

"And you." She pointed her finger at Bailey. "It's time to find you a home, chica."

She slid out of bed and wrapped a robe over her pajamas, then went downstairs. While Bailey did her morning business out in the yard, Olivia drank a tall glass of water. She chased that with a green smoothie and—already feeling better—let Bailey back in and went upstairs for a shower.

There would be no moping around for her today. She had a lot to do to get ready for her move to New York. She let the hot water pound away her reservations. Maybe her heart wasn't quite in it, but her heart had led her astray many times in the past.

Too many times.

This time, she was following her head, and the logical path of action was to jump on an airplane to New York and take this job.

Her phone was ringing as she came back downstairs. It was Maggie. Olivia's stomach clenched, wondering what Pete might have told her.

"Good morning," she said.

"Morning," Maggie answered.

"Have you talked to your brother?" she asked.

"Uh, no." Maggie paused. "Should I have?"

"Yeah. Probably."

Maggie sighed into the phone. "Did he do something stupid I'm going to have to kick his butt for?"

"Sort of. And it's over for us."

"Crap. I'm so sorry." Maggie's disappointment was palpable.

"Thanks. Maybe you and I can keep in touch."

"I'd like that. Actually that's what I was calling about. I want to adopt Bailey," Maggie said.

"Really?" In spite of her lousy mood, Olivia smiled. "That's awesome. She's such a great, sweet dog."

"I know. I've been thinking about her since I met her last weekend. I think she's perfect for me."

"Well that is fantastic news. And I'm sure Merry can fast-track you through the adoption process."

After she hung up with Maggie, Olivia called Merry to tell her the news about Bailey. Merry promised to come over later with wine to catch up on everything. Olivia then spent the next couple of hours working on her website. It had been a whim to broaden the scope of her new site to the plight of all factory-farmed animals in America, but it seemed to be taking off. She'd already attracted as much traffic to her new site as her Citizens Against Halverson Foods page had achieved after a year of work.

Many of her old followers had found the new site, and she'd garnered a whole new audience as well. People all over the country and even worldwide had clicked through the pages she'd created to detail the lives of factory-farmed animals, the abuses they suffered, and the laws needed to better protect them. They'd commented on her blog posts and sent messages wanting to know how they could help.

And she had a *lot* of ideas about that.

It was a similar story on Facebook. She'd attracted over five thousand "likes," surpassing the old Citizens Against Halverson Foods page. It was exciting and invigorating, a new outlet to funnel her passion and energy into, and maybe a way to create real change.

It sure as hell beat sitting around moping over Pete.

Merry arrived just past five, carrying a pizza and two bottles of wine. She set everything on the coffee table and pulled Olivia in for a quick hug. "I'm so sorry, sweetie. Fill me in on what went down last night with Pete, and then please tell me you're not moving to New York."

And with a sigh and a fortifying gulp of wine, she settled in to tell the whole sordid tale.

* * *

Pete couldn't imagine why his mom had asked—insisted actually—that he come to church with her on Sunday morning. It wasn't at all how he wanted to spend his day off, although maybe anything that kept his mind off Olivia was a good thing.

He walked up the front steps of the Dogwood United Methodist Church, stopping in his tracks as he saw Maggie standing just inside with his mom. Okay, neither he nor his sister regularly attended church, so what in the hell was going on?

"Maggie. Mom." He leaned in to give them each a kiss on the cheek. "Why are we all here?"

"I'll cook brunch afterward, and we can talk," his mom said.

Pete didn't like the sound of that, but if anything, there was a new twinkle in his mother's eyes. She looked more alive than she had in years.

Steve Barnes came up the steps then. He clapped Pete on the back and rested a hand on his mom's shoulder. "Elizabeth. You look lovely this morning."

"Thank you." She pressed a hand against her hair and blushed.

Pete decided he'd entered the twilight zone. They all sat together in a pew about halfway back, and after services, Pete and Maggie drove to their mother's house for brunch.

"You and I are talking later." Maggie narrowed her eyes and jutted a finger in his direction.

"What?"

"You know what." The look in her eyes left little doubt.

But how did she know? Jesus, were she and Olivia full-fledged friends now? How had that even happened?

Inside, their mom whipped up a batch of pancakes. She pulled a bacon and cheese quiche and a bowl of fruit salad out of the fridge while the pancakes cooked.

"That looks awesome, Mom," he said.

"Thanks. You can slice the quiche." She handed him a knife. "Maggie, you set the table and get out the orange juice."

They worked together to get brunch on the table and stuffed themselves with good food and easy conversation. After the dishes had been washed and put away, Elizabeth sat them down at the table and folded her hands under her chin. "I signed the papers," she said.

Maggie clapped her hands. "That's great. Good for you, Mom."

Pete released a breath. It was good news after all. "I agree with Maggie. I'm really glad."

Their mom nodded. "I went to see your father on Friday, and we had a long talk. We agreed it was time to go our separate ways. It's time to move on with our lives, all of us." She raised her eyes and gave Pete a meaningful look.

"Here, here." Maggie raised her glass of orange juice, and they all clinked in a toast.

When they left a half hour later, Maggie followed him to his car. She climbed into the passenger seat. "We need to talk."

"Okay."

She sighed. "When we were growing up, I always admired the hell out of you. I felt like an emotional mess all the time, and you always seemed to have it so together. I was so envious of you. I've always wanted to be like you."

He had no idea where she was going with this, but his throat tightened at her words. "Thanks."

"But the thing is, now that we're all grown up, I'm realizing that you don't have it together as much as I thought you did. I acted out, but you bottled it up inside, so much that maybe now you can't let go of it."

"Maggie—"

She shook her head. "Mom's ready to let go and move on. I think I am too. But are you, Pete?"

"What happened between Olivia and me doesn't have anything to do with Mom and Dad."

"Maybe not directly, but you've got to let go of the past. You feel guilty about helping get Dad off on that drug charge, but he was sober at the time. I'd have testified for him too if he'd asked me. It's not your fault he fell off the wagon afterward and drove under the influence. It's a risk the court took when they decided to put him back on the street."

He looked out the window. "I let my personal feelings cloud my professional judgment."

"No you didn't. You took the stand as his son, not as a deputy. You told the truth to the best of your knowledge. You're not God, so stop trying to put things on yourself that were completely outside your control."

"It's not that simple."

"Sure it is." She put a hand on his shoulder.

"I let it destroy my marriage."

"Maybe, but you and Rina were just kids. If your marriage had been solid enough, it would have survived. Rina should have been there for you, but she was too wrapped up in her own needs to see that you were hurting."

He shook his head.

"Forgive yourself. Move on. And for God's sake, don't let Olivia move to New York without you."

He choked on a laugh. "So you two have been talking."

"I'm adopting Bailey."

"She pees." He stared out the front window of the Forester, his mind spinning in a million different directions.

Maggie snorted. "Don't we all. But Olivia assures me she's potty trained now."

"Yeah, I suppose she is."

"She loves you," Maggie said.

"Bailey?" He rubbed his brow.

Maggie punched his shoulder. "Olivia, you idiot. And if I'm not mistaken, you're pretty crazy about her too. Don't fuck this up. Go after her before it's too late."

And with that, she got out of the Forester.

He started to drive home, but the car—or his brain—had other intentions, and he found himself parking in the lot behind the Main Street Café instead. He'd been a coward for a long time where the Hill family was concerned, and it was time to make that right.

He walked inside and asked to be seated in Tamara's section.

She approached his table with a warm smile. "Pete. It's good to see you. What can I get you today?"

"Just coffee please."

"Sure. I'll be right back with that."

She returned a few minutes later with a steaming cup of coffee and set it in front of him. "Sure I can't get you anything else?"

He shook his head. "But there's something else I need to say, something I should have said a long time ago."

Her dark eyes clouded as she sank onto the seat across from him and took his hand. "Oh, honey, I know who you are. I know who your dad is. You don't think I hold that against you, do you?"

Pete straightened in his seat. "You know?"

She nodded. "Well of course. It's a small town after all."

"He killed your husband, and I helped put him behind the wheel that night."

She squeezed his hand. "Tell me."

"He'd been arrested on an old drug charge, and I testified on his behalf, helped him get off without jail time."

"Well honey, you did what you thought was right. You didn't tell your dad to get high and get behind the wheel. He made that decision all on his own."

He shook his head. "How can you not blame me? You lost your husband."

Sadness closed over her features. "And I miss him every day. He was a good man. A damn good husband and father. I've forgiven your father. He did a terrible thing, but he took responsibility for it, and he's paying for his crime."

Pete felt incredibly humbled by her words. "You've forgiven him, and I haven't."

She looked him in the eye. "You will when you're ready. Now don't you waste another minute feeling guilty about what happened to my family. Go on, now, and drink your coffee before it gets cold."

* * *

Olivia woke Monday morning to a text message from Pete. Her heart jumped into her throat as she clicked on it.

Press conference this morning outside the courthouse. 9 a.m. Be there.

Disappointment stung in her eyes and tightened her throat. But okay. A press conference? The thrift store didn't open until ten, so she could go and see what Big Thing Pete had been hinting at all week.

Right after she got over the fact that his text hadn't included anything personal. No "miss you" or "please stay." Not that she'd expected him to, but apparently she couldn't stop herself from being an optimist.

So she got up and got ready and got to the courthouse a few minutes before nine. A crowd had already gathered, and she was happy to lose herself in it. No need to draw anyone's attention today.

A podium had been set up at the top of the steps, and local news crews were in place. Olivia frowned. What in the world was going on?

Right at nine, the doors to the courthouse opened, and several men stepped out. Olivia recognized one of them as Scott Reilly, the Dogwood County District Attorney.

Interesting. Very interesting.

The district attorney stepped up to the podium. "Good morning, everyone. I've called this press conference to inform you that as of this morning Donny Linburgh, the Dogwood County Sheriff, has been removed from office. Lieutenant Watson will serve as interim sheriff until the election."

The crowd erupted with chatter, cheers, boos, and shouted questions. Olivia clapped a hand over her mouth. The sheriff lost his job? What in the world did that mean, and what did it have to do with her?

The district attorney waved his hands for silence. "It was brought to our attention that Sheriff Linburgh broke the law, and as such, he has been relieved of his duties."

"Will he face criminal charges?" a reporter asked.

"I can't discuss specifics at this time, but criminal charges are being considered."

"What can you tell us about his crime?" another reporter asked.

"The sheriff compromised an ongoing criminal case involving the Halverson Foods chicken-processing plant and committed further illegal acts in order to pursue a personal agenda related to the upcoming election." District Attorney Reilly looked grim.

Diana Robbins, the reporter from Channel Two who'd interviewed Olivia, raised her hand. "Can you comment on any connection to the string of vandalism aimed at Olivia Bennett, the founder of Citizens Against Halverson Foods, a group that's been trying to raise awareness about the unfit conditions inside Halverson's Dogwood facility?"

"I can tell you that they are related," the district attorney answered.

Olivia rocked back on her heels, stunned. The *sheriff*

had been behind the attacks on her house and website? Why? This made no sense.

Pete had figured it out. He'd had his own boss removed from office. For her.

No, that wasn't true. He'd have done it no matter what, because Pete always stood for what was right. But he had believed in her and fought for her when no one else in his department had. And that meant a hell of a lot.

The press conference dragged on with more questions. Olivia made her way to the back of the crowd, still in a bit of a daze.

"Olivia—"

She heard a woman's voice calling her name and turned to find Diana Robbins rushing toward her, camera crew in tow. For once, she didn't want to be on camera. Her emotions were too fresh and raw. But she forced a smile anyway, because Diana had given her a lot of wonderful exposure for her cause.

"Olivia, can we get your reaction to this news?" Diana asked.

"I'm shocked," she answered honestly. "I don't really understand it yet, but I'm so glad they've caught who was harassing me."

"You must be incredibly relieved. Can you remind our viewers about everything you've gone through in the last month?"

"Well, my house and car have been repeatedly vandalized, and the Citizens Against Halvorson Foods website was hacked and later deleted completely."

Diana shook her head. "Awful. We're glad that justice has been served."

"Thank you. Me too." Olivia mentioned her new website for The Face of Factory Farming, and then Diana thanked her and headed off to get some other footage for tonight's segment.

"Excuse me."

Olivia turned to find herself facing a middle-aged man in a well-tailored blue suit. He extended a hand. "I'm Michael Hale, the CEO of Halverson Foods."

She recoiled, just slightly, but forced herself to take his hand. "Olivia Bennett."

He nodded. "I was hoping to meet you. When my local GM called me yesterday to fill me in on what was happening, I flew straight here to Dogwood."

"Oh. Where are you from?" She still had no idea why he was here, talking to her, of all people. What a bizarre morning.

"We're headquartered in Houston. I'm not involved much in the day-to-day operations of our local plants, but I've been made aware that there are some issues here in North Carolina that require my attention, and I'd very much like to sit and talk to you in depth about your concerns."

Olivia blinked. "Really?"

"I take your allegations very seriously, Miss Bennett. Are you free this morning?"

"Um." She'd probably get fired from the thrift shop if she took the morning off, but this was too important to pass up. And who cared if she got fired again if she was moving to New York anyway? "Yes. Yes, I'm free, and I'd love to talk with you about my concerns."

CHAPTER TWENTY-FIVE

Pete was going out of his mind. He'd glimpsed Olivia in the crowd that morning and seen her interview on the Channel Two news, but he'd had to wait until he got off duty at three to find her. Except when he'd gone to the thrift shop, she wasn't there. She wasn't home either.

Her house was dark.

Had she already left town?

The thought left him feeling strangled. But no, surely she couldn't have left yet. Desperate, he texted her. *Where are you?*

His phone was silent for five long minutes as he sat on her front steps, feeling like he might implode if she didn't answer. Finally, it buzzed.

MacArthur Park.

Of course. He jumped into his car and raced across town, trying hard to stick to the speed limit. He parked next to her red Prius and walked toward the big pecan tree. Beneath it, Olivia sat on a blanket, her back to him, her hair a waterfall of corn silk over her shoulders.

"Olivia." His voice was barely more than a whisper.

"Thank you," she said without turning. "You believed in me when no one else in your department did. I'll never forget that."

Her words sounded terrifyingly final, like a good-bye he no longer wanted to say.

"You're welcome." He sat beside her, his heart pounding so hard his ribs felt bruised. How had he ever thought he could give her up?

"Why did he do it?" she asked.

"Because Halverson Foods is one of his biggest campaign supporters."

"Ah." She nodded. "That makes sense now. You took down a dirty sheriff. That takes balls, deputy."

"Actually, it's Detective now. I got promoted this morning."

She turned toward him then, her brown eyes bright against the setting sun. "That's fantastic, Pete. Congratulations."

"Thanks." He'd achieved his lifelong dream. And suddenly it felt hollow. None of it meant anything without Olivia here to share it with.

"You've worked so hard for this moment." She squeezed his hand. "I'm so proud of you."

"It's been a long time coming. Why aren't you at the thrift shop?"

She ducked her head with a shy smile. "I got fired."

"Again? What did you do this time?"

"I called out for the morning. Being only my sixth day of work and with my reputation, that didn't go over well."

"Because of the job in New York?"

She shook her head. "Because I was meeting with Michael Hale, the CEO of Halverson Foods."

He sat up straighter. "What?"

"We talked for almost two hours. Nothing I had sent to Halverson Foods over the past year and a half had made its way up the chain to him, so I gave him the undercover videos and all the information we'd collected, and he gave me his direct line in case it happens again. He promised to send someone in to revamp the Dogwood plant to prevent this kind of abuse from continuing to occur."

"Liv—" He clasped her hands in his. "That's great. You did it."

She grinned, her eyes glossy. "I did."

He tugged her closer and pressed his lips to hers. "You are absolutely amazing, you know that?"

She pulled back as two tears splashed over her cheeks. "Well, I don't screw up all the time, anyway."

"You're perfect. You're everything." He gripped her hands tighter. "I'll come to New York with you, if you'll still have me."

She made a choking sound. "What?"

"I love you, Olivia, so much that I don't know what to do or who I am when I'm not with you. You were right. I was acting like a coward, but I'm not afraid anymore."

More tears splashed over her cheeks, and her chest heaved. "Did you just say what I think you said?"

He dragged in a breath, still clutching her hands in his. "I did, but you haven't said it back yet. I love you, Olivia."

She giggled through her tears. "Actually I meant that you said I was right. But I love you too."

He pulled her into his arms and kissed her, feeling whole in a way he wasn't sure he'd ever felt before. He had Olivia to thank for that. She'd changed him, challenged him, made him a better man.

"You smell like cinnamon," she whispered against his lips.

"I had trouble sleeping last night."

"It reminds me of the night we met."

He grunted. "You're never going to quit bringing that up, are you?"

Her eyes twinkled. "It'll make a great story to tell the kids someday."

He took a deep breath and blew it out with a smile. "Kids?"

She winked. "You know, if we decide to have kids."

"I'm not sure if we'd want them to know about their mother's law-breaking heyday."

She giggled again, then her expression sobered. "I didn't take the job in New York."

He sat back. "What? Why not?"

"I don't want to leave Dogwood. It was one of those jobs that would have consumed my whole life, and it dealt primarily with domestic dogs and cats. My real passion is the plight of factory-farmed animals."

He shook his head. "You are something else."

"I know." She leaned back against his chest. The sun sent long shadows across the grass before them as it began its final slide toward the horizon.

"So you're staying." That was taking a minute to sink in. He'd spent the afternoon preparing himself to leave Dogwood behind, and relief swamped him that he wouldn't have to.

"I'll find a job here. I never really wanted to go, you know. I wanted you to give me a reason to stay." She turned and smiled at him over her shoulder.

The sincerity in her eyes drove right into his heart. He pulled her into his lap and held her close, her heart thumping against his. "I'm sorry it took me so long."

"It's okay." She touched his cheek, then pressed a kiss to his lips. "We have the rest of our lives to live happily ever after."

PILOGUE

$\mathcal{O}$livia stared at the bouquet of brightly colored Gerbera daisies. To her right, Merry jockeyed for position. She'd kicked off her high heels, her bare feet visible beneath the lavender folds of her bridesmaid dress.

The two of them, along with Cara's sister Susie and a handful of other single wedding guests, had gathered on the beach for the bouquet toss. In front of them, Cara stood holding her flowers, radiant in her white dress, her strawberry blond hair pulled back from her face and pinned with jeweled clasps.

Olivia's heart ached with joy to see her friend so gloriously happy, married now to the love of her life. Matt stood nearby, watching his new wife and looking like the happiest man on the planet.

"Ready?" Cara turned her back. "Three, two, one..."

The bouquet sailed through the air and right into Merry's arms.

"Yes!" Merry high-fived Olivia, then turned to find T.J. "See this?"

He tipped his cowboy hat with a promising smile. "I see it. Let's go for a walk on the beach."

"Hmph." Olivia feigned an attitude. "You totally rigged that toss, Mrs. Dumont."

Cara shrugged with a giddy smile. "Maybe I did. You'll catch the next one...look." She gestured down the beach.

There, against the sunset with waves crashing behind them, T.J. was on one knee in the sand. Merry stood, one hand pressed to her mouth, her curly hair whipping in the ocean breeze.

"Oh, my God." Olivia clapped a hand to her mouth. "Oh!"

She grabbed Cara for a hug as they watched Merry and T.J. embracing farther down the beach.

"This is the best day ever," Cara said.

"I agree," Matt said, from behind them. "Mind if I cut in?"

"Not at all." Olivia stepped back and straight into Pete's arms.

"Hey," he whispered against her neck, "did you see what I just saw?"

"T.J. proposing to Merry?"

He nodded, looking mouth-wateringly handsome in a suit and tie, his dark hair freshly trimmed. She kissed him, inhaling his cinnamon scent. They'd been up half the night baking pastries for Cara's wedding guests. And doing other—slightly naughty—things in the kitchen.

"Looks like there's another wedding in our future." She wrapped her arms around him and rested her cheek against his chest.

"And another after that." He rubbed his thumb over her ring finger, and her heart gave a happy little lurch in her chest.

"Yes."

"Don't say yes yet." He traced a finger across her cheek. "Because when I ask, I want to do it right. Like that." He tipped his head toward Merry and T.J.

When I ask. She liked the sound of that. In fact, life was pretty awesome these days.

Not long after she'd been fired from the thrift store and reunited with Pete, Olivia was offered a job at the Dogwood County Animal Shelter as their Community Outreach Manager. She now managed the shelter's social media efforts, coordinated fund-raising opportunities, and she always dedicated at least one afternoon a week to her unofficial duty as adoption counselor. As it turned out, she had a real knack for matching families with their new best friend.

The job was fun and rewarding, and when she wasn't at work, her Face of Factory Farming campaign took up the majority of her free time. The site had really taken off, and she'd recently met with one of her senators to draft up legislation to provide better protection for factory-farmed chickens in the state of North Carolina. As for Halverson Foods, Michael Hale had invited her out to tour the Dogwood facility last month to show her the new protocols that had been put in place.

"Let's dance." Pete took her hand and led her toward the outdoor dance floor. Cara and Matt had chosen this beachside restaurant in the Outer Banks for the site of their wedding, and everything about it had been perfect.

"I love you." Olivia settled closer in Pete's arms as

they swayed to the strains of "At Last" beneath strands of twinkling lights.

"Love you too." His eyes reflected his words, making her feel all warm and gooey inside.

He and Timber had moved in at Christmastime, and they'd recently made arrangements to buy the little house on Peachtree Lane from Merry.

"I was thinking," he said, pulling her closer against him.

"Yeah?"

"When you were teaching me how to meditate, you kept telling me to find my center and my happy place, but the truth is that you're my center. Wherever you are is where I need to be."

And he brought his lips to hers in a kiss that stole her heart and melted her knees. Because as it turned out, he was her center too. At home, in a tent, or beneath the stars, as long as she had Pete at her side, the world was her happy place.

Cara Medlen has one rule: Don't get attached. It's worked well with the foster dogs she's rescued and given to good homes. But when she meets her incredibly sexy neighbor, Cara will learn that some rules are made to be broken.

See the next page for an excerpt from

Unleashed

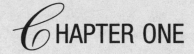CHAPTER ONE

Cara Medlen felt the growl before she heard it, rumbling against her leg from the dog tensed at her side. She jiggled the leash to break his concentration. "Easy, Casper. You may not realize it yet, but today's your lucky day."

He looked up at her with dull eyes, one brown, one blue. A jagged scar creased his face. Ribs and hip bones jutted through his mangy white coat. And, oh boy, did he stink. Cara had yet to meet an ugly boxer, but Casper... well, he had the sort of face that made people cross to the other side of the street.

That same face grabbed at a tender spot in her heart.

"It's a blessing that Triangle Boxer Rescue can take him," the woman behind the desk, a volunteer named Helen, said. "Shelter life hasn't been good for him."

Cara nodded as she handed the signed paperwork to Helen. "I've worked with a lot of dogs like Casper. I'm sure we'll have him ready for adoption in no time."

But the warning she'd received from her homeowners' association over the summer weighed heavily on her mind: Keep her foster dogs in line or face disciplinary action by the board.

The door to the kennels opened, allowing raucous barking to spill into the lobby. Casper peered around her and fixed his gaze on the man who'd come through the door. His ears flattened, and the hair raised along his spine.

Yep, this dog was trouble all right.

Cara sidestepped to block his view. "Thanks, Helen. Happy New Year."

With a quick wave, she hustled Casper out the front door. He tucked his tail against the cold air, then raised his nose and sniffed the sweet scent of freedom. He slunk onto the brown patchy grass of the shelter's front lawn and raised his leg on a tree.

When he'd finished, she loaded him into the backseat of her little blue Mazda. She smoothed her hands over her black dress, wrinkled since the funeral by hours in the car and now covered in Casper's white fur. The ache in her chest rose up, squeezing her throat, and she shoved it back.

Later, she'd grieve. Now she needed to get Casper home.

She swung into the front seat and cranked the engine. "So, you've officially been sprung from doggy jail."

He gave her a wary look, then turned his head to stare out the window. She pulled onto High Street and took the ramp to Interstate 85, headed for her townhouse in Dogwood, a small town on the outskirts of Raleigh, North Carolina.

"But listen, no more shenanigans, okay?"

Casper cocked his head, his mismatched eyes somber.

"One of my fosters growled at my neighbor's dog, and she filed a complaint against me with the homeowners' association, so I need you to be on your best behavior."

With a dramatic sigh, he sprawled across the backseat and closed his eyes. Well, she'd take that as a yes. She'd put in a few extra hours of behavior training with him in the meantime, just to be sure. Casper slept for the next hour as Cara drove them home.

The latest Taylor Swift single strummed happily from inside her purse, and she shoved a hand inside to grab her cell phone. Merry Atwater's name showed on the display. "Hey, Merry."

"Hey. Just wanted to see how you're holding up," Merry said. "I've been thinking about you all day."

Cara tightened her grip on the steering wheel, blinking away the image of Gina's pale face inside the casket. "I'm okay, or I will be."

"Oh, sweetie, I'm so sorry. Let me know if there's anything I can do. Are you still planning to go out tonight?"

"Yeah, I'll be there, just maybe late. Casper and I have some acquainting to do."

"How is he?" Merry shifted into her professional voice. As the founder of Triangle Boxer Rescue, she had a vested interest in every dog they saved. Cara had no idea where she found the time to run a rescue on top of her day job as a pediatric nurse, but Merry somehow managed to juggle the two.

"Well, he's only growled twice so far." Cara glanced over her shoulder with a smile. Casper watched, his head on his front paws.

"What happened? The shelter didn't mention aggression."

Cara flipped on her blinker and exited the highway onto Fullers Church Road. "I think he's just stressed out. I'm not too worried about it. What time should I meet you at Red Heels?"

"Why don't I come over to your place and we can get ready together? I'll help you get Casper settled, and we can talk."

"Sounds great, Mer, thanks."

"You bet. See you around seven."

Cara shoved the phone back into her purse. Truthfully, the last thing she wanted to do tonight was go to a New Year's Eve party, but she refused to sit home and feel sorry for herself. She'd go, and she'd even have fun, dammit.

It was what Gina would have wanted.

She pulled into the parking lot of Crestwood Gardens, her townhouse community, and guided her Mazda into its assigned spot, right next to her sexy next-door neighbor's shiny black Jeep Grand Cherokee. The man in question stood in his front yard, deep in conversation with a perky brunette in tight jeans and a low-cut sweater.

Cara felt a twinge of something like jealousy, which was ridiculous because she didn't even know his name. And she'd prefer to keep it that way. She shut off the engine and hurried to fetch Casper from the backseat. "Welcome home, dude."

He hopped down, tail tucked. It had been a long and difficult day for both of them. Time to get settled in and relax for a while.

One of her neighbors—Chuck Something-or-other—

passed with a nod as Cara headed toward her townhouse. She offered a polite smile, her attention focused on Casper. The dog looked up at the older man. Their eyes met. The hair along Casper's spine raised, and he released a low, guttural growl that sent Chuck scrambling into the parking lot.

Cara swore under her breath as she shoved the key into the lock and pushed open her front door.

So much for making a good first impression on the neighbors.

* * *

Matt Dumont scrubbed a hand over his jaw as his Realtor snapped one last photo of the front of his townhouse. He watched peripherally as his elusive next-door neighbor scrambled through her front door with the mangy, miserable-looking dog who'd just growled at Chuck Sawyer.

It was a different damn dog than he'd seen in her yard last week.

In fact, from what he'd seen, there was a veritable parade of dogs in and out of her home, many of them looking rough, although this one had to be the worst. Matt didn't have much of an eye for dog breeds, but it looked like a pit bull from where he was standing.

He was starting to think something shady was going on next door.

"The listing will be live later tonight. It shows well, so I'm hopeful it will sell relatively quickly." Stephanie Powell pocketed her camera and pulled a red-and-white For Sale sign from her trunk.

He shifted his attention to the business at hand. "Mind if I do the honors?"

"Go ahead." She held it out.

Matt gripped the sign. With a grunt, he shoved the signpost through the grass and into the hard, red clay beneath. At least here in North Carolina the ground was still pliable at the end of December. Boston's frigid winters would be a readjustment.

But he could snowboard again. Yeah, he missed snowboarding, and skiing, and his mom's homemade meatballs. He was ready to go home.

He nudged the sign, then wiggled it a little farther into the earth. Satisfied it wasn't going anywhere, he turned to Stephanie. "All set, then."

She nodded. "I'll be in touch, and hopefully we'll have some showings scheduled for you in the next week."

"Great, Stephanie. Thanks." He shook her hand and headed for the front door of his townhouse, his thoughts again turning to the girl next door and her odd collection of dogs.

Matt knew most of his neighbors, was friendly with all of them, yet she remained a mystery. He didn't even know her name. Perhaps that was why her face sometimes occupied his mind as he passed the long nights on surveillance.

His cell phone rang, and he swiped it from his back pocket. Felicity Prentiss. Shit.

"Mrs. Prentiss," he said as he strode toward his front door.

"I'm having second thoughts." Her voice was taut with nervous energy.

Matt held in a groan. He'd known when he met her

yesterday that she was going to be a pain in the ass. Probably, he should have turned her down, but this job would bring in a lot of billable hours, extra cash to tide him over while he got things going up in Boston.

But honestly, Felicity Prentiss was one of the most uptight clients he'd ever worked with. Since she'd hired him yesterday, she'd already called five times, looking for updates, reassurances, and advice.

The woman needed someone to hold her hand. And that was not his job.

Not her husband's, either, since she had enlisted Matt's investigative services to secure evidence of his adultery for their divorce proceedings.

"I'll be honest with you, Mrs. Prentiss. I've never worked one of these cases where it turned out the spouse wasn't cheating. You want proof, I'll get it for you. You want to call it off, tell me now before there's no going back."

On the other end of the line, she sucked in a shaky breath. "I do want to know—I *need* to know. But what if he sees you? He'd kill me if he knew I'd had him followed."

Matt closed and locked the front door behind him. "He won't see me. Is your husband violent, Mrs. Prentiss?"

"No." A long pause, then a sigh. "No, he's a sweet and gentle man, or at least I thought he was until I caught him sneaking into the house in the middle of the night smelling of another woman's perfume."

"All right, then. Let me do my job. I'll get what you need for the lawsuit, and your husband will be none the wiser. Don't worry."

"It's just . . . with the New Year and all, I'm ready to get on with my life, you know?"

Did he ever. Matt flipped on the overhead light and sank into his leather recliner. "I do, and you will. Since you'll be with him tonight, I plan to start surveillance tomorrow. Shouldn't take more than a week, maybe two."

Felicity Prentiss hoped to file an "alienation of affection" lawsuit, taking advantage of an outdated law in North Carolina that allowed a wife to sue her husband's lover. The problem was that Felicity couldn't file for divorce from her philandering husband until the necessary evidence had been gathered.

Matt planned to get the evidence she needed for her lawsuit and her divorce proceedings as quickly as possible. Because once he closed this case, he was going home.

He headed upstairs to log some background information on the Prentisses in his office. It always paid to know whose closets you were poking around in before you brought out the high-powered lens. A loud bark drew him toward the window in the hall, from which he had a decent view of his next-door neighbor's backyard.

Enough to see her outside with the white dog and another larger brown dog. She'd changed from her black dress and pumps into an ice-blue jacket and dark-colored jeans that hugged a shapely figure. Her hair was the color of his fantasies, somewhere between blond and red, a delicious apricot that shone in the sun with soft waves that brushed her shoulders.

As he watched, the white dog snarled. The brown dog hesitated a moment, then they were on each other like a couple of wild animals, growling and snapping. The sound made the hair on the back of his neck rise.

Blood streaked the white dog's fur.

Holy shit. Was his pretty golden-haired neighbor training fighting dogs?

With a grunt of disgust, Matt stepped away from the window. It was time for them to finally meet, because there was no way in hell he was going to look the other way if she was mistreating those dogs.

* * *

The dogs were fighting.

"Hey!" Cara clapped her hands and shouted, making as much noise as she could. Casper slunk off to hide behind a bush. Mojo trotted over, looking sheepish.

Cara knelt and ran her hands over him, checking for injury. She suspected the skirmish had been more bark than bite, but with Mojo's dark fur, it was hard to be sure, and she'd seen blood on Casper.

Mojo sat, tongue lolling, tail wagging, as she checked him out. Blood oozed from the gum behind his left incisor. With any luck, that was the source of the blood she'd seen on Casper. She shooed Mojo inside, then coaxed the frightened white boxer from behind the bush.

"Easy, Casper." She dabbed at the blood streaking his fur, and it came off on her fingers. He watched her with those unnervingly solemn, mismatched eyes. Other than Mojo's bloody slobber, he was unharmed.

Thank God. Cara plopped down on the grass at Casper's side, her legs rubbery, heart pounding. "You are not good for my adrenaline levels, you know that?"

Casper was going to take some work. He'd come into the shelter as a stray, and he would need time to feel comfortable again as part of a family, if he ever had been.

He wasn't a mean dog, just frightened and defensive. He lay beside Cara now, head between his front paws, weary eyes glazed.

In retrospect, she shouldn't have offered treats in front of both dogs so soon. Mojo had sniffed at Casper's cookie, and Casper had defended what was his. Resource guarding wasn't unusual for a dog like Casper, who'd been on his own for a while. Cara had made a rookie mistake. She was distracted today, but that was no excuse.

Mojo whined from the other side of the door. Casper watched, his posture relaxed.

She stood and opened the back door, keeping a close eye on her troublemaking canines. Mojo trotted out, nuzzled Cara's hand, and took off across the yard in search of a ball. After a moment, Casper got to his feet and followed him. Mojo spun around him, his front legs pressed to the earth, tail up, as he invited Casper to play.

That's more like it. Cara breathed a sigh of relief. She shoved her hands into the pockets of her jeans to ward off the cold breeze as she watched them.

Mojo was a funny-looking dog with brown brindle stripes that darkened to black along his back. He had a sturdy body, full tail, and a face thicker than a full-blooded boxer. No one knew what he was mixed with, but something in his coloration and stance suggested German shepherd to Cara. No matter his heritage, he was all fun, the most laid-back, well-mannered foster she'd ever had.

After watching Mojo try in vain for several minutes to get Casper to play, she headed for the house, chilled from too long outside in only a thin jacket. The dogs bounded ahead and waited for her at the sliding glass door.

"Lead the way, Mojo," she told the brown dog. His

tail beat the vinyl siding as she opened the door, then he scrambled across the kitchen to check his bowl, as if the dog food fairy might have filled it while they were playing outside. "In a little while. Let's get Casper settled in first."

Despite his emaciated appearance, Casper had been well fed at the shelter for the past three days, and she didn't want him to get sick from eating before his nervous stomach settled. Cara flipped on the gas fireplace, then led the way upstairs.

Casper tucked his tail as he followed her into the master bedroom.

"It'll be a while before we make it up here tonight, I'm afraid. It's New Year's Eve, and I'm going out. But I wanted you to see it first in the daylight. You can join Mojo and me in the big bed." She eyed his soiled fur, then grabbed an old sheet and spread it over her pink-flowered comforter. Before she went out tonight, he definitely needed a bath.

She kept talking, knowing that her calm voice and demeanor, as well as Mojo's, would put Casper more quickly at ease. She sat on the bed and patted it, inviting them up. Mojo leaped up and made himself at home, while Casper stood anxiously at her feet. She told him all about tonight's party while stroking his chin until, with a shy wag of his nub, he hopped up on her other side.

"That's a good boy." She lay back and closed her eyes, a dog on each side.

What was better than that? Maybe she'd take a quick nap before Merry arrived. Gina's funeral had left her drained.

The chiming of the doorbell sent Casper into fits of

hysterical barking. He launched himself off the bed and ran a lap around the bedroom. Mojo jumped down and headed for the hall, his bark mixing with Casper's as both dogs raced downstairs.

Cara glanced at her watch as she hurried after them. Merry wasn't due for another two hours. Whoever it was had lousy timing.

She sprinted into the kitchen and grabbed a handful of peanut-butter dog biscuits from the counter.

"Come, Casper." She used the biscuits as a lure, and the dog crept into his crate, still eyeing the front door with suspicion. She rewarded him with a handful of peanut-butter yummies, then draped the crate with a thick blanket, hoping the darkness would help calm him.

The doorbell pealed again. Casper's booming bark filled the room, accompanied by the sound of his body slamming into the metal bars of the crate. So much for calm.

"Shhh," Cara whispered, then hurried toward the front door. "Coming."

Mojo stood in the hallway, tail wagging in anticipation of their visitor.

Without pausing to check the peephole, she yanked the door open, then gaped at the man standing there. He filled her doorway, tall and solid in worn jeans and a black leather jacket. Dark brown hair was pushed back from his forehead with a slight wave. His brown eyes settled on hers, and a little ping of warmth traveled through her.

"Matt Dumont. I live next door." He jerked his head toward the townhouse to the left of hers.

Cara nodded. Oh yeah, she knew who he was, and she'd been doing her best to avoid him for the past year.

Well, now she had a name to put with the face formerly known as "Mr. FMH," a term she and her friend Olivia had coined back in college for a guy that was "fuck me hot." Matt sure was, not that she had any intention of acting on it.

She glanced down at herself, painfully aware of the streak of bloody slobber on her shirtsleeve and the way she was panting for breath after wrangling an uncooperative sixty-pound boxer into his crate. Of course, if they had to meet after all this time, she'd be a mess.

She pasted on the sweetest smile she could muster as Casper growled from the kitchen. "Nice to meet you. I'm Cara Medlen."

"'Bout time I knew your name, don't you think?" The corner of his mouth hitched in amusement as those cocoa eyes searched hers. He was even more handsome up close, staring at her like that, so intense she almost forgot to breathe.

"I guess so."

"So, what's the story with your dogs, Cara?"

She sucked in a breath. "What story?"

His eyes narrowed, less warm now. "You tell me."

She crossed her arms over her chest. What was it with her neighbors and their closed-mindedness about her foster dogs? "We haven't broken any rules, Mr. Dumont, so if you don't mind..."

She moved to close the front door, but he stepped forward, blocking her. "Actually, I do mind."

Cara felt the force of his stare right down to her coral-painted toenails.

"The white dog—is he receiving some kind of medical treatment?"

He was so close now she could smell the faint scent of his aftershave. Too close, but she refused to give him the satisfaction of backing away. She straightened her spine, wishing for a few more inches so she could glare at him without having to look up. "What exactly are you suggesting?"

"I can see into your backyard from my upstairs hallway." He tilted his head. "I think I know what's going on here."

Cara scrunched her nose. What in the world was he accusing her of, mowing her lawn in the wrong direction? Crap, had he been watching last week when she tripped over Mojo and fell in a pile of dog poop? She'd stripped out of her jeans right there in the backyard and run inside half naked. Her cheeks burned. "Perhaps you should be more specific."

He glanced down at the dog at her feet. Mojo sat, ears back, his shoulder against Cara's left leg. A crash echoed from the kitchen as Casper thrashed in his crate. "You fighting these dogs, Ms. Medlen?"

She couldn't help it; she snorted with laughter at the absolute absurdity of his accusation. "Are you serious?"

Matt pinned her in his laser-like gaze, looking deadly serious. "That a pit bull?"

"A boxer. Thank you for your concern, Mr. Dumont, but maybe next time you should mind your own business."

And with that, she slammed the door in his face.

Fall in Love with Forever Romance

A TASTE OF SUGAR
by Marina Adair

For fans of Rachel Gibson, Kristan Higgins, and Jill Shalvis comes the newest book in Marina Adair's Sugar, Georgia series. Can sexy Jace McGraw win back his ex, pediatrician Charlotte Holden, with those three simple words: we're still married?

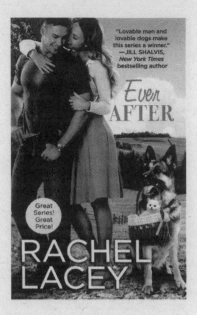

"Lovable men and lovable dogs make this series a winner."
—JILL SHALVIS, *New York Times* bestselling author

Ever **AFTER**

Great Series! Great Price!

RACHEL LACEY

EVER AFTER
by Rachel Lacey

After being arrested for a spray-painting spree that (perhaps) involved one too many margaritas, Olivia Bennett becomes suspect number one in a string of vandalisms. Deputy Pete Sampson's torn between duty and desire for the vivacious waitress, but he may have to bend the rules because true love is more important than the letter of the law...

Fall in Love with Forever Romance

YOU'RE THE EARL THAT I WANT
by Kelly Bowen

For Heath Hextall, inheriting an earldom has been a damnable nuisance. What he needs is a well-bred, biddable woman to keep his life in order. Lady Josephine Somerhall is *not* suited for the job, but he's about to discover that what she lacks in convention, she makes up for in passion.

Fall in Love with Forever Romance

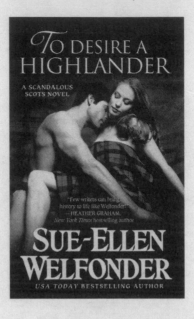

TO DESIRE A HIGHLANDER
by Sue-Ellen Welfonder

The second book in *USA Today* bestseller Sue-Ellen Welfonder's
sexy Scandalous Scots series. When a powerful warrior meets
Lady Gillian MacGuire—known as the Spitfire of the Isles—he's
shocked to learn that *he's* the one being seduced and captivated...